LIVID

ALSO BY PATRICIA CORNWELL

LIVID

A SCARPETTA
NOVEL

PATRICIA CORNWELL

GRAND CENTRAL
PUBLISHING

NEW YORK BOSTON

Grand Central Publishing
Hachette Book Group
1290 Avenue of the Americas, New York, NY 10104
grandcentralpublishing.com
twitter.com/grandcentralpub

First Edition: October 2022

Grand Central Publishing is a division of Hachette Book Group, Inc. The Grand Central Publishing name and logo is a trademark of Hachette Book Group, Inc.

The publisher is not responsible for websites (or their content) that are not owned by the publisher.

The Hachette Speakers Bureau provides a wide range of authors for speaking events. To find out more, go to www.hachettespeakersbureau.com or call (866) 376-6591.

Library of Congress Control Number: 2022939620

ISBNs: 9781538725160 (hardcover), 9781538726624 (large print), 9781538740651 (intl. trade pbk.), 9781538740101 (signed edition), 9781538740125 (B&N signed edition), 9781538725191 (ebook), 9781538740644 (Canadian edition)

Printed in the United States of America

LSC-C

Printing 1, 2022

To Staci

DEFINITIONS OF LIVID

The dark bluish-purple discoloration of skin after death;

To be enraged.

Develop your senses—especially learn how to see.
Realize that everything connects to everything else.

—*Leonardo da Vinci (1452–1519)*

LIVID

CHAPTER 1

After three days in the Atlantic Ocean during a heat wave, April Tupelo wasn't recognizable to her family.

What the cops call a floater, the former beauty queen was marbled green and bloated by gases from decomposition. The outer layer of her skin and her long blond hair had sloughed off. Her eyes, ears, lips and other delicate body parts were gone, the images displayed inside the crowded courtroom like something from the movie *Jaws*.

I wasn't working in Virginia when her remains washed ashore on Wallops Island twenty-one months ago. I didn't go to the scene or perform the autopsy. The forensic pathologist who did isn't alive to amend his egregious errors. By the time I got involved, April Tupelo's fiancé had been indicted for first-degree murder and mutilating a dead body.

He was in jail awaiting trial, held in isolation without bail, the story headline news internationally. The prosecution was a dog with a bone. It didn't matter what I said.

"Again, let me emphasize how much I regret the necessity of displaying these painful images." Alexandria's Commonwealth's Attorney Bose Flagler carries on in his lyrical drawl, and had this case been mine from the start, we wouldn't be here now. "Seeing things like this can wound one's very soul and psyche, isn't that true, ma'am?"

"I'm not sure what you're asking," I reply.

He continues repositioning himself in front of the witness stand, doing what he can to block my view of the jury. A master of choreography, Flagler is mindful of his every move, never straying far from the fixed cameras filming live for Court TV.

"No matter how difficult, we have to look unflinchingly. Would you agree with that, ma'am? That we owe it to April Tupelo to see the full extent of what was done to her at the end of her very short life?" Flagler slowly paces back and forth in front of me. "It's our moral obligation to do so, isn't it, ma'am?"

His incessantly calling me *ma'am* is anything but polite. He's dismissing me as a silly armchair sleuth guided by hormones and intuition. I've been in court with him a number of times since I was appointed chief medical examiner last year. He's always been obsequiously polite, at times flirty. Until this case I wasn't the enemy.

"I'm not sure of the question," I say yet again, and I can tell that the jurors are intrigued by him.

They always are. Charismatic and clever, the thirty-four-year-old bachelor brings to mind Michelangelo's sculpture of David or Giuliano de' Medici. But with clothes on, expensive ones. Dipping his hand into a pocket, he slides out the small touchscreen tablet that controls the grotesque slideshow around us.

"I regret the necessity of subjecting everyone to these graphic images," Flagler says disingenuously as they fill the courtroom monitors in vivid color.

He clicks through multiple photographs of the victim's body facedown on an autopsy table in the Norfolk morgue. Close-ups of her flayed back and buttocks show four long deep gashes spaced close together, yawning widely and blackish red.

"You've seen these photos before, correct?" Flagler asks me.

"Those and many others."

"And what we're looking at are the victim's decomposing remains, and the savage knife cuts to her back from when the defendant tried to turn her into fish bait—"

"Objection!"

"What this time, Mister Gallo?" Judge Annie Chilton asks from her black leather chair flanked by the state and U.S. flags, the bronze seal of Virginia behind her.

"The photos are inflammatory and prejudicial. He's testifying, Your Honor! Again!"

"Overruled. Again. Please rephrase, and let's move on."

In her early fifties, with a compelling face and short dark hair, Annie is tall and lanky, more handsome than pretty. Based on her demeanor toward me as I've been testifying this afternoon, you'd never guess we've known each other since our law school days at Georgetown. You wouldn't suppose we were roommates at the time or that she encouraged my return to Virginia last year.

In fact, she was the deciding factor, influencing Governor Roxane Dare to appoint me. All was fine until last month when Annie started avoiding me for no apparent reason.

"Thank you, Your Honor. Let me try a different way," Flagler says in his compelling baritone while people around us mutter angrily and sob. "What we're seeing is severe damage inflicted *postmortem*. In other words, after death, correct, ma'am?"

"That's correct," I answer.

"This is what April Tupelo looked like on the Saturday morning of October seventeenth, two-thousand-twenty, after three days in the ocean?" he asks to more upset sounds around us.

"In these photographs the body has been cleaned up, as you can see," I reply. "And decomposition is continuing at a rapid rate. So, she's not going to look exactly as she did when she was first found—"

"Ma'am, would you agree that most of what you experience as a matter of routine would be traumatizing for a normal person?"

"Again, I'm not sure what—"

"My point is, you're accustomed to these sorts of nightmares. The dreadful images we've been looking at since you took the stand are part of your routine, your bread and butter. It's what you're paid to do, isn't that true?"

"I don't think you ever get accustomed to—"

"One dead body after the next. Yet another stiff on the slab. Day after day, it never stops, if we're honest. Let's just call things what they are. Death is darn ugly. There's nothing pretty about it. What was that nursery rhyme? *The worms crawl in, the worms crawl out...?*"

"Objection!" Sal Gallo is on his feet.

"*...They play pinochle on your snout...?* Or something like that, ma'am?" Flagler continues stereotyping me as antisocial and morbidly peculiar while hardly letting me get in a word. "I realize that *empathizing* isn't what you're paid to do—"

"Your Honor, I'm just going to keep objecting to the commonwealth's attorney badgering the witness!" Gallo is red-faced in his rumpled blue seersucker suit and crooked bow tie. "The only reason for his ranting and harassing is to prejudice the jury."

"Overruled."

"I'd like my continuing objection noted on the record."

"So noted."

"Again, I request a mistrial." Gallo sits back down, disgusted.

"Denied."

■ ■ ■

It's obvious what Bose Flagler is doing. His strategies have been cleverly and carefully planned from the start. His intention is for me to make the worst impression imaginable on the jurors. That's why he's saved me as his last witness before resting his case.

The only reason he's called me to the stand at all is for that singular purpose. To dismantle me. To impeach my credibility and integrity, leaving negative impressions foremost in the jurors' minds. If Flagler doesn't cause reasonable doubt about my testimony, he can't win.

"Your Honor?" he offers politely, unflappably. "I think it only fair for the jury to know what services the witness receives compensation for as the chief medical examiner of our fine Commonwealth. You know, what's in her job description that entitles her to be paid a handsome six-figure salary funded by our tax dollars?"

"Objection! Here we go again, Your Honor!" Gallo erupts. "And I believe Mister Flagler is handsomely compensated by these same taxpayers!"

"Not all that handsomely," he fires back, some people laughing.

"Mister Gallo, your objection is overruled."

The restless noise inside the crowded courtroom is getting louder as Flagler carries on with his outrageous antics while assassinating my character. Annie continues to allow it. I've been in her courtroom before, and don't expect special treatment because we're friends. But she won't make eye contact, and is barely respectful. Something's wrong, and has been for weeks.

"My point?" Flagler resumes. "We want to know what's expected of the witness in this most unusual profession she's chosen. One that very few people know much about, I might add. Or want to, for that matter?"

"Your Honor!" Gallo's voice is getting hoarse. "The commonwealth's attorney is doing everything he can to impeach Doctor Scarpetta's credibility. That's the only reason he has her on the stand. He's trying mightily to make the jury distrust her because he doesn't have a case! He knows that what he's orchestrated is a witch hunt!"

"That's enough," Annie decides. "And I'm asking the jury to disregard defense counsel's comment about this proceeding being a witch hunt. Let's refrain from any further asides." She sternly peers down from her lofty perch. "What's your objection, Mister Gallo?"

"The prosecution is preaching a sermon *and* testifying!" he says as Flagler continues ignoring him, loudly flipping pages, skimming his notes. "Not to mention going after Doctor Scarpetta nonstop, and insulting her." Gallo is so angry his voice shakes. "She can't even finish a sentence!"

The prominent defense attorney has been sticking up for me with great flourishes of chivalry because what I have to say is helpful to him for once. That will change soon enough when my findings don't suit him in some other case.

"Your objection has been noted, Mister Gallo." Annie dismisses him yet again. "Mister Flagler, you may continue."

"If I could have just a few seconds, Your Honor." He smiles apologetically. "Unlike the witness, I don't have the memory of a computer. I actually have to check my paperwork, making certain I don't misspeak."

Leaning against the witness stand, he shuffles through his notes, cutting quite a figure in his vanilla suit and blue suede shoes. He's close enough that I detect the verbena eau de parfum he has custom made in a Paris shop on the Avenue des Champs-Élysées. I can make out the heraldic crest engraved on his Super Bowl–size gold signet ring.

His wealthy Virginia family traces back to the Norman Conquest. Also the *Mayflower* and Ellis Island, I've heard him boast, depending on whose vote he wants. He's been given every advantage while groomed for greatness, and I catch whiffs of his citrusy scent as he moves about. He's dragging things out, making sure he's the focus of attention, something he's perfected to an art.

"Ma'am?" Flagler retrieves the touchscreen tablet from his pocket again. "If you'd please direct your attention to what's displayed on the monitors? Have you seen these?"

"Yes," I reply.

"Please take a moment to refresh your memory." He directs my attention to images that scarcely look human.

Displayed on monitors around the room are photographs of April Tupelo's putrefying remains spangled with starfish and scuttling with crabs. I can well imagine the stench, the static of flies buzzing. Horrors like this don't happen in the cloistered part of the world where she and the defendant were born and raised, some two hundred miles south of here on a spit of land surrounded by water.

The six-square-mile barrier island's population is fewer than five hundred, and there's only one road that will get you there from Virginia's mainland. Otherwise you need an aircraft or a boat. The location is ideal for those who make a living on the water catching and selling seafood, and operating tourist inns and diners. Wallops Island's remoteness also makes it ideal for a spaceport.

Home to the National Aeronautics and Space Administration, the NASA-Wallops facility has four pads, with more under construction. Those living and working in the area are accustomed to the mighty roar of rockets blasting off. They light up the skies over the Atlantic Ocean like gigantic Roman candles, the launches so frequent that the locals barely notice.

The typical payload is space probes and other scientific instruments for NASA and private aerospace industries. Often it's research experiments, and supplies bound for the International Space Station.

In photographs of April Tupelo's body washed up on the rocky beach, I can make out the launchpads on higher ground in the distance. Starkly etched against the horizon are lightning suppression masts, water towers and generic concrete block buildings.

A rocket juts up from its pad like a colossal stick of white chalk with a sharpened tip, a satellite concealed inside the nose cone. Before taking over the Tupelo case, I had a pretty good idea of the work that goes on at NASA-Wallops. In recent months I've learned more, and some of the details are surprising. I wouldn't have guessed that often it's the locals who do the fetching when experiments touch down in the water.

It could be anything. The prototype of a crew capsule carrying crash-test mannikins. A flying car with pop-out floats. An amphibious drone that looks like a dolphin. A robotic bird that flies while it spies. The boat pilots who retrieve such curiosities rarely have any idea what they're carrying or towing back to shore. Most of them aren't interested, don't care, and the defendant was hired routinely for such missions.

At the time of April Tupelo's death, Gilbert Hooke was the twenty-five-year-old owner and operator of a forty-foot charter trawler named *Captain Hooke*, as one might expect. He and April kept busy working pleasure cruises, fishing trips and other excursions, including official ones for the federal government. On the day she died, they'd retrieved a weather balloon that had been launched 120,000 feet to the edge of space.

Malfunctioning, it hurtled back through the atmosphere, splashing down off the Virginia coast late that morning. Indirectly, this single event may have been a factor in what happened that night. Displayed on a monitor directly across from the witness stand is an image of a uniformed NASA Protective Services special agent who's young and extremely nice to look at.

He and Hooke are using gaff poles to snag a deflated bright silver balloon hundreds of feet long. Its mysterious gondola brings to mind a shiny metal satellite bobbing in the water on inflatable floats. Juxtaposed to this image is one of April Tupelo's decomposing body tangled in seaweed and rotted netting on a rocky shore strewn with plastic bottles, a faded boat cushion and other marine detritus.

Hooke admits to getting upset with April. They'd been arguing right before she died. He wrote in his police statement that the NASA special agent *paid too much attention to her, and she got off on it. She encouraged it.* The couple's exchanges got angrier as the evening wore on, and based on psychological reports and other confidential materials I've reviewed, their relationship was volatile.

They fought often and violently. It would seem she had a habit of encouraging attention from other men, and in general creating drama. It's Bose Flagler's contention that the night of her death, Hooke was in a jealous fury. While he and April argued as they sat on the boat drinking beer in the heat, he plotted how to get away with the perfect murder.

Most important was how to dispose of her body, Flagler explains in the cadence of an evangelist. The defendant had to make sure it wouldn't be found.

CHAPTER 2

Have you seen these?" Flagler asks me over the upset noise around us. He waves his hand around the courtroom like a game show host, indicating the gruesome images on the multiple big-screen displays.

"Yes," I reply.

"Do these images accurately depict the condition April Tupelo's body was in when she washed up on the beach?"

"Yes, as best I know," I reply. "I wasn't there but have reviewed the photographs and videos taken by police and death investigators."

"And you don't think she looks like a victim of violence, ma'am?"

"What I'm seeing is common when dead bodies are recovered from water—"

"*Common*? As if anything we might be looking at is *common*?"

"Objection! Argumentative commenting on the testimony!"

"Sustained."

"Go ahead, ma'am," Flagler says to me. "You were talking about how *common* April Tupelo's death was."

"I was saying that usually a dead body will float facedown and partially submerged, the extremities and head hanging lower than the torso." I explain this to the jury and not Flagler. "Often it's run over by ships or motorboats."

Those aboard them rarely have a clue, I continue painting the gory picture. Or if they do, they don't want to get involved, and keep going. They leave the gruesome discovery for someone else to manage, meaning we don't always have a history that might correlate with postmortem injuries.

"When human remains have been preyed upon by marine animals and slashed up by a boat propeller, you can understand why one might assume the death was violent." I summarize for the jury as if Flagler is invisible. "To someone untrained or no longer thinking rationally, it's easy to attribute such postmortem artifacts to torture, mutilation and murder."

"Isn't it also possible, ma'am, that a murder victim might look exactly like what we're seeing in these photographs and videos?" He again indicates the disturbing images brightly displayed on big flat screens.

"Yes, it's possible, but—"

"You can't look at these pictures and from them alone tell us that April Tupelo wasn't murdered, can you, ma'am?"

"No, not at a glance," I reply as he continues moving around strategically.

This moment I'm confronted with his dark blue crocodile belt, and the diamond eyes of the silver rampant eagle buckle. I can make out the pearly buttons of his powder-blue cotton shirt, and the gray spots where his flat belly is sweating through it.

"Of course, you weren't at that Wallops Island scene. You've been clear about that, haven't you? *You...weren't...there...,*" he slowly drawls while pacing in front of me. "I mean it's important the jury's reminded of that point. You were living in Massachusetts, busy with your life up there. You weren't even in Virginia, and never saw April Tupelo's body in person, so to speak, correct?"

"That's correct." I'm increasingly uneasy about getting out of here alive.

Enclosed by cherrywood-paneled partitions with a waist-high door, I'm mindful there's no quick way out as Flagler continues working the courtroom into a frenzy. I steal a glance at Pete Marino, seated up front on the aisle where he can get to me in a hurry. His big sun-weathered face is stony as he takes in everything around him without making it obvious.

"What about the defendant, Gilbert Hooke?" Flagler starts his next tactic, and the rumbling around me is ominous. "How many times have you met with him, ma'am?"

"I haven't," I reply.

"The two of you have never been introduced?"

"No."

"You never visited Mister Hooke while he was locked up in Norfolk jail prior to being transported to Alexandria?"

"No."

"Maybe you've spoken to him by phone?" Flagler persists, and what he's implying is absurd.

"I haven't. It wouldn't be a normal thing for me to do in this case or any other."

"Why's that?" He stops pacing, stares at me, shrugging. "Why wouldn't it be normal?"

"Determining guilt or innocence of the accused isn't up to the medical examiner," I reply.

"Then the only time you've had any direct exposure to the defendant is this afternoon inside this courtroom? Is that what you're telling us?"

"That's correct." I know better than to let my eyes wander to the defense table.

But it doesn't mean I'm not aware of Gilbert Hooke seated with his lawyers. He watches me intensely, not reacting to much, the legal pad and pen in front of him remaining untouched.

"And ma'am?" Flagler keeps ramping it up. "Since you haven't spoken to or met with the defendant, you don't have an informed opinion about what kind of human being he might really be, now do you?"

"I don't."

"You have no direct knowledge about whether he's capable of cruel acts, including murder and mutilation? You couldn't possibly know if he's the cold-blooded monster people say he is, now could you?"

"I have no direct knowledge—"

"Objection!"

"You wouldn't have personal knowledge about whether Gilbert Hooke is pathologically jealous? Of if he'd been violent and psychologically sadistic with April on other occasions—?"

"I object!"

"...You have no personal knowledge of him being out of control and vindictive when he doesn't get his way or isn't the center of attention? Especially when he's drinking, correct—"

"Objection! Asked and answered!"

"...My point is, you don't personally have a clue what the defendant's really like, do you, ma'am?" Flagler says to me while Annie watches with stunning silence.

"No," I answer. "I have no personal knowledge."

"And you wouldn't know whether any of us are safe should the jury come back with a not guilty verdict, and Gilbert Hooke is out and about, free again? You have no direct knowledge of that either, do you?"

"I don't."

"Well, the courts seem to think the defendant is plenty danger-ous, bringing to mind Hannibal Lecter—"

"Objection!" Gallo shouts, and I've never seen him this offended. "For God's sake, Your Honor!"

"It's no accident that Gilbert Hooke has been held in isolation without bail since his arrest almost two years ago," Flagler continues unimpeded. "It's clear why he should remain behind bars for the rest of his destructive and hateful life..."

■   ■   ■

All eyes are on Gilbert Hooke, clean-shaven with pale skin and short mousy hair, in a drab cheap suit several sizes too big. He could pass for a young attorney were it not for his jail-issue orange sneakers, and the shackles around his wrists and ankles.

This in vivid contrast to how he looked at the time of April Tupe-lo's death almost two years ago when he was muscular and darkened by the sun. In every image I've seen of him displayed in the court-room so far, he's wearing a tactical combat knife on his belt and a large-caliber pistol.

He's shirtless, sporting tattoos and a cocky grin, usually with a beer in hand. We see him baiting outriggers, filleting fish, blood and guts everywhere. Or shooting his gun at a shark he's gaffed while laughing maniacally, ejected cartridge cases glinting in the sun. All of this is a deliberate and effective ploy on the prosecution's part.

"Again, I'm just reminding the jury that what you see with Gil-bert Hooke isn't what you're getting." Flagler aggressively points at the defense table's team of pricey lawyers, and the upset murmuring is louder. "Don't be fooled by his mild-mannered appearance!"

"Objection!" Gallo complains.

"Mister Flagler, that's enough," Annie finally says.

He digs his hands in his trouser pockets, parking himself squarely in front of me. I'm staring at the *champs de fleurs* pattern on his blue silk tie, picking up his bright scent again.

"Ma'am? I don't care how many fancy degrees you have, you can't undo death, now can you?" he asks me.

"No."

"You can't restore to April Tupelo's loved ones what they've lost, correct? So what choice does someone like you have except to become desensitized, isn't that right, ma'am?"

"No, that's not right—"

"In fact, your earliest memories are of your father sick and dying," he says. "I regret the necessity of bringing up such a delicate subject. Because how could it have done anything but ruin your formative years...?"

"I object! Relevance!"

"While also making it difficult for you to have relationships, to connect with people. Living ones, I mean—"

"Objection, Your Honor!"

"Sustained. What's your question, Mister Flagler?"

"What type of cancer did you say?" He directs this at me.

"My father died from chronic myeloid leukemia."

"Sadly, you got started young learning how to make yourself bulletproof emotionally. Of course, growing up in a bad neighborhood in Miami, you probably needed to be *bulletproof* in more ways than one," he adds to derisive laughter around me. "Neither of your parents were born in this country and barely spoke English, isn't that true?"

"I'm just going to keep objecting!" Gallo shakes his head in disgust, and I'm more incensed than he is but no one would know it.

By bringing up details about my childhood and Italian ethnicity, the well-heeled Flagler with his prominent pedigree is reminding the jurors and everyone else that I'm an outsider. He's painting me as a coldhearted female who's barely American, and I can feel the hostility in the air like static electricity.

"Let me rephrase," he replies while Annie looks on without interfering. "From an early age you were taking care of your terminally ill father, weren't you, ma'am?"

"Yes."

"*You had to learn not to feel,* isn't that true."

"No, it's not true."

He stalls again, flipping through his notes, and people are making ugly comments that I'd rather not hear.

"Quiet in the courtroom," Annie says.

"Ma'am?" Flagler looks at me. "You've decided that April Tupelo wasn't murdered because...? Um, strike that. I'll start over... Now, let me see if I've got this straight. Your opinion is based on these little snowflakey-looking things that the jury heard testimony about earlier from someone who works at a museum... *Diatoms.* Am I pronouncing that right?"

"Yes," I answer.

"And diatoms are basically algae, the scummy stuff we see on ponds and in fish tanks."

"You can't see diatoms with the unaided eye unless there are a lot of them, a bloom as it's known," I reply.

"So, you happened to notice these teeny-tiny things called diatoms even though they're invisible to the rest of us unless there's a bloom of them?"

"The individual unicellular algae can be seen easily with a microscope." I keep my attention on the nine women and three men in the jury box, most of them retired and college educated.

"And ma'am, you were looking through that microscope in hopes of getting lucky. Sort of like finding the prize in the Cracker Jack box, is that right?"

"No, that's not right. It wasn't luck or happenstance that I found diatoms," I reply. "I checked for them specifically in lung tissue preserved during April Tupelo's postmortem examination twenty-one months ago on October seventeenth—"

"Like I've said, you had a hunch, and wanted to prove it by experimenting with body parts," he says. "Ones that had been preserved in glass jars like canned peaches all this time...?"

"Objection!"

"Sustained. Mister Flagler, let the witness fully answer the questions. We need to speed this along," Annie adds, to a distant rumble of thunder as a late afternoon storm rolls in.

"During autopsies," I continue, "it's standard to preserve sections of organs and other biological tissue in a colorless solution of formaldehyde and water called formalin."

As I give the jurors a brief morgue primer, Flagler constantly shifts his position. Moving my head this way and that, I must look ridiculous as I try to see past him.

"This is basically the same fixative that funeral homes use in embalming, and has no effect on diatoms being present or not," I explain. "Formalin wouldn't have destroyed the diatoms, in other words. The problem is they weren't looked for at the time of April Tupelo's death. This should have happened but didn't."

There's nothing I've seen in reports or been told that would make me think the subject came up. I'm sure the reason it didn't was that Dr. Bailey Carter had become incompetent. According to those he was closest to, the sixty-four-year-old forensic pathologist was suffering from rapid onset dementia. He'd become forgetful, erratic and resistant to suggestions.

Performing April Tupelo's postmortem examination and in charge of the medico-legal investigation, he didn't consider drowning as the likely cause of death or a possibility. She died from manual strangulation according to what he filled in on the final autopsy report and death certificate. I have no idea why he thought this unless it was a guess. Much of her throat's soft tissue was gone, decomposed and fed upon by marine life.

There was no apparent evidence of injury to the structures of the neck, and no reason to rule that strangulation killed her. It didn't. She may have sustained injuries that were gone or not found. But she drowned, and Bailey Carter missed the telltale signs. He disposed of the "watery brownish" gastric contents without checking for diatoms.

Had he done so, he would have found them the same way I eventually did when I examined preserved sections of the victim's lungs, I explain to the jury.

"Because of the wave action in ocean drownings," I'm saying, "victims often swallow water in addition to inhaling it. Especially if the surf is rough—"

I'm interrupted again, this time by a matronly juror waving her hand in a spirited fashion. Heavily made up and flashing big rings, she has zany winged glasses and lavender-tinted hair, reminding me of the British comedian Dame Edna.

CHAPTER 3

Do you have a question for the witness?" Annie asks the juror.

"If it's all right. Yes, please," she says in an accent that sounds more like South Carolina than Virginia.

"Go ahead." Annie nods at her.

"I guess I'm still a little confused why these diatoms are so important. For example, if the victim had gone swimming earlier in the day, could that explain your finding them?" the juror asks me.

"Not in her lungs," I reply. "Not inside intact organs, in other words."

"Well, I'm wondering if you would mind explaining what these diatoms might actually tell us that matters in this trial. And are they dangerous? If I filled a glass with tap water would they be in that too? Are they in this?"

She lifts her plastic bottle of water up to the light. Reflexively, the other jurors do the same.

"How would I know? And what if I drank them? What if my schnoodle did?" she asks with all sincerity.

"That's highly unlikely unless you're talking about drinking water from a well, a lake, maybe a stream or pond," I reply as she writes it down with pencil and paper supplied by the court. "But neither you nor your pets would want to ingest diatoms because some produce toxins."

The microscopic organisms are ubiquitous, I go on to describe. They're in rivers, bays, oceans and other bodies of water all over the planet. Like different types of pollens, diatoms can vary enormously depending on location.

"That's why they're important in an investigation," I add, and the juror who asked the question is nodding her head. "They might tell us what happened and where."

Finding diatoms in lung tissue would confirm the victim inhaled water, and that's what I discovered. When I reviewed slides under the microscope, the single-celled creatures were in abundance, bringing to mind tiny bits of sea glass and the symmetrical shapes in a kaleidoscope.

"I also had samples of ocean water taken from the area where it's believed the victim went overboard." I give the jurors the upshot of measures I took. "And those diatoms are consistent with the ones in her lungs—"

"Okay, okay, assuming you're right about all that?" Flagler has heard enough. "It wouldn't mean April Tupelo *wasn't* murdered, now would it? Maybe water got into her lungs while she was floating in the ocean for three days, isn't that possible?"

"She inhaled water. That couldn't happen unless she was still breathing, still alive when she went into the ocean." I repeat what I've been saying to him all along. "It means she couldn't have been dead on a boat for hours, and then cut up and thrown overboard to chum the waters."

As I counter the false claims in the prosecution's case, I can tell that Flagler is about to lose his temper. I recognize the warning signs. His cheeks turn red, and his right hand starts twitching like a gunslinger about to draw his weapon.

"Are you trying to let someone get away with murder, ma'am?"

Flustered, he's beginning to sputter, angrily raking his fingers through his dark wavy hair.

"Objection!"

"Your Honor, I think it's a fair question."

"The witness may answer," Annie says.

"All I'm doing is testifying as honestly and as clearly as I can," I explain to the jurors, and the one who questioned me is watching intensely, jotting her notes. "My statements are based on medical science, and had this case been mine originally—"

"I didn't ask you!" Flagler angrily cuts me off, and I interrupt him right back.

"I would have signed out April Tupelo as a drowning, the manner of death undetermined pending further investigation—" I'm silenced by the uproar.

"Order," Annie warns as spectators inside the courtroom boo while others applaud and blurt out comments. "Quiet, please."

"Now I'm the one stringently objecting, Your Honor!" Flagler scowls at me as if I'm Judas.

"You called her as your witness," Annie reminds him.

"Yes, but Your Honor, her statement is non-responsive. It's mere speculation stated as fact—!" As if he's never heard me say it before over the phone and in person.

"Order, please..."

The whispering and angry asides continue.

"Quiet in the courtroom. Ladies and gentlemen, please. Thank you, thank you..."

As the uproar subsides, the fitness tracker–type "smart" ring I wear on my right hand is vibrating silently. A swarm of messages and calls are landing on my phone, which isn't in my possession at the moment. I sneak another glance at Pete Marino. He's not supposed to have his phone, either. But rules are made for others, and whatever he's looking at is making him unhappy.

He's busy typing with his thumbs, and wouldn't be doing that right now if it wasn't urgent. Scowling, he glances up as if he senses me looking at him, and something's going on. It's not good, almost never is.

"Ma'am?" Flagler says to me, sliding the touchscreen tablet out of his pocket again. "I'm wondering if you've seen any of these? What I guess you'd call *premortem* images, ones taken before death?"

Video clips begin playing of an adorable little April Tupelo hamming it up in a number of pageants she was winning by the age of seven. More crying and murmuring in the courtroom, and I can't help but think of the murdered child beauty queen JonBenét Ramsey.

"Objection! Relevance and prejudicial!" Gallo starts in.

"Overruled."

"Are these familiar?" Flagler asks me.

"No."

"I see. I thought you said you've reviewed all of the materials?"

"There wouldn't be a reason for me to look at these videos," I reply.

"They wouldn't have helped with April Tupelo's identification?"

"She was an adult when she died, and wasn't visually recognizable by the time her remains were recovered." I state the obvious as the commotion around me intensifies. "She was identified by dental records and DNA."

New images on monitors are of April as Chincoteague High School's homecoming queen. She's slender, athletic-looking and *Seventeen* magazine pretty in a long black dress.

"How about these?" Flagler asks me. "Have you seen them before?"

"No."

"And this?"

He displays a close-up of what was left of her featureless face and hairless head. The empty eye sockets and bared teeth are intentionally shocking as death investigators and police zip the maggot-teeming remains inside a black body bag.

"Yes, I'm quite familiar with the scene photographs and videos," I answer.

"It wasn't April Tupelo's hope and dream to be turned into fish bait by her psychopathic boyfriend, now was it, ma'am...?" Pointing his finger at the defendant again.

"Objection, Your Honor! Is there a question somewhere? Anywhere at all?" Gallo protests furiously as thunder explodes directly overhead like a rifle shot. "Was it something I said?" He looks up as a hard rain begins hammering the roof.

■ ■ ■

The sudden thunderstorm reverberates like a war going on, and it couldn't be more appropriate. The courtroom is divided down the middle, April's people seated on one side, and those here for Gilbert on the other.

The Tupelos and Hookes are considered dynasties on Virginia's Eastern Shore, their competitiveness in the fishing industry passed down through the generations. During the trial, there've been only passing references to their historic hostilities. But I've seen the sordid details in confidential psychological and investigative reports.

The families have been enemies since before the American Civil War, and this added exponentially to the risk factors for the victim and defendant. Like a Shakespearean tragedy they were doomed from the start. That was part of the appeal for the two of them. It's one of the reasons the story has sparked with the media, and books have been written.

Day after day, the back wall of the courtroom is packed with journalists from the largest outlets, including the *New York Times*, Reuters, Fox and CNN. Film crews have set up camp in nearby hotels, and it's difficult evading their cameras and relentless questions. The sensational publicity was a major factor in the murder trial's venue moving to a Washington, D.C., bedroom community.

Were Old Town Alexandria any farther north, we wouldn't be in Virginia anymore. This part of the world is a foreign country compared to where the Tupelos and Hookes are from. In this area jurors could be found who have no connection to either family, but this hasn't stopped relatives, friends, supporters and the curious from showing up.

Many of them have traveled by RVs that are parked in local campgrounds. Some are living on their fishing boats moored on the Potomac River. Traveling in groups to and from court, these visitors have invaded local marinas, laundromats, liquor stores and markets. A few of them have gotten into scuffles over vaccines, gun control, abortion and other incendiary topics.

All of this is concerning to those of us who live here. Fear of COVID-19 and its variants isn't the only reason some of us haven't been going out, especially after hours. In recent days, protesters have showed up at my medical examiner headquarters. They march around the parking lot with megaphones. They beat pans with sticks while shouting *Justice for April*.

Some of these visitors have appeared in front of my house. Their vile comments and gestures are captured by my niece Lucy's hidden surveillance microphones and cameras. My husband, Benton, and I haven't been to a local pub or restaurant since the trial began. We haven't ordered takeout from our favorite spots or gone for a stroll, a jog or a bike ride around here.

"Ma'am," Flagler says to me, "how many victims of violence have you examined over the years?"

"I don't know the exact number."

"Five thousand? Ten thousand?"

"More than that."

"Well, I have a good idea what you see every day."

Here we go again. He continues painting me as a doctor to the dead. Someone who has no bedside manner or empathy, and I'm unpleasantly reminded of my mother criticizing me unrelentingly until her last breath.

You can't fix it, Kay. Dead is dead. I hear her voice in my head. *What a waste of an expensive education.* As if she paid for it.

The truth is you're antisocial. Now my sister Dorothy invades my thoughts. *A misanthrope.* She says it often enough.

"My point, ma'am?" Flagler turns up the volume. "As desensitized as you may have become? I think you would agree that April Tupelo didn't deserve being hacked up to chum the waters, now did she?"

"Objection! There he goes again!" Gallo is on his feet.

"Sustained—"

"Gilbert Hooke cut up her dead body and threw it overboard so the crabs would get it!" Flagler rails.

"Burn in hell!" Someone starts yelling.

"Order, please..."

"Fry him!"

"Quiet in the courtroom, please..."

"Guilty!" Others chime in.

"Order!" Annie picks up her gavel as thunder claps, the rain pounding in a violent percussion.

"GUILTY!"

"Justice for April...!" people begin chanting.

"Order!"

Annie bang-bangs her gavel as Gallo again calls for a mistrial, and I am reminded how quickly a riot can start. I steal another glance in Pete Marino's direction as my smart ring continues vibrating alarmingly.

"Order! Quiet in the courtroom . . . !" Annie hammers away, looking like an indignant blackbird, her robe flapping.

The uproar slowly subsides, the guards hovering and ready. I catch a shadow of uneasiness in Annie's eyes that I've not seen before. What's happening may be entertaining to watch on Court TV, but for those of us here it's another story.

"Quiet, everyone. Thank you," she says. "Mister Flagler, please continue."

"In summary, you had nothing to do with April Tupelo's death investigation until just a few months ago," Flagler says to me as if I'm the one on trial. "And yet suddenly here you are the expert? The one we're supposed to believe?"

"The forensic pathologist who responded to Wallops Island, and performed April Tupelo's autopsy, died before I moved back to Virginia," I reply.

"And it's been your testimony in depositions that the late Doctor Bailey Carter basically committed malpractice and perjury, among other crimes?"

"I've never said such a thing or accused him of a crime—"

"And as a consequence, there's been a lot of negative publicity? All of his earlier cases have come into question, isn't that true?"

"Yes. Unjustifiably and unmerited, I would add—"

"All of his cases going back decades are under scrutiny because of his questionable ethics and judgment?" Flagler body-blocks my view of the jury again.

"Doctor Carter was one of the finest medical examiners I've worked with," I reply as I imagine his widow watching this on TV. "But at the end of his life, he was impaired."

"Most notably, there are doubts about his handling of the couple killings, the Colonial Parkway murders that occurred when you were working in Virginia the first time, correct?" Flagler says. "Those cases were twenty-two years ago, and now there might be serious doubts about what really happened back then—"

"Objection! Relevance."

"Overruled," Annie says, and what Flagler intimates is largely true.

"It's correct that Doctor Carter was the deputy chief in the Tidewater district office when the Parkway murders occurred," I reply.

"And you were the chief then. He worked for you, and you supervised him."

"At that time, yes. To my knowledge, nothing was mishandled in those cases—"

"And you would know because you were in charge then. Just as you are again? Meaning the buck stopped with you?"

"Yes."

"And not long after the Parkway murders, you moved away from Virginia, isn't that right?"

"Yes."

"That's convenient. Now you're back, testifying that while you were gone, cases were screwed up like this one? Is that what you'd have the jury believing?" Flagler says.

"Objection!"

"Overruled."

"Maybe you're trying to make yourself look good at Bailey Carter's expense? Maybe that's what you're really trying to do?" Flagler says to me as he looks at the jury.

"I'm not," I reply.

"He was involved in conspiracies, and it drove him to suicide, isn't that right? That's why he hanged himself?"

"Objection!"

"Overruled," Annie says, and Flagler's statements are outrageous.

CHAPTER 4

I know nothing about a conspiracy, and never stated that Doctor Carter was deliberately ill-intended or deceitful." I keep my attention on the jurors as I think about Bailey Carter's family watching. "But he made erroneous assumptions in the April Tupelo case that couldn't be more misleading—"

"Sounds like you're doing a lot of second-guessing for someone who wasn't living or working in Virginia at the time, doesn't it...?"

"It wasn't my wish to criticize Doctor Carter or accuse him of anything, and still isn't. But he made serious mistakes," I reply. "In his original handwritten notes and diagrams, he refers to lividity, what's known as a livor mortis pattern. And there wasn't one, for example—"

"All right, thank you—" Flagler butts in again.

"Let the witness answer, Mister Flagler." Annie is fair to me, finally.

"After death, the heart no longer is beating," I tell the jury. "Therefore, blood isn't circulating and it settles like sediment."

This causes corresponding areas of skin to turn livid, a bluish-red color that looks similar to bruising. One would expect to find this had April Tupelo's body been aboard the boat for hours after her death. I don't know what Doctor Carter thought he was seeing, but what he described simply wasn't present.

"There was no livor mortis pattern, and no deliberate mutilation to chum the water." I'm emphatic about it. "The gashes to April Tupe-lo's back and buttocks were caused by a motorboat prop. They weren't inflicted by a knife or some other sharp cutting instrument."

"Yes, well, let's get to her ghastly injuries!" Flagler defiantly strides back to the prosecution's table.

He picks up a white cardboard banker's box that's the same size as a carton of copying paper. It's not marked as evidence or labeled in any official fashion because what's inside is a demonstrative exhibit. Better put, a stunt. As he moves around, we hear a mysterious sliding sound, and Gallo begins his objections.

"Your Honor, there's no probative value to this latest trick he's about to pull!" he protests.

"It's just a demonstration for the sake of clarity," Flagler assures her.

"I'll allow it, but my patience is running out, Mister Flagler." Annie doesn't put a stop to what I have a feeling will be his biggest spectacle.

The knife he's about to show the jury has a hefty handle with a guard, and a seven-and-a-half-inch carbon steel blade that's double-edged and pointed. I know this because I've examined it more than once in Flagler's presence. The defendant was a competition knife thrower trained in martial arts. I'm not surprised he would own a combat weapon or that April Tupelo's DNA was on it.

They lived together. She crewed for him during charter trips. Both of them were facile with tools and cutting instruments, using differ-ent types for various tasks and chores. The early evening of October 14, 2020, they'd been arguing while drinking beer in the heat with little or nothing to eat. It was getting dark when April left him to use the toilet, according to the defendant's written statement.

When she didn't return after *10 or 15 minutes, maybe a little longer,* Hooke started looking for her, and she wasn't on board. He began shining the searchlight over the water *in a panic,* he claimed. Finally, he radioed a mayday to the Coast Guard. April's disappearance was treated as a homicide, and it doesn't matter if she and Gilbert weren't getting along.

Their fighting likely contributed to what happened. But legally it's not why she's dead. I base this on evidence I've studied, including photographs and video of the boat itself. One of her flip-flops was found on the stern near a metal cleat smeared with blood that would turn out to be hers. The autopsy showed that around the time of her death, she suffered a deep laceration on the top of her left foot, and a fractured big toe.

Her postmortem alcohol level was three times the legal limit. Absent other injuries or any obvious sign of a struggle, I suspect she tripped on her way to the head while extremely intoxicated. The sea was choppy, the boat rocking up and down. The visibility was deteriorating as the sun went down, the safety rail low, and she wasn't wearing a life vest.

Details in the autopsy report describe the victim dying with a full bladder. This suggests she went overboard before making it to the toilet, very possibly while she was on her way there. Her death was senseless and preventable. It's the sort of tragic event I've seen all too often when people add one foolish risk factor to another, and the equation suddenly turns fatal.

Gasping for air while trying to keep her head above the heavy surf, she would have swallowed and inhaled saltwater. After that, she wasn't going to make a sound as she drowned. It's unprovable how much time passed before Gilbert Hooke realized she was gone. We know only that he radioed for help at almost eight P.M., a good hour after sunset.

. . .

"Since you're supposedly such an expert in violent atrocities, ma'am, how about you show the jury what happened that night?" Flagler says. "A picture's worth a thousand words, isn't that right? People should see things for themselves, isn't that what you always say, ma'am?"

He carries the banker's box toward me.

"I'm not sure what you're asking—" I start to answer.

"Now, I warn everyone that this may be upsetting." He bombastically raises his voice above the din of the thunderstorm stalled directly over us.

Resting the box on the polished wooden rail in front of me, he calculates his every move while countless people watch on live TV.

"I realize this won't be pleasant to imagine." What he says is accompanied by whispering and the loud creaking of benches.

"Quiet, please," Annie says.

Spectators are repositioning themselves, trying to get a better view, the tension in the air like a low vibration building to an earthquake.

"We need to bravely look at what Gilbert Hooke did to someone he supposedly loved and wanted to marry." Flagler takes the lid off the box.

"Objection! Where's the question?" Gallo shouts.

"When what he really wanted was to possess and control April Tupelo literally to death!" Flagler declares.

"Objection!" Gallo is on his feet again.

Flagler reaches inside the box, lifting out a dagger-like black steel knife that I know for a fact he found on eBay. He's shown this to the jury before, but not in my presence or accompanied by a demonstration that I know will be underhanded.

"Now obviously, as I've stated previously, this isn't the actual weapon that the defendant had on his charter boat twenty-one months ago. But it's exactly like it, the same make and model," he says.

"Your Honor, I'll continue my same objection!" Gallo begins yet another scathing protest while Annie does nothing. "There's no evidence that the knife he's parading around has to do with anything. We all agree that the victim's death is a terrible thing, but she wasn't strangled and mutilated by Gilbert Hooke or anyone else."

"Now who's testifying?" Flagler retorts.

"Mister Gallo, your objection is sustained," Annie decides to Gallo's surprise.

"Thank you." He sits back down.

"Please proceed, Mister Flagler. And maybe you're not watching the clock, but I am."

"Yes, Your Honor. Obviously, the actual knife found on the defendant's boat has been admitted into evidence. It was examined by the forensic labs here in Alexandria, isn't that right, ma'am?"

"Yes," I reply.

"And you're in charge of those labs?"

"They're in my building but I'm not in charge—"

"But you have a say about what goes on in them."

"If it relates to medical examiner cases, yes—"

"Obviously, I didn't want Gilbert Hooke's actual knife passed around the courtroom due to contamination concerns. April Tupelo's DNA was discovered on that knife, wasn't it, ma'am?"

"Objection! Your Honor, Doctor Scarpetta didn't examine the knife."

"Overruled. The witness may answer."

"I'm aware the victim's DNA was found on it."

Flagler holds up the replica of the wicked-looking knife, and the jurors crane their necks, spellbound. The protests and whispers rolling through the audience are frighteningly louder.

"The defendant never went anywhere without his combat knife, the steel blade blackened, making it invisible in the dark," he says. "Advertised as perfect for assassins, it's ideal for slicing and throwing—"

"Objection!"

Flagler offers the box, the knife to me, and I don't touch them.

"Connoisseur of violent death that you claim to be, ma'am, would you like to show us how the defendant slashed up April Tupelo's dead body?" Flagler continues goading me, hoping I'll lose my temper.

"Her postmortem cuts weren't inflicted by that knife or any knife," I repeat as he turns the box upside down.

"Well, if you won't do it then I'm going to show you what happened. And you tell me if I'm right!" With startling violence, he plunges the blade through the cardboard, stabbing and slashing, making loud ripping sounds.

People react with outbursts, clapping and whistling over Gallo's enraged objections and Annie banging her gavel. A gaunt, harsh-looking woman in a JUSTICE FOR APRIL T-shirt is crying uncontrollably, and I've seen her in the news. Nadine Tupelo is the victim's mother.

"I realize this is unbearably hard." Flagler watches as those seated nearby tuck in their legs to let her pass, patting her back and squeezing her hand.

She's joined by three other women, possibly family members, and they hurry out of the courtroom. On their heels are several journalists, including Channel 5's Dana Diletti, and she never fails to ambush me. The upset muttering picks up again, and Annie taps a warning with her gavel.

"Quiet, please."

"What I just demonstrated is what really happened, now isn't it, ma'am?" Flagler returns his attention to me. "That's what the defendant did to April Tupelo's dead body before throwing it overboard, correct? As opposed to your lame claim that a motorboat prop was to blame?"

"The periodicity of her injuries is inconsistent with the random slashes of a knife or other cutting instrument," I emphasize without looking at him.

"There's that big word again. *Periodicity*," he says condescendingly, the restless noise inside the courtroom growing dangerously.

"The incisions on her back and buttocks are exactly one and a half inches apart," I inform the jury. "The pattern is similar to what you'd see if you drag a rake over sand. The marks will be parallel and the same distance apart. That's what I mean by periodicity."

Flagler holds up the knife and shredded box, strutting around. The emotions on both sides of the aisle echo the weather. Thunder sounds in staggered explosions, the rain beating in different rhythms, the wind gusting and howling.

"Quiet, please," Annie says.

"You weren't even there!" Flagler points the knife at me, jabbing the air for emphasis, making sure it's caught on TV cameras around the courtroom. "You never even thought about this case until just months ago!"

"Objection!"

"...Maybe that's why it's easy for you to let someone get away with the murder of a beautiful young woman whose entire life was before her!"

"OBJECTION!"

More booing, only louder, and people are yelling *guilty* and *fake news*. Others join in accusing me of working for the defense, of being

35

bought by politicians. A scary-looking man in back calls me a *commie*, and a young woman shouts that I'm a *body-snatching Nazi*.

"Order. Order! ORDER…!"

"Your Honor, I have no further questions," Flagler says when the uproar begins to fade.

"Your Honor," Gallo says, standing up. "The witness has supplied all the testimony I need, and I have no questions."

"I have no further witnesses, and rest my case." Flagler pointedly looks up at the wall clock, the time nearing five-thirty P.M. "Thank you for your patience," he says to the jury. "I know it's been a long day."

"Your Honor," Gallo says, "the prosecution hasn't proven as a matter of law all the elements of this case. As I've continued to state, *that's because there is no case*. Doctor Scarpetta has stated her position under oath, and I see no need to waste the time of the court and the jurors by putting on further witnesses."

"Is the defense resting, Mister Gallo?"

"Yes, Your Honor. And due to the lack of evidence the prosecution has presented over the better part of two very long weeks, I'm making a motion for a directed verdict."

"Denied. There's sufficient evidence for this case to go forward. As for the quality and quantity of the evidence, that's up to the jury."

"Thank you, Your Honor. Nothing further," he says.

"Gentlemen, are we done for the day?" Annie asks, and they are.

When she finally addresses me directly, it's without a trace of a smile. I'm excused and may step down. Everyone else is to remain seated until court is adjourned. Annie's giving me a chance to make a safe getaway. She's released me as a witness, and I don't have to come back. At least she's doing that much after allowing Flagler's disgraceful machinations and behavior.

I get up from my uncomfortable wooden chair with its hard leather upholstered seat and armrests as she announces that the trial will reconvene tomorrow at eight A.M. Both sides are expected to wrap up, making it all the more crucial that the jurors continue following the court's strict instructions.

"...We're down to the wire, and then you'll be deliberating. The life of the defendant will be in your hands," Annie says. "Before we leave here today I again will review the rules of law applicable to this case, and remind you to be guided by them and not emotion..."

In a few minutes, they'll climb aboard the shuttle bus that awaits in the sally port behind the courthouse. It will return them to the local Marriott where they've been sequestered from the start. No doubt they'll want fresh air once the storm blows over. The temptation will be strong to venture out, to stroll along the water, to enjoy the sights.

"...Just say no...," Annie continues her instructions.

I step out of the witness stand, and Pete Marino looms large and threatening in his black cargo pants, tactical boots and T-shirt that flaunt his action-hero build. He hands over my briefcase.

"...No errands," Annie continues to instruct. "No going on a quick walk to pick up takeout food from the many wonderful restaurants in the area, and I know it's tempting. But please stay put..."

She reminds the jurors that Alexandria's historic district of Old Town has a population of fewer than ten thousand. It's not a whole lot bigger than Mayberry, she says, referring to the old TV show starring Andy Griffith.

"...Only imagine media and tourists coming in from everywhere while this trial is going on...," she's saying.

CHAPTER 5

I feel hostile eyes fasten on Marino and me as we pass through the large paneled courtroom with its coffered white plaster ceiling and glass ball chandeliers. He has a fierce expression on his face, his jaw muscles flexing nonstop, the top of his shaved head beaded with sweat.

We avoid looking on either side of the aisle. But in my peripheral vision I catch ugly gestures, people nudging each other, making snide comments.

"...So please, no wandering about. Chances are good you might run into someone connected to this case, and that could be disastrous...," Annie goes on, and I'm vaguely aware of the man who called me a *commie*.

Seated on the aisle in back, he has the ruddy complexion of a drinker who's out in the sun too much, his long gray beard reminding me of Spanish moss. An American flag tattoo covers his neck, and he's missing part of his nose and lower lip, likely from skin cancer.

"You're going down, bitch!" he snarls under his breath as his skinny leg and booted foot snake out.

Clipping my right ankle, he hisses obscenities. I stumble to a wave of gasps, feeling as if I've just been whacked by a hockey stick. My thick accordion organizer spills confidential case files, and this may be the worst day in court I've ever had.

"Whoa, Doc!" Marino grabs me, adding to my embarrassment.

People are whispering and snickering, and if Annie is aware of what's going on, it doesn't register. Her attention is intensely on the jurors as she continues instructing them while I collect my scattered paperwork clumsily, furiously. My face is burning, and I'm awkward in my fitted skirt. I've managed to snag my panty hose and almost lose a shoe.

Putting myself back together, I inadvertently meet Gilbert Hooke's stare. His eyes are pale like a Siberian husky's, the edges of his lips barely curling up in a smile that could be a sneer. He winks at me, and it's as if I've been touched by a draft as cold as dry ice. Cramming my paperwork back inside my briefcase, I limp after Marino, out of the courtroom.

"Dammit!" he exclaims, the double wooden doors swinging shut behind us. "Some motherfucking piece of shit! I should have broken his fucking leg!"

Over six feet tall and built like a heavyweight boxer, Peter Rocco Marino looks more like a bouncer or hit man than a former homicide detective turned forensic operations specialist. Originally from Bayonne, New Jersey, he's never lost his accent or early imprinting. He can be uncouth and crass, a tough-guy character straight out of central casting.

It's his nature to be overly protective, especially when it comes to me. Some would say he's been territorial as I've headed various medical examiner offices around the country over the years. He's relocated each time I have. No matter where I'm needed, he's always there, thinking of us as partners in crime, but we're more than that.

We always have been. Now he's family, and I don't mean just the extended kind. When the pandemic was surging the first time, he and my sister Dorothy got married after dating on and off for years.

Marino is my brother-in-law. I don't think I'll ever get used to the thought.

"...The dirtbag better hope I don't run into him somewhere...!" he continues in a voice that carries. "Are you hurt, Doc?"

"I'll be fine." My ankle throbs.

"The son of a bitch will pay for this...!"

"A better idea is not drawing attention," I remind him.

The corridor isn't entirely empty at this late hour, and I'm on the lookout for April Tupelo's mother, Nadine. I don't want to run into her or the companions she left with earlier, and can only imagine what they must be feeling. Nothing I might do is going to diminish their pain and hostility, and I understand why they might blame me.

I hate to think what Bose Flagler tells them behind my back. What he says in court is bad enough. I'm sure he has them convinced that I'm in cahoots with the defense. Gilbert Hooke winking at me doesn't help. Marino hurries us toward the illuminated exit sign in the distance, my heels a sharp staccato on the checkerboard marble tile.

We pass tall Palladian windows overlooking the courtyard three stories down, rain thrashing the glass. Thunder rumbles as lightning illuminates glowering clouds, the late afternoon dark enough that streetlamps are blinking on. I'm dismayed to see that the main drag of King Street is a solid strand of cars in both directions.

We're going to get drenched. I don't look forward to sitting in gridlocked traffic forever. I dig my phone out of my briefcase, and it's no wonder my smart ring is vibrating like mad. My secretary, Maggie Cutbush, is trying to reach me. So are my deputy chief Doug Schlaefer, death investigator Fabian Etienne, and Alexandria Police Investigator Blaise Fruge, among others.

"What's going on?" I ask Marino. "Because something is."

40

"We got a big problem, maybe more than one, and need to get the hell out of here as fast as we can..." He starts to explain when we're interrupted by a loud banging accompanied by impatient exclamations.

"...Shoot...!"

Veteran court reporter Shannon Park boils out of the ladies' room.

"...Oops...!"

She knocks against the door again with her pink hard case on wheels, the long silver handle extended.

"...Oh, darn...!" she says in her lilting Irish brogue, and then she spots me. "Kay? Thank goodness, there you are!"

In her early sixties, she's as small as a child, her spiky hair dyed red with hints of fuchsia that fade to pink at the tips. She typically looks like she was dressed by a tornado that hit a vintage clothing shop first, her many layers mismatched and whimsical. Today she has on a yellow bucket hat, and saddle shoes that remind me of my childhood.

She's been a fixture in the Virginia judicial system since Marino and I were getting started. We saw her regularly, often having lunch with her. Now she works when she wants, picking some cases and avoiding others.

■　■　■

"What are you doing here this late? Especially in the middle of a monsoon?" Marino asks her.

She's been covering the Gilbert Hooke proceedings during the mornings, and it's surprising that she'd be here at this hour.

"I have something I needed to deliver in person," Shannon replies as more thunder rumbles and cracks, a fierce wind flinging rain against window glass. "And then too much coffee, and I had to make a quick visit." Her old-fashioned euphemism for needing to use the bathroom. "I was afraid I might have missed you."

"We're trying to get out of here before Judge Chilton's court adjourns." I explain as kindly as I can why I'm not inclined to chat. "I'm sorry. How about I call you later? What are you doing this weekend? Maybe you can come over."

"That's probably not a good idea, and I won't be around." She lowers her voice conspiratorially.

Plastic wheels clatter noisily as she rolls her hard case closer, and it's plastered with pink ribbons and rainbow stickers. Inside are her stenograph machine, recorders and other equipment. Also, containers from whatever she brought to eat, and the latest paperback novel she's reading, probably a thriller, I can safely deduce from past experience.

"I wanted both of you to know I'm done here sooner than expected," Shannon says.

"It could be days before the jury comes back with a verdict," I remind her. "The trial isn't over yet, as much as all of us might wish it."

"It's over for me," she says flatly. "I quit. And I don't just mean the Gilbert Hooke case. I've had enough."

"No way," Marino says. "You're the best court reporter out there, fastest fingers in the East."

"I'm heading to Richmond to stay with my daughter for a while, getting far away from this ticking time bomb before it blows," she replies. "No matter the verdict, I'm afraid of violence. And with the Fourth of July coming up on top of everything else? Well, no thank you. I'm tired of being around horrible people."

"How about we walk you out?" Marino winks at her, and I'm reminded unpleasantly of the defendant winking at me. "We should hoof it before Judge Chilton adjourns all the assholes in there."

"Oh, I'm fine. My car is safely tucked away inside the parking garage, which is where yours should be."

"I like being right out front, darling. Where you park there's too many places for people to lurk in the shadows and behind stuff."

"Well, any lurkers try to bother me, they'll get whacked but good." The floral-printed umbrella Shannon is armed with looks like one my mother used to carry. "But I believe I'll wait a bit. You know how these storms are. They blow over fast. If only other bad things would."

She rummages inside her quilted pocketbook, digging out a pink envelope that has nothing written on it.

"For when you have a quiet moment, Kay. When you're not in a hurry or distracted."

She hands me what looks like a Hallmark card with something lumpy inside it. I promise her that I'll take a look when the time is right. I tuck the envelope inside my briefcase, and Shannon walks off, her sticker-covered pink hard-shell case rolling after her.

"My phone's been blowing up," I say to Marino as we resume our rapid pace along the corridor. "Maggie, Fabian, Fruge, a number of people have been trying to reach me for the past twenty minutes..."

"The judge has a sister, Rachael Stanwyck," he replies, and bringing her up in this context is a very bad sign. "Forty-seven years old, going through a nasty divorce from Lance Stanwyck, a billionaire who's probably a prick. She works for the CIA. A spy, in other words. Were the two of you friends?"

"She's the CIA's press secretary, and not a spy as far as I know. She's been staying with Annie temporarily while looking for a new place to live..."

"It's temporary, all right. Rachael's just been found dead on the kitchen floor."

"Oh God." I go hollow inside.

"The judge will hear about it soon," Marino says.

"How terrible."

"Then what happens to the trial? Imagine everybody going through this ordeal all over again?"

"Who's notifying Annie?" I ask as we pass the cafeteria, the lights low, the entrance barricaded with a metal curtain.

"Fruge, probably," he says.

"This is way over her head."

"You got that right."

"If nothing else, it's going to be a majorly complicated mess," I tell him. "A very public one. It's a good thing Fruge thinks of you as Yoda."

"As she damn well should."

The Alexandria Police Department's greenest investigator, Blaise Fruge, is talented. I believe she's trustworthy. But this isn't the case for her to cut her teeth on.

"She texted me to call her but didn't say why. What do we know so far?" I ask Marino, and we've reached the end of the corridor.

"Fruge is calling the death suspicious. That's what the police are releasing to the public. But she's indicating in her messages to me that it's a homicide." He pushes through the fire exit door that leads to the stairs.

"Based on?"

"They're thinking it might have been a home invasion gone bad." His big voice echoes, his booted feet loud.

"Someone broke in? Rachael was attacked on the driveway while getting in or out of her car? What are we talking about? A shooting? A stabbing? Evidence of sexual assault?"

"I don't know. Probably Fruge doesn't want to put stuff in writing that can be subpoenaed. I've warned her about it enough," Marino says as we reach the first-floor landing, my ankle throbbing.

He pushes through the fire door leading outside, and the downpour is as loud as a car wash, the rain splashing and sizzling. It's as if buckets of water are dashed on us as we set out across an expansive walled-in courtyard that's pleasant enough in decent weather. Usually it's crowded. But at the moment it's just the two of us slogging through puddles with our heads bent, strong gusts of wind grabbing at our clothes.

Wrought iron benches and café tables are empty beneath thrashing trees. No one else is in sight as we forge ahead through billowing sheets of rain. The storm wasn't in the cards when Marino picked me up at home this morning as he's been doing lately. We headed to court in the early afternoon, and there wasn't a cloud in the sky. The weather prediction was for hot, humid temperatures, perhaps a light rain.

But nothing like this, and he doesn't believe in umbrellas. My state-issued take-home car with my rain gear and scene case in it is parked at home. Marino has insisted on driving me while the trial is in town, acting like my bodyguard as usual. I have nothing to change into except the personal protective equipment (PPE) in lockers built into the back of his truck. That's not ideal when I have nothing dry to wear under it.

"What time was the body found and by whom?" I raise my voice above the din of the storm as we hurry through the courtyard, the rain coolly soaking through my clothes.

"All I know is the guy who takes care of the property was supposed to meet Rachael late afternoon," Marino says, and I know who he's talking about.

In his early seventies, Holt Willard has worked for the Chilton family most of his life. I've encountered him on a number of visits over the years, including recently when Annie's had me over to her house. I've sat in the very kitchen where we're told her sister's dead body is on the floor.

Images of Rachael Stanwyck flash in my mind. She was gorgeous and vivacious. But I found her vain and indifferent, her eyes unhappily distracted the few times I was around her.

"He was meeting her for what reason?" I hold my briefcase in front of me, shielding my face from the driving rain.

"I don't know," Marino replies as we reach the sidewalk, and then we say nothing more.

Dana Diletti is in front of the Georgian-style courthouse, one of the few public buildings in Old Town that's a modern reproduction. By now, she and her film crew are familiar with Marino's black Ford Raptor pickup truck. Looming over other vehicles on its oversized tires, it's parallel parked at a meter near the Starbucks coffeehouse.

"Enough already, goddammit!" Marino says much too loudly as the camera light flares on. "Let's go!"

Stepping ahead of me, he runs interference, waving his arms angrily. He's pouring more gasoline on the fire, and for all the world to see.

"This is Dana Diletti outside the circuit courthouse in Old Town, back to you live . . . ," she starts in.

Beautiful and six feet tall, the popular television journalist is larger than life in a khaki trench coat with the collar flipped up. Her crew attends to her every need, their umbrellas forming a canopy as if she's a royal.

". . . It's been another explosive day in the trial of accused murderer Gilbert Hooke . . . ," she's saying into her microphone.

LIVID

The former professional basketball star is nimble, brazen and quick. She can get into a foot pursuit without breathing hard, doing whatever it takes to score her points. That includes throwing elbows, so to speak, and committing other fouls without penalty, it seems.

CHAPTER 6

As if the case hasn't been bizarre enough, it's taken a shocking new turn that raises the question of a mistrial." And then Dana Diletti is on top of me. "Doctor Scarpetta? If I can have just a minute...?"

"Not now!" Marino barks at her as thunder cracks and lightning illuminates the volatile overcast.

"I'm sure you're aware of the breaking news?" Dana asks over the splashing rain, and I feel a sucker punch coming. "Is it true that Judge Chilton's sister has just been found dead under suspicious circumstances? Rachael Stanwyck, the press secretary for the CIA...?"

I have nothing to say, and no one who cares about her should find out like this. I continue making my getaway as lightning flashes unnervingly close, thunder splitting the air.

"...Can you confirm that foul play is suspected...?"

I'm distracted by the heel of my right leather pump becoming dangerously wobbly.

"...This must be upsetting to you personally. I have it from a reliable source that you and Judge Chilton used to be roommates, and are close friends...?"

One of Dana's umbrellas almost pokes me in the eye, her crew bird-dogging me down the sidewalk. Marino can do nothing but stay a few feet ahead, soaking wet and infuriated.

"...Are you headed to Chilton Farms right now...?" Dana's voice is right behind me like a kite tail.

Favoring my right foot and its unstable shoe, I'm hurrying along with an ungainly gait that won't translate well on camera. Neither will my ducking behind my briefcase as I'm chased down a sidewalk. My drenched gray linen skirt suit and white silk blouse are plastered to me like shrink-wrap, and that's not the look I want, either.

"...Doctor Scarpetta? Do you think the judge will recuse herself? Do you expect a mistrial in the Gilbert Hooke case, and what will that mean...?"

Dana and her crew don't quit their pursuit, and thank goodness Marino's pickup truck is in range. He remotely unlocks it, the lights flashing in the foggy deluge. He runs ahead of me as the loose heel of my right shoe detaches completely.

"Shhhh...!" I swear under my breath, almost stumbling again. "Dammit!"

I kick off my ruined leather pumps, and must look like a fugitive or crazy. Making a run for it in my stocking feet, I splash through puddles, the bricks spattered with flower petals that are slippery. Rain smacks the top of my head, my injured ankle aching.

"Let's go!" I shout above the rain as Marino opens the passenger's door, and we couldn't be more drenched had we fallen into a swimming pool.

"What the hell?" He stares at my dirty feet and shredded hose. "What happened to your shoes?"

"Never mind!" I climb up into the seat.

Dashing around to the driver's side, he slides behind the wheel. We drip all over leather upholstery that still smells new as rain loudly pummels the roof. He cranks his big truck, and I can feel its roar and rumble in my hollow organs. Emergency sirens wailing in the distance are getting closer, possibly on their way to Chilton Farms.

Where Annie lives is about a thirty-minute drive from Courthouse Square when traffic is normal. But in the current conditions and were I on my own it could take an hour or more. Fortunately, Marino isn't driving a state-owned vehicle like my take-home Subaru with the seal of Virginia on it. In his sinister-looking personal truck, he's got a lot more potential for breaking rules than I do.

An independent contractor working mostly pro bono, he doesn't have my concerns when duty calls. There isn't a median strip, private property, bicycle or pedestrian path that's off-limits. He's happy to speed, run red lights, make illegal U-turns and activate his truck's aftermarket mini-lightbar and beacons. If the situation is sufficiently dire he'll resort to a handheld siren that could wake the dead.

He's quick to display his forensic investigator badge as if he's still a cop, strutting about, and loud with his opinions while issuing orders. Unlike him, I don't get to break protocol or the law when it suits. I'd best be careful throwing my weight around. But I don't know what even Marino can do to remedy our current situation as we go nowhere in a hurry.

Hemmed in between other parked cars, we can't move forward more than a foot or two. There's less room to back up, and on our right are parking meters and the sidewalk. The only choice is to exit left. That's assuming someone will let us, and so much for Good Samaritans or even decent neighbors. The hell with the Golden Rule. Nobody will look in our direction. It's everybody for themselves.

"I don't know that even you can find a way out of this madness." I look around at a dangerous confusion of harsh lights and loud engines, and hostile people at the wheel.

"Geez-us! How damn hard is it to let somebody in?" Marino lays on the horn. "What's wrong with everyone...?"

"I'm not sure how we'll get to the scene or anywhere else," I reply as a roiling mist reflects our headlights and foglamps back into our faces.

Cars and pedestrians are everywhere, and it's mostly a younger crowd out and about this early Thursday evening. The restaurants, bars and shops are hopping regardless of the weather. People are starting the long holiday weekend early. It's happy hour at the height of tourist season, and Marino continues cursing as he tries in vain to merge onto King Street.

I dig inside my waterproof briefcase for tissues and a tube of lip balm. The pink envelope from Shannon Park is safe and dry. As are my files and everything else, thanks to Lucy. She never misses an opportunity to supply me with the latest tactical accoutrements. The black messenger bag I carry everywhere looks like a normal accessory. But the leather-like material is an ultra-high-molecular-weight polyethylene.

It's interwoven with electrically conductive micro-copper fibers, and embedded with sensors that I can't see. My briefcase can be unfolded like origami to form a shield against projectiles, knives and deadly radiation. Hidden compartments are fitted with flexible featherlight Kevlar panels, the quick-draw holster empty at the moment except for my phone. I slide it out again.

"It wouldn't be a bad idea keeping towels in here, Marino. Really." I offer the same helpful hint whenever we're caught in a downpour. "Especially since you're phobic of umbrellas because you think they're not a good look. Well, this isn't a good look, either."

Water is puddling at my feet, and soon enough I'll be freezing in the air-conditioning.

"Except I got too much crap inside my truck to begin with because of what other people think I need." He means Dorothy. "A few weeks ago, it was a fire extinguisher and a mini-fridge she thought I couldn't live without. Before that, it was some fancy designer toolkit I'd never use."

As he continues to make excuses, he gropes under our seats. I do what I can to accommodate, tucking my legs to one side or the other. The wipers thud-thud, sweeping water off the windshield, the rain steady but not as hard as earlier. Already, the storm is moving out, and that's typical during hot, humid Virginia summers.

"Here, this will have to do." Marino hands me a crushed roll of blue paper towels, maybe ten sheets left.

They're the heavy-duty type he uses to Armor All the tires and trim, to wipe down the carbon fiber or clean the glass of the expensive truck that my sister bought him. A successful graphic novelist and Internet influencer, Dorothy indulges him to a fault, buying him whatever he wants and many things he doesn't. I tear off paper towels for us, combing my fingers through my wet hair.

Staring at my reflection in the visor mirror, I wipe off eye makeup. I dab on the lip balm, looking like death on a cracker, to borrow a line from Dorothy. I reach up my skirt as modestly as possible, pulling off my destroyed panty hose. I stuff them and dirty tissues into the red biohazard trash bag hanging from the gear shifter.

"Uh-oh." Marino glares at the Channel 5 news crew several spaces away from where we're parked. "Exactly what we don't want."

■ ■ ■

Dana Diletti and her producer hurry into their van, the door sliding shut. The turn signal begins flashing, the front tires cutting left. I can feel Marino's aggression and defiance as he hands me his soggy paper towels.

"They want to get to the scene first," he says. "So they can film us rolling up, the whole nine yards."

He tries again to bully his pickup truck into traffic, and nobody lets him. My vibrating ring alerts me that my secretary, Maggie, is calling again. I'm not about to answer.

"Thanks a lot!" Swearing and fuming, Marino continues his efforts with no success. "Jerkoffs! Bunch of idiots!"

Tossing out a few other choice words for good measure, he rolls down his window, waving his muscular tattooed arm in the foggy rain, shouting at other drivers. Some of them mouth back while making offensive gestures. I hope we don't end up in a road rage free-for-all.

"What's the hurry?" he yells at everyone and no one in particular, his eyes glaring, the veins standing out in his neck. "Your damn hair on fire? You never heard of a fucking emergency? Well, I'll show you one!"

He flips on green and white strobes that I'm not sure are legal, their rapid stuttering enough to cause vertigo.

"HANG ON, DOC!"

He grabs the handheld siren from its holder, and I cover my ears.

"FIRE IN THE HOLE!"

He whelps his way into traffic as horns honk and blare in a discordant cacophony. We pass the Channel 5 news van, and it manages to dart in behind us, nearly causing an accident.

"DAMMIT!" Marino yells as we creep off in sluggish traffic, the lights dancing on the police scanner, the volume low. "I've had enough of this bullshit!"

He scowls in his mirrors, turning off the strobes, rain blowing in through the window as he closes it. He irritably tries wiping his eyes dry with the sleeve of his dripping-wet T-shirt, and I hand him several tissues. He dabs his face, then his shaved head as I begin telling him what to expect.

"Rachael Stanwyck worked for the CIA. She didn't have to be a spy for there to be an uproar," I explain. "I won't have control over much that happens next. Not the control I usually have, depending on the circumstances, and at the end of the day we may never know the whole truth about who she was. Or what's happened and why."

"What was your gut feeling about her?" Marino puts on mirrored Ray-Bans, amber-tinted for mist and haze.

"I didn't know her," I repeat. "When Annie and I were in law school together at Georgetown, occasionally I'd spend the weekend at Chilton Farms. Her sister was never there. She hated the place, and I've not gotten the sense that she's shown up for much of anything in Annie's life."

"Rachael sounds like somebody who pisses people off," Marino says. "That might be an important detail if it turns out that someone whacked her."

"I would imagine she was quite skilled at offending people," I reply. "Lucy and I ran into her once at the liquor store on Saint Asaph Street where I have a feeling Rachael was a regular."

This was several weeks before the Gilbert Hooke trial had started, and life was still relatively normal in Old Town. There were no hostile strangers camping out, no news crews or writers from here and abroad. It was safe to frequent our local haunts, and Lucy and I had gone for a bike ride on the Mount Vernon Trail.

We followed it to Gravelly Point where aircraft spotters watch traffic in and out of Ronald Reagan Washington National Airport.

On our way home, we decided it would be a good night for fajitas and margaritas, and stopped to pick up a couple bottles of tequila. We were tucking our purchases into our backpacks when Rachael walked in.

She was dressed in a fitted midnight-blue skirt-suit that was Dolce & Gabbana, and wearing a gold Rolex with a diamond bezel. Her sunglasses and big pocketbook had ostentatious Chanel logos, and I could tell she'd been crying. She declared that she'd been savaged all day by her estranged husband's *team of flesh-eating lawyers*, as she referred to them.

Arrogant pricks. Misogynistic meat puppets. Lance won't rest until I'm destroyed, you know. What she said seems ominous now as I repeat it out loud. *He's hoping the stress will kill me. Nothing would please him more.*

"It sounds like she didn't give a shit who overheard her," Marino says, the wipers dragging across the glass intermittently. "Meaning she probably did that sort of thing a lot. You'd think someone working for the CIA would be more careful about running their mouth."

"Her background was journalism," I reply. "It's been my impression that she didn't hesitate to say whatever she thought, often bluntly and with little regard for how she came across."

Reaching in front of me, he unlocks the glove box. He lifts out his 10-millimeter matte-gray Guncrafter Industries 1911, custom built with Trijicon optic sights. Old-school Dirty Harry huge and heart attack scary, it's loaded with 200-grain Buffalo Bore rounds, cocked and locked, the thumb safety on. He places the pistol and extra magazines on the console between us.

He arranges them for easy access as I turn on my phone's flashlight. I check my injured ankle, tender to the touch, the bright red bruise turning dusky. I take photographs as Marino constantly scans the mirrors, blowing out exasperated breaths. We've made it only a few blocks.

The CVS drugstore is to our left. Just beyond is Lucy's favorite bicycle shop, and the Indian restaurant that Benton likes a lot. The lights of traffic, the splashing rain are distracting and confusing. The truck's menacing-looking grill guard is alarmingly close to the sports car in front of us, triggering loud warnings.

Everywhere I look I see accidents and outbursts about to happen as stressed commuters behave like primitives. I'm reminded that Marino and I have been inside a courtroom most of the afternoon. Before that, we were inside the autopsy suite. I've not had access to my phone for much of the day. We've been in our own morbid bubble, and I suspect there's much happening that we don't know about.

"I'm not sure I've seen it this bad before. Something else is going on, has to be." I begin checking my emergency alerts and traffic apps. "Maybe a bad wreck, some other disaster in the area. This isn't normal rush hour, not even in a storm before a holiday weekend."

"You got that right," Marino complains. "This minute we're going six miles an hour, and people are acting like the world's coming to an end."

It doesn't take long to discover that the cause of the chaos is the president of the United States. He made a visit to Old Town earlier this afternoon, and there were security issues, a perceived imminent danger that resulted in his motorcade diverting. Sections of King Street and the George Washington Memorial Parkway had to be shut down for extended periods.

It's no wonder I've not heard from Benton and Lucy. Any threat to the president, and the U.S. Secret Service takes over. My husband is going to be involved. Possibly my niece will be as well. He's their top threat analyzer and criminal profiler. She's a technical subject matter expert, her title intentionally ambiguous.

"For a while, even the Woodrow Wilson Bridge was closed in both directions," I relay to Marino.

"What security issues? Are there any details?" he asks as I glance through news articles and other information.

CHAPTER 7

The president was supposed to visit Ivy Hill Cemetery for a service at two-thirty but the motorcade was turned around." I keep looking for news updates but there's almost nothing. "It returned to the White House. There's not much else I'm finding, including on government sites."

"Must be something they're keeping hush-hush," Marino says.

"Whatever it is they're taking it seriously."

"I'm betting the feds have boxed in Alexandria, maybe the entire greater D.C. area, because they've got a suspect. Maybe more than one." Marino has both hands tensely on the wheel, red taillights blearily stretching ahead endlessly.

"Unfortunately, stories about Rachael Stanwyck's *suspicious and shocking* death are popping up all over the place already." I tell Marino what else I'm finding as we make our way in the awful traffic. "Conspiracies are brewing about the *privileged and peculiar Chilton sisters,* and I quote."

Annie's address has been published. There's gossip about her passive behavior on the bench during the Gilbert Hooke trial. She's accused of showing favoritism toward Bose Flagler while treating Sal Gallo deplorably. Rumors are flying about why she's never married and lives like a recluse in the family's eighteenth-century *haunted mansion.*

"Forget any semblance of privacy," I pass along to Marino. "Everything about this would be terrible for anyone. But it's especially dangerous for a judge, and unfortunately she's lax about security, as you're about to discover."

He hasn't been to Chilton Farms, and won't be happy when we get there. It may or may not have ghosts. I can't swear to that, although I've heard my share of strange noises. I've seen peculiar shadows, and glimpsed strange images in mirrors I pass. What I can state categorically is that the overgrown property is a safe haven for gnats, ticks, mosquitoes and other antisocial insects.

Annie rules against pesticides, including natural ones like garlic spray. Outdoor lighting is basically nonexistent. As I'm describing this, Marino reaches for his gun. He places it and the extra magazines in his lap.

"Get ready, Doc!" His attention is everywhere, jaw muscles clenching.

I notice a brick wall on our right in the swirling fog. Just beyond is an alleyway Benton and I have walked through when it was still safe to take long strolls in Old Town.

"HANG ON!" Marino yells.

That's my cue to grip the armrest, pushing my head against the back of the seat so I don't bang into the window or wrench my neck during one of his NASCAR maneuvers. He floors it, cutting the steering wheel hard, rubber squealing, the engine gunning, the force of the turn shoving me against the door.

"BOOM! Now we're talking!" He folds in the side mirrors.

He snakes his big truck through a narrow lane originally meant for pedestrians and horse-drawn carriages.

"Be careful of the stone column coming up on the left." I point it out in the mist.

"No way anybody's following us back here."

Pleased with himself, he carefully bumps us along, foglamps reflecting off water and wet pavers. If I opened my window, I could reach out and touch the back walls and gates of grand old residences. The branches of ancient evergreens and English boxwood hedges are inches from us.

"Not the smoothest ride, sorry about that." He glances at me, and I see my distorted reflection in his mirrored glasses. "But better than sitting on King Street for the rest of our lives."

Turning around in my seat, I look for Dana Diletti and her crew. The narrow passage behind us is empty and foggy, no sign of the white van with the news station's logo on it.

"I think you lost Channel Five and everyone," I confirm. "Not that I'm surprised. I don't believe cars are allowed back here. Nothing with an engine or much bigger than a golf cart."

"I figure you could use a hit right about now." Marino slides open the ashtray. "You and me both."

He digs through his stash of retro chewing gum that reminds him of better days. The familiar aromas of Teaberry, Juicy Fruit, Bazooka and Dubble Bubble bring back powerful memories of my childhood when I would help out in my father's neighborhood grocery store.

"Thanks." I take the Wrigley's Spearmint Marino offers, both of us recovering smokers.

He rolls up three sticks of gum, cramming them into his mouth at once. The inside of his truck smells sweetly minty as he navigates through the alleyway, past wrought iron fencing and walls. I glance at my phone, scrolling through messages.

"Did Lucy tell you what she's doing today?" Marino is nonchalant as if it doesn't bother him that they aren't as close.

"We had coffee before you picked me up this morning but she

didn't mention anything specific," I reply. "She had on her bike gear and backpack, though, headed out somewhere."

"At least she's not holed up in her crib twenty-four-seven talking to an avatar as if it's a real person," he says unpleasantly.

"That's not fair. Or accurate."

"I just don't want her getting any weirder on us, Doc. Riding her tricked-out bike all over the place like it's the X Games, chasing radio signals and things that go bump in the night."

He's not really worried about how my niece spends her time. What's under Marino's skin is that she's sworn law enforcement again, and he's not. It rankles him that he no longer can arrest people and lock them up, and she can. This on top of his relationship with her cooling considerably after he married her mother.

■   ■   ■

Traffic isn't nearly as bad now that we're on South Royal Street with its pristine detached homes and rowhouses, many with American flags over the entrances. Bronze historical plaques attached to siding are a reminder that nothing much can be done to your property without permission from a preservation committee.

The low sun shimmers through the lifting overcast as we get farther away from congested neighborhoods. We're headed to the largely uninhabited stretch along the Potomac River where Annie and Rachael Chilton grew up. The haze is burning off, steam rising from pavement. A band of fiery gold light spreads along the horizon, and I recheck my messages, sending Fabian Etienne another one.

"Let him know to avoid King Street unless he wants to sit there until he turns into a skeleton," Marino says.

"There's no point in telling him much when he's not bothering to answer us." I've about had enough of this.

"Hell, it's exactly what he fantasizes about," Marino says. "A big case that's all over the news, and he rolls in like the Grim Reaper. He's probably been primping in the mirror for the last half hour, putting on eye makeup, redoing his nails."

"Fabian doesn't respond to me in a timely fashion unless it suits his purposes," I reply, and my problem with the death investigator isn't the way he looks.

It isn't his taste in attire. Or even his favorite cliché, *Our day begins when yours ends,* that's silkscreened and printed on T-shirts and coffee mugs he sells on the Internet. I can't control Fabian. It was bad enough when I first got here. But after a year it seems close to a lost cause.

I have no doubt who's influencing him, and it's been escalating. I think of recent encounters with the former physician's assistant who claims he's always dreamed of being a death investigator. Yesterday, I couldn't find him for hours, and finally took the elevator below ground to the anatomical division.

Phones don't work very well down there, and that's his excuse when he's not answering. I discovered him injecting formaldehyde into the femoral artery of the most recent body donated to science. He was doing an embalming with no one else around.

"This is the third time I've caught him," I remind Marino. "God only knows what the real number is. Fabian has decided he doesn't answer to me, not to either of us. And I don't think he's the only one who's decided it."

I send him another text, warning about traffic. I instruct him to head out, adding that I hope he got my earlier messages. He's to bring extra PPE, and on his way to grab scrubs and a pair of surgical clogs for me. I don't want him in my office digging through more personal clothing. I don't want my secretary touching my belongings, either.

"Screw this." Marino checks traffic all around us.

He nudges his truck ahead barely, and I can tell he's about to bust another move.

"Hold on, Doc!"

He flips on the strobes like a cowboy cop. Flooring it, he cuts into another side street as I clutch my briefcase, holding on to the armrest again.

"You're going to have to do something about her." Marino is talking about Maggie. "Before it's too late. And maybe it already is."

"You know how hard it is to fire anyone who works for the state," I reply. "Especially if that person is protected the way she is and has been for decades. Should we go after her, it will be an all-out war. One we won't win because she's in Elvin's pocket."

"You mean in his pants."

"We can't prove that or much of anything," I reply.

"We've got to find something to nail her with like leaks to the media. Because we know damn well it's her. What's she getting in exchange for her favors to the Dana Dilettis of the world? Our office is hemorrhaging like a damn sieve."

"And who's going to do something about it?" I reply, and it's a tired argument. "Elvin oversees everything that pertains to public health in the Commonwealth. That includes how people die. I answer to him." It's a loathsome thought, and Marino can't accept it. "Elvin has all the power, and he set things up to be exactly like they are. I'm sure he's enjoying himself royally."

My predecessor, Elvin Reddy, won't forgive or forget. He'll never stop paying me back for dropping him from my forensic pathology fellowship program. This was decades earlier when I was new on the job in an all-boys club. The first woman chief medical examiner of Virginia, I had very decided ideas about doing no harm. Death shouldn't be political. It's not something to be exploited or trivialized.

I refused to mentor Elvin or so much as write a letter of recommendation, and would do the same today. When I agreed to replace him as chief medical examiner last year, I didn't know the rest of the story. It wasn't until I'd moved here that I realized his secretary, Maggie, wasn't leaving with him. I'd inherited her. Then he was appointed health commissioner. I'd been lured into a trap is the way Marino describes it.

I grip the armrest again as he careens into another alleyway. This one isn't as narrow as before, and we're a few blocks from the river. Sunlight breaks through clouds, and a perfect rainbow arcs across the sky over the steeple of the Basilica of Saint Mary. I've not been to church since the pandemic started. Before that I had other excuses, if I'm honest.

"Let's see what Maggie has to say for herself, what poisonous stew she's been stirring up this time." I call her mobile phone, and it barely rings before she answers instantly.

"It's about time you got back to me," her voice sounds rudely from the truck's speakers.

"I've been a little busy, as you well know," I reply.

"I left you a message that the health commissioner needs a word with you." My secretary's polished British accent belies her basic incivility.

I can tell from the background noise that she's home from the office. It sounds like she's outside walking her dog, and she asks me to hold for a second. I hear her picking up after her Corgi named Emma as Marino glances at me, shaking his head hatefully. Then Maggie resumes telling me how frustrating it is when I'm missing in action.

"As usual you're nowhere to be found, flitting about with your personal investigative partner in his gas-guzzling truck," she's saying, and I sense her resentment like a bomb off-gassing. "And his reimbursements for fuel and such are something you and I need to discuss..."

"You know exactly where I've been." I make no attempt at sounding gracious, barely polite. "I've not had an opportunity to deal with much of anything since escaping a volatile situation in court a few minutes ago—"

"I have no doubt that you could use a vacation, a rest from all this madness." Maggie is quick to cut me off, and I have no doubt who she's been conferring with. "Today in particular has been...Well, there's no other word for it other than *deplorable*."

"What do you want, Maggie?"

"I understand you've yet to call Doctor Reddy?"

"Call him about what?"

"If you'd bothered to return my call in a timely fashion you would know." The way she addresses me, you'd think she was in charge. "Well, it won't be possible to reach him now."

Elvin no doubt has plenty to say about Marino's outbursts, and my running shoeless along the sidewalk in Courthouse Square. Every public embarrassment, mistake and misfortune is a gift when one's adversary has the obsessiveness of a stalker.

"Doctor Reddy is having dinner at the governor's mansion, and waited as long as he could. I'm afraid you lost that window of opportunity." Maggie's arrogant voice inside the truck.

"What's so urgent?" Anger continues heating me up. "Why is it more important than what Marino and I are on our way to deal with—"

"I'm afraid your public spectacles a little while ago are everywhere." Maggie continues to interrupt. "He and others aren't happy about your investigative partner's behavior, either. It's simply disgraceful the way he bullies and threatens—"

"You've got to be fucking kidding me!" Marino feels compelled to interrupt as profanely as possible.

"Such language," she goes on to chide him, and I imagine her imperiously pretty face as sharp as a blade.

I can see her smug, satisfied smile as she walks her spoiled dog through her cloistered Old Town condo development. I tell her that Channel 5 knew about Rachael Stanwyck around the same time Investigator Fruge notified our office.

"Dana Diletti was on the air first with the breaking news, ambushing me yet again." It's obvious what I'm accusing. "And this has been happening all too often. It's been escalating."

"Just one of many things Doctor Reddy has concerns about," Maggie says. "But far more troubling is your very clear conflict of interests."

Rachael Stanwyck is linked to a controversial trial that's international news. She's the sister of the very judge in the case. Apparently, Annie Chilton and I have a long history, Maggie goes down the list.

"You know better than most that there's not much one can't find out these days." Her tone turns insidious like the hiss of a snake. "And apparently it's come to the health commissioner's attention that you and the judge once lived together in a lovely place that I wouldn't think was in your price range back then."

CHAPTER 8

Maggie informs me that Channel 5 has been digging up all sorts of interesting information about Annie's and my past. Including specifics about the rented rowhouse we shared while at Georgetown Law, two bedrooms and a patio. It's not far from the Four Seasons Hotel, my secretary says, and that's true.

I paid Annie one dollar per month in rent, and I don't know how Maggie found that out. I won't confirm or deny. I feel as if I'm on the witness stand again as I listen to her comments and unseemly assumptions sounding over the truck's speakers. I'm not about to divulge that Annie enjoyed my company, and benefited from it. Both of us were helpful to each other.

She was happy to have somebody around who cooks, gardens, does laundry, yardwork, and so many things that she never learned and avoids at every opportunity. I derive pleasure from taking care of my world and those in it. She's missing such tendencies in her DNA, it seems. But she more than makes up for it with her honesty and decency.

"I think it is glaringly apparent that one of our other medical examiners should respond to Judge Chilton's property. Someone other than you." Maggie gets to the punch line with maddening presumption. "There are just so many reasons why you should stay away from Chilton Farms."

"That's not up to you." I feel my pulse picking up, and she's one of the few people I know who can make me livid.

"But it is indeed up to the health commissioner. He wants you to turn around now. You're not to continue on to the scene, and that's an order, Doctor Scarpetta." Maggie says this with perfect calm in her posh London accent.

I'm to go home and enjoy the July Fourth weekend with my family. From this point on, all media requests are to be handled by Elvin Reddy's office. I'm to have nothing to do with the Rachael Stanwyck case, period. Marino isn't, either.

"I informed Doctor Schlaefer that he needs to respond to the scene," Maggie continues with a plan that isn't hers alone. "He'll be heading to Chilton Farms in a few minutes, and I've sent Fabian on his way."

"Which you have no damn authority to do," Marino blurts out.

"Doctor Schlaefer will take care of the autopsy first thing in the morning." Her haughty voice sounds through the truck's speakers, and Elvin must be in a good mood right about now. "He'll deal with the police and others who have an interest, and all will be fine."

"All wouldn't be fine, and it's not happening," I reply. "You can tell Elvin that I'm continuing on to Chilton Farms. It would be most appreciated if I could do my job without interference and undermining. Once I understand what we're dealing with, I'll give further instructions about who's doing what and when. Let me be clear, Maggie. It will be me who does that."

"I'll let him know how you've responded." She ends the call.

"Fuck her." Marino's hands clench on the wheel. "Her and Elvin both."

"I'm nipping this in the bud right now," I reply. "I'm telling Doug that we're handling the case. I'm sending him the message in writing so he can't deny he was told."

My instructions are to respond to the scene personally, my deputy chief texts me back a few minutes later. *Maggie says the health commissioner thinks it's a problem if you show up. Because of what's all over the news.*

I'm in transit now. I make sure Doug understands who's boss. *Do not head out. I'm handling Rachael Stanwyck. If you have questions, call me.*

I just don't want trouble with powers that be, he replies, and clearly, I'm not the one he worries about.

"We'd better give Fruge a heads-up about what's going on," Marino decides after I read the texts out loud. "That she'd better expect a shit show if she hasn't figured that out already."

He reaches for the touchscreen on the dash display, placing a call, and Investigator Blaise Fruge isn't picking up. Of course, she isn't. Unquestionably, she can't. Someone is making sure of it. The question is who, and for what reason. It could be Maggie or Elvin. It might be someone else.

You've reached Investigator Blaise Fruge with the Alexandria Police Department. If this is an emergency..., her voice mail begins.

I'm more aware of her lilting Virginia accent because she's not in front of us. She sounds formal and stilted, as if trying too hard to be taken seriously. Marino leaves her a message. We're having trouble with leaks and people meddling, he says. Should someone else from our office show up at the scene, don't allow access without checking first.

"Doesn't matter if it's Fabian or Doctor Schlaefer, the cops aren't to let them in unless we say it's okay, and right now it's not," Marino explains in his message. "We're almost at Belle Haven Market. If they're still open we'll hit the john, and see you in a few."

Set back from the road amid lush trees and shrubbery, the barn-like country store is ahead on the left, its red siding paint-peeled. The tin roof glints like pewter as the sun settles closer to the horizon, and the wraparound porch with its big swing is empty and shadowed. Until recently, Benton, Lucy, my sister, all of us were regular customers.

On weekends we'd sit at the picnic tables in back, feasting on salads and sandwiches. We'd leave with bags of locally grown produce, homemade baked goods and other specialty items, including fudge for Dorothy and retro gum for Marino. It's one of my favorite places to shop, but in recent weeks I haven't been here once. It wouldn't be smart.

The market is a local landmark, featured prominently on tourist maps. You can buy beer, wine, lottery tickets, and there's an ATM. People come from all over, and I suspect business has surged since the Gilbert Hooke trial started.

"At least there are a few things you can still count on," I say to Marino as he slows down. "This place hasn't changed since my law school days, and still has the best sandwiches in Alexandria."

"Don't remind me. I'm so hungry my stomach is digesting itself."

As he says this mine grumbles. The last thing I ate was the fish fillet and fries from McDonald's in the early afternoon. I could handle twice that right now, and would pay a king's ransom for an iced tea, a coffee, anything with caffeine.

"I'm betting the judge and her sister have been coming here since they were kids." Marino flips on his turn signal. "Wally's probably waited on them forever."

"Annie's a regular. I have no idea about Rachael's shopping habits beyond her visiting the local liquor store."

"That's another question," he says. "Her habits. Not just shopping but booze, for example. Was she drinking a lot? Maybe more than before because of the stress of the divorce? What else was she doing?"

■　■　■

Marino drives into the market's parking lot, and handwritten on a big A-frame sign is today's lunch special. My mouth waters as I imagine the roast beef and chutney on toasted sourdough, the cup of chilled spicy gazpacho.

It's 6:15, and often the market closes early when big storms are rolling in. But we may be in luck. Unless Wally Potter got a ride home it would seem he's not left yet. His blue Malibu Classic is parked inside the wooden carport in the shade of crepe myrtles and jacaranda trees. I can't help but think of my father whenever I see the vintage wagon. Only Papa's was a Ford with faux wood side panels.

I remember the smell of vinyl in the Miami sun, the interior door locks reminding me of golf tees, the hot air rushing in when we'd hand-crank the windows down. There are no other cars, no one in sight as Marino drives past the island with its self-service gas pump. While running errands you're welcome to top off your tank and clean the windshield. You can check the oil and put air in the tires.

Off to the side is a big unpainted shed that has firewood during cooler months, and fresh wreaths, pumpkins and potted lilies depending on the holiday. There's a restroom that can't be used without getting a key from the counter, and a dog potty station with biodegradable bags. Like the grocery store my father ran before he was too sick to manage it, Belle Haven has a little bit of something for everyone.

Marino pulls up front, and I notice the CLOSED sign hasn't been displayed. But it isn't always, depending on who locks up at day's end. Especially if that person was the owner. Wally can be forgetful, and through a window I can see his empty ergonomic chair behind the checkout counter.

"I'm not getting the sense that they're still open," I say to Marino.

"Maybe he's in back. He's probably frapping around, getting ready to head out."

"He doesn't hear very well but should see us on the security cameras," I reply.

"Assuming they're working and that he or anybody's checking."

I look up the store's phone number. Calling it, I'm disappointed by a busy signal.

"He must be on the phone," I decide. "If he's heard about Rachael, I would imagine he's calling people or they're calling him."

"I'll try the door," Marino says.

He removes his arsenal from between his legs where he's held it securely while careening in and out of side streets and alleyways. I hope he never does this when his big pistol's safety is off, and he returns it and the magazines to the console between us. He climbs out of the truck, and I call the store's number again.

I have no better luck as Marino's feet sound on wooden steps leading to the covered porch. He walks past the empty swing suspended by ropes, then the ice machine, and the trash can made from a wine barrel. He tugs on the front door, and it's not budging.

"HELLO! YO! ANYBODY HOME?" He bang-bang-bangs with his fist. "HELLO! HELLO...!"

Cupping his hands around his face, he peers through the glass, shouting and knocking some more. He walks across the porch, and at the far end is the office window. The blinds are drawn, the glass covered by a screen. Marino knocks on the wood siding.

"YO, WALLY? YOU THERE?"

Yelling and thumping some more, Marino gives up with a frustrated shrug. He returns to the truck, his clothing damply clinging but not dripping anymore.

"Dammit!" He climbs back behind the wheel. "There's nobody here. I'm sorry, Doc."

"I appreciate you trying." And it's not that I don't know how to rough it.

I learned long ago to forgo modesty when left with no choice. During my early career it was typical for me to be the only female at a crime scene except for the victim. But I could do without another indignity or discomfort this day. Once we arrive at Chilton Farms the options don't include helping ourselves to bathrooms or anything else. We don't get to eat, drink, wash up or even toss our trash.

It has nothing to do with being polite or respectful of private property. Not even Annie can give permission for us to make ourselves at home. We can't. Everything is about the eventual trial. Whatever we decide to access can ruin evidence and change the story. As is true of an archaeological excavation, once something is disturbed, there's no going back. Or if you do it's not without a lot of explanation.

The Bose Flaglers and Sal Gallos of the world wait for people like me to make a false move. They pray I'll do something foolish like borrowing a toilet and leaving my DNA. If they're lucky I'll change my clothes in a bedroom where the killer had been earlier. Or I'll step in blood. In the old days, it was dropping cigarette butts, and I'd stuff them in my pocket.

"The only other bathroom option is going to Raven Landing,

and I'm not optimistic." Marino continues trying to solve a problem that's trickier for me than him. "Usually places like that are going to close early when it storms. But if someone's still there maybe they can unlock a ladies' room."

"Let's just get where we're going and I'll figure it out," I reply. "You've got toilet paper, I assume?"

"You know what they say, never leave home without it."

"Good, because it's looking like I'll be grabbing a roll and disappearing into an overgrown thicket. Which I'm not looking forward to. But I guess I'll manage."

"Nope, not me," Marino says. "No spiders or snakes, and I'm betting there's poison ivy. I realize it's not ideal, but the pee bottles in back are better than nothing."

"It depends on who you're talking to," I reply.

The portable urinals he orders from camping websites aren't compatible with female factory settings or equipment.

"As often as you drive me in your personal vehicle . . . ?" I start to say that he could do better.

How hard is it keeping appropriate accoutrements in his truck's many storage cases? But complaining about such things is similar to my telling him not to be aggressive. He refuses to be thoughtful in a caretaking way, and it's worse since he got married.

"I'll remember to put a field case in back that has other stuff," he promises. "But for now, we've got limited choices that include a pee bottle or a large to-go coffee cup. Door number one or door number two, so to speak. At least you can take care of the problem inside the privacy of my truck."

"It will have to be taken care of one way or other in the not too distant future," I assure him.

As we continue on our way, the terrain becomes rougher and

more rural, the low-lying road prone to flooding and freezing over. Cars are increasingly infrequent, the low sun slipping in and out of tattered clouds, the silvery light mirrored by puddles the size of small ponds.

Driving slowly in stretches, Marino is careful not to hydroplane as water drums the undercarriage. At times I can't see the edge of the pavement, and it's a good thing his big truck doesn't mind potholes.

"I wouldn't want to drive this every day." He digs in the ashtray again.

"You don't want to be out after dark around here either if you can help it." I decline his offer of gum.

"I hate to think how much time the judge spends in the car. In traffic and bad weather, this would be a crappy commute." He peels open several sticks of Clove that remind me of Christmas, of potpourri.

"Her habit is to leave for the courthouse at the crack of dawn, and head home early evening," I reply. "That way she avoids the worst of rush hour."

"Sounds like all she does is work," Marino says. "That she doesn't have a life."

"Annie doesn't get close to people easily," I reply.

Businesses and residential communities are few and far between the deeper south we go. Weed-infested meadows give way to jungles of undergrowth choked by creepers, and loamy clay is the brownish red of bone marrow. Scattered between woods and fields are small churches, most of a conservative persuasion.

They've been around longer than I have. The gentleman's club and adult bookstore near the truck stop have survived the vicissitudes of time. The Bunghole package store and Top Value pawnshop haven't gone anywhere. Neither has Carl's Cash Express or the Colonial

Smoke Shop. We pass the bones of a barn with a rusty silo, and all that's left of the house is a freestanding chimney.

Fallow cornfields have long since been harvested, then we're crossing the old covered bridge that spans a dry creek bed filled with rocks and trees. Next is a construction site where a 1950s motel used to be. The trailer park on our right has been around forever, and beyond it is the small cemetery with leaning headstones and plastic flowers.

Absent is the Sears department store where I shopped on occasion when there were sales. The site is now occupied by an industrial center with a pontoon boat dealership, and a bakery thrift store. Fields of balding grass are followed by tidal marshland and swamps with cypress knees.

CHAPTER 9

I remember how unsettled I felt when I drove to Chilton Farms for the first time since finishing at Georgetown and going on with my life.

I returned to this part of the world last summer because I'd been offered the job I have now. I was given the opportunity to come back to where I started long ago, to be the chief medical examiner of Virginia again.

"And I was torn." I'm telling Marino details I've not shared. "My decision was hugely influenced by Annie. On the occasion I'm telling you about she'd arranged a cone-of-silence meeting with Governor Dare. The three of us had a sit-down conversation at Chilton Farms. No notes taken. Nothing recorded."

Marino wasn't with me. Neither was Benton. I traveled to Alexandria alone, and ironically was in the Old Town Marriott where the jurors for the Hooke trial are staying. I hadn't been to Annie's family homestead in more than three decades, and as I followed the same route that Marino and I are on, I was depressed by what I saw. Everything felt run-down and unsafe.

"It was different during law school when I'd spend a weekend with Annie's family now and then." I continue passing along what I know firsthand. "There were all kinds of fun places like seafood shacks and diners around here. I remember a Hardee's, a Dairy Queen, an Army-Navy store."

"Well, there's nothing much now. I wouldn't want my truck to break down out here," Marino says.

"Back then you didn't think twice about driving around at any hour of the day or night," I reply. "And Annie had a car."

The rowhouse we shared in Georgetown was close enough to Chilton Farms that we'd drop in often for an early dinner with her parents. If the weather allowed, we might eat in the formal garden, and the landscaping was splendid and controlled. In those days you could see the water.

"Now you wouldn't have any clue, the place is so overgrown," I add. "You wouldn't know you're close enough to the Potomac that you practically could throw a rock and hit it. You'd never guess there was once a formal garden for that matter."

While the parents were still around and healthy, Chilton Farms was quite the showplace. Staff included housekeepers and chefs, and there were all kinds of social events. Birthdays were occasions for dazzling parties, and I was invited to Annie's twenty-fifth.

"As I think back on it now, I'm struck that Rachael wasn't there for that, either." I'm telling Marino the story. "I remember these huge Baccarat chandeliers, and an amazing art collection, all of it gone now. In storage or sold, I assume, because Annie doesn't want to live with it, and I would imagine her sister couldn't be bothered."

"Did the parents leave everything to both of them?" he asks.

"I don't know. But Annie's the one who cares about the place. As I understand it, her sister wanted nothing to do with it until recently when she asked to stay there for a while."

"What did the father do?" Marino takes off his mirrored glasses, clipping them to the back of the visor.

"A lawyer," I reply. "I don't know how busy his practice was or how much time he actually spent at the office. Like a lot of old aristocratic families in this part of the world, he was a professional descendant. The very thing Annie doesn't want to be."

"We know Rachael married someone super rich," Marino says. "I'm sure she was angling for a huge settlement. The question is how much Annie might be worth."

"If she has a lot of family money you wouldn't know it. She doesn't appear to spend it," I reply. "Certainly not on upkeep or improvements. Not a dime on privacy or security that I can tell. And the place wasn't in the best of shape by the time she moved in. What you're about to see is nothing like it used to be."

"How long's she been living there?"

"It's been at least ten years since her parents died."

"I know the judge is starting to sound a little kooky," he says. "You wouldn't guess it from watching her in the courtroom. I'd never think someone like that would be careless about their safety. Especially coming from money and all that goes with it."

"What she comes from is the problem, and she's had her fill of my lectures going back to when we were living together."

Georgetown was my final graduate school stop by the time I met Annie in the late 1980s. I'd finished my pathology residency at Johns Hopkins. I'd attended my first homicide school and forensic academy at the Baltimore medical examiner's office. While she existed in her idealistic tower, I'd been to crime scenes and up to my elbows in autopsies.

"It drove me to distraction when she left windows open or doors unlocked," I tell Marino. "And it did no good to say anything, although I did often enough."

"I assume she has a security system at least."

"A silent alarm, God knows how old," I reply. "She's not going to add to noise pollution."

"If you want to stop some asshole from breaking in, a silent alarm's not a deterrent."

"It's even less of one if you don't bother setting it," I reply. "Annie refuses to do anything that might disturb the wildlife, including making noise. Or that's the excuse she gives."

"Like the tree-huggers who run Raven Landing," Marino says. "No motorboats allowed, and if you have one they give you the stink eye as you go by their candy-ass sailing club."

"No security cameras on Annie's property either," I tell him as we cut through dense stands of pines, headed east toward the river. "She doesn't even have a doorbell camera."

"That's too bad. If we're talking a homicide then most likely the killer was on the property. It would be nice if we had video," Marino says. "After all she's seen as a judge you'd think she wouldn't live like this. She's locked up her share of dirtbags who eventually get out of prison. Maybe someone decides to come back with a score to settle."

"It takes a lot of energy to worry about the next thing that might maim or kill you," I reply. "She chooses not to."

"Stupid when you're a highly visible judge. These days no public official is safe from being attacked," Marino says. "Including in the middle of a courtroom like you just were."

"Denial, a need to control," I reply. "And Annie's altruistic causes become the focus instead of dangers she has little or no power over. She's always had a worldview that's different from yours and mine. She insists on believing people are inherently civilized."

■ ■ ■

We've picked up the George Washington Memorial Parkway, and the traffic delays would seem to have been resolved. We're moving along at a decent clip, and I check my phone.

Benton has sent a text. He'll be in D.C. for a few more hours, he says. I don't know if he's at Secret Service headquarters or the White House. Wherever he is, he's in the midst of something intense, I have no doubt. By reaching out he's communicating that he's aware of what's going on. He's okay and thinking about me.

Still nothing from Lucy, and not a peep from Fruge or Fabian. But Maggie insists I call her ASAP. Magically, the health commissioner has a free moment to speak to me after all, and I wouldn't think of it.

"I'm assuming Rachael could afford to stay anywhere she wants." Marino continues making his point that it's strange she would move in with Annie. "Why not get a presidential suite in some ritzy hotel? Why not get a short-term rental in some luxury condo complex?"

"I've wondered the same thing and don't know the answer," I reply. "My assumption has been that she needed something last minute, and returning to Chilton Farms was the path of least resistance."

"Where was she before?"

"The D.C. penthouse she was living in with her husband. A fifteen-million-dollar place with a rooftop terrace and solid rosewood doors." I've heard Rachael mention it when complaining about the run-down family homestead.

"Why last minute? And why did she move out instead of the husband doing it? What are they accusing each other of in the divorce?" Marino chews his Clove gum vigorously. "Was she physically afraid of him? Why was she the one who had to relocate?"

"Hopefully Annie will have some answers."

"Well, if the judge didn't give a shit about security before, she'd better care now," Marino says. "If we're talking murder then the question is who was the intended victim. I don't know how she's not thinking about that. Because she ought to be."

"It was very apparent that Annie was on the bench today until just a little while ago." I argue that anyone stalking her should have known she wasn't home. "The person also would know that she hasn't been living alone in recent weeks."

"Right. Rachael was there, and late this afternoon the caretaker was supposed to meet her for some reason," Marino says as we pass a billboard for Raven Landing that must be five stories tall.

One can tell by the graphics of sailing yachts and the beautiful people aboard them that the place is exclusive. I'm reminded of photographs I've seen in Bose Flagler's office. He or his family keep an expensive sailboat somewhere around here.

"Do Annie and Rachael look much alike? Would it be easy to confuse them?" Marino asks.

"Both are dark," I reply. "They're slender, although Annie is taller and has more of a runner's build. Rachael is three or four years younger, and with long hair. Annie's is graying and short. She drives a white Prius."

"What a shock. Probably an old one."

"Rachael has a red Mercedes sports car," I add. "That's what I saw her driving when Lucy and I ran into her at the liquor store. It's what I've seen parked in Annie's driveway. As I've mentioned, her sister didn't shy away from attention."

"There's always a chance the murder was random. A crime of opportunity. A burglary or robbery gone bad." Marino continues through his menu of scary possibilities. "A home invasion. And Rachael was in the wrong place at the wrong time. Maybe somebody broke in not realizing anybody was there..."

He continues cutting his eyes to the rearview mirror, and I turn around to see what's grabbed his attention.

"Some rent-a-cop from Raven Landing." Marino talks with

no expression on his face as the white Dodge Durango follows too closely. "He's been behind us ever since I turned off Fort Hunt Road. Only now he's tailgating and getting on my last nerve."

He says all this without scowling or cussing. He barely moves his lips, making sure the private security officer behind us can't tell that we're talking about him.

"Let's hope he doesn't decide to pull you over," I reply.

"Fuck that noise. No way I'm doing it if he's stupid enough to try." Marino fishes the gum out of his mouth, flicking it into the trash bag, getting ready for a fight.

"Would someone like that be armed?"

"He shouldn't be. But Virginia's open-carry. I just assume everybody's armed, and nothing worse than a fucking wannabe."

"We're not in an official vehicle." I keep an eye on my side mirror, monitoring the SUV barely one car-length behind us. "He might think you look suspicious for some reason," I add with a trace of irony. "Maybe because your truck is blacked out, with oversized run-flat tires. And I'm not certain the window tinting or all of your lights are legal."

"Nothing he can do about it. We could be Bonnie and Clyde, and it's not his damn business. He's just a private citizen with a fancy uniform and enough training to be dangerous."

"Let's hope he doesn't try to show us he's more than that," I reply as two Virginia State Police cars go by in the opposite lane, blue lights flashing, sirens silent.

"You hear it?" Marino cracks his window, and I detect the distant thud-thudding of a helicopter. "They're looking for somebody. Got to be. There's some kind of search going on."

"Whatever it is, they're keeping it off the air."

"No kidding. If the scanner was any quieter I'd think it was broken." He closes his window. "Something big is going down."

"This is when we'd be better off in my car. With its state seal and government plates, it's obvious who we are." I glance in my mirror again at the Durango on our bumper. "If he runs your tag what will it come back to?"

"He can't run shit. You've got to be the real deal to do that, and I've had my fill of people acting like assholes. Well, fish or cut bait, Deputy Dawg!" He snarls under his breath, slowing way down, opening his window.

Sticking out his arm, he impatiently waves for the white Durango to go around us. *Raven Landing Private Security* is on the doors, the officer wearing a khaki uniform with red-and-gold patches on the shoulders. He's bearded, probably somewhere in his fifties, staring boldly as he passes. Marino stares right back, shaking his head slowly, implying the guy's an idiot.

The sound of rotor blades beating the air has gotten louder, the helicopter close by. I can tell that it's a big one, possibly police or military. It's flying low and slow in the area of Raven Landing, and the sound becomes fainter when Marino rolls up his window. Tall pines are etched darkly against the pale sky, the sun dipping lower as we follow a bend in the river.

Moments later, we're confronted by blue and red lights flashing at the next intersection. Parked on the shoulder are four Alexandria police cruisers. Nearby are two unmarked white Tahoe SUVs, and as we slow to a stop their doors open. Sawhorses and a DO NOT ENTER sign with reflectors barricade the access road that leads to Chilton Farms.

Long ago, the mile-long paved lane was the grand formal driveway to the former five-hundred-acre plantation. All but Annie's small parcel of overgrown property now belongs to Raven Landing, and for years she's been pressured to sell off what's left.

"How about tucking my heat out of sight?" Marino says to me as he slows to a stop.

Four uniformed officers are standing guard at the barricades. Dressed in blue with bulletproof vests on, they're keeping up their scans from various positions as two women in black cargo pants and shirts open the back doors of the Tahoes. I get a glimpse of shiny steel cages, and it's odd that the K-9 handlers are plainclothes.

I might not know they were police were it not for their ballistic vests, the guns on their hips. I can't tell who they're with, but I don't believe it's Alexandria City or the state police. Possibly they're CIA or FBI.

The female handlers get their Belgian Malinois shepherds out of the SUVs. I tuck Marino's pistol and the extra magazines inside the glove box. He rolls down his window, a muscular male uniformed officer walking toward us.

"How's it going, Officer Cagley?" Marino makes a point of looking at the silver name tag, *B. Cagley* stamped in black on it.

CHAPTER 10

T his road is closed." Officer Cagley is no more than thirty, I'm guessing, with red hair, a devil's lock curling over his brow. "Where is it
you're trying to get to?"

"We're being met at Chilton Farms, and I can tell you on good
authority that there's media headed this way," Marino says. "Channel
Five will be rolling up any minute."

"They won't get in."

"What's going on at Raven Landing?" Marino asks. "You got a
few uniforms down there, I hope? Otherwise, it's easy access by the
water. I go up and down this stretch of the Potomac all the time
in my powerboat. Mainly to piss off the Richie Riches at the yacht
club."

"Who are you with?" Cagley isn't smiling, and I'm fairly certain
he's playing dumb.

I have little doubt that he and his comrades already know who we
are. If they follow the news even a little, for better or worse Marino
and I are all over it. The Alexandria police certainly have been
informed that the chief medical examiner and head of investigations
are responding to the scene at Chilton Farms.

The question is what anyone has been told, and mainly I'm thinking the worst. I'm wondering if the cops are aware that I'm not supposed to be here, depending on who you ask. I've been ordered off the

job, to go home. Marino explains who we are, and Cagley asks to see identification.

"And your registration," he says, after Marino hands over our badge wallets. "You need to step out of the truck. The dogs are going to have to search it."

The two K-9 officers are standing by with their Malinois shepherds on leads. Marino and I open our doors and climb out as the dogs begin to circle.

"Go, go, go...!" The handlers encourage them, and instantly one of the dogs sits by the passenger's door I just exited.

"I got my firearm in the glove box," Marino lets everyone know. "And ammo in back like you might expect. Plus, inside the truck bed are cases of forensic equipment, tools and other shit, including a box of road flares."

One of the uniformed Alexandria officers begins searching the undercarriage with a long-handled mirror. A K-9 handler opens the tailgate.

"*Quincy, LLC*?" Cagley says to Marino with a hint of sarcasm, returning the truck's registration and our badge wallets as we stand by on the wet pavement. "My grandmother used to watch that show. The one about the coroner."

He looks at me, and I don't acknowledge that I'm familiar with the 1970s television series or its star, Jack Klugman. I don't appreciate being mentioned in the same breath as the officer's grandmother. I'm reminded of how dreadful I must look in my damp wrinkled suit, my hair flat, no hose on, and barefoot.

"It's just the name I've got my truck in." Marino never bothered with limited liability companies and other accounting sleights of hand until he married Dorothy. "I used to have a rescue named Quincy. The most worthless cadaver dog you ever met."

The K-9s are finished searching the truck. They're rewarded with playtime and quiet praise.

"Good boy! What a good boy you are...!"

"Good dog, good dog, that's a good girl...!"

"You can return to your vehicle," Cagley lets us know.

Marino and I climb back into our seats and shut the doors. I'm waiting for what's next. No doubt the police are about to inform me that I'm not on the list. They've been told that I'm not allowed entrance. I'm to go home and enjoy the holiday weekend as Maggie threatened. Doug Schlaefer will handle everything just like she promised.

"Sorry for the inconvenience." Cagley bends down, peering at me through Marino's open window. "But we're under strict instructions how to handle things. You got this checkpoint and two more once you get up there. The next one is at the driveway, and the final one is up at the house. That's what I understand. I've not actually been on the property."

His attention continues drifting back to the two K-9 handlers, the two white Tahoes. Then he looks at me, and his stare is intense.

"Nice to meet you, Chief. I couldn't help but notice your bare feet," he says. "I've seen the video. It's all over the Internet. Pretty disgraceful the way Dana Diletti was chasing you down the sidewalk."

"I've had better days," I reply.

His eyes are locked on mine as blue and red lights flash around us.

"Sorry for all the formalities," he says. "But as you can see they've got this buttoned up tight, and it's only going to get tighter."

"Who are you talking about?" Marino asks.

"The feds."

We're maybe thirty feet from the barricade and the other uniformed officers. They've got earpieces in, communicating on their phones, keeping up their scans while talking to each other. I can't make out what they're saying, and Cagley doesn't want them hearing us.

"What are we about to drive into?" Marino indicates the narrow access road cutting through trees and marshland. "What's going on at Raven Landing?"

"It's been shut down for hours," Cagley says. "Nobody there but cops. Some of the private security guys, and the FBI. Also, a couple of state police investigators. I don't know who all, because the feds aren't telling us anything."

"I figured it was going to be like this," Marino says. "Rachael Stanwyck worked for the CIA, so you can imagine."

"I heard on the news that she was more like a PR person for them."

"None of these people are who they say they are," Marino replies as if it's common knowledge and beyond dispute. "What's happening at the judge's house? Some of your guys are up at the scene, right? What are you hearing about Rachael Stanwyck?"

"Investigator Fruge's there," Cagley says. "I'm not sure who else or how many."

The K-9 officers are rewarding their dogs with more playing, tugging on ropes and jumping around. They head back across the road to their Tahoes as Cagley watches. He tells us there are Zodiac boats on the river.

"Plus, they got a chopper up, as you've probably noticed," he says, "and I've seen a few drones buzzing around."

"You got any idea who or what they might be looking for?" Marino asks. "And are they thinking maybe someone's hiding out in the Landing? Maybe in the woods at Chilton Farms?"

"No one's telling us crap, like I said." Cagley hitches his thumbs in his shiny black duty belt. "But I've heard things. And apparently the victim didn't hide the fact that she had money. An expensive car, flashy jewelry and clothing. Plus, she came across as snooty."

"They thinking that money's the motive?" Marino asks. "Rachael Stanwyck's a robbery that went really bad?"

"Maybe that. Maybe other things," Cagley says. "I've never seen the victim. My patrols don't usually bring me down here unless we get called. The rest of the time we're not welcome."

"Yeah, tell me about it." Marino knows how to empathize with those who feel marginalized and put upon.

"But I've been hearing a few stories," Cagley says.

■ ■ ■

He informs us that Rachael might have been a player. She's been seen driving home at lunchtime on occasion.

"Like maybe she's hooking up with somebody while the judge is in court," the Alexandria officer confides while keeping his eye on everything going on around us.

"Just because she comes home at lunchtime doesn't mean she's screwing around," Marino says.

Cagley glances at his comrades standing guard near the saw-horses, at the two K-9 handlers sitting inside their Tahoes with the engines running.

"From what I understand, she definitely was meeting someone," he says.

"Any idea who?" Marino asks.

"You didn't hear it from me. Bose Flagler," Cagley says, and I think of Annie's behavior in court. "He's been spotted driving in and out."

If Rachael was involved in a romantic relationship with the com-monwealth's attorney, it might be making more sense why she wanted to move back to Chilton Farms for a while. There are no cameras. The property is overgrown, and Annie's not home much of the day. Cars parked up at the manor house aren't visible from the street.

"Who told you stories about the commonwealth's attorney sneaking around out here?" Marino asks.

"And do we know whether Flagler or his prominent family might be members of the yacht club?" I inquire. "I've seen photographs in his office of a very nice sailboat, and the backdrop looks a lot like Raven Landing."

"Makes sense," Marino says snidely. "The Landing is the kind of place someone like him would belong."

"The security officer's name is Dogg, with two g's. He stopped by here a little while ago, and we were talking," Cagley says. "He pulled in a few minutes before you did, and is probably down there at the Landing."

"I think he passed us while we were driving here," Marino says. "White guy, dark hair with a beard. I didn't get a good look at him but he had a thick neck, seemed big."

"That's him."

"I called him *Deputy Dawg*. I guess I'm clairvoyant," Marino says. "He was riding my ass. Playing cops and robbers."

"The people working down there at Raven Landing aren't happy," Cagley says. "You think the local cops like us get dissed when the big guns roll in? You can imagine how private security gets treated..."

"Worse than a dog with two g's," Marino says.

"Like shopping mall cops," Cagley adds.

Marino opens his badge wallet, fishing out one of the business cards he had printed after I hired him as my forensic operations specialist.

"I don't know why Deputy Dogg thought it was all right to

tailgate me," he says in case it's lost on anyone that he didn't appreciate it. "You might tell him not to pull shit like that again if he knows what's good for him."

"I'll make sure to pass along the message," Cagley says. "And I'll let Fruge know that you and the chief are here."

"One of our vans should be showing up fairly soon," Marino replies. "Black with no windows, you'll know it when you see it. The investigator driving it is Fabian, and don't be put off by his appearance."

"I'll be looking for him." Cagley steps back from the truck.

Marino closes his window. He puts on his ventriloquist act again, no expression on his face, barely moving his lips as he reacts to the latest information.

"As if things weren't fucked up enough?" he says. "Wait until the media gets hold of this. Bose Flagler? Holy shit."

Cagley and the other officers move the sawhorses, the DO NOT ENTER sign, and we're waved through.

"Nothing like a violent death to air everybody's dirty laundry," Marino says. "I wouldn't want to be the commonwealth's attorney right now. And he's got the election coming up in November."

"I wouldn't want to be him for a lot of reasons. Especially if he cared about Rachael. Especially if they had something special," I reply as we drive through woods and wetlands.

We can't see the river as we get close, just the different way the sky looks, pale like pearls and shimmering with light. The sun is fiery on treetops as the helicopter flies loud circuits somewhere along the water. We pass another sign for Raven Landing, this one ironically with a cawing crow sitting on it.

"It's easy to be cynical," I remind Marino. "And people like us can be the worst because of what we see routinely. Not to mention Flagler is an opportunist of the first order. But we don't know that he didn't have deep feelings for Rachael."

"Even if he was head over heels," Marino replies, "he's going to save his own ass first, last and always. What I want to know is how he and the judge are going to finish the trial. Because Flagler's calculating that as we speak, you can bet on it."

"Personal problems aren't supposed to interfere. Technically, they're not grounds for recusing oneself," I reply. "Unless you claim you're unfit to serve, and Annie won't do that."

"Flagler won't either," Marino says, and we can see the manor home's four tall brick chimneys peeking above trees. "I wonder if the judge has any idea that her sister was screwing around with him."

"If she didn't know, she will soon. That might explain why she's been steering clear of me of late," I reply.

"And why she's playing favorites in court," Marino says. "Bending over backwards to go easy on him."

"I hope not. That wouldn't be like Annie. One thing she's never lacked is integrity. I've never known her to be a sellout."

The road in front of her old estate is lined with four Alexandria police cruisers parked with their lights off. There are two more unmarked white K-9 Tahoes. Uniformed officers are standing guard at the foot of the driveway. Moving out of the way, they motion us to drive into a wide apron of cobblestone pavers, what Annie calls the *turnaround area.*

"Already I'm seeing what you mean about this place." Marino parks in front of two tall brick pillars choked by dead creepers.

On top are large carved stone owls eroded by the centuries, their vague eyes staring. The copper signs for Chilton Farms are patinated green and obscured by honeysuckle that's brown and missing most of its blossoms. Rhododendrons crowding the entrance also appear to be dying. When I was last here last, the place didn't look this neglected and blighted.

The driveway is long and winding, disappearing in the forest. Beyond the brick pillars is a bright yellow spiderweb of crime scene tape lashed between thick cedar trees. On the other side of the ribbon barricade are more sawhorses.

"Looks like this is as far as we get for now," Marino says. "And that's fucking unacceptable."

He irritably shoves the gear shifter into park. We open our doors as two more Malinois shepherds and their K-9 handlers appear, dressed the same as their colleagues at the first checkpoint. We climb out and go through the routine again, the dogs circling the truck.

They alert on the same areas as before, and Marino explains about his guns, ammo and road flares. He reminds them he used to be a cop, and they're not interested. Then the handlers in their generic field clothes are praising their dogs and playing as they return to the generic white SUVs parked on the street.

"CIA." Marino watches the handlers. "Maybe FBI, but that would be weird because they almost always make sure you know it's them. You can see their fucking flak jackets from outer space."

We're quite alone and ignored sitting inside his truck. No one's coming over to talk to us. Marino removes the pistol and extra magazines from the glove box. He returns them to the console between us, and opens his door.

"Stay here," he says, as if there's anywhere else I might go.

CHAPTER 11

I open my window a crack to hear what goes on as Marino approaches the officers at the edge of the driveway. He flashes his badge wallet again, and the shiny gold shield winks in the slanted light. The Alexandria cops barely look.

We've been cleared ahead by Cagley no doubt. If the police didn't know who we are they wouldn't have allowed us to enter the property. But Marino rarely passes up the chance to flaunt his credentials. The less he thinks he's going to be appreciated, the more he's going to do it.

"We've got to get up to the house," he informs the officers. "We have a lot of gear, and pretty soon our van will be here to transport the body. We have to be able to drive to the door." He looks up at the four chimneys in the overgrown distance. "We can't be wheeling the body all the way down here to the street."

"We've told them you're here," one of the officers says.

"Who's *them*?"

"They're sending someone down."

"*They?*" Marino is getting feisty. "Who the hell are we talking about?"

"In the meantime, you're going to have to leave your truck. I'm sorry for the inconvenience."

"You're fucking kidding me."

"No, sir."

"This is bullshit. All we've got to do is take down the crime scene tape and move the sawhorses. I'll drive through, and you can put all the shit right back where it was."

"No can do."

"You got a reason? Or are you just jerking us around?" Marino demands answers, and I wish he'd back down.

"We're doing as instructed, buddy."

"Yeah, well, tell Fruge we're heading up one way or another," Marino threatens, stalking off.

He returns to the truck as I roll up my window. He opens my door. Reaching across me, he collects his gun and ammo off the console, his big arm brushing against my legs.

"I don't know what the shit's going on. I hope we're not in for another setup by Maggie and Elvin." Marino tucks his pistol in his waistband, the extra magazines in a pocket. "I guess we should have expected we'd get jerked around like hell if we didn't do what they said."

Opening a back door, he rummages for something on the floor behind me, and I hear the rattle and crackle of paper. A mosquito lands on my bare thigh and I slap it, leaving a small bloody smudge. Digging inside my briefcase, I find the packet of tissues and there's only one left. Marino approaches my window, and I open it.

"Here we go." He hands me a used to-go cup with a lid. Extra-large, thank God. He gives me a roll of toilet paper, less than half of it left.

"Don't look," I tell him as if we're twelve.

I close the window, and he stands with his back to the tinted glass. It takes me a few minutes in the cramped conditions. When I'm done, I open the glove box where he keeps extra biohazard bags, red plastic, neatly folded.

"Now what?" I ask as I open the door, uncertain what we're supposed to do.

"I'll handle it." He takes the lidded cup, the biohazard bag from me. "Not ideal, but who's going to know?"

He walks to the edge of the driveway, finding a tangle of thorny briars and poison ivy that nobody's going anywhere near. I hear him make the deposit as I wave off mosquitoes. If the officers standing guard are aware of what just happened they show no sign of it. Marino returns to the truck.

"Thanks for that," I tell him.

"What are friends for?" He stuffs the empty coffee cup, the lid inside the red bag.

Tying a knot in it, he leaves it on the floor for now. I step out of the truck shoeless, slinging my briefcase over my shoulder, the humid air fragrant with lilacs and jasmine. I'm aware of wet pavers cooled by the rain. They're littered with dead foliage and bugs, and I have an eerie feeling already. The sort that hollows me out and pricks up my hair.

"I don't blame Rachael for griping like hell." Marino looks around unhappily. "I wouldn't want to stay here either, based on what I'm seeing so far."

He surveys overgrown foliage tangled with kudzu and grapevines. I can almost read his mind. My advance warnings haven't quite prepared him for what he's finding.

"I'm really not getting why Rachael wanted to be out here in the middle of an overgrown haunted forest unless it's the obvious," he says.

"I think that's right." I spot dead grasshoppers floating in a puddle as if they drowned.

"Bose Flagler."

"It's making sense the more we talk about it," I reply as he inspects the withered creepers choking the entrance's brick pillars.

He takes in the huge rusting hinges where majestic gates used to be, black wrought iron with the Chilton coat of arms in blue and gold. When I used to visit here with Annie in days of old, there was a polished brass intercom on a post. You'd push a button and buzz the house. If you were expected, the gates opened like welcoming arms, moving with a slow gravitas that I found thrilling.

But there's nothing inviting or exciting about Chilton Farms now. The cast iron lamps haven't illuminated anything since Annie moved in and removed the bulbs from every outdoor fixture. The big lanterns on top of their poles look like sad empty faces, many of the glass panes cracked or missing. After the sun goes down, the driveway is as dark as a black hole.

When fog rolls in from the river the conditions are extremely hazardous. You have to be careful where you walk under the best of conditions. Granite pavers haven't been power-washed in years. The smooth river rocks are slippery when wet, some of them coated in moss, and others have weeds sprouting up between them. I've never known the property to be this strangely still.

I survey thickets of perennials blooming in blue and yellow. Nothing stirs in them or the looming magnolias with their dark green leaves and waxy white blossoms that smell lemony. There's no bird-song. No squirrels or rabbits darting about. No deer or other animals bounding through the brush. I don't see the usual red-tailed hawks or bald eagles perched high in the branches of huge hardwoods and evergreens.

It's as if nature is in hiding and has been shocked silent. The only sound is the steady drip-dripping of water from trees, and the whine of mosquitoes finding me as I step barefoot around puddles and plant debris and dead insects.

"It doesn't look like the caretaker, what's-his-name, spends much time on this place," Marino observes. "What does he do? Because it isn't yard-work or maintenance, that's for damn sure. What'd you say his name is?"

"Holt Willard." I look at several dead butterflies. "He does what Annie tells him, and it doesn't include landscaping, yardwork, that's correct. But he's been with the family forever."

I step closer to blue and pink hydrangea bushes, some of the branches bare. The ground beneath them is showered with brown leaves as if it's winter.

"As I've said, Annie keeps the place *wild,* as she describes it," I explain to Marino.

"This is worse than wild." His eyes are everywhere. "There's prob-ably a lost world under all this shit."

■ ■ ■

Marino wanders closer to the crime scene tape and parked police cars. He looks at the driveway winding through trees and foliage, notic-ing the slippery and missing bricks, the puddles, the sloped uneven terrain. Walking around some more, he's concentrating on the brick-pillared entrance.

He's noticing what's in puddles and scattered in some places but not others. Stopping and starting, he searches the ground as the stone owls atop their columns blankly stand guard.

"Is it just me? Or is something weird going on?" Marino points out hundreds of dead ants under a rhododendron that has damage.

"I've been noticing the same thing ever since I got out of the truck," I reply.

He inspects dead spiders, white-faced hornets, yellowjackets, tiger moths and ladybugs littered about. They're congregated in areas where damaged foliage is in brown swaths and splotches. Nothing about the pattern is uniform, and I might know what's happened. I might know why the driveway has been closed to automobile traffic.

"And you're positive the judge doesn't use insecticide?" Marino asks. "Any possibility the caretaker or somebody's been using it or another poison? Maybe squirting stuff around like an exterminator?"

"I can't imagine it. Annie would never allow such a thing," I reply. "But I wouldn't know firsthand."

"Or maybe a powerful weed killer. Some kind of strong chemical. Almost like the splash patterns you see in arsons." He walks around, trying to figure it out. "When someone tries to burn down a place. That's almost what it reminds me of."

"I don't think arson or an attempt is what we're talking about." I'm looking around at warning signs I recognize even as I hope I'm wrong. "I don't believe anyone came out here to burn down Chilton Farms."

"Yeah, I'm not smelling gasoline, no type of accelerant," Marino decides, increasingly jumpy.

"The damage is in some places and not others based on what we're seeing so far," I reply. "Mostly here around the pillars where the big entrance gates used to be. I didn't notice anything along the road, and nothing when we first pulled in."

"The thunderstorm earlier could be another possibility." Marino looks up at the scrubbed blue sky as the sun settles lower. "When it rains hard enough it can kill things like bees, butterflies if they don't take cover. Especially if it hails. I used to see it all the time when we lived in Florida."

"Everywhere I'm looking there's plenty of cover. A jungle of it."

I stare past him into woods so dense in places that light barely filters through. "And here and here?" I point to the wilted honeysuckle, the rhododendron's curled dead leaves and withered pink blossoms. "Rain didn't do that."

"Lightning could," he says.

"Or something similar that's manufactured by humans." I direct his attention to dead beetles and bumblebees.

"I'd sure as hell rather it was the storm that did all this."

"I have an ugly suspicion about what we're dealing with." As I find a dead hummingbird.

Next, I find two more.

And a goldfinch.

"Dammit." Marino looks around anxiously.

"I'm going to need some pillboxes. Cardboard, not plastic, about a dozen should do it," I let him know as we return to the back of the truck. "Plus a pair of forceps and gloves. Also, a small bag. Paper, not plastic, because everything we're collecting is going to be wet. We don't want the evidence decomposing before we can get it to the labs."

He unlocks the covered truck bed in back. It's tightly packed with heavy-duty black storage cases, and I tell him that the first order of business is insect repellent. I'm getting chewed up, and he's not in my same hurry. His blood type is less tasty than mine, and he has a bigger bladder.

"Bug spray coming up." He begins opening storage cases.

He makes a lot of noise sliding things and thumping around. Finding the plastic bottle, he peels off his shirt, and I catch the officers at the foot of the driveway staring. Also the K-9 handlers as they sit in their Tahoes. It's hard not to gawk. I find myself doing it if I'm not careful, and that's especially unsafe when my sister is in the area.

Marino is obsessed with his *bigness,* as I refer to his relentless muscle building, fine-tuning, sculpting, and wearing clothing that flaunts. Inside the waterfront townhome Dorothy found for them is all the equipment needed to be action-hero huge and cut. He belongs to a boxing gym, jogs, jumps rope, pounds down protein supplements, and has the body of someone half his age.

He's happy to show it off. Flexing and bulging like he's doing now. Strutting about like the cock of the walk when there's an audience, and I can't say that I blame him. Gone are the days when he had a beer gut, the inside of his car a landfill of fast-food trash and cigarette butts.

"Close your eyes and don't breathe." He takes the cap off the spray bottle of insect repellent.

Standing on the driveway bare-chested and brawny, he envelops us in a mist that makes me cough. I take the bottle from him, spritzing my legs and feet some more as he resumes rooting through the storage cases.

"Do you have any extra?" I hold up the bottle.

"Yep. I always keep plenty on hand. Dorothy's like you. If there's a mosquito anywhere it's going to find her."

"Put gloves on before you touch anything, please," I remind him. "We want to be careful we don't contaminate the evidence with our own insect repellent."

I tuck the extra bottle into a pocket. He pulls on a pair of black nitrile gloves, and I do the same. Then he hands me the cardboard pillboxes, a paper bag and plastic forceps.

"Also, a surgical mask," I add. "And a Sharpie."

"Just be careful. You don't want to step barefoot on anything that has a stinger. Or fangs, even worse. Or toxins like some frogs and lizards secrete." Marino's warnings are punctuated by the loud snaps of plastic clasps opening. "Even if something's dead, that doesn't mean it can't get you good."

"I'm all too aware," I reply, and he hands me the items I requested. "What about Tyvek booties?"

"Nope. But the police should have shit like that up at the house. Fruge should." He continues rooting through lockers.

"That doesn't help me now."

"Here. This will have to do." He gives me a pair of blue papery footies, one size fits all. They're intended for indoor crime scenes only, and aren't meant to get wet. Not much better than wearing disposable hairnets on my bare feet, the shoe covers won't protect me from cuts and bruises. They won't prevent me from stepping on a wasp and getting stung. But better than nothing, as the saying goes.

"I'd put them on now if I were you," Marino tells me. "Like I said, they should have plenty of PPE up at the house. They'll have a pup tent set up, the whole nine yards."

I stare down in dismay at my wet, dirty bare feet.

"Don't worry if you go through a lot of them. I've got a whole box," he assures me as if it's helpful.

"Remind me never again to leave home without my scene case." I put on the footies anyway, and can feel everything I step on.

I'm not looking forward to wearing Tyvek over my clammy clothes once I get to the alleged pup tent that may or may not have been set up at the manor house. Assuming that's where Marino and I are headed as we continue to wait on the barricaded driveway, everyone ignoring us.

CHAPTER 12

There's no sign of anyone but the four uniformed officers, talking in low voices. They fall silent as I walk toward them.

"I don't know about you, but I'm feeling like steak tartare out here." I hand over the bottle of insect repellent.

"Hey, thanks." With a surprised smile.

"Much appreciated."

"They're bad enough to airlift you away."

"It's also got sunblock in it," I let them know. "You're welcome to keep it."

They spray themselves as I scan a battlefield of carnage littering pavers and floating in scummy puddles. I'm noticing earthworms everywhere, and that's typical after a hard rain. Significantly, they're not dead. Taking photos and video with my phone, I suspect Rachael Stanwyck died around the same time the birds and the bees did.

Then the rain started, and the worms surfaced. Whatever caused the damage I'm seeing was no longer a threat by the time the thunderstorm started some two hours ago. I return to the former grand entrance, taking photographs as I go. Squatting down and using the forceps, I pick up ladybugs, a dragonfly, a sparrow. I place them in the pill boxes, and the cops are watching my every move.

I feel their eyes on me as I closely inspect the area around the brick pillars where the honeysuckle is withered. Branches of a pink trumpet tree have been denuded of leaves and flowers, and I understand what Marino means about a splash pattern. But it's more like someone has been out here with a flamethrower. Except there's no lingering odor, no hint of anything blackened, sooty or charred. Nothing has been singed or burned. Not by fire.

I make my sad collections, writing the date, time and location, noting what type of specimen is tucked inside. Stepping into the street, I find no other victims. Just a toad that was run over much earlier. Probably days ago. The K-9 handlers inside their SUVs watch my progress with no expression on their faces.

"Looking for anything in particular, ma'am?" one of the Alexandria officers finally asks, and I see myself the way they do.

In my damp skirt suit and paper footies, I'm wearing a surgical mask and black exam gloves, holding plastic forceps like chopsticks. Bending over to look at puddles, I inspect under shrubs, checking areas of brown foliage and shriveled leaves. I'm picking up fragile dead things and gently tucking them into small white coffin-like boxes.

"Just checking the damage," I explain. "Dead plants, dead bugs and birds."

"Uh-huh."

"Lightning, maybe," one of them offers.

I return to the truck in my worthless wet footies. Marino is setting two large rolling hard cases on the pavers, and he pulls out their retracted handles.

"Fabian sent me a message," he says.

"At long last." I'm unhappy for many reasons.

It would seem I have *Mutiny on the Bounty* at work, and what's happened on Annie's property is beyond awful and troubling.

"He's at the roadblock with his knickers in a knot because they made him get out of the van," Marino tells me. "They searched it with the dogs, and all the rest. He's pretending he's pissed off."

He rolls the big field cases closer to the crime scene tape barricading the driveway.

"Just the drama Fabian loves," I reply. "No matter how much he might protest to the contrary."

"I told him that when he gets here they're going to do the same damn thing again," Marino says. "And then he's to keep his ass inside the van unless we say otherwise."

I open a back door of the truck, placing the brown bag of evidence I just collected on the seat next to an ammunition box.

"We'll need to get this to Doctor Allemand as quickly as possible," I explain.

Bug Man, as Marino calls him, is an entomologist at the Smithsonian's Museum of Natural History in Washington, D.C. One of the world's foremost authorities on insects, Albert Allemand also knows a thing or two about arthropods (centipedes and scorpions), arachnids (spiders), crustaceans (shellfish) and the microscopic aquatic organisms called diatoms.

He and I have had plenty of conversations about April Tupelo over recent months, and he testified during the trial. Flagler went after his testimony and credibility the same way he went after mine but a few short hours ago. Albert and I also serve together on a federal task force known as the Doomsday Commission, and it looks like I'll be *bugging* him again, as I put it, whenever he hears from me.

"Someone will have to drive the evidence to the Smithsonian first thing in the morning, the sooner the better," I explain to Marino. "Maybe Fabian if we can trust him with the job. And right now, that's a very big if."

Taking off my soiled gloves, I drop them and other trash into a biohazard bag. I put on new footies as Marino opens another locker, finding a dry polo shirt that has our office crest on it. This is followed by black tactical briefs with *Always Be Ready* on the waistband, and I have no doubt who bought those for him.

It's the sort of thing Dorothy would pick out for her *trophy husband,* as she likes to call him. He pulls the shirt over his head. He carries a dry pair of khaki cargo pants, the briefs and one of his camping urinals to the other side of the truck. He sets his gun and ammo on top of an oversized tire.

"Don't look." Now he's the one saying it while making himself as invisible as possible.

■ ■ ■

I turn my back to Marino, and am startled by my niece Lucy riding toward us on her racing-green e-bike with its fat tires and integrated lights.

For an instant, I wonder if my eyes are playing tricks on me. She's coming from the direction of the manor house. Pedaling right behind her is Sierra Patron, or Tron as most know her, the two of them Secret Service cyber investigative partners.

"Holy shit!" Marino steps out from behind the truck, his boots unlaced, his pants unzipped. "What the hell are they doing here?"

"I'm as surprised as you are," I reply.

Nimble and quiet, Lucy and Tron maneuver around puddles, weaving between the sawhorses. Dismounting, they duck under the crime scene tape, walking the rest of the way in pursuit shoes that don't clip to the pedals or make any noise. They gently prop their bikes against Marino's truck.

"We promise not to scratch the paint," Lucy deadpans to him.

"What the hell?" Marino doesn't like this surprise for a lot of reasons. "What's the Secret Service got to do with Rachael Stanwyck? Or were you just in the neighborhood with nothing better to do, and thought you'd drop by?"

"How's it going?" Tron replies with a smile.

"Why are you here?" Marino acts as if we've been invaded while he resumes getting dressed. "When the cops complained about the damn feds showing up, it didn't dawn on me they were talking about the two of you." As if he takes it personally that the Secret Service might not advise him in advance of its every move.

"We're not the only damn feds involved. Just the damn most important ones." Tron smiles again.

"The Secret Service, the FBI, who else?" Marino glares at the four chimneys darkly etched against the early evening. "That figures. We're left stranded in the heat, picking up dead bugs and shit while everybody's up there."

"We've got a lot to brief you about before we escort you to the house." In her subtle way Tron's letting us know who's in charge, and that there will be no argument.

"Glad you've got bug spray on and are good to go." Lucy points two fingers at her eyes, and her meaning couldn't be clearer.

The Secret Service has set up hidden surveillance devices at the entrance of the property and who knows where else. It's not a happy thought as I envision Marino handing me the roll of toilet paper. Then emptying the coffee cup in a thicket. Before changing his clothes while taking care of other personal business.

I have no doubt that my niece and Tron have been monitoring our every move and utterance since we got here. They aren't medical examiners and don't work for me. They don't have my concerns and aren't in my hurry. The police have other priorities when someone is dead, especially if the body is indoors and protected.

"We regret the necessity of keeping you in the dark until now." Tron continues to apologize as we talk by Marino's truck. "Sorry about all the inconvenience." She's not just saying it. "But we also wanted you to have a few minutes to absorb without the distraction of us hovering. I have a feeling you understand why."

Tron directs this at me, knowing I'd pick up on the same clues they have. I'd notice the dead insects and animals. I'd be aware of the damaged foliage. I'd draw my own conclusion, and it's the same as theirs. Only I came up with mine independently, and it can be proven. Everything I've said and done was viewed in real time and recorded.

"This is just the four of us talking." Tron cuts her eyes at the cops guarding the driveway. "We can't tell them the same things we're about to tell you."

"And the FBI?" Marino snarks. "What are you telling them?"

"It's not for you to worry about." Tron won't be pushed around by him.

Her easygoing politeness is disarming, and her strong-featured good looks can be exotic when she puts her mind to it. In my husband's words, Tron is charming and can talk someone off the ledge. But you wouldn't want to mess with her. You wouldn't want to mess with Lucy either, and she takes off her helmet, looping the strap over her bike's handlebars, her face keenly pretty.

I notice that her shaggy mahogany hair is bone dry. Her clothing and gear don't look rained on. I can see no sign that she and Tron got caught in the storm earlier. I recall the traffic delays. I think about the president's motorcade diverting, and major roads and bridges closing. I have an idea what the two of them have been doing in their stretchy bike clothes and black shoes that could pass for everyday trainers.

They've been ghostbusting, going after the invisible, and you wouldn't guess it to look at them. They come across as serious cyclists who carry enough gear for camping. They don't look armed, dangerous and assisted by artificial intelligence. I expect that in their saddlebags are MP5 submachine guns with folding stocks. In fanny packs are pistols, extra magazines, possibly other weapons.

Concealed by their big backpacks are signal analyzers and omni-directional antennas that can pick up a broad range of radio frequencies for many miles. These are tracked by satellites and mathematical calculations. That and other information is displayed nonstop in the sport glasses they have on, the lenses this moment tinted gray.

Such wearable devices, including our smart rings, are connected to the only stand-alone cloud computer in the U.S. government. The Secret Service maintains this at their training facility in southern Maryland where Lucy and Tron spend a lot of time. If they're not in the cyber lab, they're on the driving, cycling and firing ranges. They're being put through their paces in mock-ups of towns, presidential motorcades or Air Force One.

"What interest does the Secret Service have in what's going on here?" Marino retrieves his gun and ammo from the truck tire where he set them. "You don't get to roll up just because you feel like it."

"We have jurisdiction," Lucy replies.

"How come nobody bothered to answer our calls while you've been sitting up there spying on us?" Defiantly pocketing the extra magazines. "Whose bright idea was that? Yours?" Scowling at Lucy.

"Take it easy, Marino," she says.

"Who invited you, and why? To chase down signals with your magic wands?" He tucks his gun into the back of his pants.

"We don't need to be invited. The case is ours" is Lucy's simple answer.

"What about the FBI?" He keeps pushing, the way he does when threatened. "I hear they've got agents snooping around. I assume it's their Zodiac boats and helicopter."

"Most of what you're seeing right now is ours," Lucy says. "The K-9s, for example."

The white Tahoes and field clothes are unmarked because the Secret Service doesn't want to draw attention in public areas like intersections and roadsides, she explains. Thus the reason for the word *secret*, Benton likes to quip, except it's not funny. It's the truth, the objective to protect and prevent instead of showing up after the fact with an army of agents in flak jackets.

Almost always by then it's too late, the evil deed done. Law enforcement performs its usual task of cleaning up what can't be fixed, and meting out punishment. It would be better avoiding the calamity to begin with. But non-incidents don't make for good news stories or TV viewing. You rarely hear about what didn't happen.

"Key people, those with a need to know, have been informed that what we're dealing with is a matter of national security." Tron gets to the reason it's their jurisdiction legally. "This relates to the attempted attack on the president of the United States earlier today."

"How is that possible?" Marino says. "What the hell would Rachael Stanwyck and Chilton Farms have to do with something like that?"

"What we know is that the same type of high-energy weapon was involved in both incidents." Lucy verifies what I suspect caused the damage I've been seeing and collecting. "That much we're sure of."

"We don't even have a guess how the incidents are related," Tron explains. "Only that they are somehow."

A microwave weapon was used near Ivy Hill Cemetery. Also,

in this area, including here at Chilton Farms. She and Lucy believe Rachael was deliberately attacked while alone inside the kitchen, the motive to injure severely or kill.

"The goal wasn't to vandalize some historic estate by ray-gunning it," Lucy says. "The bad guy arrived with the intention of doing harm to her or whoever he thought was inside the house. He positioned himself in the backyard, and blasted away at the kitchen window."

CHAPTER 13

Any evidence the killer went inside the house?" Marino asks as I detect the rumbling of big engines headed in this direction.

"No," Tron says. "We don't believe he did."

"Hit and run," Lucy adds. "I doubt he stuck around."

"They usually don't in these kinds of attacks, typically executed from vehicles, we're fairly certain," Tron says. "As far as we know the bad guys haven't been on foot. But it now appears they have weapons that are more easily transportable. And that's pretty damn scary."

"Intermittent rapid bursts of microwaves were fired here on the property between three-forty and four o'clock this afternoon," Lucy informs us. "That's the interval when we were able to detect the two-point-three-oh-five-gigahertz signals. It's a frequency allocated to radio amateurs, and not at all typical."

She and Tron first became aware of this rogue signal earlier at 1:45 P.M. while on routine patrol along the presidential motorcade's route. The terrorists didn't realize their microwave radiation would be detected. Most likely that's because they had no expectation that anyone was looking for it. The funeral service was for a retired U.S. senator who'd suffered a stroke earlier in the week.

"The president's visit wasn't announced until late yesterday," Tron explains. "There was very little time for anyone to plan an organized attack. They weren't expecting that we'd be looking for something like this. Fortunately, it didn't occur to them that we'd have people out with signal analyzers."

Almost an hour after detecting the 2.305 GHz frequency, they picked it up again. This time it was miles from the cemetery. Triangulating with signal analyzers in other locations, they determined the rapid intermittent bursts were coming from the general area of Raven Landing.

"We followed the signal to an intersection about a mile from here, and then it was lost," Lucy says. "Buildings, trees, other objects can block the line-of-sight trajectory. And the weather may have been a factor."

It wasn't storming yet but was getting very overcast. This might have caused interference or degradation of radio waves, Lucy explains. She and Tron didn't detect the 2.305 GHz signal again until approximately a half hour later at 3:40. The bursts of energy lasted ten minutes, and the general location was the access road that leads to Chilton Farms and Raven Landing.

Lucy and Tron called for backup to respond, and were met at the intersection where the first checkpoint was now. They put their bikes inside the cars and drove toward the river. When they reached the entrance of Chilton Farms, they noticed the odd pattern of dead and wilted foliage.

"I saw the same things you did," Lucy says to me as the sound of big engines gets closer. "I realized what it likely meant, that we were looking at damage caused by the unusual microwave signal we'd been picking up."

They headed up the driveway with weapons drawn, clearing the area every step of the way, making sure no one was lying in wait to ambush them. When they reached the house, they saw Rachael's car parked in front.

"We spotted her body through a kitchen window," Lucy says as two tactical BearCats appear on the street. The guttural grumbling of the diesel engines seems to shake the air as Alexandria officers direct the armor-plated SUVs to park behind Marino's truck.

"Crime scene and more K-9s aren't too far behind," Lucy informs us.

The thudding of rotor blades continues, but more faintly, the helicopter somewhere north of here. She and Tron continue monitoring the latest communications they're viewing in the tinted lenses of their AI-assisted sport glasses. They update us as ten Secret Service uniformed division police officers in ballistic gear roll out of the two BearCat SUVs. They begin opening storage lockers, paying no attention to us.

"Are we about to get invaded?" Marino is more impressed than he wants anyone to know.

"We're making sure that doesn't happen. Keeping the scene and all of us safe and secure won't be routine. There's a lot going on at once."

Tron continues telling us what to expect. They have it on good authority that some of the unhappy and none too savory people from the Gilbert Hooke trial and their friends and allies are headed this way. Possibly as many as fifty. But it could be more.

"A number of them are armed to the teeth," Tron says. "They plan to show up as soon as it's dark. There are all kinds of threats circulating about vandalizing and looting Raven Landing and Chilton Farms. They're saying it's all part of the same corrupt and privileged plantation, and there are some scary comments about you." This to me.

Included in the potentially violent mob is April Tupelo's mother. Crying and fleeing the courtroom one minute, Nadine Tupelo is now on TV encouraging vigilante justice. She's accompanied by the man who kicked me, and just thinking about it reignites my anger, my ankle throbbing.

"We're making sure none of these people can get anywhere near here. The FBI and Secret Service have Raven Landing closed off," Lucy says as we talk by Marino's truck. "We'll be adding other units and barricades to the roadblock you came through a few minutes ago."

No one can access this area by land, air or sea unless authorized. Based on criminal records and what's being said on social media, there's reason for serious concern.

"We're seeing all sorts of inflammatory theories, including that the trial's going to be unplugged and Gilbert Hooke will be found not guilty," Tron says. "He'll walk because of what's happened to Annie Chilton's sister. *Will he get off the hook?* is the quote of the day."

"Supposedly, the judge will recuse herself, and a mistrial will be declared," Lucy summarizes.

"Has she actually said anything publicly?" I inquire. "Has she released a statement to that effect?"

"No," Lucy replies as I worry about where Annie is and how she's faring.

"It's just more of the usual conspiratorial nonsense." Tron goes on to give examples: *What's happening is about politics and money. The system is rigged.* And as bad as this is, I have other things weighing on me. I pass along what we've been told about Bose Flagler and Rachael possibly having a romantic involvement.

"We heard the same thing from the Landing's private security," Tron says.

Neither she nor Lucy seem surprised, and I ask who's on the property besides us and the crowd of officers, the dog handlers and everybody else I'm looking at and hearing about. My focus is Rachael

Stanwyck's body, and who might be around it. I'm concerned about who found her and pronounced her dead.

"There are two FBI agents at the house. Also Fruge and two of her uniformed officers. And three of our people, the backups we've mentioned." Tron gives us a headcount.

"Everybody is outside." Lucy assures us the body hasn't been disturbed. "A tent has been set up, and certain outdoor areas have been secured and photographed for evidentiary reasons."

"Fabian needs to bring the van up there," Marino tells them. "I understand not wanting a lot of traffic because the killer may have been on the driveway and all the rest. But we've got no choice."

"When are you thinking you'll be ready?" Tron asks me.

"I need a few hours." I look up at the low sun. "About the time it will be dark. About the time the armed and violent mob is supposed to show up."

■ ■ ■

The Secret Service will take care of getting the van to the manor house. But the body transport will be carefully monitored and heavily supervised, we're told. Mostly the worry is explosive devices. The multiple checkpoints ensure that nothing is introduced into the mix along the way.

Theoretically, a drone could attach a bomb to a vehicle's roof. Or someone could emerge from the woods when the car is moving slowly, and attach a device that way. As Benton's always saying, just imagine the worst scenario someone might dream up. Then be prepared for it to happen. Because it will. Probably it already has.

"The van will be searched at each checkpoint," Lucy continues to inform us. "Then one of our agents will ride with Fabian up to the house, where the van will be searched by the dogs a final time."

"No doubt you're already noticing the telltale signs of what we believe happened." Tron says this to me. "We've been talking about it enough on the Doomsday Commission, anticipating this very sort of nightmare."

The Emergency Contingency Coalition, or Doomsday Commission, as it's known, is a White House–appointed task force. Benton and I serve on it along with other experts, including Albert Allemand, Tron and most recently Lucy. The objective is for top people in law enforcement, the military, the sciences and various disciplines to help predict and mitigate the gravest dangers to life on the planet.

The most dangerous villains are the ones we can't see. Viruses, poisons, chemicals, hacking and other cyberattacks. Also, bigotry and the sorts of misinformation that result in violent rampages, wars and genocide. Most troubling at the moment is electromagnetic energy that can cook our food or give us a phone signal. It also can be used as a hideous weapon.

Anyone can get hold of microwave motors and various types of antennas. Building your own radio frequency (RF) high-energy ray-gun is inexpensive. The pieces and parts are legal, and there's plenty on the Internet to offer guidance. Historically such weapons required a vehicle for transport. But technologies continue to get smaller and more convenient.

Eventually such sadistic inventions will be wireless, and charged like a mobile phone. They'll be worn on your hip like a stun gun or fit in a pocket like a *Star Trek* phaser. We aren't there yet, for which I couldn't be more grateful. But it's just a matter of time.

"I suspect that the guts of the weapon system will fit in a normal-sized carrying case. A big backpack not so different from what we have on." Lucy continues explaining the nightmarish scenario. "I know it's possible to build such a thing."

The microwave power source would be connected to a radio antenna, most likely a garden-variety Yagi. The single long metal rod is connected to a series of short ones in a shape that brings to mind a sawfish bill. The gun barrel antenna is enclosed in a metal cone or wave guide. The result resembles a garage-made blunderbuss, and I've seen videos of the damage such a thing can cause.

I tell Lucy and Tron about the paper bag inside Marino's truck. They'll have someone deliver it to the Smithsonian, they promise before I can ask. I'm reminded that Secret Service surveillance devices would have picked up my suggesting that Fabian drive the evidence.

"If something needs to go to specialists outside your labs or ours, we'll take care of it," Tron explains. "We don't want members of your staff doing it."

"I'm happy with that," I reply. "Relieved, in fact. I don't care to have my office the source of any further leaks."

"Anything to keep Maggie *Cutthroat* out of the loop," Marino agrees.

Tron surveys the brown foliage, the brick pillars strangled by dead creepers. "We've seen similar damage at other attack sites, now that we know what to look for," she says mostly for Marino's benefit.

He knows very little about our work on the Doomsday Commission, and doesn't like the reminder that I can't tell him everything about my life. I can't share all of the details, and lately there has been a rash of these microwave attacks in the capital area. Most often this has happened when White House and other key staff are walking to their cars.

But government officials have been blasted through the walls of their residences. Victims report feeling extreme pain as the room begins spinning and hearing weird clicking sounds and other noises.

Lights flickered, the power going out. Electricity arced, metal heated up, becoming mildly magnetized.

Victims report ending up on the floor, on the pavement in a parking lot. Usually the first thought is that they're having a stroke.

"And depending on how and where the attack occurred, we might find wilted plants, dead insects and birds that were in the line of fire," Tron continues briefing Marino about the Havana Syndrome, as it's been dubbed.

The first reported cases were in 2016. Canadian and U.S. embassy personnel working in their Havana, Cuba, offices heard loud booms and other noises. Victims suffered severe pain, dizziness and visual disturbances, a number of them claiming they've been permanently damaged.

Complaints range from mild to severe, and include chronic migraine headaches, fatigue, ringing in the ears, hearing loss, insomnia and cognitive impairment. The Havana Syndrome is no longer dismissed as imagined or due to other causes, including group hysteria. I've seen the medical evidence myself, MRI scans showing necrosis and changes in brain structure and connectivity.

For decades the Chinese, the Russians and other nations, including the United States, have been developing directed high-energy weapons. Microwaves are a type of radio wave, and like x-rays can do a lot of damage if one isn't properly shielded. To fire such a thing brings to mind ray-gun attacks from UFOs in science fiction. The horrific potential is the stuff of H. G. Wells's *War of the Worlds,* penned more than a century ago.

It was inevitable that the technology would be real one day and find its way into the general public. A homebuilt microwave gun isn't so different from making improvised explosive devices (IEDs) from Crock-Pots and ball bearings. It's similar to 3-D printing a 9mm pistol.

Next thing you know such monstrous fabrications are going on in your neighbor's house. Maybe inside your own basement, depending on what the kids and their friends are doing to entertain themselves.

"Based on intelligence gathered, we think the plan was to fire these microwave weapons during the graveside service earlier today. The terrorists would attack when the targets were out of the presidential motorcade," Lucy tells us about the aborted assassination attempt.

Likely the shooters were in various locations outside the cemetery, and on cue they planned to sweep the crowd with waves of intense microwave energy. Much like multiple shotguns firing at once and spraying hundreds of pellets. Maybe you kill people. Maybe you only injure some of them, brain-damaging them forever. Most of all you terrorize the public, and that's the goal.

"I guess the big question is how close would they have to be to the targets," Marino says. "Far enough away that the potential victims can't see somebody shooting at them, I'm assuming."

"We can't be certain," Tron replies. "The heat-rays the military deploy to scatter crowds typically have a range of at least a thousand meters, about ten times the length of a football field. But it's hard to say when we don't know exactly what we're dealing with."

"It depends on the power system, the size of the antenna," Lucy explains. "It depends on the location, the weather, a lot of things."

CHAPTER 14

We have less than an hour of daylight left. The uniformed Secret Service officers have MP5s slung across their chests, and are ready for anything.

Some of the crime scene investigators have disappeared along the driveway with armloads of gear. Others are setting up wireless auxiliary lighting at the entrance and various key locations. They're placing orange-striped sawhorse barricades in the road out front as Marino and I continue being briefed by his truck.

"The insect and plant evidence, the dead critters you've collected," Tron says to me, "there's more of the same up at the house except it's worse. We'll show you when we get there. But when the bad guy rolled up at this location, his first target was here at the entrance."

She directs our attention to the brick columns wound in withered creepers, the stone owls widely staring.

"He probably drove through when no one was around." Lucy continues painting the scenario. "He powered up his weapon and discharged it at the pillars and all around them. Probably shot it out his car window, then drove on. Likely that was the bursts of energy that we detected at around three-forty."

"Why? To knock out security cameras if there were any?" Marino surveys the damaged foliage.

"Typically, the entrance is where you're going to find surveillance devices," Lucy says. "The bad guy electromagnetically disabled anything like that while entering the property."

"You sure it was only one person?" Marino asks.

"Only one weapon was detected," Lucy replies. "Most likely, the bad guy showed up here alone."

"But we don't really know," Tron says.

They suspect the killer drove all the way up to the house where his vehicle wouldn't be spotted from the street. Then he launched a second attack, this time on foot from the backyard behind the kitchen. He was on the property a total of twenty minutes at least, and likely not much longer than that.

"Well, if he was trying to fry surveillance devices like cameras, that tells me right off that he didn't know a whole lot about this place," Marino says, and I'm having the same thought. "Anybody familiar with the judge or Chilton Farms would be aware she doesn't care about security. She doesn't have cameras. There aren't even any outdoor lights that work."

"Driving up to the house is incredibly brazen," I point out. "How did the assailant know someone wouldn't pull in right behind him? How did he know he wouldn't be spotted coming and going?"

"Maybe it was someone you wouldn't think twice about if you saw his car in the driveway," Marino suggests, and I have a feeling he's wondering about the caretaker.

"Or the person is increasingly aggressive and taking bigger risks." Lucy meets my eyes. "Ask Benton about it. He'll tell you what he thinks about this particular asshole. Charging in like a drunk gunslinger blasting away, and getting off on it. You can see it in the damage to plants and bugs and other things. Overkill."

"I'm assuming anyone shooting weapons like this must be wearing some sort of Faraday cage protection?" I ask. "Otherwise there's no way to prevent microwaves from flowing through one's own body if there's inadvertent contact while firing."

"You buy something like shielded clothing and fabric, and it's not hard to track. Especially if it's being purchased in bulk," Tron says. "So far, we're not seeing that kind of movement, and we're always looking for it."

"These bad guys are stealthy and quick on their feet," Lucy says. "I doubt they're hauling around cumbersome chainmail, and the metalized fabric suits people wear when working around stuff like high-voltage power lines. It would be hard getting in and out of gear like that quickly, and you'd be conspicuous."

"What happens if you fire something like that? Do you hear or see anything?" Marino looks slightly panicked.

"You won't hear or see the actual microwaves as they travel through the air," Lucy answers. "You might hear the motor running if you were really close, depending on the power source."

"You might see steam as the foliage withers before your eyes," Tron describes. "And of course, you'd see the wildlife affected."

It's a kind way to put it. I know all too well what happens.

"The rapid bursts of energy basically cook things the same way a microwave oven does." I give Marino the ugly upshot.

"A bad way to die." He makes a face.

"There aren't many good ones," I reply, and I ask Lucy and Tron when they arrived on their bikes. I'm trying to figure out who got here and at what time as my suspicions deepen about my niece's role.

"Our three plainclothes agents were first on the scene," Lucy answers. "The ones up at the manor house, they were the backups who met us."

"Which was when?" I ask again.

"We first rolled up a little more than three and a half hours ago,"

Lucy says. "At four-twenty to be exact. The times, locations and such are documented, of course."

"All the fun things we carry around with us and wear on our person." Tron indicates her heads-up display sport glasses, her smart ring as examples. "We couldn't lie about where we've been and when. It's all captured by computer."

"What time did the caretaker get here?" Marino asks. "I'm assuming he found the body."

"He didn't. Tron and I did, but we didn't access the property alone, not even once. And like we've said, everything is documented," Lucy explains. "There's nothing we've done that's going to come back to haunt us."

■ ■ ■

They arrived at Chilton Farms before Rachael's body had been found, before it was known that she was dead.

That wasn't long before it started raining. The reason my niece and her investigative partner don't look as if they were out in the storm is because they weren't. They were inside the manor house by then. They were with the body in the kitchen and anywhere else they thought they should search.

As they're telling me what they did, I detect a distinctive high-pitched whining overhead getting louder. I gaze up at the drone soaring high over the trees like a giant six-legged robotic insect. Silhouetted blackly against the smoldering sun, it carries gimbalized cameras among other technologies, including miniature ultrasonic devices, explaining why Chilton Farms is silent.

"We have these small repellent devices on the drones," Lucy says. "And we've also placed these same devices in certain areas of the property."

The transmitted ultrasound waves humanely keep critters away, and the major concern is raptors like hawks and eagles. Lucy doesn't want them dive-bombing and grabbing the drones out of the air. It's bad for the autonomous aircraft, and can injure or kill anything getting too close to the spinning props.

"Too bad your gadgets don't work with mosquitoes," Marino says snidely.

"Ultrasound waves can actually make them worse," Tron tells him. "Everything's got its downside."

"We've got drones up in several locations monitoring the protesters and other potential threats," Lucy explains as the one I can see makes a U-turn, sailing over treetops, off into the sunset. "Also, we've been searching the woods between here and the river."

"Who are you thinking was the intended victim?" Marino's attention is on the police, the activity at the foot of the driveway.

"We believe Rachael was the target," Tron says as Marino barely listens.

He's itching to help the cops set up, to shoot the breeze, to be one of them. More to the point, he doesn't like being briefed by Lucy. In his mind, it's a role reversal that's intolerable. He opens the front passenger's door of his truck, retrieving my knotted red biohazard bag from the floor where he left it.

"How's Fruge reacting to you showing up and taking over?" He grabs the roll of toilet paper.

"She's been doing as we've instructed," Lucy says. "She notified your office and you personally. She listened to Maggie's bullshit but didn't really. Your secretary thinks she's got Fruge buffaloed, but she doesn't. Fruge's doing what we've asked."

"That's good. Because I'd about crossed her off my Christmas list." Marino walks to the back of the truck. "But it's making sense. I figured the feds were bossing her around, and I was right. It's not her fault."

He's relieved and pleased Fruge isn't dissing him. Depositing my biohazard trash, the toilet paper in the truck bed, he slams shut the tailgate, locking it.

"How's this going to work going forward?" I want to know. "I can't have multiple parties from multiple agencies pulling at me constantly. And what I'm getting ready to do isn't a spectator sport."

"You'll be dealing directly with Lucy and me. Of course, Benton, and some others," Tron says.

An unmarked white van parks in front of the police cars. Doors open, and six Secret Service officers climb out dressed in black fatigues with CRIME SCENE UNIT emblazoned in yellow on their backs. Soon enough there will be FBI agents all over the place as well, we're told.

"You know, checks and balances," Tron adds. "And when it's terrorism the FBI has to be involved."

"Get any evidence you need." Lucy locks me in her intense green stare. "I know we have and will. Because once it ends up in the FBI labs or elsewhere, you lose control."

Another white Tahoe arrives, another Secret Service K-9 handler, and he looks familiar. I may have seen him in a training video. I'm all but certain he was the one wearing a bite suit, a Secret Service dog going after him. He crosses the street, carrying a rope toy, his sleek brown Malinois shepherd on a lead.

"I'd better check on the troops," Tron decides. "I need to get some of these folks up to the house and give them the lay of the land."

She retrieves her bike, walking it to where her colleagues are congregated. She greets the officers, and says something to the K-9 handler. The dog grabs at the rope, desperate to play, reminding me of Marino and his driving need to be put through his paces.

"Someday I'm getting another one." He can't stop staring. "Maybe call him Quincy. I don't see any reason why you can't use the same dog name twice as long as it's not at the same time."

"Why don't you go on," I suggest to him. "I'll meet you up there shortly."

"Good idea. I'll get the lowdown," he says. "I'll find some PPE for you, a decent pair of booties." He tries to be more thoughtful.

Grabbing the handles of the two big scene cases, he hurries after Tron and her compatriots. The hard cases loudly roll behind Marino as he awkwardly tugs them along. The beefy plastic wheels have a mind of their own, bumping and swiveling, getting caught between old pavers.

"Dammit!"

One of the cases flips over with a dull thud, and he sets it right.

"Shit!"

It happens again, both of them at once. Giving up with a streak of profanities, he carries them as if they're nothing. Each must weigh at least thirty pounds. Breaking into a trot, he catches up with everyone.

"I might have a partial solution for your wardrobe failure, Aunt Kay." Lucy never calls me that when her colleagues are present.

Unzipping a compartment of her backpack, she pulls out a pair of sneakers with balled-up socks tucked in them.

"For when I'm stuck somewhere and don't want to be wearing my tactical bike shoes," she explains. "Or if they get wet."

Fortunately, her feet are only slightly bigger than mine. Sitting on a running board of Marino's truck, I start putting on the shoes and socks.

"Annie's power is out. Meaning no air-conditioning or anything else."

"That's unfortunate," I reply. "But I'm not surprised if someone's firing away with a microwave weapon."

"We've brought in portable generators, and set up auxiliary lighting inside the house. I did it myself," she says.

"Annie can't stay here, for every reason imaginable," I reply.

Lucy puts her backpack back on, and we set out along the driveway.

"Benton and I were thinking she could be with us tonight, maybe for a few days," she says.

The same thing has been on my mind as I've worried about my old friend. At our place she'll be safe, Lucy explains as we pick our way around slick pavers and broken ones.

"There are some nasty people out there who would like to hurt her. And just as many would like to hurt you, Aunt Kay." My niece continues warning me of the dangers.

Shadows deepen as we walk to the whispery clicking of the bike wheels turning. I text Annie with the invitation, reminded of the caretaker she's known her entire life. I tell Lucy we need Holt Willard's DNA for exclusionary purposes.

"Even if he didn't touch the body, he has access to the property," I explain. "His DNA's going to be all over the place."

"We've already done it," she replies. "He got here at five o'clock on the nose, exactly when he was supposed to meet Rachael. By then she was dead, obviously, and we'd been here for a while. One of the agents intercepted him at the entrance. Holt Willard was never up at the house."

"Did he have any idea what was going on?"

"Not at the time. But he realized something seriously bad was," she says as a Secret Service crime scene officer appears around a bend, walking briskly toward us.

CHAPTER 15

He's older and tough-looking with a gray crew cut, and he carries a tactical-looking black hexacopter. I don't know if it's the same drone that flew over earlier, but it could be.

"Everything all right?" Lucy stops walking her bike.

"We had an unsuccessful launch," the Secret Service officer says.

"Damn, that's too bad." She inspects the broken prop.

"The motor started spinning at different speeds, and it wasn't responding to right-stick inputs."

"Sounds like Pixhawk problems again," she decides, and he heads along his way, cradling the drone like a broken bird.

"We should have at least four up," Lucy explains to me. "That explains why I'm seeing livestreams from only three."

Not noticing drones flying anywhere at the moment, I'm reminded that she's wearing her AI-enhanced sport glasses, the lenses clear as the light fades on the driveway. Information in her heads-up display includes images from drones we can't see from here, and we resume walking.

She tells me that it wasn't possible to deploy the drones until the weather cleared. The Secret Service is using them for aerial surveillance of Chilton Farms, the Landing, and also the protesters gathering in a church parking lot not too far from the Old Town Marriott where the jurors are sequestered for the night.

"The drone cameras can zoom in on a lot of things. License tags, for example." She wheels her bike around a puddle chartreuse with pollen. "We can do facial recognition in some instances."

"When you were with the caretaker"—I get back to that—"did he mention anything important? Had he noticed anything unusual going on here of late?"

"He seemed pretty clueless," Lucy says. "Is pretty badly shaken up, wouldn't stop crying. Tron and I sat him down inside one of our vans, talked to him briefly, then told him he was free to go home. There's no way he has anything to do with this unless he's involved with those responsible. Domestic terrorists, in other words."

"As well as Holt Willard knows this place, he must have noticed the damage to the entrance the same way you did," I reply. "Even if he wasn't allowed to access the property, he would have seen at least some of the same things we're picking up."

"He didn't mention it, and we didn't, either."

"What did he tell you about why he was meeting with Rachael? And what about proof that he actually had an appointment?"

"There's a light out in the kitchen pantry," Lucy says. "Changing it requires a ladder."

He promised he'd take care of it. He showed Lucy and Tron the texts between Rachael and him from early this morning when she notified him about the problem. She told him to meet her at the house at 5 P.M. *sharp,* and that he couldn't be inside long because she was in the middle of a *mountain of work.*

"She wasn't much for saying please and thank you," Lucy adds. "But I saw that for myself when we ran into her at the liquor store, as you well remember."

"Holt Willard showed up at five as promised, after Rachael was already dead," I reply. "But what I'm wondering is, what about earlier?

Was he on the property earlier today? While she was here working, presumably?"

"Rachael didn't want him on-site because she didn't want to be disturbed," Lucy says. "She needed quiet and privacy. That's the story. And according to him it wasn't the first time she'd done this, telling him not to come to the property. She would order him to stay away because she was working from home."

"Or that's what she claimed. But I'm wondering if that's the real reason she wanted to stay in." I'm thinking of Flagler. "Did Holt mention how often this was happening after Rachael moved in with Annie?"

"It was more frequent earlier, maybe once a week. Of late, not as often."

"Not since the Hooke trial started, let me guess," I reply. "If Flagler was coming to see her in secret, I doubt that's been going on in recent weeks, as consumed as he is. Why did she stay in today? Why really?"

"The caretaker told us that Rachael was worried about traffic being terrible because of the holiday weekend," Lucy says. "That's the gist in the text messages he showed us."

"She couldn't have been staying in to have a rendezvous with Flagler," I reply. "She must have known he'd be tied up in court all day with the world watching on live TV."

He was going after me on the witness stand at the very time Chilton Farms was under siege by whoever showed up with a microwave gun.

"Unless Bose Flagler can be in two places at once, he wasn't here," I add, old oak trees arching over the driveway like the vaulted ceiling of a cathedral.

The sun burns brightly behind the tall chimneys, and in the early days the property wasn't nearly this obscured by foliage. Sweat trickles down Lucy's face as she pushes her bike. The temperature is still in the eighties but a breeze is kicking up.

"Obviously, you didn't call nine-one-one or request a rescue squad," I assume.

"We didn't," she says.

"How did Fruge find out?"

"I called her."

"And there's no question it's Rachael Stanwyck whose body is inside on the floor?" I ask.

"None."

"Who decided she was dead?" I get to what's nagging at me.

"I did," Lucy says. "I was wearing gloves and a mask, and it was obvious she was gone. No heartbeat. She wasn't breathing, her pupils fixed and dilated."

As she explains what she did and didn't do, I treat her as objectively as I would any colleague experienced in dealing with crime scenes and dead bodies. The difference is that my niece knows more than most. When she was coming along, her field trips included spending time at my office, where I'd park her in the library for hours. The medical and scientific tomes held her attention for only so long.

Inevitably Lucy would get into things she shouldn't, including instructional videos of autopsies, and cases awaiting entry in the office computer. She was Marino's ride-along when he was still a Richmond homicide detective, and she couldn't get enough. She witnessed what most kids don't.

"I saw her body through the kitchen window," Lucy is saying. "I was inside checking her a few minutes later, and she hadn't been dead long. We have a good idea because of what our signal analyzers were picking up during that interval between three-forty and four o'clock."

"I don't think it will be difficult determining time of death in this case," I reply. "It's everything else that's going to be hard."

Around another bend, and the manor house is before us, two-story and boxy, a perfect example of Georgian symmetry with its steeply pitched slate tile roof. The chimneys are disproportionately tall like they were long ago, and I remember my visits during the early years. Annie's estate seemed impossibly grand.

Now it's tired and unkempt, on the way to ruination. Ivy covers brick siding like glossy green scales all the way to the dormer windows, threatening to one day overcome the roof. Brick and mortar have been cracked by the invasive roots. Should anyone remove them, I worry the house might disintegrate. Like so many things, the infestation has gotten out of hand because Annie's done nothing about it.

The only car in front is Rachael's red Mercedes-AMG GT, the sleek roadster cordoned off with bright yellow ribbons of tape attached to traffic cones. Nearby, Secret Service crime scene officers have set up a canopy tent. They're busy unpacking hard cases and gear bags, getting out PPE, evidence markers and a variety of forensic necessities for when they're allowed inside the house.

That won't be until the body is on its way to our office, and Marino and I are done collecting our evidence. I pause by the cordoned-off sports car, beaded with rainwater and plastered with leaves and flower petals. Bending down, I peer through a window at black leather upholstery with red diamond stitching. It doesn't look like Rachael had the car detailed very often.

I'm noticing dirt, plant debris, food crumbs on the mat in front of the driver's seat. There are crumbs on the console and passenger's seat as if she routinely grabs meals to go, eating inside her car. In the upper left corner of the windshield is a gummy residue, possibly from a parking decal that's been removed, possibly for CIA headquarters in Langley.

I would imagine it hasn't been only the Secret Service inside this car checking out the electronics and who knows what else. I look around, feeling uneasy and spied upon.

"We've already interrogated the GPS," Lucy tells me. "The last time someone entered a destination was this past Saturday, June twenty-fifth. At close to seven P.M., Rachael or someone wanted directions to a D.C. address that you, Benton and I are more than a little familiar with."

The Mercedes was driven to the Navy Yard some eight miles from here depending on what route you take. Rachael's car was parked until midnight at Mollie's Underground, a popular watering hole for the intelligence community and high-ranking members of the military. More like a secret society than a bar and grill, it's located inside a repurposed former Civil War foundry that has a waterwheel and plugged cannons.

Known for its food and libations, the Underground has spirited karaoke competitions that include bringing in ringers depending on who's performing in the area. Not so long ago it was Paula Abdul. Before that it was Cyndi Lauper, and you never know who might saunter up to the stage, grabbing the mic.

Benton and I usually stop in for lunch or dinner after meetings at the Pentagon. When possible, we hang out with Mollie, her last name Gunner. As in the wife of Jake, the four-star general who's the commander of the U.S. Space Force. Benton and I work with him on the Doomsday Commission. The four of us have gotten to be friends.

"I'm not surprised Rachael would patronize the place," I say to Lucy as we walk away from the Mercedes. "A lot of CIA people do.

The question is who she was meeting. Or who might have been driving or riding with her."

■ ■ ■

Blaise Fruge and two uniformed Alexandria police officers are waiting outside the tent, and I ask Lucy to give me a minute.

"I'll be right there." I explain I need to speak to the investigator alone.

Fruge's eyes are masked by mirrored Ray-Bans similar to the kind Marino wears, and she's in cargo pants and a polo shirt, her dark hair short. Since I've seen her last, she's bulked up in the gym with him as her trainer. She looks a lot more formidable than I suspect she's feeling at the moment.

"How's it going, Chief?" She greets me without smiling, and the two officers with her move off, giving us some privacy.

"Things are complicated, as you no doubt are figuring out," I say to her mirrored glasses. "I have a feeling your day has been about as bizarre and unpredictable as mine, and I appreciate you rolling with the punches."

"You know I'm here to help if there's anything I can do," she says. "It doesn't matter that it's not Alexandria P.D.'s investigation anymore. Tough shit if my first time out of the gate I get demoted."

"That's not what's happened, and this has nothing to do with you."

"What I'm saying is I'm here," she answers. "You and Marino need anything, all you gotta do is ask."

"You're already doing plenty." I can tell it pleases her to hear me say it. "Marino and I are grateful that you notified us. Thank you."

"Maggie figured that she and Doctor Reddy could boss me around, and I think they've gotten their comeuppance." Fruge takes off her sunglasses as her defenses lower. "The Secret Service took charge, and your secretary didn't know that. Not that I would have listened anyway when she told me point-blank not to allow you and Marino on the scene."

"It's good and bad to know Maggie really did that as opposed to just threatening it," I reply.

"She did it all right," Fruge says. "And let's just put it this way, certain parties know all about it."

She has a friend. If you know Fruge long enough you'll realize she has plenty of them, and is nosy as hell. She tells me this particular friend is someone she grew up with in Richmond. Her name is Echo, and she's now the head chef at the governor's mansion. She cooked dinner tonight, beef Wellington and asparagus for six.

"One of Governor Dare's guests was Elvin Reddy. Enough said." Fruge parks her sunglasses on top of her head. "You don't need to know the rest."

"The rest of what?" Lucy has returned, carrying a black plastic field case the size of a regular tacklebox.

"The usual story about what assholes Elvin Reddy and Maggie are," Fruge says, and my secretary would be shocked to hear it.

"You got that right," Lucy replies. "But on a more important subject, the protesters are leaving the church parking lot in a caravan as we speak. Eighteen vehicles so far, at least fifty people presumed to be armed and dangerous. Some are waving Confederate flags out the windows."

The *Justice for April* movement has morphed into something bigger and worse, Lucy explains. The authorities don't expect these people to be well behaved. They should reach the first checkpoint soon after dark.

"That sucks," Fruge says. "I knew when the Hooke trial was

moved up here that they were towing a damn Trojan horse into our backyard. I was totally against it. Why not other places like Roanoke, Charlottesville, even Richmond? Why way up here where traffic is a nightmare already? Why lure some of these rough people this close to D.C.? Because you ask me, that's not smart. Not that anybody cared about my opinion."

"What would be most appreciated is if you and your officers could help secure the perimeter," Lucy tells her as if they're friends and comrades. "We've got things squared away up here. Maybe reinforce the troops at the entrance. That would be really helpful. The more the merrier."

She's communicating in the most respectful way that she appreciates Fruge and her officers. She's grateful for their help but they need to get the hell out. Fruge doesn't say a word, simply nods. She seems more than happy to do something useful. Lucy and I cover our phones with antimicrobial protective sleeves. We put on gloves.

"What have you shown her?" I ask when Fruge is out of earshot.

"The same thing I'm about to show you except that she doesn't have any idea what it means," Lucy replies. "For her purposes, I pointed out where we think someone was waiting in the bushes. But I didn't get into the dead bugs or plants. She and the other cops think the storm is somehow responsible for it."

"What do they think went on here? What impression does Fruge have in particular about what happened to Rachael Stanwyck?"

"That someone was hiding, and maybe got her to open the door. Possibly, the killer is someone she knew, someone stalking her. Maybe even her estranged husband. And after the fact, this person staged the scene to make it look like an attempted sexual assault or robbery or both."

I'm careful where I step as we follow a flagstone walkway that's slippery when wet. It leads around the back of the house, the dense woods to our left. Lucy and I put on face masks.

"That's a pretty good story," I reply. "Based on what exactly?"

"Fruge and her buddies were looking through the kitchen window, and misinterpreted the evidence. No one can blame them," Lucy says. "You'll see in a minute why that would be easy to do. At first glance what they're thinking would seem to make perfect sense, because they don't know anything about a microwave weapon. They have no idea."

CHAPTER 16

As we reach the back of the house the moon is a pale crescent in the darkening blue sky. The wind quietly stirs the trees as we duck under crime scene tape encircling what's left of the formal garden.

The path leads through a riot of pink and red shrub roses, lavender lilacs, blue hydrangeas and other flowering vegetation, all of it in shadows. The trellis is overwhelmed by fragrant wisteria and jasmine near a stone table that's stained and pitted. The teak loveseat is weathered the silver gray of ashes.

Annie and I have sat out here together on a number of occasions since I moved back to Virginia. We've had conversations about cases while watching her eclectic hamlet of birdhouses. She'd tell me the proper names of every winged creature visiting the feeders or the butterfly bushes.

I'm not finding anything magical about this place now. My heart is heavy while getting harder, the devastation between here and the back door painful and infuriating. The word *monster* flashes in my head, and I'm more offended by the moment as I take in the carnage. Annie's garden has been murderously vandalized, and I dread the thought of her seeing it like this.

But there's not a depressing image that will be left unrecorded. More will follow when I deal with her sister's body here at the scene, and later during the autopsy. Inevitably Annie will bear witness to all of it. That's the way criminal cases work, and now her personal life is part of one.

Lucy snaps open the clasps of her small scene case. She finds a pair of plastic forceps, a ruler to use as a scale in photographs. I take samples of wilted foliage. I collect more insects and birds, not expecting Albert Allemand at the Smithsonian to discover anything different with these additional specimens.

No doubt they'll have nothing more to say than the ones I found at the entrance. But if I don't gather samples from where the fatal attack occurred, some attorney's going to give me a hard time about it. I make my way to one of my favorite birdhouses, built of brightly painted reclaimed wood, and on top of a squared teak post.

Dread wraps around me as I get close to the tiny red front porch with two bird-sized blue Adirondack chairs. Below the hole with its perch is a cheery red front door that I open with my gloved finger. Saddened but not surprised by what's inside, I hope it was quick. I always think the same thing whether it's people or chickadees.

As microwaves bombarded the backyard, there was no protection in feeders or habitats made of non-metallic materials such as plastic and wood. But at least a few of the neighbors had a fighting chance. Near a cluster of mountain laurels is an enclave of copper birdhouses on copper poles of varying heights. The *hotels,* as Annie calls them, are tarnished like old pennies, with peaked roofs and whimsical embellishments.

The metal enclosures would have acted like Faraday cages, deflecting the microwave radiation. I stand on my tiptoes. Looking through the holes, I catch moving flashes of fluttering indigo, and lively dark eyes and shiny black beaks. My mood lifts considerably.

"Where were you while it rained?" I ask Lucy.

"In the kitchen."

Following me with her field case, she has her phone ready. She bends close, taking one-handed photographs for me while I move about, placing the plastic ruler next to whatever I'm collecting. Without a scale, it's impossible to know what size something was or the distance between objects.

"Unfortunately, the rain started while we were inside the house, literally while I was checking the body," Lucy says. "We hadn't seen the damage back here by that point."

She didn't need to notice what's still obvious despite the downpour. Flowers and leaves are wilted and brown where the microwave weapon was discharged through them. I can make out the point of origin behind a tall boxwood hedge. This is where Lucy believes the assailant was positioned like a sniper with a rifle, waiting for a clear view of his target.

"He would have had to be back here at least several minutes finding the right spot," she says. "Unless he knew the terrain because he'd been here before. Whether he was familiar or not, he had to do some setting up. He had to put on protective gear or clothing, assuming he bothered. He had to power up his weapon. He had to wait until he was sure where the victim was."

"How did the killer know Rachael would go into the kitchen at some point?" I continue collecting hapless creatures, placing the tiny white boxes in the paper bag. "Unless he had some expectation of it he might have been sitting out here for a very long time."

"That's a missing piece of the puzzle," Lucy says. "For some reason he made the decision that this was the spot. He set up behind the hedge, waiting until she appeared in the window over the sink. He pulled the trigger, firing in rapid bursts like a machine gun."

The discharged waves of powerful energy followed a straight line through tree branches and other foliage. The swath widened the farther it traveled from the weapon, reaching the kitchen window, the ivy around it parched and brown. The microwaves passed undisturbed through the six panes of old wavy glass, and it's a shame there's no mesh metal screen.

Few of Annie's windows have them. Had that not been the case, Rachael might have been able to seek cover before she was debilitated and dead. Lucy shows me the disturbed area behind the hedge where she believes the killer was crouched, and I'm going to guess he was wearing something that blended, such as camouflage. I can see the broken branches, the crushed underbrush where he waited with his anarchist death ray.

From here to the kitchen window is maybe a hundred feet. If the range of the weapon is significantly more than that, as Tron has suggested, then Rachael was radiated by a concentrated beam. I wonder if she saw anything amiss before experiencing searing pain and collapsing to the floor.

"We've collected samples of vegetation the piece of shit would have been brushing up against," Lucy says, and I sense the bristling hostility beneath her coolness.

She hates whoever it is. When people are cruel enough, after a while she takes it personally the same way Marino does. My niece is just stealthier, more polished about it. She doesn't show the emotional cards she holds. But I intuit what's going on with her, and I'm not feeling any more charitable.

"I don't think we'll have much luck with DNA," she says. "That's probably not going to be the silver bullet that solves this case, because I doubt Rachael and the killer had physical contact. I doubt he touched anything except the great outdoors."

"Even without the rainstorm, DNA would be a long shot," I agree. "Unless he injured himself and left blood or skin cells that didn't wash away."

. . .

The slate walkway leads to the kitchen door. To the right of it the six-paned window glows invitingly because of the auxiliary lights Lucy set up inside.

"And you've done whatever was needed over here?" I ask before getting closer. "Because there's a chance the killer might have looked through the window. He might have wanted to see his handiwork."

"We've already checked for fingerprints and swabbed for DNA," she says as I change my gloves. Stuffing the soiled ones in a pocket of my skirt, I put on new ones and another surgical mask.

"But I doubt he would have gotten this close. He ran the risk she might have been conscious and gotten a look at him," Lucy says.

Careful to avoid thorny vines near the window, I smell the delicate perfume of the climbing red roses as I peer through the glass. Rachael is curled up on her left side between the sink and the door leading out to the garden. She's dressed in a beige warm-up suit, socks and sneakers.

Her clothing isn't disturbed, but I notice jewelry scattered on the red-and-white marble floor. Earrings. A necklace that looks open or broken. A ring. I understand what Lucy means about how easy it would be to misinterpret.

"Is what I'm seeing the way everything looked when you got here?" I ask.

"I didn't touch anything beyond what I've already said. And we took photos, video." Her voice is behind me as I look through the window. "Confusing, right?"

"Very."

"You can see why Fruge and the cops think it looks like a home invasion gone bad."

"And it was. Only the invader was invisible." I back away from the window.

Returning to the path, I pause in front of the kitchen door, solid wood and painted white. It has a Victorian-era crystal doorknob that Annie calls *aftermarket*.

"Was this locked or unlocked when you first got here?" I ask.

"Locked."

"And the front door?"

"Affirmative," she says as we walk back through the garden. "We had to pry it open."

"What about the alarm?"

"Disabled," she says. "The microwaves created a power surge that cooked it like everything else."

"Did the alarm service get any sort of notification that there was a malfunction?"

"No," she replies. "The company gets an alert only if the silent alarm is triggered."

"I guess the big question is whether it was set at the time of the attack," I reply as we return to the front of the house.

"Tron's already contacted the company," Lucy replies. "The system was unarmed, and not used all that often."

Apparently there had been a number of false alarms since Rachael moved in, resulting in the police responding, Tron was told. That's the problem with a silent alarm. You don't realize you've set it off until a police car arrives, and that would be most unfortunate if you're inside the house with your secret lover.

"Rachael may have been more afraid of false alarms, of being surprised by the police, than of the alternative," Lucy explains, and we've reached the tent the police set up.

Tyvek makes crinkly sounds as we step inside while Tron works her legs into a pair of coveralls. Marino rummages in an ice chest for a bottle of water.

"Doc?" He offers me one, and he's suited up and sweating.

"I think I'll wait."

I don't want any more extra-large coffee cups in my immediate future. Taking off my wrinkled linen suit jacket, I drape it over a scene case, setting down my briefcase. I step into a pair of coveralls one leg at a time, pulling them up, working my arms into the sleeves, trying not to fantasize about an eventual shower.

I snatch more gloves out of a box, tucking them, several surgical masks and a permanent marker in a pocket. I zip up the coveralls to my neck, put on the hood and a pair of safety glasses. Shrouded in white, the four of us make slippery sounds as we move around. We head to double front doors that I remember from my past.

But back in the old days there was a housekeeper to open them, and they weren't splintered from a prybar. The noise of generators is loud inside, electrical cables snaking across Italian marble flooring, the grand entryway garishly lit up.

"We tried to be as gentle as possible," Lucy says as I look at the damaged centuries-old wood, at the brass ram's head knobs that are original to the house. "A prybar was the best solution."

"Better than shooting the lock or caving in the door with a battering ram. Or kicking it open." Marino offers his expert opinion.

We pull booties over our shoes before walking into the glare of auxiliary lighting. I would know the musty smell anywhere, a bouquet of old odors. Dust, wood, candles, furniture polish. The acrid hint of soot from the fireplaces in every room. The air is still and stale as if the house has been closed up and empty forever. Some of it's my imagination fired by deep emotions.

The boiserie sculpted paneling in the entryway was carved in France centuries earlier, Normandy as I recall. The wood needs oiling, and I mention it to Annie every time I'm here. But it's not a priority, and she won't ask the caretaker to do that or much else.

"Then what does she have him for?" Tron asks as I tell them what I know from personal experience.

"By now Holt is like family. And as Annie puts it, you don't fire family because they get older and have arthritis," I reply while we look around the entryway. "I think he does light chores and runs errands."

I stare up at the tarnished silver mount in the molded plaster ceiling where one of the Baccarat chandeliers used to hang. Through an archway is the great room, as Annie's always called it, and the French oak flooring is scuffed. The boards are badly separating in spots, the rug threadbare. Over the limestone fireplace the wall is blank where a Picasso once hung.

Behind the sofa was a Constable landscape, and I remember where sculptures were displayed on risers and pedestals. Lavish meals in the formal dining room play like movies in my head. The elaborate fruitwood table is still here. Only it's dull and probably hasn't been used in years. The needlepoint seats of the twenty matching chairs are faded and stained.

Plate racks are missing their fine blue-and-gold china with the Chilton crest. The blue walls are as empty as the sky, the Baroque oil paintings of religious scenes gone. I remember eating rare roast beef and drinking a fine red Bordeaux while staring at David beheading Goliath.

"It must have been pretty cool hanging out here in the old days. But it doesn't feel very lived in now." Marino rarely realizes the irony of what he says, the kitchen before us.

Through the doorway I can see the old wooden cabinets, the deep brick fireplace with its carved gray marble mantel. Rachael's body is some ten feet to my right, not far from the back door that leads outside. Her arms are tucked in close, her legs drawn up.

"This is how she was when you got here?" I ask Lucy. "In a fetal position?"

"Yes, and like I've said, we've documented everything. You'll get all the photos. But with the exception of a few minor adjustments, what you're seeing is what we found."

"It's the *few minor adjustments* I'm worrying about," Marino says to her.

"Nothing that affects you."

"Not for you to say. How do you know what the hell we might be looking for?"

"Give it a rest." Lucy shuts him down, the two of them bickering like the old days.

"Her being positioned like that? In a fetal position?" Tron asks me. "What does that tell you?"

"It's what I often see when someone suffers severe trauma but can still move," I reply. "They bend their backs, drawing in their limbs like this as they're dying."

"Then she wasn't dead when she hit the ground, so to speak," Tron says.

"Unless you're vaporized, blown to bits by a bomb, or something else that causes instant obliteration?" I reply. "People don't literally drop dead. It takes a minute or two for everything to shut down. But that doesn't mean they're conscious."

"I'm betting she wasn't." Marino opens the field case he brought with him.

He hands me a new pair of shoe covers. I put them on, also a new surgical mask, and gloves. I step deeper inside a kitchen where I've spent a fair amount of time since returning to Virginia. It was here where I had my secret meeting with Annie and Governor Dare a year ago. I agreed to return to Virginia in this very room.

CHAPTER 17

Ancient cookware and baskets hang from exposed beams in the ceiling. The fireplace in a plaster wall is as deep as a cave. On the hearth are cast iron tools and bellows that look like something from an ancient castle.

To the right of the back door is a simple shaker table and four chairs in front of the window where Annie and I have had many conversations. In any other setting the kitchen appliances would look antiquated, the gas cooktop at least twenty years old. The refrigerator isn't much newer, nor are the electric skillet or toaster.

I take in the scene from the doorway, noticing the black Chanel shoulder bag and sunglasses, the keys on the butcher block. It catches my attention that the drip coffeemaker's glass pot is full of a tan liquid that might be tea. Nearby is a mug.

"With the power out, it's difficult knowing what lights were on or off at the time of the microwave attack," I say to Lucy and Tron. "I can see that the wall switches near the doors are in the up position."

"It looks like the lights were on in here," Tron agrees. "But we'll have to do additional analytics to be certain. Same with other areas of the house."

She and Lucy leave us for now, and Marino sets a glass mercury thermometer on top of the butcher block. Next, he finds the infrared (IR) gun, because I like to take the temperature with both for redundancy. We work quickly and quietly, needing little instruction or explanation, and he shakes open a disposable white sheet as if setting a dinner table.

"I see what you mean about what happens when it's the intelligence community." He arranges the sheet on the floor next to the body. "For all we know the CIA's been in here."

"Nothing much would surprise me, and I've already concluded that's exactly what's happened. For one thing, Tron's on loan to them. For all I know Lucy is too. And we know they were in here before anybody else."

"We have no clue what the hell is going on for real or who's watching." Marino is looking around irritably, uneasily. "And everybody lies. Even Lucy. But that's not new."

"Spying and lying are the same thing. Out of necessity."

"It bothers me they're the ones who found her." He glances back at the doorway as if Lucy and Tron might still be there. "How do we know they didn't . . . ?"

"I think it wise to resist spinning theories."

I stop him from finishing the thought, mindful that there probably are surveillance devices. Marino is wondering if Rachael Stanwyck was a hit. Maybe she was taken out by the CIA, our own people, and he hands me the IR thermometer gun. I point it at her forehead, clicking the trigger. The digital readout shows a temperature of 96.5 degrees Fahrenheit.

"That can't be right, Doc." He stares baffled at the number glowing red.

I take another reading, and it's the same. I point the IR gun at the empty air, and the ambient temperature in the kitchen is 78 degrees.

"Her head is hot because of the high-energy radiation," I explain.

"Holy shit, if she's been dead more than four hours and is still that warm? She must have really been lit up at the time it happened." Marino writes down the details I give him.

"If the killer was close range and aimed at her head, then the energy was concentrated there, causing thermal damage that I should be able to see microscopically," I reply. "The radiation could have heated up the targeted area ten degrees or more."

"And it wouldn't have heated up her entire body like that?"

"No."

"How come?"

"Think about a casserole in the microwave oven." I kneel next to the body. "It's hot in places and not in others. Especially if the oven doesn't have a stirrer, a rotating plate."

"You're starting to freak me out a little, Doc."

"In cases of Havana Syndrome that we know about we believe the target is the head." I inch up Rachael's warm-up jacket to her waist. "That's where you'll find the most intense internal damage, to the brain, the eyes, spreading out from there like shockwaves."

I point the IR thermometer at the exposed skin of Rachael Stan-wyck's waist. The result is what I would expect.

"Ninety-point-one," I tell Marino, and he writes it down. "Her body's cooled seven or eight degrees, and that's about right when you think of when Lucy and Tron picked up intermittent bursts of energy between three-forty and four P.M. And it's after eight now."

"Meaning that when she died her head temperature might have been as high as a hundred and ten?"

"Possibly. But there's much we don't know about these kinds of attacks."

"Well, it must have hurt like hell."

"She would have felt severe pain in her head, her eyes. She might have heard weird sounds as the room began to spin. I doubt she was conscious long, possibly only seconds, maybe a minute," I reply. "Let's take her core temp because it's going to be the most reliable for telling us when she died."

"I think we have a good idea," Marino replies. "Probably around three-forty, three-forty-five this afternoon."

"If I don't do it..."

"I know. Damn lawyers." Returning to the field case, he looks through trays and drawers. "We'll never hear the end of it."

He places a scalpel and a long glass chemical thermometer on the paper sheet where I'm kneeling. I turn Rachael flat on her back, and she's limber and warm to the touch. A trickle of blood drips from her nose, her eyes partially open and staring blindly. The beautiful and vain Rachael Stanwyck wasn't wearing makeup when she died, not even lipstick.

Her luxurious black hair is pulled back in a scrunchie. She smells like onions and garlic when I lean close. It certainly wouldn't seem she was expecting company. Pulling her designer warm-up pants below her navel, I notice that her belly seems distended.

"That's a little odd," I comment.

"What if she was pregnant?" Marino offers.

"We won't find that out here, but the autopsy certainly will tell us." With the scalpel I make a small incision in the right upper abdomen, and a drop of blood slides down her side.

■　■　■

I insert the long glass chemical thermometer into the liver to get the most accurate reading. More blood spills, spotting the white sheet I've tucked partially under her. I bend her slender fingers, and they've begun to stiffen. I move her head from side to side, and her neck is still relatively limber.

"Rigor mortis is in the early stages." I continue reporting my findings, and Marino makes notes while taking photographs. "Lividity isn't fixed yet."

Changing my gloves, I turn my attention to the jewelry scattered over the flagstone floor.

"One silver metal ring with embedded blue stones. Likely white gold and sapphires," I explain.

I place the ring inside a small evidence bag, and collect a pair of earrings next. One is in front of the sink, the other several feet away.

"A pair of silver metal clip-on earrings with clear stones." I continue giving Marino an inventory.

More white gold and diamonds, I'm supposing, while aware of the metal's subtle attraction to the smart ring on my right gloved hand. I know what it means. But the sensation is creepy.

"I need a magnifier," I tell Marino, and he hands one to me.

I collect the necklace from the floor in front of the sink. As I hold it up to the light I see the clasp is bent open, and the jeweler's mark is for 18-karat gold. I feel the chain move like something alive, attracted to my nickel-plated smart ring.

"The necklace appears to have been forcibly removed." I drop it into another plastic evidence bag, labeling it like all the rest. "As if yanked hard."

"Now you're seeing how easy it would be for people to think she was grabbed, that she struggled with someone while he was trying to rob or sexually assault her. Or maybe both," Marino says.

He waits near the open scene case, watching what I'm doing, his sweaty face framed in white, a surgical mask on. His safety glasses keep fogging up.

"And then someone like the caretaker or ex-husband is blamed," Marino says. "The cops figure Rachael let the person in because she knew him. Then things went south. When in fact nobody was inside the house with her when she died."

"She removed the jewelry herself because it was burning the hell out of her," I reply. "And all of it is magnetized, which makes sense after being bombarded by electromagnetic energy."

I unzip the warm-up jacket, and she has nothing on underneath except a sports bra, a pair of bikini panties. Moving her hair out of the way, I find four tiny red burns around her neck. Both earlobes have similar red marks from the clip-ons, and I take her hands in my gloved ones, inspecting them carefully front and back. I find another tiny burn, this one on her left ring finger.

I imagine Rachael standing in front of the window over the sink. I suspect she was making a pot of tea when the assailant started firing his weapon from the backyard. The current of microwave energy was conducted by the metal jewelry she was wearing. Suddenly, it was burning her, and she yanked it off. Her head was heating up and hurting before she collapsed.

"Or she might have been down on the floor when she started ripping off her jewelry," I explain. "We'll probably never know, but I suspect she was still standing when she did it, having no idea she was being fired upon. Only that something was horribly wrong."

I ask for a tape measure, and the necklace she had on is twenty inches long. The burns on her neck and upper chest are approximately five inches apart. The distance tells us the wavelength of the current.

I explain to Marino what I've learned from working with the Doomsday Commission. "The wave of energy peaks every five inches, and that's when it burns." I draw a microwave in the air, up and down, up and down. "We've seen similar injuries in recent victims of Havana Syndrome if they're wearing something like a watch, a bracelet, a jacket with a metal zipper."

The metal conducts the positively charged current, which then tries heading to the negatively charged earth. But it can't. The current has no place to go because the ring and the necklace aren't grounded, and heat up rather much like tires do when they're spinning in place.

"That's why you get burned," I explain, and I'm no electrical engineer.

But as people like me continue dealing with the latest threats to human life, I've had to learn about high-energy guns. I've had to educate myself about poisons, to become facile in my understanding of chemical and biological weapons of mass destruction. The conversations Benton and I have over drinks are the stuff of dystopian horror stories.

"It's a lot easier dealing with guns," Marino decides. "I don't like not being able to see what you're being shot with."

"Unless you're Superman you're not seeing a bullet before it hits you, either." I remove the thermometer from the small incision in Rachael's abdomen, wiping off the glass with a corner of the sheet.

Her core body temperature is 92 degrees, and that sounds about right for having been dead four to five hours in these conditions. I take off my gloves, walking around the kitchen, waving my right hand like a symphony conductor. I move close to the antique copper faucet and its figurine handles. Then the swan neck brass pulls, the stainless steel blender, the stove.

I check the silverware and other metal items in drawers, feeling the gentle tug of the magnetic attraction to my smart ring. I walk into the pantry with its built-in oak shelves, cabinets and drawers. The only light source is the bare overhead bulb, and it's pointless pulling the string. Since the power is out we can't know whether this light was working or not at the time of the attack.

But based on what Holt Willard told Lucy and Tron, the bulb

needed changing. He was supposed to take care of it for Rachael at five P.M., and the stepladder is folded and leaning against the wall. On the stone countertop is a box of four 100-watt lightbulbs as if Rachael left them out for him. The sides of the corrugated cardboard are brown from the bulbs getting hot before burning out.

Had she been conscious and aware at the time, she might have noticed the box glowing inside the pantry like something from Stephen King. She might have tried to call for help, and found her cell phone wasn't working. The lights might have flickered and gone out as the air-conditioning quit.

"Her entire kitchen basically has become magnetized," I continue, telling Marino what I'm seeing.

Electrical currents cause magnetic fields to form around them, and that's what happened inside Annie's kitchen, I explain. Microwaves are electrical and magnetic energy moving together through space. That's what electromagnetic energy is, I add, changing my gloves again, dropping the used ones in a biohazard bag.

I turn my attention to Rachael's leather Hermès sneakers. The tread has bits of purple material stuck in it. I use paper bags and rubber bands to cover her hands and feet. Then Tron and Lucy are back, and I update them on what we're finding.

"All of it consistent with a microwave attack." I walk over to the butcher block, interested in the black leather Chanel pocketbook and sunglasses. "Hers, I presume." I remember them from bumping into her at the liquor store, and nearby are keys.

"Yes," Lucy says. "No sign the pocketbook had been rifled through or that anything such as money or credit cards might be missing."

"Again, arguing against the killer ever being inside the house," Marino says. "We know the front door was locked since you had to pry it open. And this one?" He indicates the back door near the body.

"Locked when we got here," Tron says.

"The keyless remote is to Rachael's Mercedes," Lucy tells me. "The other keys we're not sure about yet. Except one of them is to the front and back doors. It opens both of them."

"God only knows the last time the locks were changed," Marino says. "Or how many people might have a key."

"What about medications or anything else that might be important inside her pocketbook?" I ask.

"I can show you." Swapping old PPE for new, Lucy walks into the kitchen.

CHAPTER 18

Lucy spreads a paper sheet over the butcher block, and removes everything from the pricey Chanel tote. A crocodile-skin wallet, lipsticks, a hairbrush, breath mints, hand sanitizer, a black cloth face mask, a small can of Lysol. As Lucy does this I check the coffeemaker, and the three herbal tea bags in it are typically used as a laxative.

"Nothing exciting." Lucy digs inside the pocketbook, pulling out chargers, possibly for a cell phone, a computer. "Obviously, I've been through her personal effects already. Everything's been photographed and processed."

She unzips another compartment, pulling out several packets of moist towelettes, a stack of napkins, a cosmetic bag. Also a bottle of a fiber supplement, and sugar-free gummy bears that are important to note.

"Eight ounces, cinnamon flavored, and containing maltitol," I tell Marino, and he writes it down. "Also, a bottle of psyllium." I spell it for him, and mention the tea bags.

"Does that mean something to you?" Tron asks from the doorway.

"It might," I reply. "The maltitol in the sugar-free candy, the psyllium can act as laxatives. As will the tea."

"Tell me about it," Marino says. "Remember that time I ate sugar-free chocolate turtles?"

"I won't touch shit like that," Lucy replies.

"I was doubled over with cramps," Marino continues his story. "It was like a Roto-Rooter going through me."

"She was probably one of these people who always worried about her weight," Tron decides.

"I assume you've been through her wallet," I say to Lucy.

"Yes, and you're welcome to look."

The first thing I check is how much cash Rachael was carrying. I count more than eight hundred dollars, most of it in crisp new twenties that are sticking together.

"I'm wondering if she might have used an ATM, possibly recently. It looks like she got cash from somewhere," I suggest. "It also appears she had a habit of buying food to go, possibly eating in her car."

I indicate the napkins that were inside the pocketbook. I mention the crumbs I noticed inside her Mercedes.

"If she goes to ATMs, maybe waits in line at fast-food places?" Marino says. "And maybe the wrong person spots her? Let's be honest, someone who looked like her? She must have been stared at everywhere she went."

I glance through credit and ID cards, and notably absent is anything that might indicate Rachael worked for the CIA. If I didn't know what she did for a living I couldn't possibly tell from what I'm seeing. All I'd conclude is that she appeared to have money. She was beautiful, ostentatious and weight conscious. There's not much of a trail for me to follow.

No doubt her communications exist in cyberspace, and I'm not going to have access. Gone are the days when I might find a pocket diary to flip through. Or an address book. Maybe an envelope of photographs that were just developed at the drugstore. One never knows what might be important. Possibly notes or letters that divulge murderous intentions or suicidal thoughts.

Even a horoscope or slip of paper from a fortune cookie can be telling. It might hint at what someone feared or dreamed about. The smallest thing might speak to someone's state of mind or activities. But I can't glean much from what I'm looking at. No doubt Rachael's life, like mine, has been managed electronically, and I'm not seeing a single device to account for that.

"I don't care what you've taken, moved or otherwise altered unless it interferes with what I'm doing." I say this to my niece the way I would to anyone else I'm working with. "You have your purposes. But I have to see what might be important for mine. Is there anything else I should know about?"

"Her computer tablet was in her bag," Lucy replies. "It was damaged by the microwave attack, as you might expect."

"And her phone?"

"I have photographs of where it was." Lucy continues informing me of how much has been tampered with. "It's cooked, probably hopeless. We're already after records from the provider."

"Where was her phone exactly when you first got here? Before anything had been done?" I ask.

"On the floor, her right hand was touching it." It's Tron who answers.

"I need to get her out of here and to my office," I decide. "I've done what I can for now. Where's Fabian?"

"At the entrance of the driveway," Lucy says. "The dogs are searching the van, and not alerting on anything. He's standing off to the side looking up at the news choppers."

"I'm surprised he's not waving at them," Marino says.

"This very second he's walking around making sure he's visible," Tron replies. "He may as well be waving."

"How do you know what the hell he's doing this very second?" Marino asks gruffly.

Tron points to her AI-assisted sport glasses.

"Yeah, better you than me," he retorts. "It would make me crazy wearing something like that. It's hard enough dealing with TV remotes and my damn phone at the same time."

"Multitasking at the next level," Tron replies.

"Really? And what happens if you can't do shit or think for yourself anymore?"

"That wouldn't be good," she replies, and it's not possible for Marino to get a rise out of her.

"I assume you've checked the trash in here," I say to Lucy.

"Nothing that's interesting," she replies, and I don't wait for an invitation.

I know where to look, and opening the cabinets under the sink, I pull out the plastic trash basket. Inside are wadded paper towels, used tea bags, eggshells and other detritus. But I'm seeing no sign of recent meals eaten, certainly not substantial ones, and Annie doesn't have a garbage disposal.

I check inside the refrigerator, finding bottled fruit smoothies, yogurts and prepackaged lean cheeses and deli meats. Several bottles of champagne are in a drawer. There's nothing much in the freezer except two bottles of vodka. I'm not surprised I'm not seeing much in the way of foods that have to be prepared.

Annie can't cook. She never learned, didn't have to, isn't interested and takes no pleasure in it. I know this all too well from having lived with her. When I'd prepare a dish, no matter how simple, you might have thought I'm a magician. Whipping up spaghetti or a frittata was as foreign and impossible to her as flying a plane or composing a symphony.

She's not changed much over the decades. It's been my observation that Annie gets her meals from the courthouse cafeteria and local restaurants or she might stop at a drive-through. I'm not seeing any indication that Rachael was industrious in the kitchen, either. As spoiled as she seemed, I can't imagine it.

"What else have you checked inside the house?" I ask Lucy and Tron. "I'd like to take a look at her bedroom. Most of all her medicine cabinet. Or did you empty that too?"

"We had to check every room when we first got here in case anybody was hiding inside," Lucy says. "We didn't take anything from the medicine cabinet."

"That doesn't mean we didn't look," Tron adds. "To be certain something is what it appears to be. That what's supposed to be inside boxes and bottles really is. The usual."

They aren't going to tell me everything they've done or why. They won't say who's been inside the house, and how many times. Maybe I don't want to know, and I head out of the kitchen alone. I don't wait for Marino or anyone as I walk through the dining room, then the great room, returning to the entryway staircase.

The worn limestone steps, the black wrought iron railing bring back memories from the early years. On the second floor, walls are blank where rare sconces and art once hung. I walk past a series of shut oak doors. Behind them are bedrooms filled with boxes Annie's yet to unpack since her parents died. I've told her that she doesn't have to sort through things alone, and once it's done she can move on.

But she won't hear of getting rid of what she can't let go, and it's true about the enemy you pick. It's who you become most like if you're not careful. Despite her hard work and accomplishments, in some ways she's as much a professional Chilton as her father was.

■ ■ ■

The door I want is at the end of the hall, and the old seeded glass knob is cool through my glove. I walk inside, detecting the scent of perfume. The elegant maroon bottle of Casablanca Lily is on top of the dresser, the exotic floral scent lingering on furniture and fabric.

But Rachael wasn't wearing that perfume or any other when she died. Everything I'm finding is consistent with the story that she wanted to work from home today, and wasn't as invested in her appearance as usual. It would seem she wasn't expecting to see anyone, most of all Bose Flagler. I doubt she intended to deal with the caretaker Holt Willard, either. Not in person.

She placed the box of lightbulbs inside the pantry for him. He knew how to let himself in, and his way around. Perhaps she intended to stay upstairs while he took care of his chore, and at his age he's not as limber as he was. No doubt she didn't plan on offering to help hold the ladder. It probably wouldn't have occurred to her. If it did, she wouldn't bother.

It crosses my mind that she might have been taking care of more than her so-called *mountain of work* while she was here today. Maybe the untenable traffic she expected isn't the real reason she chose not to drive to CIA headquarters. Maybe it's an excuse. I wonder if she and Flagler were getting along. Likely she's not seen much of him while the trial's been going on.

Maybe she's been watching him on TV, and has been missing him terribly. Or possibly they've been at odds. I wonder what she was feeling while supposedly working in her bedroom all day. Her desk is in front of the window. Had Rachael been sitting here when the killer entered the backyard, she could have seen him. And he could have seen her.

The bedroom window is directly above the one he shot her through, and I notice the dead bugs on the white-painted sill beyond the wavy glass. I take in damage to foliage not visible from the ground. The killer may not have known that his target would end up in the kitchen. He may have had no idea she was working from the upstairs guestroom.

He didn't need to know who was inside the house or what the person might be doing as a matter of routine. He didn't need to possess special information. All he had to do was watch for lights, and I'm betting the ones in here were on. But not in the master bedroom downstairs or the great room. Not in the closed-off bedrooms that face the front of the house.

It may have been that the only windows lit up during this afternoon's gathering overcast were the ones in the kitchen and also up here. As I look around, I don't see a single electronic device, including a laptop, a hotspot or a router. If Rachael was overwhelmed with work as she claimed in her text message to the caretaker, it's not apparent what she might have been doing.

I'm not finding printed materials, no notebooks or file folders, not so much as a scrap of paper. Whatever was here has been spirited away, there can be little doubt. The desk drawers have nothing in them except paper clips and several rollerball pens. There's nothing inside the wastepaper basket, and I understand all bets are off when the intelligence community is involved.

The canopied four-poster bed is neatly made, and I open the small chest of drawers on either side. A packet of tissues, a phone charger. On the upholstered rococo armchair is a dry cleaning bag, and inside are one of Rachael's designer suits and several blouses. The painted armoire fills half a wall, and her expensive clothing is neatly hung inside, her shoes lined up on the wide board floor.

In dresser drawers are lingerie, socks, panty hose and other apparel that doesn't need to be hung or ironed. Wrapped in a pair of leggings is a large leather jewelry box that I place on top of the bed for later. I pause in the bathroom doorway, remembering the tile marble floor, the pedestal stone sink. The antique copper bathtub might have saved Rachael's life had she been inside it during the attack.

A walnut vanity has been repurposed as a cabinet. I open drawers filled with cosmetics, over-the-counter remedies and also diet pills, fat burners and laxatives. I find more packets of moist towelettes like the ones in her tote bag, and tubes of hemorrhoid treatments like Preparation H.

"Whatcha got?" Marino is behind me, his face flushed and dripping, not a breath of air moving in here. "Anything good?"

"That's a strange way to put it, considering," I reply.

"Fabian should be out front in five minutes. What do you want to do?"

"He stays with the van," I reply. "You and I will get the body out, and I don't want him inside the house. For every reason that's a bad idea."

I step back inside the bedroom as Marino looks at surroundings once beautifully appointed with fine artwork and tapestries. Linens were high thread count and monogrammed, the room fragrant with arrangements of fresh-cut flowers from the garden.

"When you spent weekends? Did you stay in here?" he asks.

"This was Annie's room back then," I reply. "Now she's in her parents' former bedroom downstairs."

"Where would you stay?" He sets down the scene case, opening it.

"In one of the closed-off rooms down the hall. But it didn't matter where you stayed if you were a guest," I reply. "Everything was elegant, everyone treated as special."

"What are you finding up here? Because knowing you, you're finding something." He holds out a biohazard bag, and I drop used gloves in it.

I show him that the wall switch by the bedroom door is in the up position. This doesn't prove the lights were on in here when the micro-wave attack occurred. But I'm betting they were.

"It might be why the assailant knew to hide in the backyard. He could see the lights on upstairs." I share what I'm thinking.

The lights may have been on in the kitchen too, as gloomy as the day was by midafternoon. Maybe Rachael came downstairs to make a pot of tea.

"It's looking like she had a problem with laxative abuse," I explain. "People get into this sort of thing to lose weight, and it takes more and more for the same effect."

"Sounds like me and bourbon," Marino says.

"High-fiber tablets, sugar-free candies, herbal teas," I explain. "In excess such things can induce diarrhea."

"Dorothy does that sometimes. Now and then I do. I guess every-one does if they're honest about it."

"Sometimes is one thing," I reply. "Chronically is another. And it's not an activity you engage in at the office or other public places. You don't drink a pot of laxative tea if you're planning on playing ten-nis, going out to a bar or having a tryst with your lover."

CHAPTER 19

"Are you thinking this is why she stayed home today?" Marino asks. "To take laxatives?"

"It may not be why," I reply. "But it may have been convenient for her to engage in such behavior, assuming I'm right."

It's similar to people who day drink because they happen to be working from home. Or it's a snow day, a holiday.

"You do it because you're alone in your safe environment. And you find reasons to be there so you can do it," I explain. "Often disorders like this flare up in times of stress. As you and I both know from our years of smoking."

"I'd kill for one right about now," Marino says. "And the minute I'm off the clock I'm pouring a double bourbon. I don't give a shit."

I open another drawer. This one holds a variety of condoms, and several boxes of tampons. Assuming they were intended for Rachael, one can infer that she was sexually active, and capable of having periods. Returning to the bedroom, I put on clean gloves. I open the leather jewelry case I placed on the bed.

"We won't be taking this in with us, obviously," I explain as I look at the dazzling collection. "There's probably close to a million dollars in timepieces alone."

None of them are working. Chronographs with self-winding mechanisms might not have been running anyway when microwaves bombarded the back of the house. But quartz watches should have been keeping time as long as the batteries were good. I suspect some were running before they were rendered inoperable. The cliché of a stopped watch telling the time of death isn't always a joke.

Sometimes it's true, depending on what killed the person. All of Rachael's battery-powered watches quit within a minute or two of each other. The gold Breitling and Rolex, the Audemars Piguet, the Breguet stopped working at around 3:45 this afternoon, during the interval when Lucy and Tron were picking up bursts of microwave energy from around here.

"Rachael was going to have a major problem whether she was in the bedroom or the kitchen," I tell Marino as we head back downstairs. "She was going to be killed or badly injured in either location unless she was ducked down in the copper bathtub maybe."

"How are we supposed to guard against shit like this?" he says. "I don't know how anybody protects themselves anymore."

I don't answer because I don't have a satisfactory one, and what we face isn't a new problem. Clubs and spears were replaced by crossbows and firearms, and on it goes. There will always be the next thing weaponized, more efficient ways to cause inhumanity and destruction. It's coded into our DNA to discover them, and the way the planet is programmed.

If you ask Benton he'll tell you that fearing for our lives is motivating. People get more done when pitted against opposing forces. Wars can bring us together, and pain creates poetry. It would have been better if diligence, exquisite engineering and empathy were what inspired. But I didn't write the algorithm.

Marino and I step outside to the loud rumbling of our black windowless medical examiner's van, its headlights illuminating the overgrown boxwoods. Auxiliary lighting blazes as police and plainclothes agents move around the driveway in a chiaroscuro of blinding bright and inky dark.

Three helicopters hover high overhead, shining like planets, and I suspect they belong to TV news stations. Marino opens the van's tailgate as Fabian's window rolls down, his face angry and enthralled. His passenger up front is a uniformed Secret Service agent in tactical gear, and she's not smiling or here for a good time.

"Evening, ma'am," she says to me, keeping her eyes on our surroundings.

"Thanks for getting our van up here." I almost call her a lifesaver, deciding it's not a good choice of words when someone is dead inside the house.

Fabian's Secret Service escort has her seat belt off, her window cracked, her MP5 in her lap. She's ensuring that no explosive device somehow got attached to our vehicle between the first checkpoint and the house. She's making sure of a lot of things.

"I realize this isn't pro forma," I say to Fabian. "We don't get to do things in the usual way, and I appreciate your cooperation."

"You don't want me to help load her up?" He stares off toward the front door, and for him this is a crushing blow. "I can take care of everything, and you can go home if you want."

"You need to stay outside. We have to do things in a very decided way," I explain as the Secret Service agent listens while keeping up her scan of the driveway.

"I get it." Fabian sweeps his long hair out of his face, and I catch a glimpse of smoky eye shadow and black nail polish. "I just feel torn." He never hesitates offering how he's impacted personally. "Maggie tells me one thing. Then you tell me another. I don't feel anybody trusts me anymore, and it makes me really uncomfortable."

"We'll talk about this another time...," I start to say, but he's not finished.

"Don't blame me for what Maggie does. Imagine the position she puts me in." Fabian flicks his hair again the way he does when there's an audience.

"We're not getting into this now but I'm happy to talk about it later," I inform him, but he's not listening.

"This job is really stressful. Especially when nobody tells me what to expect, especially now, for example. What happens after we get to our office with the body, and all the cops leave?" He says this to me while glancing at the agent next to him. "What if the violent mob shows up while I walk alone to my car, which by the way attracts a lot of attention?"

"You should spend the night in the on-call room." Marino is behind our black van, talking to us through the open tailgate as he slides out the stretcher. "That's the smart thing to do." Aluminum clinks and clacks as he opens the legs.

"I'm worried about someone vandalizing my car, the more I think of it," Fabian replies. "It's inevitable. Oh God, I hope it hasn't happened already."

"Move your damn El Camino into the bay, and crash in the on-call room," Marino says as if it's decided. "The TV works fine. And I know there's food in the fridge because I made myself a sandwich earlier today."

"Well, I guess I could." Fabian watches him in the rearview mirror.

"Get some shut-eye, and the rest of us will see you first thing in the morning. Once you're inside the building, nobody's going to bother you." Marino closes the back of the van with a heavy clang.

"As long as you and yours get us there safely." Fabian says this to his Secret Service escort, flirting with her openly while she doesn't seem to notice.

"I'll be sitting right here during the drive to the morgue," she says without looking in anyone's direction. "And we'll be in a convoy, making sure nobody tries anything funny."

"What do you mean, *a convoy*?" Fabian brightens up as if someone flipped a switch. "You mean a lot of cop cars with lights and sirens?"

"Probably not sirens."

"Oh my God. It will be like a parade." Fabian can't help himself. "My lucky night. I know I shouldn't say it ..."

"Yeah, you probably shouldn't." The agent keeps up her scan of the driveway.

■　■　■

The stretcher bumps and stutters as Marino wheels it to the front of the house. I open the splintered double doors to let him through, and it's a terrible sight when a mortuary cot is pushed through the living room of someone you know.

"Right about now I could rip Fabian a new one." Marino grumbles and complains, struggling to pilot and navigate his unwieldy trolley.

Swivel wheels can be problematic when one of them sticks, and that happens more often than not. It's like trying to steer a damaged grocery cart. Marino is forcing and cussing, starting and stopping, hot and bothered in Tyvek, a face mask, his safety glasses continuing to fog up.

He's careful not to bang into old walls and doorframes as he fumes about Fabian, who's rather useless when it comes to the devil in the details. He's not going to check on the wheels or brakes of a stretcher before loading it into one of our vehicles. He forgets to replace batteries in IR thermometer guns, flashlights or magnifiers. Usually, there's something.

Inside the kitchen, Marino and I spread sheets on the floor. We're gentle as we wrap the body in layers that we tape together. Zipping up the heavy black vinyl pouch, we lift it to the stretcher's thin pad, and I buckle the two restraint straps. Flipping up the handrails, I release the brakes, and we fishtail back through the house.

Out the front door we roll our grim cargo around to the van's tailgate as Fabian opens it. He's put on gloves, a mask, his designer safety goggles black-framed with rose-tinted lenses. His long straight hair is pulled back, reminding me of Rachael. Except his scrunchie has a goth spiderweb pattern.

"Good job with the stretcher," Marino says to him sharply. "Maybe next time make sure everything's working worth a damn."

"I keep telling you we need new ones that aren't hospital hand-me-downs, state surplus, Goodwill or wherever they come from." Fabian stares up at the helicopters, the thudding of their blades barely audible over the rumble of generators. "You think they're filming us right now? I've got to tell Mom. If it's national news she can pick it up in Baton Rouge."

We lift the stretcher and collapse the legs, sliding in the body. Then the van is disappearing down the dark driveway, its headlights slashing through dense trees and undergrowth sparking with fireflies. I'm removing my PPE under the tent when Lucy appears by my side. I retrieve my suit jacket, my briefcase from where I left them earlier, and we start walking back along the driveway to Marino's truck.

He carries the scene cases, and it's as if someone turned on nature again. The ultrasonic repellent devices were removed as it got dark,

Lucy tells us, lighting our way. The Secret Service is done flying drones for now, and are wrapping up. They'll be clearing out soon, leaving others to do as they see fit, and mainly she's talking about the FBI.

We follow the bright beam of her tactical light, the woods alive around us. Owls hoot and whistle balefully as cicadas saw monotonously. Frogs bark while fireflies flicker like quasars. Katydids rasp and sizzle in varying waves and rhythms, and their electrical-like sounds make the hair stand up on my arms.

"I'll be heading home soon." Lucy shines her flashlight on pavers, and a small green frog hops out of the glare. "Then I'll be on the computer. When are you doing the autopsy? Not tonight, I hope."

"No need for that," I reply.

"I wouldn't go to your office now. No way." As if she's the adult. "Not with all these bad people dressed up in rage and ready for trouble. And you need some rest."

"We've done everything we can for now, collected the evidence that can't wait," I reply. "So yes, I'm going home."

"We've got officers patrolling the property." Lucy shines her light on puddles we dodge. "You'll be okay there, and you need something to eat, and decent sleep. Tomorrow's going to be a long day."

"I'll start her first thing in the morning. I'm assuming we shouldn't expect any interference?" I reply, and Lucy knows who I'm talking about.

"Not from the usual sources," she says, and I check my phone.

There's no word from Maggie. Nothing from Elvin, either. But Doug Schlaefer has texted that he's at my disposal should I need him. I answer back that I'll see him in the morning. While I'm sending it, a message from Benton lands.

Almost home, he writes. *Annie's spending the night.*

Excellent, I write back as I pick my way along her driveway.

Around another bend, and the entrance to Chilton Farms is illuminated like a parking lot. The crime scene tape is down, and one of the Secret Service transporter vans has been moved so that Fabian could get in and out. The street is crowded with police vehicles, including additional armored BearCats that might be FBI. I'm seeing at least a dozen Alexandria cops in riot gear.

"Where are these protesters now?" Marino asks as we head to his truck. "Are we going to be okay trying to get out of here?"

"You'll be fine, and you won't be alone during the tricky part," Lucy says. "Most of the assholes turned around and disbanded. The half dozen or so vehicles left are on the shoulder of the Parkway, and we've got a lot of police out there."

She says that Blaise Fruge and other Alexandria officers will escort Marino's truck, and he unlocks the back of it. He shoves in the scene cases.

"Be careful." I look at Lucy, resisting the impulse to hug her.

"A late supper?" she suggests with a shadow of a smile.

"I know just what to make," I reply.

Moments later, Marino and I are driving along the access road through the dark countryside. I'm thinking about the sausage patties I'll cook in the air fryer, and the cheese omelets I'll throw together. With or without Bloody Marys. I should have spicy V8 juice, and plenty of limes. I tell Marino that he and Dorothy are welcome to join us.

"As long as you don't mind camping out in the smaller guestroom upstairs," I apologize. "Annie will be in the other one."

"I'm thinking the same thing. Maybe send Dorothy a note and let her know the plan," he replies, emergency lights flashing on his face as he drives. "With what's going on, it's best if all of us are together."

Fruge leads the way in her Ford Interceptor. Behind us are three cruisers with light bars rolling. The first checkpoint is now a sea of strobing red and blue. There must be at least twenty police cars pulled over on the shoulder of the Parkway. Additional barricades have been set up, and news crews are here with satellite trucks, the noise of helicopters relentless.

Police direct traffic through the intersection, stopping each vehicle, checking identifications. K-9 handlers and their dogs are standing by as officers in tactical hard-shell gear stare down angry-looking men gathered around vans and trucks. Some of their female passengers are waving Confederate flags out the windows, and holding JUSTICE FOR APRIL signs.

Dana Diletti is filming outside her van, interviewing a young tattooed woman who looks familiar. Whatever the celebrity news correspondent is saying, the woman is nodding and answering vigorously while angrily pointing her finger at the police. She might have been one of the family friends who left during the Hooke trial when Nadine Tupelo did.

I don't see her but don't want to be obvious about scanning the crowd. I'm certain a number of the protesters were inside the courtroom today. They're dressed in camouflage and tactical clothing now, and have pistols on their hips or assault rifles slung across their chests, glaring as we drive past. I catch a glimpse of a neck tattooed with the U.S. flag.

It belongs to the man who kicked me. His eyes are wild, his sundamaged face flashing viciously in our headlights. He's pumping his fist, flaunting an AR-15 assault rifle because he can. In Virginia, like most states, it's legal to carry firearms openly, including high-capacity semiautomatics.

"Don't look at anyone," Marino says as we drive with our police escort, their emergency lights going full tilt. "Maybe they won't notice us."

"Oh, they notice us all right." I feel hateful stares like insect bites.

CHAPTER 20

The angry crowd is behind us. Then we can't see it anymore as we follow the Parkway, headed away from Raven Landing and Chilton Farms.

We haven't gotten far when our police escort's emergency lights suddenly go dark ahead and behind us. Fruge must assume we're safe from this point on, and the four cars turn off at the next intersection. I check various news sites to see what we've missed in the past few hours.

I'm not surprised that the mob scene we just witnessed is head-lining, trending, going viral. Nothing like murder and anarchy to grab the world's attention, and Rachael Stanwyck's life is described as full of twisted plots, espionage and other intrigue. Possibly her suspicious death is related to her work with the CIA, and the Russians are behind it.

Maybe she's a paid hit because of her estranged husband and the dangerous secrets she would know about him. Or she's a hate crime that's really directed at her prominent judge sister, and possibly related to the Gilbert Hooke trial. It's all over the news that the Secret Service is at the helm of the investigation, and the FBI has stepped in because of terrorist threats.

Federal officials are linking Rachael's "suspected murder" to the attempt on the president earlier today, and I could have predicted that Bose Flagler would rise to the occasion.

"He never misses an opportunity to turn a situation to his advantage," I continue informing Marino as we follow the dark road we were on earlier, headed home. "Let's see what he has to say."

I begin playing the commonwealth's attorney's televised soundbite. It's been distributed to major news outlets and posted on his social media, his statement long and self-serving. I fast-forward to the relevant part.

"...I've spoken to Judge Chilton, and of course she's shocked and heartbroken," he's saying into the camera. "But we're in agreement that what must come first is honoring our commitment to the public. Our top priority has to be the citizens of Virginia who have entrusted us to bring about justice for all..."

He's seated at his desk in his office before a backdrop of legal tomes and his degrees and commendations. Surrounded by flags on tall poles topped by rampant brass eagles, he looks like the leader of the free world, and that's his intention. Since he confronted me in court, he's found time to change into a black suit with narrow blue pinstripes.

He wears an American flag pin in the lapel. His white shirt has French cuffs, his red tie perfectly knotted. He informs us that the Gilbert Hooke trial will resume tomorrow morning as planned. We're shown an exchange of e-mails in which Annie states unequivocally that she has no intention of recusing herself.

She's bound to perform her judicial duties as long as she's able, and promises to be on the bench in the morning when he and Sal Gallo make their closing arguments. But mostly what Flagler's doing is showing his command of the situation, and implying that he and Annie are allies.

"So, as you can see, the rumors about the judge and I recusing ourselves are fake news." Flagler's eyes flare with righteous indignation, and I pause on the image.

I zoom in on his handsome face to see what else I notice, looking for the slightest suggestion of grief. A shade of sadness. A flicker of fear. But the dashing commonwealth's attorney lives up to his nickname and campaign motto: *Unflagging Flagler, he'll never let you down.*

He's steady and solid. I see no indication that he's destroyed by Rachael's death. Or even cares as he stares into the camera.

"Tomorrow I expect the jury to begin deliberations in short order, everything carrying forward." His unrelenting focus is the trial he intends to win. "And these protests going on right now? Well, that's just not acceptable, folks..."

He dramatically gets up from his desk, walking around to the front of it, giving us a much better view of him in all his glory. He unbuttons his suit jacket.

"We're not going to tolerate any violent behavior here in Alexandria or anywhere else, not on my watch," he says. "I've spoken to Governor Dare, and if need be she'll call out the National Guard. We're fully prepared to lock people up and throw away the key...," he says, and I close the file on my phone.

"Not so much as an allusion to him knowing Rachael," I tell Marino. "Assuming it's true."

"I got the impression that Lucy and Tron think it is."

"Then Flagler's an even better actor than I thought," I reply. "Or just colder and more selfish."

"He's figuring out how to spin her death. That's why he's not saying anything yet."

"You're probably right," I reply. "He'll figure out a way to turn it to his advantage somehow. That's his special sauce."

"It will be just our luck that he ends up in the White House someday." Marino begins slowing down at the red light ahead.

Just beyond is the billboard for Raven Landing that we passed on our way to Chilton Farms. It cuts blackly against the night like a small skyscraper, and I think about what Lucy said. She talked about trees, buildings and other tall objects blocking high-energy radio frequency transmissions such as microwaves.

■ ■ ■

It was around this area that she and Tron detected the 2.305 GHz signal, and then lost it for more than an hour. The billboard is plenty big enough to have caused a problem. I can see why Lucy might assume that's what happened. But I don't think so.

"I'm not liking this." I look out at the dark void where Belle Haven Market is tucked in trees across the street, not a light on anywhere.

"Shit, me either." Marino swings into the parking lot, and Wally Potter's vintage blue Chevy wagon is where we saw it last. "Dammit! This isn't good."

Already Marino is second-guessing himself, wondering what the hell he missed when we were here the first time. I'm thinking the same thing. We creep to a stop at the self-service concrete island, and my pulse has picked up, adrenaline kicking in again. Marino collects his pistol from the console.

He climbs out, the headlights glaring on the glass windows in front of the store. Removing the gas pump's nozzle, he works the lever up and down. Nothing happens. Turning around, he looks at me, shaking his head. The power is out on the entire property, and it's too much like what we just came from at Chilton Farms. Marino has his pistol ready by his side.

He shines his flashlight around the empty parking lot, its outbuildings and the surrounding woods. He's looking and listening, getting increasingly tense. Climbing back into the truck, he places a call, and this time Fruge answers.

"We're at Belle Haven Market, and need to make a wellness check," he says over speakerphone, a dog whistle of urgency in his tone. "The lights are out here. The gas pump isn't working..."

"Turning around as we speak."

"Everything's in a blackout, but the owner's car is still here," Marino says in a voice that bodes serious trouble. "Wally Potter. That old Chevy wagon he drives..."

"Ten-four. On our way." Fruge ends the call as we hear sirens in the distance.

They get louder as we sit tight, our headlights glaring on the gas pump and the dark empty store behind it. Marino has his gun in hand, and his eyes don't stop moving.

"When we were here earlier," I say to him, "were the lights off inside the store?"

"It was my impression they were," he says, and neither of us wants to believe the unthinkable. "That was one of the reasons I assumed Wally was gone for the day. I figured maybe he got a ride, and that's why his car was still here. We didn't have a reason to think he or any-one was inside the store. But I wasn't sure at first."

I envision what it was like when we pulled up earlier tonight. It was around 6:15 when Marino tried the door, hoping the store was still open or that Wally would let us in. The overcast had lifted. There was plenty of daylight. It wouldn't have been obvious if lights were on inside the store.

"I figured the same thing, that he was gone for the day," I reply as we sit inside Marino's truck, the sirens getting close.

"When I walked past the ice machine on the porch I thought it was unusually quiet." He continues doubting himself. "I have a feeling it wasn't working, and I'm realizing now that the motor wasn't running. The whole place was quiet the more I'm thinking about it. I should have been paying closer attention, dammit...!"

Then four Alexandria police cars are flashing and wailing into the parking lot. Cutting their lights and sirens, they pull up next to us. Fruge and three uniformed officers climb out, doors shutting at once. Everyone is armed with tactical flashlights, their guns drawn. I'm the exception, and I tuck my phone in a pocket. I leave my briefcase inside the truck.

"The doc and I stopped by on our way to Chilton Farms, as you know, because I left you a message about it." Marino directs his comments to Fruge.

He says we intended to "borrow" the bathroom if the store was open or someone was there to let us in. No one answered when he yelled, banging on the locked door and also the siding near the office window. When I tried the store's landline several times, I got a busy signal. I don't have Wally's mobile number. Not his daughter Clemmy's either, I explain.

"I know them pretty well." Fruge is scrolling through her phone. "I used to stop in here all the time before I got promoted." She places the call. "But I don't get out this way as much as I used to, and now I'm sorry I haven't." The phone she's calling begins to ring. "I used to make a point of keeping an eye on this place..."

"Hold on...! Hello...?" The woman answering over speaker-phone is laughing.

I hear music and loud talking in the background. It sounds like she's in a bar or a restaurant, and having a rollicking good time.

"Is this Clemmy Potter?" Fruge asks with gravity.

"Yessssss...?" The mirth in her Southern drawl fades with uncertainty. "Who wants to know...?"

"Investigator Blaise Fruge here with the Alexandria police." She's all business.

"Oh! Gee. Uhhhh, how are you? Is everything okay?" Clemmy sounds a little uneasy, and she's had a few. "Did the alarm go off at the store? Oh no. Not again. Dad's at home. Did you try him? Because you know, if he's watching TV he can't always hear the phone..."

"Clemmy?" Fruge asks as we listen in the blacked-out market's parking lot. "Where are you? Are you here in Alexandria?"

"In Newport News visiting my sister and her husband. We're out to dinner. I'm spending the holiday weekend with them. It's my birthday...," she adds inanely, and Fruge doesn't wish her a happy one, thank the good Lord.

"We're standing in front of your store," Fruge says, "and your dad's station wagon is still here in the carport. I'm wondering if maybe he got a ride home...?"

"What...? Oh God!"

"Clemmy? I need you to call Wally right now while I have you on the line," Fruge says.

"How can I when I'm on the phone with you?" She's starting to come unglued.

"Clemmy? Have your sister call Wally on her phone while you stay on the line with me," Fruge says calmly, kindly, but she's in charge. "Don't hang up. I need you on the line with me while we figure this out."

"Okay." Her voice is shaking. "Hold on..."

Marino, Fruge, the three officers continue to have their guns drawn, pointed down by their sides, their index fingers ready above the trigger guards. They're shining their lights on flowering trees and shrubs, searching around us as Wally Potter's mobile phone rings and rings in the background.

"He's not answering!" Clemmy is in a panic.

I can hear her upset sister exclaiming that they have to go. Chairs scrape, and the husband yells at someone for the check.

"Something must have happened!" Clemmy is crying. "Oh God! Oh God! Dad's car wouldn't still be there. I should have checked on him! Made sure he got home! I knew I shouldn't have left him alone this weekend...!"

"Try to stay calm," Fruge says. "I'll get back to you when I know more." She ends the call. "Come on," she announces to everyone, and for now she's the investigator.

She's leading the charge. But if what I suspect is true, she won't be for long. Should we find what I expect once we look inside the market, Fruge's next call will be to the Secret Service. It will be to Lucy.

"I'd tell you to wait in the truck," Marino says to me as we start walking across the parking lot. "But you won't, and I wouldn't let you if you wanted to. It's not safe with all these angry assholes on the loose and looking for trouble."

"No way I'm sitting out here by myself." He won't get an argument from me.

I pause by the carport without getting close to the Malibu Classic inside it. A gift from Wally's parents when he graduated from high school in 1965. He's kept it in mint condition. He had the carport built because of it, never failing to tell me the story whenever I'd comment on his prize vintage wagon.

"It doesn't look like anybody was around here messing with his car or anything else," Marino says. "No sign anybody's touched it."

He illuminates the elongated low-slung rear with its big round taillights. The powerful beam of light whites out the blue paint, flaring on chrome and glass. He searches the pavement, and it's littered with plant debris from the storm. Finding the rusting metal trash barrel nearby, he shines his light inside it. He checks each one we pass.

The night is alive with the music of nocturnal creatures tuning up like an orchestra. The sawing of cicadas, the twitter and trilling of nightingales are amplified, fireflies glowing and fading like an electrical short. Somewhere along the river, coyotes begin to howl and bay as we walk around the corner of the old wood-frame market. In back is additional parking, and picnic tables surrounded by jacaranda trees that shed purple flowers everywhere.

The walk-in cooler has a padlock on the handle, another indication that Wally had closed for the day. Next to the wooden ramp used for deliveries is a pedestrian door, and it's also locked. On either side of it flies crawl on the window screens as Marino and the police check with their flashlights. They see no sign of anyone inside alive or otherwise.

"Well, he's got to be here," Fruge says. "Where else would he be unless he's been kidnapped?"

"Flies are never good," Marino says. "Out of the way!" He back-kicks the door open, and no one stops him from going in first.

CHAPTER 21

Fruge is right behind him, and they hold tactical lights high, their weapons ready. I can hear them talking and moving as they disappear inside, checking the back of the building. I wait by the open door with the three uniformed officers. I can tell by Marino's sudden swearing that the news isn't good.

"We found him!" he calls out to us. "We're going to keep checking around! Don't come in here!"

He doesn't want anybody accidentally shot, and I wait with the three officers some distance away from the open door. We can see flashes of light in windows as Marino and Fruge move around, checking every area. After minutes pass and there's no further sight or sound of them, I get increasingly uneasy.

Then two figures with flashlights appear from around the corner of the market, heading toward us. Marino and Fruge exited through the front door, leaving it unlocked, we're told, as they reach us.

"So, crime scene and whoever else can get in without accessing from back here," Marino says, and his face is stone.

Fruge is upset, I can tell by her stiff demeanor, her thousand-yard stare and staccato attention. She's trying too hard to seem cool and confident. I can almost see her thoughts racing. She's stopped by Belle Haven Market countless times for takeout food, necessities and treats. All of us have, the place familiar and warm like a favorite old sweater.

"He's bound with duct tape and in a chair." Marino's voice is flinty he's so angry. "It's like he was being interrogated before his throat was cut from ear to ear. Probably to get the combination to the fucking safe that's open in the office. It looks like a fucking mob hit. We didn't get close because there's no question he's dead, and has been for a while. Nobody goes in there until we gear up."

As he's saying this, Fruge is on her phone, requesting the crime scene unit. She informs whoever she's talking to that we need more backups. She needs them *now*, she says aggressively, and SWAT should respond because of the armed protesters in the area. She's overplaying her authority because she's scared.

"Lucy and Tron need to know what's going on." Marino tells Fruge what she doesn't want to hear.

He's typing on his phone, his flashlight tucked under an arm and shining aimlessly on the back of the paint-peeled store.

"Probably you want to do it." The way he says it isn't a suggestion.

He looks at her, giving her a pause to fill, waiting for her to do the right thing.

"I'm not seeing what the Secret Service has to do with this," she finally says, hoping he won't make the call, maybe not yet.

Fruge knows what Marino is about to say. She doesn't want to be preempted by the Secret Service, the FBI or anyone else yet again this day. It's not lost on her that the two crime scenes likely are related. If the feds were involved with one, chances are good they'll be showing up for the other.

"It has to do with them whether we like it or not." Marino reminds her that she doesn't get to choose her cases.

"You telling me that what happened to Wally is a matter of national security?" She probes the dark with her light, moving it around angrily.

Her first time starring in the investigative rodeo, and she's about to be thrown off her horse twice. It's disappointing and humiliating.

"You need to talk to Lucy, tell her what's going on," Marino says.

"What are the feds pinging on? Their cell phones?" It's one of the uniformed officers who asks.

"I'm sure they're pinging on all sorts of things," Marino answers.

He's not going to mention the microwave signals detected near Ivy Hill Cemetery, Chilton Farms and Belle Haven Market. That's the missing piece Fruge and the police don't have. But like Rachael Stanwyck's alleged affair with Bose Flagler, the information isn't for us to share. It's up to the Secret Service.

"Assuming there may be a link between the cases, we have to be more careful than ever of cross-contamination," I remind Marino and Fruge. "We'll take extra precautions."

"Everything needs to be brand-new and disposable if possible," Marino replies.

"I also don't want us using the same field cases we just had with us inside the house at Chilton Farms," I add. "Nothing from there can be used here."

"I've got forensic stuff that hasn't left my trunk," Fruge volunteers. "I haven't had the chance to use it yet. But it's all set up and ready to go."

"It ought to be, since I'm the one who packed it for you," Marino says to her. "Between your gear and what I've got, we should be okay. Come on, let's move our trucks back here."

They return to the front parking lot of the store while I walk away for some privacy. This is beyond what I intend to manage on my own, and I call Doug Schlaefer.

"How's it going?" he answers. "Is everything okay? I've been following the news, holy moly. I hope you weren't anywhere near all those thugs with assault rifles..."

"There's a new development, and I need you to head out to a scene near Chilton Farms." I get straight to it.

"That doesn't sound good."

"It's very bad, and likely related to Rachael Stanwyck's murder. I know you're familiar with Belle Haven Market."

I've seen Doug eating their takeout at the office. He talks about how much his wife loves the produce and soups.

"Oh no." His voice in my earpiece as I pace in the market's dark back parking lot. "Don't tell me something's happened there."

I inform my deputy chief of what we have so far while an owl clucks and whistles a warning somewhere in the woods. Fireflies spark as if giving me their alarmed impressions.

"We're going to have to tag-team," I'm telling Doug over the phone.

As we discuss the best approach, I have my flashlight pointed down, and it shines on a clump of white tuberoses where a luna moth has landed. The moth slowly fans its long-tailed pale green wings, the brown eyespots staring. I think of the small cardboard boxes headed to the Smithsonian, and anger smolders.

"I'm just not getting the connection between the cases," Doug says in my earpiece. "Why do you think there's one? Rachael Stanwyck's throat wasn't cut, was it?"

"As far as we can tell the killer had no physical contact with her," I reply.

"It seems like a different sort of crime..."

"In both cases some sort of radio frequency weapon was used to ruin the cameras," I reply. "And that's why the power is out."

I explain the link between Rachael Stanwyck and Wally Potter, and that Doug mustn't mention this to anyone. But my deputy chief has to have some idea what we're dealing with. He can't help me if he doesn't know, and I'm going to have to trust him.

"The same weapon likely is what caused Rachael's death. This is why the FBI and the Secret Service are involved," I continue to explain. "We need to be extremely mindful of confidentiality, not saying a word about the details. Including to our own people."

"Are we safe working the scene?" Doug's young wife is pregnant with their first child, and it doesn't take much to make him skittish.

"There are ways of monitoring such things." I'm not going into any more detail than that. "I think it best to do as little to the body as possible here."

"You won't get an argument from me. Why would someone hurt Wally Potter? He couldn't have been nicer, if you ask my wife. What did he ever do to anyone...?"

"Trace evidence is going to be crucial because the killer was inside the store." I don't have time for Doug's emotions. "The person had contact with the victim, with Wally."

"I'd bag everything." He's happy to agree.

"Head, hands, feet, the entire body before pouching it," I reply. "Then we can take our time looking with the appropriate forensic equipment and lighting."

I don't want the two bodies inside the same cooler, room or vehicle at any given time. We'll keep the two cases completely isolated and separated, I explain. In the morning, Doug will take care of Wally Potter's autopsy, and I'll deal with Rachael Stanwyck. We won't share morgue assistants or equipment. We won't be on the same ventilation systems.

■   ■   ■

"Maybe you can deal with Fabian," I say in conclusion. "He needs to decon himself before heading out again. I don't want him driving the same van he's using to transport Rachael Stanwyck's body. He should be back at the office by now."

"For sure we don't want to be transferring DNA from one case to the other," Doug says, and I can hear him walking outside to his car. "Good God, talk about a shit show."

I watch Fruge and Marino drive around back. They park so their headlights shine on the market.

"We've had enough shit shows lately," I reply, and Doug knows what I'm saying.

"All is quiet on the Western Front. Crickets from Maggie and Elvin."

"As it should be, and maybe if we're lucky it will stay that way," I say to him. And how quickly people change alliances. Or at least they decide it's best to be your defender because the bully has left the building. For now, anyway. For tonight at least. Doors thud shut, and Marino and Fruge are walking away from their trucks.

"While we're waiting for you to get here, I'll go ahead and get started," I inform Doug. "I'll take care of the usual preliminaries, and everything we do will be well documented."

"I'm in my car." His voice in my earpiece, the sound of the engine starting. "Barring anything unusual, I should be there in a half hour. And I'll deal with Fabian."

I get off the phone as Marino and Fruge set down a scene case and a big box of PPE. We start suiting up in the uneven illumination of headlights, the truck engines rumbling. I notice that my borrowed sneakers are filthy with mud and bits of foliage. I rinse the tread with a bottle of water before pulling on shoe covers.

"I'll leave you to do your thing," Fruge says to Marino and me. "I'm going to check the front of the store, especially the cash register and area around it. Let's see what all the asshole did while he was in here."

"Keep an eye out for paper receipts that might tell us when the last purchases were made." Marino can't resist coaching her. "And when are the Secret Service crime scene guys getting here?"

"They're on the way." Fruge has talked to Lucy. "They'll be setting up lighting, a tent and everything."

"They need to search the parking lot front and back." Marino hands me a stack of white paper sticky mats, a flashlight. "The killer likely was getting in and out of a vehicle. I don't see how else he could be moving around otherwise. I doubt he's taking Uber."

I follow him inside the market, our flashlights showing the way, and directly ahead is a small cluttered office where I've never been. Just inside the doorway is a table with a hammered metal ashtray that looks like something a child would make. Inside it are keys on a Civil War Minié ball keychain that I've seen before.

When I first met Wally it was with Annie during our law school years. He had the same keychain and vintage car then. Last time I stopped by the market was maybe a month ago, and he gave me fresh basil and oregano, insisting it was on the house. I do my best to shake the image of his sparkling eyes, his friendly face and wispy white hair.

From the office doorway, I shine my light at the green metal desk, and the chair is missing. I take in piles of what look like invoices and receipts, the obsolete princess-style phone, the old-fashioned Rolodex. The intercom station on a shelf is for communicating with customers at the gas pump while watching them through the window.

The security camera video display is like others inside the store. When working they show cars driving in and out of the parking lot, and customers entering and leaving. I wonder if Wally might have been sitting in here doing paperwork when the killer took out the power.

"That's assuming the rogue signal Lucy and Tron picked up and then lost came from here," I explain to Marino. "I'm going to venture a guess and say that the burst of energy they detected at ten minutes past three P.M. was the killer firing his microwave gun at the store. And there would have been a fair amount of protection for anyone inside."

I shine my light on the window directly left of the desk, and the Venetian blinds are partially open. From here I can see that they're made of metal.

"You tried to look through this same window when we stopped here earlier," I remind Marino, "and I got the impression it has a screen on the outside."

"That's right," he says.

"Opened or closed, the aluminum blinds would have offered shielding, as would the metal window screen," I explain. "The steel filing cabinets on either side of the window would have blocked the radiation. As would the large floor safe that's wide open."

The thick door has a combination dial on it, and our lights probe empty galvanized metal and carpeted shelves. The safe has been cleaned out, and it's unlikely everything in it would have had value to the killer. I get the sense of someone in a hurry, grabbing what he could to sort through later like looters during smash-and-grabs.

Beyond the office is the *employees only* bathroom, and I pause in the doorway. I paint my light over the white porcelain toilet, the sink, the linoleum tile that probably goes back to the 1970s. On a shelf are over-the-counter medications. There's a dispenser of hand sanitizer, a bar of soap and a bottle of Old Spice cologne.

"He's in the next room," Marino says, and I can hear the ominous droning as we reach it.

The missing desk chair is in the middle of the floor, Wally's body slumped back in it. His severed neck is bloody and gaping, flies buzzing and alighting. Gray duct tape is wrapped around his wrists, ankles, and covers his mouth. I smell musty cardboard, rotting produce and the sweetly putrid stench of coagulating blood that's decomposing.

It's pooled around the chair and gleams like blackish-red glass in my light. Marino and I wait in the doorway until we're certain what our Tyvek-covered feet will be treading on. The killer was inside this building. He was inside these very rooms not so long ago. Marino squats down, shining his light obliquely over the scuffed heart pine flooring.

He looks for footwear impressions, for anything that might have been dropped or tracked inside. The storage room is about the size of a two-car garage. The closed door opposite the one we came through leads into the front area of the market where Fruge is searching. I can hear her talking to someone. But I can't make out who it is or what's being said.

"It's pretty clean in here, no dust or dirt on the floor to speak of, and we're not going to see footprints easily," Marino tells me. "The unvarnished old wood flooring isn't going to show them all that well, either. But I'm wondering what that is."

He angles his light, and it catches something glittery behind the chair. We start covering the floor with sticky mats before venturing in any farther, laying them in front of us as we work our way across the room. Reaching the body, I find a dust bunny hiding behind a back leg of the chair, and I approach slowly, cautiously.

"I need a paper envelope and a pad of Post-its." I ask for the usual items. "And an illuminated magnifier."

Marino brings me what I need, and I kneel on paper mats that capture whatever is tracked in and out. I'm barely breathing, moving as little as possible because dust bunnies are easily scared off. They're a skittish cosmos of spiderwebs and debris held together by static electricity, this one about the size of a tennis ball.

It crouches behind the chair leg, peeking out, glittery like a distant galaxy in the glare of my flashlight as my gloved hand gets closer. Then the airy nebula tries to make a weightless getaway, rolling and shimmering like a frightened spirit.

CHAPTER 22

I capture the dust bunny gently with the adhesive strip on the back of several Post-its. Tucking them inside the envelope, I put on the illuminated magnifiers to take a sneak peek. Bug pieces and parts. Bits of black thread, snarls of fibers and tangles of hair.

"Also, shards of something shiny that's irregularly shaped and multicolored." I continue describing what I'm seeing under low magnification. "Dozens of tiny pieces, very reflective. Sort of like Christmas glitter but not exactly. Green, black, silver, copper, brown, gold."

"Metal shavings maybe?" Marino asks as he holds his light on what I'm doing. "Paint?"

"I can't tell but don't think so." I seal the back of the envelope with red evidence tape that I label.

"Maybe it's glitter from the holidays or a birthday or something when they had decorations up in the store."

"I don't know what it is but we'll find out," I reply.

Retracing my steps across the mats, I place the envelope inside the field case Fruge let us borrow. The killer likely carried the office desk chair in here. The dust bunny could contain the microcosm of another world. We may discover a collection of debris from the killer's residence, workplace, his vehicle.

Dust bunnies are electrostatically elusive but they're also clingy. Possibly, this one hitched a ride on whatever the killer carried with him into the store. I envision a tote bag, a murder kit. I think of the duct tape, and that would be my vote. The edges of the roll would be sticky, and the body was bound with tape while in the chair the dust bunny lurked behind.

It's right about where the killer would have been standing while cutting Wally's throat. As Marino gathers thermometers and other equipment, I shine my light around some more. There are several things wrong that couldn't be more apparent. I keep wishing Benton was here. I can imagine some of what he'd say, starting with the way the body is displayed.

The killer deliberately has created an impression that's false, the amount of visible blood not enough to account for Wally's death. The front of his blue-checked shirt is thick with dry and coagulating drips. There are but a few speckles on his khaki-covered thighs and his bound hands in his lap.

On the floor are puddles with the consistency of pudding, and I estimate that maybe a unit of blood was spilled at most. That's it, and not possible. When carotid arteries are cut they can continue spurting for up to half a minute. I've seen spatter on walls and furniture as far as twelve feet from the victim.

A gallon of blood might be hemorrhaged, the arterial pattern following the rhythm of the heart and unmistakable when present. I'm not seeing anything like that. Not even close.

"I don't believe his cause of death is going to be his cut throat or exsanguination. He didn't bleed enough." I can tell Marino this much already. "It doesn't appear that he resisted when he was bound or that he was violently forced to sit in a chair. No scratches or bruises, no signs of a struggle so far."

I shine my light on the blood-streaked tape around the wrists, wrapped twice and not tight enough to dig into the skin.

"Usually when someone is about to die, they panic. You and I have seen it more times than we care to remember." I continue explaining what I'm thinking. "The tape is twisted, often cutting into the wrists, the ankles as the person resists like mad. The same thing if the mouth is taped, especially if the victim is having trouble breathing."

"And if someone comes up behind you with a knife? Now you're really going to freak out." Marino directs his light on everything I'm doing. "You're not going to just sit there with your head thrown back. Even if you've got duct tape around your hands and feet you'll still try to get away or fight like hell."

"As long as you're alive and conscious," I reply.

The transected carotids and other blood vessels bring to mind severed hoses, and the strap muscles and airway are cleanly sliced through. I check the neck front and back, looking from every angle as best I can without moving the barely attached head.

"This room might be where his throat was cut," I decide. "But I suspect it isn't where he died."

"I'm thinking the same thing." Marino carries over thermometers, a scalpel. "He should have been spraying blood everywhere."

"And he didn't because he was already dead," I reply. "That much I can say with reasonable certainty even as we stand here."

"Maybe a heart attack. Maybe when the killer got out the duct tape, the knife, and Wally realized what was about to happen? Whenever it was, he was scared literally to death." Marino's anger glints again. "We've seen it before when someone dies in the middle of being murdered."

"We'll want to do touch-DNA on all of the clothing." I unbutton the barely bloody khaki pants. "The killer had physical contact with him, positioning the body, taping him up, cutting his throat." I pull down the zipper.

I feel something hard and flat in a side pocket of Wally's pants. Dipping in my gloved fingers, I find a generic-looking steel key that has no tag. I give it to Marino. Holding my tactical light with one hand, I make a small incision in the right upper quadrant of the abdomen, inserting the long glass chemical thermometer.

"I don't know what this might be to." Marino shines his light on the key. "Definitely not to the store or his old Chevy wagon."

"What about to the cash register?"

"It doesn't look like a cash drawer key to me, but we'll check," he says.

I manipulate the arms and legs, and they're resistant. Rigor mortis is well advanced, and the body feels tepid. Marino alternates between taking photographs and handing me supplies while helping light my work. I continue hearing people talking and moving behind the closed door leading to the front of the store.

I don't know who Fruge is with or what's being said. I remove the thermometer from the small incision I made. The body's core temperature is 82 degrees.

"Consistent with him being dead approximately seven or eight hours in these conditions," I tell Marino.

"I got a few degrees cooler than that on infrared," he says.

"To be expected."

He struggles with his flashlight, the notepad and pen while swatting at flies, and there are more of them. I shine my light on Wally's lace-up tan leather shoes, noting the absence of blood, and that the tread is clean. I look at the duct tape wrapped around his ankles three times, catching a whiff of his cologne that hurts my heart.

Paper crackles loudly as I work a large bag over his lower legs, and the door leading to the front of the store opens. It's as if my wish has been granted. Benton walks in carrying an LED tower that's connected by a cable to a generator.

"You've got company." He looks at me. "Let there be light."

■ ■ ■

My husband's handsome sharp-featured face is framed in white Tyvek, and he sets down the light tower. Turning it on, he floods the storeroom in a horror show of brightness and shadow.

Fruge walks in next with Doug Schlaefer in tow, their PPE making whispery sounds.

"Stay on the sticky mats and don't touch anything." Marino never hesitates reminding everyone that the body and anything associated with it is our domain.

"Lucy and Tron are here as well." Benton directs this at me, his expression unreadable behind his face mask and safety glasses. "They're outside making sure nothing and no one shows up uninvited."

"Jesus God." Doug stares at the body, and outrage flares. "What the fuck is wrong with people?" For an instant his eyes are touched by tears.

"You're just asking now after all the shit you've seen?" Marino impatiently waves his gloved hands at flies.

"Why the fuck was it necessary to do something like this to him?" Doug is getting a look on his face that I've seen before.

"It's got nothing to do with necessity." Marino hasn't much patience for my deputy chief's fragile sensibilities. "The asshole who did this is a fucking coward and a bully. He should pick on someone his own fucking size."

"Amen to that," Fruge says, and she goes on to give us her latest update.

She called the daughter Clemmy to inform her that Wally Potter is dead. Fruge told her it appears he was killed during a robbery, his body found in the storage area.

"I didn't want her hearing it on the news," Fruge explains, "and nothing stays secret for very long anymore. I said that someone was inside the store and obviously stole stuff, and the electricity is off. I told her there's some damage to the property."

"Did she have any idea who might have done something like this?" Marino asks. "Was there anybody who'd caught her attention of late? Anybody hanging around, causing trouble, anything at all?"

"She didn't have a clue," Fruge replies. "They'd been crazy busy during peak hours, and there are a lot of tourists around. She did say some of the people coming in during recent weeks are associated with the Hooke trial, and are rough-looking. But nothing jumped out."

"When's the last time she heard from Wally?" I ask as I work a paper bag over his bound hands.

"She worked with him today," Fruge says. "They got here around seven this morning but drove in separate cars because Clemmy planned to leave early. She said when things got quiet around two P.M., she headed to Newport News. Someone else who works here part time was going to cover for her over the holiday weekend."

"What about the safe?" Marino asks. "What was in it?"

"That's where Wally kept the stock of lottery tickets and gift cards, anything valuable or important like property deeds, the title to his car, bank statements, the usual," Fruge reports. "But the cash likely wasn't in there. You probably noticed the big walk-in cooler in back, and that the door is padlocked. Clemmy's asking about the key."

If Wally hadn't been to the bank in a while, he'd hide the cash pouch. His secret spot was a nonworking electrical box inside the walk-in cooler at the back of the store. It wasn't a place that anyone would think to look.

"Then he'd lock the key to the padlock inside the safe here in his office," Fruge says. "Probably the same thing he's been doing for fifty years. But not a bad system, if you ask me. Of course, it would have been better not keeping a lot of cash on the property. But it wasn't unusual. Clemmy says she expects there to be at least five thousand dollars inside the cooler, assuming the killer never went in there."

As Fruge continues telling us what she's discovered, Benton listens, staring at the body. He takes in everything around him, often gazing up at the ceiling as if receiving signals from above. Then he looks at all of us the way he does when he has something to say.

"When the killer showed up, Wally was alive and alert," Benton begins like a prophet. "He was forced to open the safe, which had some things of value but no cash. He had the presence of mind to hide the key in his pocket without the bad guy noticing. Wally was mindful there was considerable cash. He didn't want the intruder to get it."

"In the end, he's thinking about his family," Doug says.

"Except the piece of shit's going to wonder what the hell happened to the money from the cash drawer," Marino replies. "Now he's really pissed."

"That's exactly right," Benton says. "He cleans out other items of value such as cash equivalents. Lottery tickets, gift cards. But he wanted the money. He wanted to be in control and have all the power."

"And maybe that's what we're seeing, and why he did this. Rage."

I shine my light on Wally's neck, the wound gaping like a screaming mouth.

I explain that the postmortem injury was inflicted by a single cut from right to left that begins at the lobe of the right ear. I step behind the body to show them.

"The incision travels almost straight across the front of the neck, terminating approximately half an inch below the left ear. And rarely have I seen this when someone's throat is cut," I explain, and mostly Benton needs to hear this. "Typically in such cases the attack is from the rear, both the killer and victim standing. The trajectory of the slash is downward, not straight across the throat."

As I describe all this inside the hot airless room, the stench of decomposition is foul and will get only worse. The expected blowflies continue finding their way to the body, and the droning is infernal. They make their greedy orbits in the harsh glow of the light tower, and I shoo them away as best I can while I continue to show what I'm finding.

"He was taped up and arranged in a seated position after death," I explain. "The assailant was standing behind him where I am."

Slashing the air horizontally with an imaginary knife, I demonstrate what I'm talking about. I suggest that unless the killer is ambidextrous, he's probably left-handed just like I am. This person is reasonably strong, and used a substantial cutting instrument.

"Something he brought with him, and left with after the fact." Benton states this as if he knows.

"We've not found a weapon, a roll of duct tape or anything else he might have used while he was here," Marino reports.

"They're likely in something the bad guy uses to carry what he needs," Benton says. "Possibly something he keeps inside his vehicle. Or inside his residence or place of work, wherever he spends his time. He won't dispose of such things. He won't assume he needs to. He likes and relies on what he knows and trusts. This is someone who has rituals and habits that have worked for him. But he's getting careless."

"Careless?" Doug's eyes are wide and angry. "This looks pretty damn premeditated to me. The asshole showed up with a plan."

"It was impulsive," Benton says. "But that doesn't mean he hadn't thought about robbing this place in the past. He struck when he did because it was emotional. He's compulsive, and never leaves home without certain things he might need."

"What about a box cutter?" Fruge asks. "Usually there's one or two of those lying around in storage areas. I'm not seeing any. I'm wondering if the killer might have helped himself to them."

"He wouldn't hesitate to take whatever he wanted," Benton says. "But this isn't someone who's going to show up and look for the nearest thing he can use as a weapon."

"A box cutter didn't do this." I indicate the savage neck wound. "The blade's not long enough. He's been cut all the way to the spine. His windpipe is transected, which is an awful way to die. Normally on autopsy we'd find that he aspirated blood. Basically, you're gasping for air, you're inhaling your own blood, drowning while bleeding to death."

"Assuming he was still alive when his throat was cut," Doug says, and he's sweating profusely. "I fucking hope for his sake he wasn't."

"I don't think so," I reply. "I'm all but certain we're going to find he wasn't."

"For what logical reason does anybody do something like this?" Doug blurts out alarmingly.

"What makes you think shit like this is logical?" Marino's voice has the ring of metal.

"Why go to all this trouble if he was already dead?" Doug is getting angrier and more upset. "Saying he'd gone into cardiac arrest? Why do this to him after the fact, for God's sake? To send a message?"

"That's a big reason, yes," Benton says. "But not the only one."

CHAPTER 23

Sometimes I fucking hate the human race!" Doug declares, and he's only forty.

He gets worked up like a lot of forensic pathologists still new enough to be shocked and traumatized. I've witnessed him kicking a plastic bucket across the autopsy suite, cursing. I've seen him sit down and cover his face with his hands, trying to get hold of himself, especially if it's a child on the table.

When the invasion of Ukraine began, he had to stop watching the news or he couldn't sleep. There were some atrocities he wasn't sure he could handle if asked, he's confided in me. Maybe he picked the wrong profession, he admitted over lunch one particularly bad day. I said I'd worry if he didn't feel that way.

"I believe I've seen enough," Benton decides. "If you're ready to go?" He looks at me, and I look at Doug, checking that he's up for the task.

"Will you be okay?" I ask my second in command, and he knows I mean it seriously. "I can stay."

"We can handle it from here." He takes a deep breath.

"Don't worry, Doc," Marino says to me. "I know what to do. Why don't you go home with Benton, and I'll hang here with Doug, and will see you a little later."

"My briefcase..."

"Yeah, I know, it's in my truck," Marino replies. "Give me a couple of minutes and I'll bring it out to you."

In the front area of the store, electrical cables snaking across the tile floor connect to more LED light towers. The portable power stations are loud.

"I'm assuming you didn't show up to give me a ride home," I say to Benton. "As nice as that is, and as glad as I am to see you."

"It's not my only motivation. But an important one," he replies, and we've reached the counter where food is ordered and prepared.

Homemade cookies, muffins, breads and fudge are inside glass display cases. Wally or someone put away perishables, adding to my suspicion that he closed early. I look through a refrigerator glass door at plastic containers of roast beef and chutney sandwiches, and the spicy gazpacho I love.

The labels have today's date, and list the ingredients. Other luncheon foods such as tuna fish and egg salad were made this morning, and I resist thinking about how hungry and thirsty I am.

"I believe the attack here was opportunistic," Benton says. "As was what happened at Chilton Farms afterward."

He begins to tell me more of his assessments now that we're alone. Robbing and murder weren't in the cards until the attack on the president failed. That was a huge frustration and disappointment for the terrorists. But this particular psychopath wasn't done showing what a tough guy he is.

"If the earlier assassination attempt on the president had been successful, this wouldn't have happened." Benton means that the market wouldn't have been targeted, and likely Chilton Farms wouldn't have been, either.

The killer showed up here first. He intended to eliminate whoever was working inside the store, and would have known that Wally was here alone.

"But the killer wasn't expecting what happened," Benton says. "He was denied the chance of brutalizing, of seeing fear and making someone suffer. He wanted that sense of power, and didn't get it. Wally died before his killer had the chance to have his sadistic way with him. That was a red flag to an already enraged bull."

"And Rachael? Why her?" I ask as we pass through an aisle crowded with canned goods, and bags of coffee beans you can grind yourself. "Because his compulsion wasn't satisfied?"

"Yes," Benton says. "And maybe she was on his radar for some reason. The big question is why he headed over to Chilton Farms to begin with. Why did he pick it? Is he familiar with the place? And I'm going to say that the answer is yes. The killer is decompensating."

"Just what we need. Someone out of control with a microwave gun. Someone doing drive-by shootings with it, taking out security systems, causing brain damage and death to whoever and whatever is in the path," I reply, and we're in the retro candy and gum section.

"He's in a cooling-down period that won't last long," Benton says. "I would expect that by now he's returned to wherever he lives. I remind you that he has friends and neighbors, possibly family who have no idea about his secret life."

"You talk as if you know who he is."

"I know what he is, and we're not talking about just one person," Benton says. "He works with his pack. He also works on his own, is secretive and doesn't get emotionally close to people."

Freezers full of ice cream and other frozen foods are melting, as if enough harm hasn't been done. Much of what's inside the store will be ruined, and I wonder if I'll ever be back here again. I wonder if it will reopen. It would be terrible if Belle Haven Market disappears after all these years. It would seem Alexandria has lost a part of its soul.

Near the suntan lotions and insect repellents is a barrel of flip-flops. Then a rack of paperback books, and finally the checkout area and cash register. The empty drawer is open and sooty with dusting powder. Behind the counter is a pegboard partition, all of the hooks bare.

"Cash or its substitutes, that's the name of the game," Benton says. "Gift cards you can use. Lottery tickets you can sell anonymously on the Internet. You can get rid of almost anything that way, including stolen goods and counterfeit money."

This is how terrorists help fund themselves these days, he explains. And in recent years they've been increasingly subsidized and supported by the Russians.

"The person who did this knew exactly what to take, and where it was." I survey dozens of empty hooks.

The lottery tickets and gift cards behind the counter wouldn't be visible from outside the store if you were looking through the windows or glass front door. You need to be close to the register to notice the pegboard, and that would seem to be an important detail. The killer knew what was here that he might want to steal.

"Which is another argument that he's familiar with the place," I add.

"He'd been in here before," Benton says. "I think that the cash drawer was already empty, the store closed by the time he fired his microwave gun, taking out the cameras and everything else."

The cash register was unlocked when Fruge first saw it. There was nothing inside except a paper receipt of the day's total that was tucked under the cash partition, Benton tells me.

"Wally must have done this after removing the money," I reply as

I stare at the ergonomic chair behind the counter, envisioning him sitting in it. "Whoever opens up the next morning will have the details from the day before. Another old habit, I'm guessing."

"Business was booming from eleven this morning until around two P.M. Almost fifteen hundred dollars' worth," Benton says.

After that there was little activity, the last purchase made at 2:37 P.M., he says. That's when someone paid fifty dollars for gas, using a gift card that wouldn't be linked to the customer's name or any other identifying information.

"It's the final transaction on the cash register receipt," Benton explains.

"Meaning we don't know who it was since it wasn't a personal credit card. And he didn't need to come inside to pay," I reply.

"I've got a strong feeling it was the killer filling up his tank," Benton says. "He was getting the lay of the land while he was at it, making sure there were no eyes or ears."

"The electrical power was still on at that time. It had to be if the gas pump, the cash register was working," I reply. "Whoever filled his car would have been caught on the cameras, assuming they were recording."

The one on a wall across from the checkout counter is dead, staring blindly at the front door. The only other one I'm aware of is outside on a light post at the self-service island. The microwave attack destroyed the security system, and Benton doesn't expect to get anything off the cameras.

■ ■ ■

The front door has been propped open, and a crime scene officer is dusting for fingerprints. I envision Marino cupping his hands around his eyes, peering through the glass.

No doubt the police will find evidence he was here, but I'll let him be the one to explain. Benton and I emerge into a rapid stutter of red and blue lights, the parking lot crowded with law enforcement vehicles and vans, marked and unmarked. The FBI has shown up, at least a dozen agents wearing flak jackets.

Helicopters are hovering. I suppose it was inevitable the media would find out that something awful has happened but a few miles from where Rachael Stanwyck was found dead. Channel 5 is here. All of the major networks are, their satellite trucks lining the street out front as film crews stalk Belle Haven Market's barricaded entrance.

The Secret Service crime scene unit has set up lighting, and I notice the two e-bikes propped against the open-sided tent. But I see no sign of Lucy and Tron as Benton and I pull off our Tyvek and gloves.

"If I never wear this again it will be too soon." I drop PPE in the biohazard trash.

"The shoes are a nice touch." Benton eyes the wrinkled linen outfit I wore to court, and Lucy's borrowed bike socks and sneakers.

He's wearing the same suit he put on early this morning, charcoal gray with a gray-striped shirt, a gray tie, and he's sweated through every layer. His platinum hair is damp, and he pushes it off his forehead as Marino emerges from the door we just came through. He has my briefcase as promised, and hands it over.

"Don't worry, I changed my gloves before touching it," he says.

"Speaking of?" I indicate the officer dusting the front door. "You'd better let them know about our earlier visit."

"Already have," Marino says.

He tells us that Fabian will be here any minute, and I walk inside the crime scene tent, grabbing several bottles of water from the ice chest. Benton and I set out through the parking lot, and the emergency strobes are harsh and disconcerting. I shield my eyes with my hand, squinting as if staring into the sun.

The constant rumbling of diesel engines is like the heaving of a stormy ocean, and I avoid looking at the cameras pointed our way. I can hear Dana Diletti talking into her microphone about *the legendary Benton Wesley.*

. . . The serial killer whisperer, she refers to him. *Just like in* Silence of the Lambs . . . , she's saying.

My husband's black Tesla SUV is parked between two unmarked cars, and as we climb inside, I take the caps off two bottles of water, giving him one. I don't want to track flower petals, dirt and other debris onto the carpet. I rinse the bottoms of my sneakers. Benton does the same, and we shut our doors. The electric engine is quiet, and police move the sawhorse barricades to let us leave as TV cameras film.

Sometimes I forget that my smartly dressed, psychologically minded husband spends as much time on the Secret Service's tactical driving range as Lucy. He speeds off as if we're being shot at, and nobody's going to give him a ticket. There's not much traffic on the Parkway, and he passes everyone without seeming to try, his touch light but sure.

"Hi." His profile is sharply outlined in the glow of the glass cockpit, and the stubble on his jaw looks like sand. "I'm glad to see you." He reaches for my hand.

The woods are pitch black between here and the river. I continue looking back and checking the mirrors, relieved no one seems to be following. No doubt Benton would lose whoever tried, and it's the first time I've begun relaxing even slightly all day.

"I'm glad to see you too," I reply. "I was wishing you were with me, and then there you were. I'm glad you showed up. There's no substitute for seeing something yourself."

"That's not the only reason I'm here." He finds a menu on the touchscreen, adjusting the temperature of the air blowing on us. "I thought you might need a lift home. Or I was hoping you would. And I've got a few updates."

They're not encouraging ones, he says. The terrorists we're up against are new at what they're doing but clever and sophisticated. They're smarter than Benton wants to believe, he explains as we drive home. What's happened today is worse than the public's been led to think.

"That's not what I was hoping to hear," I admit.

"We didn't see the attack coming," he says. "Not the Secret Service, the FBI, the CIA, nobody. We know nothing about the people responsible. And that's very disturbing, Kay."

"It's beyond disturbing, and way too close for comfort." I think of the many hours we've spent talking about this very thing.

We're accustomed to worst-case scenarios, and vital to protection and readiness is information. Calamities are avoided because of advance warnings, and almost always there's chatter on the Internet. There are cell phone activities and satellite images. Spies and snitches give a heads-up, and the modus operandi often is predictable and recognizable.

"But not with these bad guys," Benton says. "We didn't ping on anything until the last minute. And it wasn't their phones we were detecting. It was their damn weapons firing up, and as you say, that's way too close for comfort. We weren't looking for these people, and have no idea who they are."

"That's not what the news has been reporting, you're right," I reply. "By all indications in the media you were tipped off."

"What was released to the public is what we want the terrorists to believe. That we got an alert. That we weren't blindsided. But we were. I don't want to think about what might have happened had the motorcade not diverted. If the president and others had gotten out of their vehicles...? Well, I don't need to say it."

CHAPTER 24

I t sounds to me like you're trying to make the terrorists paranoid and even more enraged." I look at my husband's sharp profile, his quiet fury like heat rising from an overworked engine.

"I want them to turn on each other," Benton says. "I want them as scared and destabilized as they want us. Then they overstep, and we've got them."

"It sounds personal."

"Of course it's personal." His face is hard in the glare of oncoming headlights, and he rarely talks this aggressively. "Whoever they are, they tried to take out our president and God knows who else today. Annie's sister and Wally Potter are murdered right in our own backyard, and what's done to one is done to all."

"I worry what's next," I reply.

"Two-point-three-oh-five gigahertz," he reminds me. "That's what no one saw coming."

Except for the two young women on bicycles with signal analyzers in their backpacks. They were all that was between the president and the terrorists when the trap was laid. The first 2.305 GHz frequency Lucy and Tron detected was the only indication of what was to come, and thank God they were paying attention.

Benton believes the snipers lying in wait were alerted to abort the mission the instant the motorcade diverted. But he doesn't know how this might have occurred. There was no cell phone activity detected that would explain how three shooters at three separate locations got the message simultaneously, shutting down their weapons instantly. They disbanded and went silent, except for one. His violent act had been interrupted. He was like a fire burning out of control.

"When the signal was picked up again," Benton says, "I believe this was the killer firing his microwave gun at Belle Haven Market. This particular terrorist is smart, technically savvy, and on a violent bender. He's arrogant and overly confident. The risks he takes will become only bigger and scarier. He must be stopped, and I mean now."

"He went after the president, and then killed two people in a span of several hours. How much bigger and scarier does it have to get?" I reply.

"This is someone who's capable of anything, and he's experienced," Benton says. "I suspect he's older. Possibly in his forties, early fifties. He has a history of violent behavior but has never been arrested or spent time in jail. I suspect he served time in the military but washed out."

The killer doesn't have a police record because in the past he's been methodical and careful. He goes through dry runs, resisting impetuous behavior, Benton predicts as we drive toward Old Town.

He describes this particular offender as fueled by violent fantasies. It's someone who doesn't brag about his crimes, and feels no need to share the details. He lives alone, and is skilled at not drawing attention to himself. Those around him probably would describe him as quiet, nice, possibly helpful.

The sort of neighbor who comes over to jump-start your car or shovel the snow off your driveway, he doesn't look evil. Violent psychopaths rarely do, and the most common reason they get caught is they talk. They tell war stories, showing off, especially when under the influence of alcohol and drugs. They do something stupid like getting a parking ticket or giving a girlfriend the victim's jewelry.

"But not this guy," Benton says. "He's been supremely careful until now. I'm wondering if his exposure to radiation could be having an effect on him. He and his compatriots must be training, researching and experimenting constantly the same way they would with any new weapons and technologies."

"Exposure to microwave radiation could be a problem if one isn't always properly protected," I agree. "And it's easy to become complacent. Like people who stop bothering with hard hats or safety harnesses, and that's when the bad thing happens."

"He's isolative, living his own malignant reality. His compulsive behavior will escalate as he spins further out of control." Benton tells me what he sees in his hellish crystal ball. "He's like a lust murderer on a rampage. He's no longer mindful of consequences or he wouldn't have done what he did today."

"I would think if he's gone haywire the other members of his terrorist cell would find him a liability and do something about it," I reply.

"That's my hope if we don't get him first," Benton says. "But I wouldn't count on it. He's also creating a carnival of media attention, and terrorists feed on that. A bigger threat is these heinous acts become a recruiting tool."

As he's saying this, I check Marino's text that just landed. He's letting me know that Wally Potter's body is safely wrapped up and inside the van. The police will accompany it to my headquarters, and Fabian must be in heaven. His exotic physical appearance has ensured that he's everywhere. Mostly looking up at the TV news helicopters. Or conspicuously standing by the van.

In other headlines I'm scrolling through on my phone, Annie Chilton was escorted by the FBI into her house through the splintered front doors hours earlier. She was allowed there long enough to gather certain belongings, and not left unattended for a moment.

"I can't imagine what Annie must make of all this," I comment to Benton.

We're driving along Patrick Street now, and not far from home. It's almost midnight, and Old Town is mobbed. Restaurants and bars are overflowing, and people are out on the sidewalks talking in loud voices and laughing. The sight seems surreal as Benton and I discuss the day's atrocities.

"At least she's safely at our house," he says. "And Dorothy's with her."

"Not exactly who I would have put Annie with at the moment," I reply.

My sister likes nothing better than to dig into business that isn't hers. But Benton didn't have the time to get Annie settled, and Dorothy came right over, for which I'm grateful.

"I'm wondering what Annie knows about Rachael's alleged relationship with Bose Flagler." I look for a sign that Benton is aware. "Are you familiar with the rumors?"

"I know about their romantic involvement," he says.

"Then it's more than gossip or speculation."

"Flagler admits that he was dating her discreetly but not exclusively. He's stunned and upset, but I didn't get the impression he's heartbroken."

"You talked to him yourself?"

"I didn't," Benton says.

He watched the interview remotely while cueing the investigator who was doing the questioning. Bose Flagler wasn't in love with

Rachael Stanwyck. But he admitted that she was in love with him. During recent weeks he'd not seen her much, and it wasn't only because of the Gilbert Hooke trial.

"Flagler's family keeps a yacht at Raven Landing, but he hasn't had time for sailing either," Benton says. "I guess it was easier seeing Rachael if he was doing something else he liked while he was at it. What's known as a twofer."

"She must have been miserable."

"He worried that Rachael had gotten serious way too fast," Benton says. "She was looking for the perfect place to move, and was hoping they were going to be a couple. If he's to be believed, he claims she'd begun hinting at what a good first lady she'd be."

"That sounds like something he'd say, humble guy that he is," I reply. "Is he the reason she decided to get divorced from her billionaire husband?"

"Flagler denies it, but I don't think there can be any doubt."

■ ■ ■

As we get closer to our old place on the river, we pass Alexandria police cruisers patrolling the neighborhood. The cops nod at us as we pass. Benton says they'll be watching our property until things calm down.

"When might that be?" I stroke his hand with my thumb.

"I don't know."

"Do you think Rachael's relationship with Flagler has anything to do with her death?"

"Everything has to do with everything," Benton says. "If that's why she decided to move into Chilton Farms for a while, she made herself vulnerable. She was staying in a place she didn't like or feel safe in, all because of him. There's no security to speak of, and being there made it easy for a predator."

"It would make more sense if the killer had taken her jewelry, the cash in her wallet, tried to burglarize the house the way he did the market," I reply. "I'm not understanding the motive."

"Not that or the victim selection," Benton agrees. "And that's because we're missing something important."

Carriage lamps glow at the entrance of our brick driveway, and the black iron gate is closed. Lights from the house wink like tiny flames through thick trees moving in the wind, and Benton touches the display inside his electric car's cockpit. The gate begins to slide open along its track, everything recorded and monitored by Lucy's AI software.

Infrared cameras I can't see grab our plate number and other data at lightning speed. Concealed microphones pick up every sound as algorithms recognize types of vehicles and who's inside them. Hidden antennas capture signals from all directions. They're analyzed nonstop by equipment in various locations, including the white brick guest cottage where my niece lives.

Her blackout shades make it impossible to tell if she's home with lights on or off. I happen to know she's not here at the moment but hope she will be soon enough. I'll be glad when Marino arrives and everyone is safely accounted for, including Lucy's cat, Merlin. One never knows where he might turn up. I keep my eye out for him as we follow the driveway.

"We're not bothering with the garage," Benton decides, and the former carriage house has wooden doors that have to be swung open manually.

It can be a lot of fuss, and my state-owned Subaru inside makes it a tight squeeze. We pull up to our two-story house, white brick with a gray slate tile roof. We've not done much to it since moving in beyond cleaning up the garden. Recently we replaced two broken chimney pots, and repainted the doors and shutters a rich blue called Everard that's in keeping with the period.

Parked in front are Annie Chilton's white Prius and my sister's racing-green Range Rover. As Benton and I climb out, Dorothy opens the front door, and she has a fondness for onesies. Fortunately, she's resisted the usual themed outfits that might not be appropriate considering who's visiting and why. A skeleton, a zombie and jail stripes would be bad ideas.

Her Judge Judy leggings and hoodie would be in poor taste, as would glowsticks. Dorothy is somberly dressed in plain black. She's toned down the bronzer and eye makeup, and isn't showing much cleavage. Her pale blond hair is short and brushed straight back like Annie Lennox's, her earrings small diamond studs.

"Talk about the day from hell." My sister steps aside to let us in. "Honestly, what's all over the news is absolutely unnerving. And it would appear that once again you were captured at unfortunate moments, Kay." She stares at the pair of Lucy's sneakers I'm wearing. "I couldn't believe you left your shoes on a sidewalk."

"How does Annie seem to be doing?" Benton asks as I close the door and reset the alarm.

"She's stoical but confused," Dorothy says. "Why would someone kill Wally? Why her sister, and was she sexually assaulted? What was done to them? Were they strangled or stabbed? Dear God, I hope they weren't tortured, that it wasn't some dreadful *Helter Skelter* sort of thing. Everything is so mysterious and cryptic..."

"I know you understand that we can't talk about it, Dorothy." I place my briefcase on the entryway table. "Please don't take it personally." Because she always does.

"You must be exhausted." She can go from warm to chilly very quickly.

"Thanks for helping out with Annie." Benton takes off his suit jacket. "It's very much appreciated."

"Should we be frightened? Well, I know you're not going to tell me." My sister still pouts the same way she did as a kid. "But it's only fair that you do or give a hint. I'm staying under the same roof with you. What happens to you, happens to me."

She complains anew that ever since the Hooke trial moved to Old Town Alexandria, life has unraveled. She refers to the visiting riffraff, as she puts it, the disgusting mob screaming and waving guns on TV. Nothing good will happen when *warring factions invade your home turf,* and she's not used that language before.

"The Tupelo and Hooke families are like the Hatfields and McCoys, the Montagues and Capulets." Dorothy continues holding forth. "What do you think they'll bring with them if they camp out in your neighborhood for a while? They'll bring their damn feud with them. They'll bring their bigotries and criminal behavior, that's what. And clearly they have."

I'm wondering where my sister got her information even as suspicions swirl like a funnel cloud. Details about the Hookes and Tupelos not getting along hasn't been the focus of the trial. It's been barely a mention. When April and Gilbert started seeing each other, I suspect it was exciting and forbidden until it wasn't anymore. The arguing and fighting on the boat the last night of her life wasn't uncommon.

Benton would say that their pathology is what bound them. They were birds of a feather, as Dorothy puts it, and she's probably right based on what I've reviewed in confidential reports. But such details didn't come out during the trial. It wouldn't be in Flagler's best interest if *pretty is as pretty does* didn't apply to the victim we're supposed to pity.

It wouldn't be helpful if the jurors decided she was little or no better than the one accused of killing her. Sal Gallo has to be careful, too. He wouldn't be well served by denigrating a young woman whose gruesome photographs are all around the courtroom. He won't win points by implying April Tupelo deserved what she got. But after all I've reviewed, I can understand someone thinking it.

"Destructive, horrible people, in other words," Dorothy says. "I have a feeling you're going to discover that everybody's rotten without exception. The victim, the defendant and all associated."

I have a feeling I know what my sister was doing while home for hours with no one else here except Annie. Had I expected the day to end this way I would have been more careful. I would have *Dorothy-proofed* the house, as I think of it.

"That trial has dragged all this into our backyard. Then one awful thing leads to another, ruining life for the rest of us," she's saying. "I don't know how I'll ever go back to Belle Haven Market after this."

"It won't be an option anytime soon." Benton pulls off his neck-tie. "A lot of damage was done." He opens the entryway closet.

"Someone tweeted that they drove by and the power was out. The place was vandalized. A lot was stolen, and Wally was found inside the storeroom," Dorothy reports. "And at the peak of the season? They'll be shut down the rest of the summer, I'm betting, and it's so depressing."

She acts as if she cares more than anyone you've ever met. But what she's really doing is gathering information.

"I hope you and Annie had something to eat?" I ask.

"I warmed up your lasagna and garlic bread from the freezer," Dorothy says. "I brought up a nice single malt from the basement, and made sure she has everything she needs."

"That was kind of you," I reply, and I ask Benton if he's hungry.

"I had a tuna melt in D.C., my usual," he says, and that likely means he ate at the White House. The Mess Hall in the West Wing has a grilled albacore tuna sandwich that Benton gets at every opportunity.

"Annie and I ate, had a few drinks while chatting." Dorothy tells us they've had a fine and meaningful visit.

"Did you two discuss anything we should know about?" Benton asks.

"Well, it's interesting," she says. "Rachael suddenly dying before the divorce was over means the plug gets pulled. You can't divorce someone who's dead, and how convenient for Lance Stanwyck. God only knows what he just saved in settlement money? Hundreds of millions, no doubt. And he's spared a long, drawn-out legal battle that was going to cost him in every way imaginable."

"Did Annie tell you this?" Benton stuffs his suit jacket, his tie inside the nylon bag that goes to the dry cleaner.

"I asked her what would happen with the divorce. She said that legally, Lance and Rachael are still married. Legally and officially, he's now a widower. The two of them will *never* be divorced for all perpetuity. Imagine that." My sister likes nothing better than being the bearer of important news.

"Is Annie suspicious that Lance Stanwyck had something to do with Rachael's death?" Benton takes off his shirt, and it goes into the dry cleaner bag.

"She didn't say but I don't have that impression." Dorothy boldly enjoys the view of my athletically built husband stripped down to his slacks and tight undershirt. "She didn't have a bad word to say about Lance, and if I didn't know better I might wonder about the judge and him. But I don't think he or any other man is going to tip Her Honor's scales."

As she's making this insinuation, Lucy's Scottish fold cat slinks in, gray with white spots and full-moon eyes. Merlin's flat ears give him an owlish appearance, and he makes his way straight to me, rubbing against my legs.

"Purrrrrfect timing." My sister looks me up and down as if just now noticing my appearance. "I was about to say that you look like something the cat dragged in."

"I'm headed up for a quick shower," I reply. "Benton and I have to spend some alone time with Annie. I know you understand. I hope she won't mind staying awake a little longer so we can talk to her."

I'm telling Dorothy to respect our privacy. She needs to stay out of the kitchen in more ways than one, I let her know nicely.

CHAPTER 25

Our modest estate was built by a sea captain in the 1700s, and he would moor his sailing ship on the Potomac at the back of the property. At low tide you can still see what's left of the pier, the pilings visible from windows facing the water.

Benton and I have been fastidious about staying true to the house and its maritime theme. Exposed beams in the ceiling are like the ribs of a ship, and lanterns hang from some of them. Nautical lights are spaced along the ceiling, and they glow softly on paneling as I follow the hallway's pumpkin pine flooring.

The antique maps of the Chesapeake Bay were Benton's and my housewarming present to ourselves. We found the caged copper sconces in Cape Cod while living near Boston. The nineteenth-century James Gale Tyler maritime paintings of sailing ships and moonlit seas are handed down from Benton's family, and I didn't marry him for his money.

He didn't marry me for mine, that's for certain. I have no fine art or antiques from long ago, very little from my childhood beyond memories. I reach the bedroom where Dorothy and Marino will stay the night, and she's left the door open, and lamps are on. Merlin silently follows as I step inside, checking that there are bottles of water, soap, toilet paper.

My sister's overnight bag is open on the bed, and I can't help seeing what's on top of clothing she packed for herself. Black silk boxer shorts with a Harley-Davidson flame theme. A jar of hemp-infused massage cream. Other items that are none of my affair. The dark blue medical tome on the bedside table is unmistakable, and as I suspected, my sister is up to her usual tricks.

I know what she's done in my absence, and next along the hallway is my office. The door is open, and stepping inside, I look around at the stack of thick case files next to the computer. I find the empty space on the bookcase where volume one of *Goldman-Cecil Medicine* was removed. It's classic Dorothy to be cleverly manipulative about her snooping.

She's creative with her alibis, orchestrating ploys such as borrowing something from a place that's off-limits. Then she leaves doors open, items out in plain view as if she has nothing to hide. If and when confronted, she claims she has no idea anything was inappropriate or wrong.

I scan for what she might have done in here, and my attention lands on the four white banker's boxes stacked in a corner. Inside are materials relating to the April Tupelo case. The lids aren't taped closed because I've needed to refer to what's inside as the Hooke trial has unfolded.

"That's most unfortunate." I walk over to inspect, and Merlin is on my heels. "Dammit, and excuse my French," I say to him. "But I think somebody was prowling and prying, and you and I both know who."

I lift the lid off a box, and inside are thick manila envelopes of eight-by-ten-inch photographs. There are thumb drives of videos, and reams of official communications and reports. Near the top of one box are the confidential psychological evaluations and other documents that refer to the bad blood between the Tupelos and Hookes.

"If I'd known we were having company tonight," I explain to Merlin, "I would have made sure to lock my door."

I send Dorothy a text: *A reminder that my office is off-limits, please.*

The master bedroom is at the end of the corridor. Merlin is my shadow as I enter, and the first stop is the bathroom. I flip on the light while he mutters and mumbles like a grumpy old man, and I pause in front of the marble washbasin. My reflection in the mirror looks the way I feel. Indistinct, shapeless and not completely beamed in.

I pull off my loaner sneakers and socks. I drop my suit jacket, my skirt to the subway tile floor. Closing the toilet lid, I sit on it. I examine my throbbing ankle, and the bruise is dark blue on the way to purple. Taking photographs with my phone, I swallow my fury. It climbs up my throat like bile, and I hate that I let someone do this to me.

"Just in case," I tell Merlin as I take more photos. "I hope it's not broken." I stand up painfully. "You and I know all too well how nasty people can be. You don't have to be a cat to be mistreated for no rational reason."

Dampening a cotton pad with makeup remover, I get rid of the last few stubborn smudges of mascara. My eyes are bloodshot, my collar-length hair an Andy Warhol blondish mop. My clothes go into the hamper for now, I'll sort them out later, and I step into the shower. I brush my teeth while hot water drums the top of my head, my back and shoulders.

I scrub and shampoo away the day with antibacterial soap that's followed by something kinder and more fragrant. Moments later, I emerge in a cloud of lavender-scented steam. I begin drying off with a towel. Wrapping up in it, I blow-dry my hair while Merlin guards the doorway like the Great Sphinx of Giza.

"You've met Annie when she's been over. And just because she's a judge and can seem aloof doesn't mean she doesn't have feelings."

I walk into the bedroom. "She's very sad and confused. She might be scared, and all of us are going to be extra kind and attentive. That includes you, Merlin. Please be nice."

I put on blue silk pajamas reminiscent of scrubs, and over them a matching bathrobe that ties in front like a surgical gown.

"I realize Annie doesn't come across as a cat person." I continue talking to Merlin. "She didn't grow up with cats of any description, and hasn't been around them much if at all. You'll have to teach her, and she's bad about taking the initiative."

I slip my feet into a pair of rubber surgical clogs that have good arch support. Catching myself in the full-length mirror, I'm reminded that no matter what I do, I always look like myself.

"The problem is that she's a bird lover, and unfortunately so are you." I turn off the closet light. "I don't want any gifts left on the doorstep or dragged inside like you did last time she was here."

Merlin is a rescue, and the product of early imprinting like the rest of us. As a kitten, he survived on his own, spending considerable time outside in harrowing conditions. A scrounger and a fighter, he was all but feral before having the good fortune of ending up with my niece. It's in his programming to be an indoor-outdoor cat, and when the urge strikes it's the call of the wild.

He's going outside. Otherwise he'll yowl and shriek nonstop while tearing things apart. There's no therapy or tincture that will cure his cleithrophobia, his fear of being trapped, as Benton has diagnosed the disorder. The only solution was to install cat doors in appropriate locations. Merlin can access these auto-locking metal flaps with a radio frequency identification (RFID) chipped collar that Lucy 3-D prints in bright red.

Her feline companion can't be cured of some bad habits and is notorious for stalking the neighbors' birdfeeders. If Annie lived closer, he'd be a regular trespasser at Chilton Farms. But it's impossible to get angry with a cat that looks like a cartoon character, and I find myself confiding in him as if he understands every word.

Nearing the guestroom, I can hear Dorothy behind the shut door talking to Marino over speakerphone. As I pause to listen from the hallway, I can tell she's annoyed with him. He's at home eating a sandwich, getting cleaned up while dealing with Fabian and his usual dramas. He's spending the night at the office and "wigged out about it," Marino says.

"...Well I do wish you'd hurry," my sister complains, and I can hear the floorboards creaking as she paces inside the guestroom. "I'm upstairs in this old cramped broom closet all by my lonesome because Annie's downstairs in the place where we always stay. The mattress is better, as is the view. I guess if you're a judge you get treated more special than the rest of us. It's just so boring having no one to talk to. As if none of my opinions might have merit just because I don't have a badge to flash around..."

"You know the drill by now, babe. You don't work with law enforcement, and the rest of us do." Marino's voice. "We gotta do what we gotta do, and you can't be in on every conversation."

"I'm damn tired of Kay treating me like a lesser than. And she's miffed as usual because I borrowed a book from her office. *Well, excuse me for having a seeking mind...*"

"You're not supposed to go in there, and you know that," Marino says as I stand outside the shut door hearing every word.

"Did I mention how bored I've been since getting here?" she again says, but with growing irritation, most of it directed at him. "While you're running around having all your thrilling and dangerous adventures, and now taking your sweet time getting here?"

"The doc has a lot of private shit in her office. You need to respect that. Digging into what's none of your business could be bad for her and me both."

"The door was open. What do you expect...?" Dorothy never appreciates it when he sticks up for me, and I've heard quite enough.

■ ■ ■

Downstairs, Mozart's *The Magic Flute* plays quietly, and no doubt Benton put that on. I hungrily detect the aromas of garlic, ricotta, basil, and it seems like some other person's cooking since it's not me warming it up.

Inside the living room the ceiling is low, the furniture simple and minimal but comfortable. Sofas are leather or fabric in earth tones, and table lamps have mica shades that glow warmly. Impressionistic works of art are arranged on plaster walls that are worn in places, the original bricks showing.

I stop to peek behind the drapes as if the boogeyman might be hiding, acting paranoid and weird as always. What I'm confirming are window screens as Lucy's signal analyzers constantly sweep the property silently, invisibly. I'm grateful that the metal mesh that covers our windows and doors will keep out invaders far more dangerous than flies and mosquitoes.

But it would be better to have a copper roof, and high metal fencing around the entire property. If I were remodeling the place, I'd have copper microfibers woven into the wallpaper, window treatments and the pads under rugs. New construction would include the same shielding. But I'd have it incorporated into the very structure, and it's hard knowing where to stop.

One can do only so much to protect against the dangers we know about. It's not like I can live inside a metal box, a cavern, a lava tube. Or as my forensic pathology advisor at Johns Hopkins would say, the safest thing, the best prevention is being dead. Then you have no further worries, and that's humorous but not an option I'd choose.

It used to be that my biggest preoccupation was locking up and setting the alarm. It was checking that smoke and carbon monoxide detectors were operating properly, and making sure a firearm was within reach when needed. But that's not the simple world we live in anymore.

As I walk through the house I can't rid myself of a growing sense of urgency. It's rare I see Benton nervous. I know when he is. I'd like to be alone with him or even with my thoughts. Both of us could use some restorative attention and rest. We're not going to get it anytime soon, and I think of the data constantly uploaded by my smart ring.

Microsensors spy on my sleep, stress hormones, blood sugar, physical activity and other information that might indicate my readiness to serve. Everyone on the Doomsday Commission is equipped with wearable computers. Many government officials and military leaders have AI-assisted rings and similar devices monitoring their every breath and heartbeat.

If you fail certain parameters, someone else gets the call in an emergency. I'll probably receive an automated warning message any moment. Benton will too if he hasn't already. They land with an annoying audible vibration when we don't exercise, eat or sleep properly according to the judgmental software. Eventually this is followed by a phone call from an overbearing human, and we're asked to explain ourselves.

It isn't the best idea to sit up drinking most of the night. But that's the likely scenario I'm facing since we don't get to choose the timing of broken hearts and other disasters. Having Annie here right now is a complication nobody needed, most of all her. I wish the timing were better. I wish she, Marino and my sister weren't staying over even as I'm glad they are.

I wish a lot of things right now, and can see my father's face while he clucked his tongue. He'd wag his finger disapprovingly when I'd wish my life away. Usually, my magical thinking was about him getting better. It was about him not leaving me for all eternity. If I could defeat death one day maybe it would bring him back. Or I'd discover he'd never left to begin with. I'd wish it constantly. I still do.

Merlin shadows me through the dining room where I never tire of the Queen Anne table discovered during a visit to Scotland Yard. The Murano glass chandelier is from working serial murders in Venice and Rome. Benton and I found the antique French stemware while visiting Interpol. The colonial-era hutch was in a Tennessee curiosity shop near the anthropology research facility known as the Body Farm.

Since moving to Old Town we've continued unpacking boxes in the basement, excavating our treasures. We've been redecorating even as I've worried that it was a mistake returning to Virginia. Beyond the dining room are swinging doors that are closed, and this is my husband's doing. He's reminding Dorothy not to enter should she decide to wander back in this direction.

My rubber clogs are quiet on the terra-cotta tile when I walk into the kitchen. Pots and pans hang from exposed oak beams over the butcher's block, the ceiling low. The brick fireplace is deep, and in cooler weather we use it often. Benton is checking on what's in the oven while Annie sits at the breakfast table where there's a view of the garden when the curtains are open.

"Thanks for staying up." I give her a heartfelt hug before anything else. "Do you have everything you need?"

"They broke the mold when they made him." She renders her verdict as Benton has a drink ready for me while topping off hers. "In case nobody's told you."

"I don't need to be told," I reply. "Annie, I'm sorry I wasn't able to greet you earlier."

"I can't thank you enough for everything, Kay. The guestroom is lovely, and your cooking? Just when I didn't think it could get any better."

She has an unemphatic way of speaking on the bench and off, deliberate in her choice of words and how she delivers them. The average person wouldn't know Annie Chilton is from Virginia or the South. Early on she worked hard to eradicate the lilting accent of her youth, not wanting to come across as privileged and provincial.

If you grew up in a former plantation mansion that's been in your family for centuries, she'd explain, it's best not to sound like *Gone with the Wind*. Most people have no idea where she's from but guess it's Florida or California. Possibly Arizona.

CHAPTER 26

I was telling Benton I've not eaten anything so delicious since the last time we were together," Annie says to me. "I don't know how you do it. I can barely boil water. But I think you were born knowing how to cook."

Fond of khaki pants, oversized safari shirts and sneakers, she brings to mind the unassuming law student I remember. She doesn't look like a prominent circuit court judge presiding over one of the biggest trials in the history of Alexandria. Overall, Annie hasn't changed much since our Georgetown days, having little use for fashion or shopping.

The only jewelry I've seen her wear in recent memory is her late father's gold posie ring engraved with the inscription *Honi soit qui mal y pense. Evil to him who thinks it. May you get what you deserve. Karma's a bitch. What you do to others you do to yourself.* Or that's Annie's loose interpretation. That and *Fuck you.* But it's really more about being shamed.

The family heirloom has been passed down by generations of Chilton males, and genetically dead-ended with her. She wears it on her left middle finger as if flipping the bird at an unseen enemy. Most people who don't know much about her assume she's married, and that her wedding band doesn't fit anymore. It may be truer than they know.

"Hopefully, you two have had a chance to catch up while I was making myself presentable," I say as Benton's mitted hands set a hot baking dish on top of the stove.

"I've been on the phone." He pulls out the foil-wrapped garlic bread next. "And I thought it best if both of us chat with Annie. She understands that we can listen to anything she wants to say. But we can't necessarily offer all of the details she might want."

"You don't need to talk about me as if I'm not here or just fell off the turnip truck." She has an edgy sense of humor that's not easily detectable. "Of course, I understand. Maybe better than you do."

Her steely-gray eyes are impenetrable, but at least she's looking at me. We're talking to each other, acting like old friends again.

"I'd be the first to advise you to stay away," she says. "I told Benton that in no uncertain terms when he kindly insisted I spend the night. Somebody will find out I was here and make a big stink out of it just like everything else."

"We don't turn our backs on friends and extended family," Benton says while Merlin jumps up on the breakfast table even though he knows better.

It's as if he listened to my earlier instructions, and is well aware he has me over a barrel. I'm not about to order him to get down as he stares at Annie, his tail twitching. And she reaches out and pets him tentatively. And then he's purring in her lap.

"Merlin's good company. Lucy calls him her spirit animal," Benton says.

He sets a plate of lasagna, slices of garlic bread in front of me. In his formfitting undershirt, his apron, suit trousers and socks, he looks sexy and ridiculous. Next, he sets down the shaker of red pepper flakes, the dish of grated Parmigiano Reggiano.

"How can I help?" Annie asks. "Whatever it is, I'll do my best."

"I have an idea, which we'll get to shortly. We have to think out-side the box. Whoever did this to Wally and your sister is going to do something worse." Benton says it bluntly. "The goal is nothing less than senseless slaughter and anarchy. To terrorize and overpower. To create chaos while overthrowing the existing order."

"I worry these people might be connected to the trial," Annie says. "I don't like what I'm seeing day after day." She looks at me. "I hope your leg's okay, that you weren't hurt when that son of a bitch kicked you. I would have raised hell, but that wouldn't have been wise under the circumstances."

She was aware of what had happened but afraid of a riot. Annie goes on to confess that she wanted to get out of her courtroom as badly as Marino and I did.

"We need you to be open with us, as open as you've ever been, and to feel safe and comfortable while doing so," Benton says to her. "You certainly don't have to answer questions or talk at all. I realize the late hour, and everyone's tired. To say the least, you've been through an emotional wringer."

"As long as we're not recording anything." She knows exactly what he's saying.

"We're not taking notes or making a record of any kind." This is Benton's way of Mirandizing her without doing it at all. "We're just old friends having a few nightcaps, talking about whatever comes to mind."

He's giving her fair warning she best not have anything to hide.

"As long as it's okay with you and you're comfortable." He says that again.

"I'll tell you and Kay anything you want to know," Annie replies without hesitation. "I've no illegal secrets, not even exciting ones. Maybe my life would be more interesting if I did."

"I'm sorry we can't be as open with you in return. Not as much as we'd like." Benton makes himself a drink, neat.

"Of course you can't be open with me." Annie rubs Merlin's spotted belly. "At the moment you don't know who's guilty or innocent of a goddam thing. Rachael was living with me, and I have motive."

"Which is?" Benton asks.

"Where do I start?" Annie says. "I hated having my sister in the house even more than she hated being there. We've never gotten along. How do you know I'm not involved in a conspiracy to get rid of her? Perhaps with the billionaire she's divorcing? How convenient that she dies before the case has been settled. Lance's lawyers must be thanking their lucky stars. One might suppose he's most grateful of all."

She scripts it like the brilliant jurist that she is, and prosecutor she once was. There isn't much the three of us haven't seen when it comes to crimes and those who commit them. People will do the unthinkable when the need is overpowering, and often it's a mundane one. Revenge. Rage. Envy. Lust. Greed. The usual.

■　■　■

"I was loyal to my sister but didn't like or respect her. Truth be told, I'm partly to blame for what's happened." Annie doesn't sound bereft or even all that sorry Rachael is dead. "I shouldn't have allowed her to move in with me to begin with. It's always been easier giving in than squabbling."

"Speaking of enabling?" Benton says to her. "How about a refill on your drink, and maybe some chocolate?"

"I won't say no to either."

"Dark with hazelnuts, please." I place my order in advance as I eat lasagna.

"Rachael called me right before Easter saying she didn't feel safe with Lance. She must move out immediately, and I knew it was bullshit," Annie says. "But what was I supposed to do? Say no when she was crying, claiming she was terrified? Her profession was all about appearances, and so was her life. Like the spies she worked with, she lied for a living. Maybe all of us do."

"We lie by omission if nothing else." Benton walks into the pantry. "You can't tell people everything." He opens the small refrigerated wine cabinet where we keep guilty pleasures. "For their own good you can't."

"Is it for my own good that you're lying to me?" she asks us pointblank. "I saw the damage done to my property. You think I didn't notice the dead foliage that wasn't there this morning? It's like someone sprayed the entrance with Agent Orange."

Benton returns to the table, setting down napkins and a box with a deep red foil lid as I order Merlin to hop down from Annie's lap. Cats and chocolate can be a lethal combination, and he alights on the floor with an indignant loud trill. He starts cleaning himself the way he does when offended.

"What else did you notice?" Benton asks Annie.

"Something had knocked out the power." She helps herself to a Belgian praline. "It was suggested that I'll probably have to get the entire place rewired. What's happened is a disaster."

"What have you been told about Rachel's death?" I use garlic bread to sop up sauce. "What did the police, the FBI, anybody say today when you were with them at Chilton Farms?"

"The implication is that my sister was stalked and murdered during a home invasion. Someone tried to steal her jewelry and fled." Annie sets down her drink glass with a sharp tap that reminds me of her gavel.

"Meaning, you've been told what's in the news," I reply.

"Meaning, I've been told bullshit."

"And the explanation for the power outage?" Benton asks.

"It was suggested lightning might be to blame from the sudden storm we had earlier." She takes another sip of her drink. "Again, bullshit. I've seen lightning strikes on my property and other places. That's not what they look like." She stares at us. "It was some kind of weird weapon, wasn't it? That's why the feds are crawling all over the place. I'm not naïve about attacks around the White House and elsewhere, that microwaves are suspected."

"Stay here as long as you'd like." Benton carries over the bottle of Scotch, the bucket of ice.

"Havana Syndrome," she says. "Whatever you want to call it. I realize you can't tell me if that's what we're talking about."

"This may not be the Ritz, but it's about as safe as Fort Knox," Benton says.

"Fortunately, it won't be necessary for me to wear out my welcome." Annie stares off, her face haunted. "Lance has a furnished place at the Watergate he's letting me have until I know what I'm doing. I need to sell Chilton Farms, probably to Raven Landing. They've been after me for years, hoping to turn the house into a lodge, a restaurant, an indoor climbing wall. A fucking spa, who knows...?"

"Is Lance aware of Rachael's affair with Flagler?" What Benton's really asking is if Annie is, and she doesn't act surprised.

"It's not the first time. In fact, I'd call my sister a serial cheater," Annie says as I refill our glasses with ice. "But Lance would put up with almost anything to keep her, and they decided on having an arrangement, as some couples do."

"She told you this?" Benton asks.

"He did."

"Sounds like you two are pretty close."

"Lance and I met at Harvard, and I knew him before my sister did," Annie says. "He's always told me everything, using me as a sounding board, asking my advice."

He and Rachael agreed they could have their sexual dalliances as long as the person didn't mean anything. That worked well enough because she never gave a shit about anyone, Annie says.

"Until she encountered Bose Flagler some seven or eight months ago at a charity gala," she adds. "Rachael finally had met her match, the one who could undo her."

"How did you find out? Did she tell you?" I ask. "Did Flagler? It seems an important detail he might have thought to pass along since you're the judge in the biggest trial of his career."

"One critical to his reelection and political future," Benton adds.

"I returned home from a trip and there was a condom in a toilet," Annie says. "Then I come to find out that Flagler's Lamborghini SUV was spotted on my driveway while I was gone, and also on other occasions."

"What about Holt Willard?" I ask if the caretaker might have noticed that Rachael was having company.

"Whenever she *worked from home*"—Annie makes quote marks in the air—"she'd tell Holt to stay away. He wasn't to come to the property. She'd deal directly with him, usually through a text."

"That's not why she stayed home today," Benton says. "Flagler was tied up in court, busy showing off on live television. He wasn't sneaking around, driving to Chilton Farms."

"Rachael was out of sorts. She said she was worried about traffic because of the holiday weekend. Then it was announced that the president was visiting Old Town, and that would make traffic only worse," Annie says. "She'd been more depressed than usual, and I think we know why."

"It sounds like she broke the house rule," I reply. "She fell for the person she was having her dalliance with. It wasn't just physical."

"It also wasn't reciprocal," Annie says. "Flagler did to her what she's always done to others. And Rachael simply wasn't used to it. I dare say it had never happened before, not once in her life. I would call it poetic justice if it didn't sound callous and mean. But she's not the only one who's lost everything."

"How has Lance been feeling about Rachael now that she broke the house rule and then decided to sue him for divorce?" Benton asks.

"He'll never stop loving her," Annie says. "He believes Flagler made it his ambition to turn Rachael's head, to get her to fall for him in a big way. This was all for his manipulative and ambitious purposes. And I believe it, too."

The commonwealth's attorney wanted Annie to find out. He probably left the condom in the toilet on purpose, and damn well knew his flashy car would be spotted, she says. As opportunistic and conniving as he is, he assumed that if he and Rachael were seeing each other it would make Annie feel positively inclined toward him inside the courtroom.

"Some might say that what he did worked," I reply. "I was surprised by some of your rulings, or lack of them, while I was testifying. You're being accused of going easy on him, of being helpful."

"I've been giving him a long leash to run with, and plenty of rope to hang himself. He'll find out soon enough how easy and helpful I've been," she threatens. "I never wanted that damn trial here. It's not luck of the draw that the venue moved to Old Town. I didn't recommend it, and wouldn't have allowed it. But it wasn't up to me."

The implication is obvious. Had the Hooke trial not ended up here, Bose Flagler wouldn't be the commonwealth's attorney in the case. It was his chance to win the Super Bowl, and Annie was warned not to interfere, she says.

"By whom?" Benton asks.

"Pressured by Flagler himself," she replies. "This was followed by a call from the chief justice of the Virginia Supreme Court, Chuck Hamper. The venue needed to be Alexandria, and of course it would be wonderful for Virginia if the trial not only was set in a historic area popular with tourists but was covered live on Court TV."

"I get the drift," Benton says.

"Chuck Hamper is an old friend of the Flagler family," Annie says.

"He's also pals with the health commissioner," I reply as the pieces slide together just like that. "I'm not surprised Elvin would be somewhere in the mix if there's corruption to be found."

CHAPTER 27

Bose Flagler is being groomed for governor, and plans to run in four years." Annie tells us the rumors she's hearing. "Whether or not he wins his reelection as commonwealth's attorney this fall, he's going to run against Roxane Dare. That's his plan even though he's not announced it."

"I can't imagine your sister was having a very nice time while staying with you," Benton decides. "Flagler has one obsession, himself. He was using her. She had to know he didn't feel about her the way she did about him, and here she's sacrificed it all. Walked out and moved into a place she hates just for the chance to see him when he can find the time or interest."

"Not that Rachael was ever happy," Annie says. "But of late she was about as miserable as I've ever seen her."

"I noticed that she seemed to be taking laxatives. Teas, sugarless candies and such." I bring that up. "I'm wondering if you were aware of that or anything else unusual about her health habits?"

"Overdoing laxatives, starving herself, bulimia, also she was drinking more. But food was my sister's big devil, and always was," Annie says. "Her diet was one of the few things she could control."

"Or she thought she could." Benton picks up his phone, looking at the display as an "unknown" call comes in. "I need to take this."

He walks away, turning his back to us as he answers. He says little, mostly listening, and Marino's truck pulls up at the entrance. I watch him on camera as he waits for the gate to slide open. I vaguely make out he's on his phone, the expression on his face sour. My smart ring vibrates as he sends a text.

He's heading straight upstairs to the guestroom. He'll see me in the morning, and that means my sister is breathing down his neck. I watch him drive through in a glare of headlights as Benton ends his call, walking back to the kitchen table.

"We need to talk about where Rachael was last Saturday night," he says to Annie.

"I don't have any idea where she may have been," she replies.

"Where were you?" he asks.

"I worked in my courthouse chambers all day and into the early evening," she says. "I was asleep when Rachael got home at some point. I rarely had any idea what she was doing."

"I'm wondering if she might have mentioned Mollie's Underground." Benton asks about the Washington, D.C., bar and grill in the Navy Yard.

"I know she's a regular," Annie says. "A number of her CIA folks go there, and I've been a few times. But I wouldn't imagine she was meeting Flagler unless they wanted their relationship to be a topic of conversation. Of course it would end up in the media if the CIA's press secretary was going out with Alexandria's most desirable bachelor."

"Your sister wasn't meeting Flagler," Benton says, and he's gotten information I don't have. "She was there at a cozy table for two with Dana Diletti. I was just on the phone with the Underground's owner, Mollie Gunner. That's who I was talking to while you were upstairs cleaning up." He says this to me. "She's been checking into a few things."

He informs Annie that the GPS inside Rachael's Mercedes

indicates the car was driven to the Underground this past Saturday, the night of June 25. The reservation was in Dana's name for two people for 7:30 P.M. Mollie talked to Elizabeth the hostess, gathering the details.

"Apparently, Channel Five is working on an investigative television story about you that Dana expects to be huge," Benton says, and I recall what Maggie told me over the phone.

Elvin Reddy is aware that Annie and I were roommates during law school. He knows I paid one dollar monthly for rent in a pricey Georgetown rowhouse, that it was free if you don't count what I did to earn my keep. There can be little doubt what's implied, and who's been helping Dana Diletti with a titillating story that's mostly fiction.

A big TV exposé that creates a scandal for Annie and me would have pleased Rachael to no end. She didn't need encouragement when contacted about it, I have no doubt. She was insatiably insecure and vain. It was her job to be on camera. It was where she belonged, was most comfortable, and she had countless scores to settle.

"Elizabeth kept overhearing the words *explosive* and *award-winning*." Benton passes along what he's learned.

"Jesus," Annie replies. "I guess I didn't realize how much my own flesh and blood wanted me ruined. As if implying Kay and I were more than roommates would do it. I'd almost laugh if there were anything funny right now."

"Rachael wanted attention just as she always has," Benton says. "Especially of late, she wasn't feeling good about herself, and here you are on live TV every day. You're chummy with her estranged billionaire husband while Flagler ignores her. Rachael must have been seething and humiliated."

"And jealous," I add.

247

"I wonder if she was so brazen as to go on camera and openly talk about me?" Annie acts as if she doesn't care what people think of her.

But she does, and that's always been the problem. Maybe the so-called character-assassinating TV piece will get her over her fears. I suspect she'll find there's no monster hiding in the closet. Only herself.

"Or was she offering behind-the-scenes guidance?" Annie is saying. "You know, secretly steering the train she's trying to wreck as opposed to coming across as the treacherous person that she was?"

"We'll find out if there are any recordings." Benton rinses my plate. "I'm going to predict that Rachael is on camera plenty, narcissist that she was. But she won't be the one who's saying anything critical or disloyal about you or Kay or anyone else. She's the sort to set it up so others do her dirty work."

Benton pulls out a chair at the table, sitting down with us, getting around to the last item of business he mentioned earlier. He needs Annie's help.

The public statement he wants her to write should be from the heart. She's to thank people for their condolences about the tragic murder of her sister, and also of Wally Potter, whom she has known since childhood.

...Please be assured that we will bring swift and certain justice to those responsible, she composes with careful assistance, mostly from Benton. *We can't discuss the tips and leads the authorities are following, but even as we speak these terrorists are being hunted down...*

■ ■ ■

"Are you sure about this?" Annie asks as we proofread the tweet multiple times.

"Propaganda, the good kind," Benton replies. "We'll blast it from social media platforms, circulate it everywhere, let the games begin."

With that he kisses me good night, headed up to shower and bed. I open a kitchen cabinet, finding the bottle of Advil.

"It would be smart to take some prophylactically," I tell Annie.

"Doctor's orders, and I always follow them. Except all of your patients are dead, and that should be a warning." It's been her joke since we first met. "So I'm not sure why I listen to a damn thing you say. But I always have, Kay."

"I'm not sure why either, Annie." I get each of us another bottle of water. "Except I'm your friend and care about you. Always have, always will."

I shake out the ibuprofen gel caps for us as Merlin hops up on the fireplace hearth. Annie stares down at her drink, blinking back tears.

"You were kind and generous to me when others weren't." I don't need to remind her what it was like.

At the time there were very few women forensic pathologists. That was a man's game. People like me weren't supposed to involve ourselves in such messy horrors, and I wasn't always greeted warmly. I was an oddity, a bit of a freak, by the time I arrived at Georgetown. But Annie and her parents included me as if I were their own.

"Both of us have been around a lot of people who didn't want us to succeed," Annie says.

"Still are." I'm thinking of Elvin Reddy.

"It's the green-eyed monsters you've got to watch for," she agrees.

"Yes, and it's not a new subject. At times it feels like nothing changes much."

"I've decided that at the end of the day there are no new stories," Annie says. "Cain slaying Abel. Jacob cheating Esau. Joseph's brothers throwing him into a pit. Anybody looking at Rachael and me would never believe that she was the jealous one. Who would think she'd envied me instead of the other way around?"

"Your father set up a difficult dynamic from the start."

"Mostly it was difficult for my sister. Benton's right about the timing of the TV investigative piece. Or maybe we should just call it a hatchet job. Because you know it will be, Kay. You won't be happy, either."

"I probably won't watch it."

"Sticks and stones," she says.

"Except words do hurt, and both of us know it, Annie. We can't let sensational news get to us, the latest flash in the pan. We have to move on."

"Well, it's already bad enough." She takes another swallow of water. "I've been in the news for months. I can't even go out in public because the trial has made me so recognizable. My sister couldn't tolerate it if the spotlight was on me."

Rachael didn't get as much of their father's attention as she should have because Annie was born first. She was the only child for the better part of five years, the heir apparent. Except Annie wasn't a boy.

"What went on wasn't fair to Rachael," Annie says. "It really wasn't."

"It wasn't fair to either of you, let's be honest," I reply.

Rachael and I never met until several months ago, but I vividly recall Annie's comments while we lived together during law school. Annie's story was the incarnation of *The Ugly Duckling*, so sure she was of her inferiority because she didn't look like Rachael. Annie wasn't the son her father wanted, either. She's never seen herself as a swan.

"And then he gave me this." She holds up her left hand, showing me the posie ring he used to wear.

Her father gave it to her when he was on his deathbed. He slipped off the ring, placing it on Annie's finger while Rachael watched.

"She wanted his ring something awful, and that simple gesture turned her even more covetous and contemptuous. This was dramatically worsened when she realized the truth about the family money," Annie explains. "Which was all Rachael cared about, and in her mind the only reason to be a Chilton. She was waiting to inherit a fortune that she didn't know wasn't there anymore."

The upkeep of Chilton Farms is impossible, Annie confides to me what she hasn't before. There's little left from selling art and other valuables. Not spending a dime on security and improvements isn't only because she's an ardent conservationist. It's not that she's cheap, careless or peculiar.

"For all practical purposes, my parents died broke and in debt. When you met them, Kay, they were already well on their way," Annie says. "They didn't live like it but were running on fumes. Just the insurance policies on the artwork and antiques alone were untenable."

"It sounds like I should have been paying more than a dollar for rent every month," I reply.

"At that time, I didn't realize the truth."

"That both of us were poor?"

"You're right. I should have charged you more," she says, and we begin laughing at something so preposterous. "Both of us poor as a church mouse..."

Annie can barely talk. We're laughing so hard, tears are streaming down our faces, and then the kitchen's double doors swing open.

"Did I miss something good?" Lucy walks in, showered and in running clothes, her hair still damp. The fanny pack around her waist conceals one of her guns, no doubt, and she has on her AI-assisted sport glasses, the lenses clear and barely visible. Merlin saunters over to her purring and mewing.

"Depends on what you mean by good." Annie gives my niece a penetrating look. "If you're referring to the company, the food and drink, then it couldn't be better."

"I came to collect my two-timing cat." Lucy picks him up. "Have you been behaving yourself?" This to Merlin, and they're eye to eye. "Because Judge Chilton can lock up your furry ass in cat jail. She may not know you're on the Top Ten Most Wanted List for the Audubon Society."

"We're old friends now," Annie says.

"Your tweet's going crazy," Lucy tells her, and of course she would be involved in Benton's scheme. "It's getting picked up everywhere."

"Let's hope what we just did doesn't blow up in our faces," Annie says. "The problem is we're not sure what we're poking a stick at. And when you poke at something, it's going to poke back."

"Poke away, we're ready and waiting." Lucy is content to hang around chatting to Annie, and I get up from the table.

Nobody seems particularly distracted by my departure. Merlin doesn't follow me this time, and it's quiet inside Marino and Dorothy's room as I walk by. Benton is asleep, and he's left the bathroom light on for me. The door is open a crack, the mirror above the sink still fogged up a little from his shower.

I can smell his soap in the humid air, and hear his quiet breathing a few minutes later when I slide into bed. My smart ring complains about the late hour and my bad behavior. I take it off, placing it inside the bedside drawer next to the gun I rarely think to carry.

CHAPTER 28

The early morning sun glows around the edges of the closed window shades, and I reach for the other side of the bed. It's empty and cool beneath my hand, and I panic over the time. Sitting straight up, I find my phone. It's almost 6:15 and I need to get going.

"You're okay. We're not leaving for about an hour." Benton appears indistinctly in the dimness, and I smell the strong coffee he's carrying. "Everything's under control."

"I don't see how that's possible, and since when?" I reply. "The sooner we get to the office the better."

"We have a schedule, and it's not up to you." He kisses me as I take the steaming mug. "For once you're not in charge."

"Fine, then, and good, because I don't want to be." I sip the coffee, black and bold with a touch of agave nectar. "Not in charge of this fucking mess, no thank you. I'm more than happy to fly copilot or ride in the back, for that matter."

"You say that but never mean it." He sits down, and I lean against him.

He's shaved and dressed, and no doubt has been awake for a while. Opening the bedside drawer, I retrieve my smart ring, putting it on.

"Marino and Dorothy will be heading out in a few." Benton begins his morning update, telling me what's happened since I was last conscious. "Annie's having breakfast with Lucy. Cops are out front, all going according to plan for whatever that's worth."

"Having breakfast where?" I take a sip of coffee and unlock my phone.

"I get the impression they were up most of the night. Now they're having smoothies that Lucy's making in the blender."

"Where?" I again ask, but I already know.

"In her cottage."

"Let's just complicate things further." I begin glancing through messages.

As I suspected, my unhealthy living has prompted several auto-mated responses. These are programmed into software that Lucy is developing with the Secret Service, NASA, the U.S. Space Force, the CIA, the Defense Advanced Research Projects Agency (DARPA) and other government and military entities.

Knowing all this only makes it worse when my smart ring rats on me with a noisy, somewhat violent vibration reminiscent of a stinging insect. It's as if my niece is looking over my shoulder. When I read the message that lands on my phone, it may as well be from her.

You've been up 18 hours.

It's time to go to bed.

Your total sleep was only 2.1 hours, is the most recent alert.

I feel chastised, just like I always do when I'm reminded to stretch my legs, eat a snack or get some shut-eye.

"How about you?" I ask Benton if his ring ratted on him too. "Did you get sent to the principal's office?"

"I was better behaved than you," he says as we get up from the bed, and most days my meticulous husband wears a suit and tie.

One might assume he's a successful businessman or a lawyer. He could be a politician, and I often say he looks like an actor playing someone like himself, a smart and sexy Secret Agent Man. Even my sister will admit that he's *deliciously pretty.* He has *gorgeous taste except for his wife,* she likes to quip. But this morning he's dressed for getting dirty.

His cargo pants and polo shirt can be thrown into the wash later when we get home. His black tactical shoes are comfortable on hard floors, and easily disinfected. He picks up his gun, the pancake holster from the top of his dresser, sliding them into the back of his waistband. He tucks his badge wallet into a pocket.

"The threat level is higher than it was last night." He watches me pad barefoot to my closet. "Things could get violent, and Annie will have a police escort to court. As will we to your headquarters."

"Oh, God. More cop cars and flashing lights. Just when I thought life couldn't get any duller."

I try to figure out what to wear, deciding on khaki pants and a button-up white cotton shirt. I pick out a woven leather belt, and loafers that have a comfortable heel even as I'm mindful of my aching ankle.

"Protesters are already gathering at Courthouse Square, and around your building." Benton continues filling me in on what I've missed in the scant few hours I was asleep.

"If Elvin was unhappy before, he must be beside himself now," I reply.

"He's unhappy for a number of reasons. That's what you get when your reach exceeds your grasp."

"Maybe it will come out that our lovely health commissioner had something to do with the Hooke trial ending up here in Alexandria. That it was a political manipulation he's been involved in from the start," I continue while getting dressed. "No doubt for favors. Or promises of them to come."

255

"Hard to prove, and not everybody will care," Benton says.

"Our governor might." I think back to what Fruge mentioned about her friend, appropriately named Echo.

She's the chef in the governor's mansion and can be trusted to repeat certain information. I have a feeling that by now Roxane Dare is well aware of Elvin Reddy's Machiavellian machinations. She might even know that Bose Flagler is plotting and planning to defeat her in the next gubernatorial election.

"All I ask is that people see Maggie and Elvin for what they are. That's all I ever ask about anyone." I stand in front of the full-length mirror, tucking in my shirt.

"You'll be happy to know that we've limited who can be present this morning." Benton means the Secret Service has.

Few are on the list, he tells me. Elvin Reddy and Maggie Cutbush aren't among them. They've been told politely but in no uncertain terms to stay clear of my building and these cases. They are not to interfere with anything at all.

"It sounds like I'm without a secretary today." I'm relieved I won't have to deal with her, but it's a weird feeling. An odd disconnect like having a gangrenous limb lopped off. Or getting out of prison.

"You've been without a secretary ever since you took this job. What you inherited was the gargoyle left to guard Elvin's empire," Benton says.

"If that's what Maggie really is to him, I'd feel sorry for her if I were able," I reply.

"Time for breakfast, and then we're off to see the wizard," Benton says. "Per orders of the U.S. Secret Service, the medical examiner's investigation into the deaths of Rachael Stanwyck and Wally Potter will be witnessed. We'll be your partners in anything needed."

"Who's *we*?"

"I'll be your sidekick this morning."

"Who else is showing up?" I ask.

"I think I'm more than enough."

"You mean you're my sole chaperone."

"Your friendly witness and helper, at your service. Or your wizard behind the curtain, depending on how you feel about it."

"I don't mind unless you get out of line." I wrap my arms around him, and we hold each other.

■   ■   ■

I finish getting dressed, and the house is quiet when I join him in the kitchen a little later. The curtains are open. It's a beautiful day, the sun winking on the deep blue water of the Potomac showing through trees. Birds are busy at the feeder beyond the window, and I'm not hungover. But I've been better.

"Are Lucy and Annie still here?" I ask Benton as he cracks eggs into a bowl one-handed like a pro.

"No. I saw them on camera leaving a few minutes ago," he says. "Lucy walked Annie to her car. They were quite friendly with each other, and seemed none the worse for wear."

"I'm not sure how I feel about it." I tie on an apron.

"They have a lot in common. Life has dealt both of them some pretty hard blows, and I was glad to see them smiling and energetic despite everything."

"It's my turn." I take the whisk from him. "You're in charge of coffee and keeping me company. Fill me in on every detail of what to expect this morning."

Fruge and other police are out front waiting until we're ready to leave, and we'll be escorted like a head of state. Secret Service advance teams will be clearing the way along our route, and the idea of it is disheartening. I'd prefer walking out to the garage and driving myself to work or anywhere. I'd prefer a lot of things.

I whisk eggs vigorously, mixing in pinches of basil, sea salt and pepper. Benton sets a mug of coffee next to me, and carries his to the breakfast table where Annie and I were sitting not long ago. I slice open onion bagels and place them in the toaster oven as he tells me that unfolding developments are rapid and alarming.

"As of twenty minutes ago, a terrorist organization that calls itself The Republic has taken credit for yesterday's two homicides in Alexandria. They released a statement to the media, and wouldn't be doing that unless they want publicity.

"That means they'll strike again soon while the iron's hot," Benton says.

"Were you familiar with this particular group before?" I find the bottle of olive oil I want.

"No. That likely means they're probably in the early stages of organizing. Recruiting resources and people, getting money, weapons, training, and that doesn't happen overnight. We're hearing about them now because they're riding the publicity wave," Benton says, and I wonder if he regrets adding to it.

He used Annie to taunt the terrorists, to goad them into recklessness by making them fear they're about to get caught. But I have a feeling that may not be what's happening. Possibly, they've been emboldened and further motivated in a way that might end very badly.

"It sounds like Annie's statement that's all over the media simply gave these assholes what they want." I check the bagels.

"Most likely it will inspire them to do something," Benton says. "But it won't get them what they want. Not in the end."

"Are they also taking credit for yesterday's attempted attack on the president?"

"Nobody will take credit or even admit it was planned. Who wants to brag about a failure? But what happened at Belle Haven Market and Chilton Farms is another matter," Benton says. "The terrorists are claiming these were well-orchestrated hits. The message is that no one is safe."

"Do they mention microwave weapons?" Dripping olive oil into a pan, I turn up the flame.

"They didn't and may not realize we know about that." Benton sips his coffee, staring out the window at a bright red cardinal on the birdfeeder.

"Where are these horrible people located? Where do they train and experiment with their sadistic weapons?" I ask.

"We don't know, but most likely it's somewhere around here. That doesn't mean they don't have terrorist cells elsewhere."

"Such as the Eastern Shore where the Tupelos and Hookes are from. And all their scary-looking relatives and friends." I envision the protesters Benton and I passed while driving home late last night.

"Lucy's tracked the fifty-dollar gift card used at the gas pump yesterday," he says. "Stolen from a mom-and-pop pharmacy in Arlington, about ten miles from here. Someone hooded and wearing camouflage robbed the place at gunpoint last month, made the manager lie facedown on the floor. No one was hurt."

"What about cameras?"

"Not working. Apparently, there was a power surge right before the gunman entered the pharmacy at closing time when no one was around. Just the manager."

"I think we know what happened." I spread a thin layer of egg batter over the sizzling-hot pan. "And now robbery has escalated to murder."

"I expect activity within the next twenty-four hours, another violent event. Possibly more," Benton says. "We're taking every precaution."

The Alexandria police have set up a perimeter around my building and parking lot. Barricades are in place, and officers are in riot gear. Chatter on the Internet indicates a mob will storm my headquarters if Gilbert Hooke is found not guilty today as pundits and top legal analysts are predicting.

"Almost exclusively they're basing this on your court testimony," Benton says. "They don't see how a jury can convict him unless it completely disregards science."

"As if I wasn't popular enough." I turn off the toaster oven.

After eating and taking a few minutes to finish getting ready, we head out to Benton's car, driving off in a salvo of red and blue flashing lights. Three Alexandria cruisers are in front, three in back, and staggered at intervals are state troopers on motorcycles. The George Washington Masonic National Memorial rises nine stories from the top of a hill. Its soaring tower gleams white, seeming to follow us in the bright morning sunlight.

We move along at a steady pace, sirens whelping only occasionally, our convoy drawing intense stares. Cars pull over to let us pass as we drive northwest out of Old Town. My commute to work can take anywhere from twenty minutes to an hour depending on traffic. I have no doubt we'll make it there in record time this morning as we divert away from King Street.

We're avoiding the area around Courthouse Square, and my smart ring alerts me of a call coming in. It's Albert Allemand at the Smithsonian's Museum of Natural History.

"Benton and I are driving to my office, and you're on speaker-phone," I let him know as I answer. "What's going on?"

"Can you believe it? Already I'm getting squeezed," he says in his strong French accent.

He informs us that the Secret Service dropped off my insect and plant evidence several hours ago as planned. He arrived at his lab early to start preparing the samples, and all would be fine were it not for the interference he's getting.

"I don't want to be caught in the middle." Whatever has happened, Albert is indignant about it. "I want to answer the questions as honestly and accurately as possible. I don't want conflict or personal agendas. Like I'm always saying, I don't have a horse in the race."

"Caught in the middle of what?" I ask him.

"If you can't prove a microwave weapon was used it puts the Secret Service in a difficult position. Especially now that terrorists have just claimed responsibility for the homicides you're working."

It would seem the only evidence linking the alleged attempted attack on the president to the murders at Belle Haven Market and Chilton Farms is the unusual 2.305 GHz frequency picked up by signal analyzers. If that should prove to be a misdirect, a mistake, then there's a problem with the jurisdiction. Absent the signal, there was no attempted attack on the president at all, one might argue.

"And technically, I shouldn't be talking to the Secret Service because it's not their case," Albert is saying.

"Who told you this?" Benton asks.

"The FBI called a few minutes ago."

"Who with them?"

"A woman I don't know. I wrote it down . . . Let me make check . . . She was quite insistent . . . Special Agent Patty Mullet."

"She's with their joint counterterrorism task force," Benton replies, and saying he's not her fan is putting it mildly. "I knew her well when I worked for the FBI, and have dealt with her a number of times since."

"If we find traces of pesticides, we have a problem. This has been made clear." Albert summarizes what Special Agent Patty Mullet threatened.

CHAPTER 29

He explains that the FBI is waving the neurotoxin carbofuran as a battle flag. One of the deadliest pesticides on the planet, it's illegal in this country but still widely used, with ghastly consequences.

"The FBI has been investigating cases involving it, most of them in California," Albert says over speakerphone. "But recently around here there have been falcons, eagles, swans, owls poisoned. And family pets like dogs and cats have gotten hold of it. Ingesting as little as a quarter of a teaspoon can kill a large animal like a bear in minutes, and a human in less time than that."

Victims of the powerful pesticide become part of the *circle of death*, Albert explains as Benton follows our police escort. Animals and insects feed on a food source that has been laced with carbofuran, and within minutes go into convulsions and respiratory arrest. Those carcasses then are fed on, and the hideous ripple effect continues to spread.

"Such terrible chemicals are almost everywhere," Albert says. "They're carried on the wind and in rainwater, which is why colonies of honeybees and other wildlife are being wiped out. And I told the FBI agent that repeatedly. These sorts of things are ubiquitous and pervasive. One must consider many factors and be very careful before making determinations based on finding traces of them."

Evidence testing positive for pesticides and herbicides don't necessarily mean a microwave weapon wasn't used to commit a crime, Albert says he explained to Patty Mullet. But her mind was made up before she talked to him. She didn't care what he said, only that it reflected her wishes.

"She asked if I'd reviewed photos or videos that show the damage to flora and fauna at the entrance of Judge Chilton's property and also behind the house," Albert tells us. "And I replied but of course I have studied many such images carefully since I was first contacted."

The FBI wants him to submit a signed statement. He's supposed to say it's his expert opinion that the destroyed insects, animals and vegetation very likely are the result of an exposure to carbofuran or something similar. Benton's face is angry as he listens, watching his mirrors, the flashing police lights mesmerizing.

"Christ," he replies after Albert finishes telling us what Patty Mullet has coerced and tried to leverage. "She shouldn't have done that, and I hope you don't intend to listen to such bullshit. Because that's what it is, Albert. What was your response?"

"I told her the truth," he says. "That what I'm seeing is consistent with microwave attacks."

Depending on where they occur there will be dead bugs, birds, mice, other animals. The line of fire is visible through foliage no matter the time of year. Metal objects get magnetized. The wiring is fried by what's essentially a huge power surge. There are many signs if you know how to interpret them. Albert recites some of the very things we discussed during our last Doomsday Commission meeting at the Pentagon.

In one case he worked, the pet parrot in a metal cage was fine. But the houseplants were cooked, the power knocked out. The attack left a trail of parched foliage and dead insects outside the window the microwaves passed through. The government official inside at the time suffered cognitive impairment and hearing loss, and can't work anymore.

"The Russians are involved in a lot of this sort of nasty business, as you know," Albert says. "Most recently Saudi Arabia has been developing these types of weapons, and the Chinese have been perfecting them for decades. But it could be anyone, and no doubt they're getting better at it."

"If anybody wants to argue jurisdiction, I'm happy to set the record straight," Benton replies. "I'll deal directly with the FBI, you don't need to concern yourself about them."

Albert isn't to answer if Patty Mullet calls again. He's not to let her into his lab should she show up at the Smithsonian.

"I'm not really surprised," I say to Benton when we end the call. "I hate it when people go behind our backs, and that's what she just did. An end run."

"Her specialty." He keeps an exact distance between his car and the flashing police cruiser in front of us.

"At least you know what you're dealing with."

"Albert will find some kind of insecticide or chemical that has zero to do with anything," Benton predicts. "It's inevitable. This is just a slick trick, and Patty's full of them, always has been."

"You represent everything she's ever wanted that hasn't wanted her back," I reply.

She's his Elvin Reddy, and is just as blatant and obvious. Her ambition was to be a Secret Service investigator, but her application was rejected. The intelligence community didn't hire her, either. Eventually, Patty Mullet ended up with the FBI, where she washed out of the Behavioral Analysis Unit when Benton was the chief during our early days.

"She didn't make the cut, still wouldn't, and this is why," he says as drivers move to the side, our strobing convoy turning onto West Braddock Road.

As we get closer to my headquarters the scenery is less than charming, a lot of distribution and fulfillment centers, tow lots and cemeteries. Shady Acres Funeral and Cremation Services is my nearest neighbor, and they must have Maggie's cell phone number. The long-winded text she's just now sent claims that they keep calling her.

They're upset about the protesters around my fenced-in parking lot, my exiled secretary has the nerve to pass along. I'm being asked to keep the noise down, she writes in her text. I'm sure it gives her pleasure to alert me of a problem while she's been ordered to stay away from my building. I can imagine her on the phone with Elvin, and what they must be saying and conniving.

"A service is about to start in the cemetery across the street." I tell Benton what Maggie has passed along and possibly instigated. "Maybe the protesters marching around my headquarters could be humane enough to stop for an hour. What am I supposed to do? Walk out there and ask them nicely?"

"She's rubbing it in that she's been left out in the cold," he replies. "She's letting you know that in return so are you. You're on your own without her to help."

"As if she's ever been any help at all," I reply.

We're maybe a minute from my headquarters, passing an oil company, warehouses and a recycling center. I can hear the protesters before the Northern Virginia government center is in sight. We share the location with the Departments of Health, Public Safety and Emergency Medical Services, and the Bureau of Vital Records, among other state entities focused on life and death.

All of them are acres away from my building, and it's by design. Not only do fences make good neighbors, but in this instance so does distance. The more the better. I'm used to nobody wanting to be around us. I wouldn't want to be either, protesters or not.

"...JUSTICE FOR APRIL...!"

"SELLOUT...!"

"FAKE NEWS...!"

They shout to the beating of wooden spoons and drumsticks against metal pans and five-gallon plastic drums. They're crowded outside the police line, and it's the same scary-looking bunch as before. Only in recent days it's been maybe a dozen of them marching, verbally abusing those driving in and out, including Marino and me.

Now it's more like three times that many, mostly men. I don't like it that a number of them wear guns on their hips and have assault rifles on slings. An older woman has a bandana tied around her long gray hair, and carries a pump shotgun. She's accompanied by a young man similarly armed and hateful.

The police don't let anybody close as we approach the entrance, and I can tell the protesters don't recognize the electric car or its driver. But that doesn't stop them from yelling at us. Our escorts peel off, and we're waved through the security gate, nothing more than a wooden arm that goes up and down. It closes behind us, protesters shouting slurs and insults.

■　　■　　■

The medical examiner's northern district headquarters and forensic labs are in the four-story tan brick building ahead. A tall smokestack rises above the flat roof, and I always know from a distance when our anatomical division's oven is running. It isn't, thank God. This would be a bad day to incinerate dead bodies, most of them returned to us from medical schools. We need no other visuals that are sensational and morbid.

The state and U.S. flags flap and clank against metal poles, and there are planted trees on islands and along the aggregate concrete sidewalk. Our glass front door with its painted seal of Virginia has been locked for years, and is mostly accessed by employees.

"Let's hope this doesn't go on much longer," I say to Benton as the noise of the protestors follows us like the roar of a tidal wave about to crash.

"...JUSTICE FOR APRIL!"

"JUSTICE FOR APRIL!"

"JUSTICE FOR APRIL...!" Over and over again.

My parking lot is full, only the visitor's spaces empty, and I see that Marino is here. His truck is in its usual spot near where Maggie parks. But her old silver Volvo is missing. Benton stops in front of the massive steel bay door, not having a remote for it because he doesn't work here. Of course, mine is at home inside my car.

"I'll take care of it." He releases his seat belt.

"No. It's better if I do." I'm opening my door, stepping out before he gets the chance.

Depending on who's checking the security cameras, my Secret Service agent husband might not be recognized. Since we moved here, he's been to my office but a few times. His car won't be familiar to most people, and I head to the squawk box as the agitators spot me.

"SELLOUT! SELLOUT! SELLOUT...!" They turn up the volume, chanting through bullhorns while beating their pans and plastic drums frantically.

I've never gotten used to ugly name-calling and being accused of horrendous things I would never dream of doing. I'm unaccustomed to people screaming that I belong in jail or worse, and I push the intercom button. Instantly the loud electric motor engages. The rust-stained heavy metal door begins to clank and creak as it's slowly rolled up by chains and pulleys.

"...SELLOUT! SELLOUT! SELLOUT...!"

I hurry back inside Benton's car as the vehicle bay's square opening widens, the technology old, the door slow. Now and then it goes off track, getting stuck on its way open or shut. This would be an unfortunate moment for that.

"You have to wait until it's done or the safety mechanism will halt it," I remind Benton as the din of the hostile crowd crescendos.

"A good thing nobody's shooting at us," he says as the door screeches and shudders, taking forever.

My building dates back to the 1980s, and is tired. Things are broken that don't get fixed, and finding what we need is a constant scavenger hunt. What Fabian gripes about is true. I'm not above begging area hospitals, medical facilities and funeral homes for supplies they don't want. I'm resourceful where I shop. But there's only so much I can do on a bare-bones budget.

As challenging as the job is under normal circumstances, after twenty years of Elvin Reddy, we're barely managing. He never fought for anything important, most of all his people. We're short scientists, clerical staff and forensic pathologists. Equipment is old, and much needs to be replaced and added.

When I was the first woman chief medical examiner of Virginia before moving on many years ago, Elvin was a shadow figure, a nuisance. He had no power. He hadn't ruined anything yet, and wouldn't for a while. Our statewide medical examiner system is the one of the oldest and most established in the United States. It used to be the gold standard, and I intend to restore what he's tried to destroy.

The bay door has stopped, and Benton drives inside a cavernous windowless space about the size of an aircraft hangar. The concrete walls and floor are sealed with beige epoxy that can be disinfected and hosed off easily. There are storage areas with pallets of supplies such as PPE and body pouches, and drums of disinfectant and dangerous chemicals like formaldehyde and bleach.

Parked out of the way are a Zodiac boat and our crime scene mobile unit, old and in need of significant upgrades. In the very back is the forensic bay where we can enclose large objects such as vehicles inside tents for superglue fuming and other evidence collection. Benton parks off to the side near Fabian's 1970s El Camino. *Sick*, as he describes it, black with red stripes and rims.

At the top of the ramp, I unlock the pedestrian door leading inside. We enter the brightly lit receiving area where the dead are admitted to our hopeless medical clinic. Across from the floor scale are massive stainless steel coolers and freezers. Next to them is the security office, and Wyatt Earle is at his desk behind a bulletproof glass window that has a drawer and a speaker hole.

In his sixties, wearing a khaki uniform with brown pocket flaps, he isn't a sworn officer. He's what Marino rudely calls a rental cop. Unarmed, Wyatt can't arrest anyone, and couldn't do much if we were under siege. He doesn't like the morgue, and when I started here I felt he liked me less. But we're growing on each other. We have an understanding.

"Good morning, Wyatt," I greet him.

He's eating a Bojangles steak biscuit and hash browns, his attention on the security monitors mounted on the cinder block wall above his desk.

"I don't think there's much good about it, Chief." He dabs his mouth with a napkin. "All those protesters out there?" Reaching for his coffee. "If we didn't have a lot of police we'd be in big trouble."

I introduce him to Benton because they've not met, and the cooler door opens with a loud rush of refrigerated air. Fabian emerges from a fog of foul condensation, rolling out a gurney with a pouched body on top. He's typically dramatic in black scrubs, his long hair tucked up in a black surgical cap that has blue skulls on it.

"Thanks for staying over last night," I say to him. "I hope you got some rest."

"Not much, but I'm ready with bells on," he replies cheerily, vibrating with excitement. "Can you believe what's going on out there?" He shoves the cooler door shut.

"It's not a good thing," Wyatt says, and he and Fabian aren't compatible. "I know you like being on the news, but maybe the rest of us like it quiet."

"My phone's blowing up!" Fabian is almost breathless. "It's unbelievable! I've got TV producers calling me. Even a reality show! *Death Quest* is the working title, and they'd like to follow me around on the job. But I said I wasn't sure that would be allowed."

"It wouldn't," I reply. "Who have you got here?" I look at the pouched body he's ferrying somewhere.

"A pickup," he says. "The jogger hit by a car from the other day."

Fabian informs Benton and me that Marino is upstairs in the fingerprint lab with examiner Andy Patient. They're trying to figure out the best way to deal with the duct tape, and it's not rocket science, Fabian informs Benton and me.

"Doug just gets so nervous. And of course, with all that's going on? My God, can you believe how many people are out there with guns?" Fabian gushes while Wyatt eats his breakfast behind glass. "I don't know how anyone expects me to get home eventually while these violent thugs are marching around."

Not even fifteen minutes ago there were news choppers hovering over our building. He continues painting a scene that would be routine if he had his way about it.

"Apparently a fight broke out in front of the courthouse. I just saw it on Instagram," Fabian says. "Explaining where the choppers suddenly buzzed off to, but they'll be back, I'm betting."

"Don't expect anything to get calmer or better throughout the day," Benton informs everyone. "Especially when the Hooke case goes to the jury, we can expect a lot of trouble."

"Have we had any uninvited visitors or attempts?" I ask Wyatt as he keeps an eye on the security monitors.

"Not so far," he says. "Nobody's here you don't know about, Chief."

"Some FBI agent called investigations, leaving a message," Fabian tells us.

"Saying what?" Benton asks.

"That she'd call back."

"Her name?" he asks, and I have a feeling I know.

"I'd have to pull it up on my computer," Fabian says. "Patti... hmmmm? I keep thinking Patti LuPone, but that's not it. You know how something gets stuck in your head...?"

"FBI Special Agent Patty Mullet," Benton replies.

"That's it. She's pretty full of herself. Bossy, treating me like the help. I didn't like her worth shit."

CHAPTER 30

Outside the morgue's security window, the big black logbook is anchored by a thin metal chain to the chipped Formica ledge. Attached to cotton twine is a ballpoint pen. Nearby is a dispenser of hand sanitizer, boxes of surgical face masks and gloves.

Since the medical examiner system in Virginia began, we've always kept a handwritten record of pickups and deliveries, and it's my habit to check the entries. I do it first thing when I get here, and open the big book to the last filled-in page. I glance at cases that have come in or been released as Benton continues explaining who's calling the shots.

"I'll deal with Patty Mullet." He directs this at Wyatt, and also at Fabian. "No visitors without my approval. I don't care who it is. No one unauthorized is allowed inside the building right now without my saying it's okay."

"What's been done with my case?" I ask about Rachael Stanwyck.

"She's in the CT scanner," Fabian says.

"She's still inside her pouch, I'm hoping?"

"I said it couldn't be opened except by you."

"Good. Her body can stay in the CT room while Benton and I get changed," I reply. "I'll roll her to my station when we're ready."

"I've got it set up, and Doctor Schlaefer's already in the decomp room," Fabian replies. "Am I helping you and him? One or both?"

"No going back and forth because we must be exquisitely careful about cross-contamination," I remind him. "You can help only one of us, so you stick with Doctor Schlaefer. I'll be fine on my own, but I'm going to need Jane Slipper to do me a favor."

She's my histologist. I could use three of them, but Elvin got rid of the other positions. Jane is all I've got, and she won't be happy paying a visit to the morgue. She may work with dead human tissue daily, but that doesn't mean she's a fan of autopsies or even the idea of them. She doesn't want to put a face on a case, and the less she needs to know the better.

"Time is of the essence, and slides need to be prepared as quickly as possible. She's going to have to pick up the sample herself and get started while I'm still doing the autopsy," I explain to Fabian. "I'll let her know when I'm opening the skull, and she can come downstairs."

"Uh-oh, she'll hate that," he says. "She's all right with pieces and parts. She just doesn't want to see where they came from. Kind of like me not wanting to see the lobster before it's dropped into the pot of—"

"I know Jane won't like it and I'm sorry." I don't want to hear his analogies at the moment. "We'll need to set up a secure video conference so Doug and I can communicate remotely."

"Off to take care of it," Fabian says, and Benton and I head to the locker room.

We follow the white-tiled corridor, and inevitably there are blood drips and smears from leaky body bags. There's always an abandoned gurney or two with pouches folded on top. The walls are an insipid pale green, the fluorescent lighting garish, strips of flypaper hanging from the ceiling. We near the CT suite, and through the observation window radiologist Johnny Hahn is sitting at his console, surrounded by an array of video displays, talking on his phone.

On the other side of leaded glass is Rachael Stanwyck's pouched body on the tray inside the CT scanner's wide bore. The next room is where we do full-body x-rays, and the door is shut, the lights out. After that is the evidence room where bloody clothing hangs in glass drying chambers. On an examination table covered by white butcher paper are bloody shattered glasses, keys, a wallet, an asthma inhaler from a recent shooting.

Outside the decomp room the red light warns not to enter, and most people wouldn't want to anyway. When bodies are badly decomposed, contaminated, in the grimmest of shape, this is where we work on them. There's no observation window for good reason, and it takes a lot of self-control for me not to walk in and check on Doug Schlaefer. But I don't.

Next is our small anthropology lab where skeletal remains are laid out like a puzzle, and there's nothing much sadder than dying alone and unknown. In back is a storage area with more than eighty boxes of bones going back many decades. During his time as chief, my predecessor greatly added to our skeleton closet. If the case wasn't easy or politically to his advantage, Elvin didn't care.

Benton and I have reached the autopsy suite, and through closed doors I can hear people working inside. I know from glancing at the morgue log that we have six cases so far this morning, including Rachael and Wally. In addition are a motor vehicle accident, and two victims from a suspected murder-suicide by shotgun. Next is the locker room, and using my elbow, I push a hands-free button on the wall.

Our changing area is functional and simple, just three white porcelain sinks, three showers with flimsy white plastic curtains and shelves of PPE, the air heavy with the cloying odor of disinfectant. Filling a wall are steel lockers painted institutional green and numbered. The chief's is "1," as you'd expect. I place my briefcase inside, and the door banging shut sounds like school.

On a normal day, I would lock my belongings and change my clothes upstairs in my office's private bathroom. But there's no time for that. Benton and I put on coveralls, the rustle of Tyvek quiet, the smell of industrial deodorizer strong. Covering our shoes with booties, we won't bother with gloves, safety glasses and hoods quite yet.

■ ■ ■

Johnny Hahn sits at his console surrounded by images of Rachael's brain. In his thirties, he's attractive in an unusual way with his closely spaced eyes, his nose pointed like a gunsight.

Brought up in Colorado, he's a black diamond skier, and a gaming enthusiast. Were it not for his insatiable curiosity and love of adrenaline, I couldn't have poached him from an area hospital with the promise of a forensic radiology fellowship. He's overqualified, and I can't pay him nearly enough.

"I'm making a house call." It's my way of wishing Johnny a good morning, and I introduce him to Benton. "We're here to pick up Rachael Stanwyck's body ourselves."

I explain that the Secret Service is in charge of her investigation, and also of Wally Potter's.

"Woohoo, that sounds big and bad," Johnny says.

Behind him, a wall-mounted flat-screen TV is playing breaking news on CNN with the sound muted. Bose Flagler is making his closing argument, and then Sal Gallo will follow. Then the case will go to the jury, and the protests are bigger and more agitated. Additional police are being called in from neighboring counties, and helicopter news images show the hostile mob, the cops in riot gear.

LIVID

"I thought I'd see what you've got before we take her away." I'm asking Johnny what he's found before I roll away Rachael's body.

"For sure you'll be interested in this." He directs our attention to CT images that show a linear skull fracture of the parietal occipital bone.

Rachael Stanwyck suffered a serious head injury right before she died. Johnny points to images that show the contusion of the brain's right frontal lobe.

"A classic contrecoup injury. The blow would have knocked her out if she wasn't already unconscious," I reply. "But it's not what killed her."

Blood shows up on CT as a dense dark area, and there's not much of it. Most likely Rachael fell, striking the left side of her head on the marble kitchen floor. Probably this occurred while she was bombarded with microwave radiation. The small amount of hemorrhage indicates she was alive only briefly as her temperature soared beyond survivable.

"When I checked her at the scene," I explain, "I found no evidence of injury to her scalp. It's not lacerated, but I've seen that before when people fall. I'll know more when I can take a better look."

Benton and I put on gloves, safety glasses and hoods. I open the door that connects the control and scanner rooms, and we lift the pouched body onto its gurney. Then we're pushing it along the corridor, and he opens the double doors of the autopsy suite. Water drums loudly into deep sinks, and steel rasps against a whetstone as a technician sharpens a knife.

Medical examiners and their assistants are busy at workstations where x-ray and CT images are displayed on video screens. The floor is beige tile, the cinder block walls the same ugly green as the hallways.

Everything else is metal or glass, the high ceiling bare except for electrical cord reels and light panels. There's nothing to absorb sound, the large open work area an acoustical nightmare.

Fabian has rock and roll playing that I can barely hear above a din that outsiders would find jarring. There's nothing gentle about the morgue. Often it sounds more like an automotive body shop than a medical facility or laboratory. Voices are calling out weights, measurements and other information, the noise blending into tiresome nerve-jangling static.

It's always cold in here even when it isn't, and the energy is bad despite one's best intentions and efforts. People seldom laugh. Or they laugh too much. We don't cry when anyone's looking. It's an unspoken code to keep personal feelings to ourselves. We try not to lose our tempers, but it happens, and nothing smells pleasant.

My workstation is the first one, and Fabian has surrounded it in freestanding privacy partitions, the sort used between hospital beds. We do this when cases are unusually sensitive. Celebrities and other deaths that are sensational news, for example, and most of all if it's someone we know. The partitions can't eliminate the background noise, but they'll help considerably.

This is important since we'll be connected by a secure video link to a camera inside the decomp room. We must have the ability to communicate clearly. Doug and I have to talk to each other without my being present. We need to be sure about what we're doing, no mistakes allowed. Benton moves a partition out of the way.

I park the gurney next to the autopsy table where I always work, one of six. Old-style, they're L-shaped and permanently attached to pedestals in the floor. A monitor is set up on a surgical cart that I roll closer.

"Before we do anything else I need to see what's happening inside the decomp room," I tell Benton. "We should be linked."

Rolling the video cart closer, he turns on the camera and unmutes the speakers. The display blinks on to the sound of paper rattling loudly. The screen fills with Marino's big gloved hands removing the bag that covers Wally Potter's head.

"Hello, hello?" I let everyone know we're connected. "Marino? I believe that's you and your tattoos I'm seeing."

"I'm in here with Doug and Andy." Marino tilts the screen so I can see my deputy chief and the fingerprints examiner.

"I'm here too." Fabian looms into view, fluttering his black-gloved fingers.

He's holding a clipboard, a camera, everyone suited up in PPE. They're circled around Wally Potter's body on the table, a surgical light shining on his gaping cut throat, dryer and a darker red than it was last night. He hasn't been undressed yet, and won't be until the duct tape can be dealt with.

The single strip covering his mouth is approximately eight inches long. It doesn't overlap, and hasn't been wrapped all the way around the head as I often see. We need to remove the tape without ruining possible evidence on the top layer or adhesive backing.

"Usually the underside of the tape is going to be wet from saliva and purge fluid, and that will make it easier to remove," I explain. "It's also helpful that he's been in the cooler all night. The colder the adhesive, the less sticky."

"That's what I'm hoping for, too," Andy Patient says, balding and stooped, his blue eyes faded as he peers at me in the monitor. "The ultimate goal will be to superglue all of the duct tape for prints."

"That, swabbing for DNA, checking for any trace evidence,"

Doug says. "And the question is the best order so we don't fuck up anything."

"Which is why we're talking about it first," I agree. "For now, we're going to focus on removing the tape from his mouth. We're going to peel it off very carefully."

"We could use liquid nitrogen first to get it really good and cold," Andy considers.

"I'm hopeful that won't be necessary," I reply, and were I in the room with them right now, what we're discussing would have happened already.

It's not that hard if you've done this a few times and aren't overly cautious, losing sight of common sense. But I need to stay put. And Doug needs to learn. Maybe so do I when it comes to trusting people again, letting them do their jobs, and believing they can.

"…That's what we'll do with the tape around his wrists and ankles," Andy is explaining. "We'll cut it off and freeze it. Then we can peel it apart."

"One thing at a time. Let's just try getting a purchase on a corner of the tape over his mouth and see what happens," I suggest to Doug.

"It's harder with gloves on." His face is tense.

"Pinch the tape between your thumb and index fingertips, and yes, it might stick to your glove, but that's okay as long as you don't start touching other areas of the tape. Begin pulling very gently and slowly," I tell him.

"Okay, total transparency? This is my first duct tape case," Doug confesses.

"I know I feel better," Marino says.

I watch the monitor as Doug works off the duct tape, part of Wally's lips showing.

"Looking good," I encourage.

"It's coming...," Doug says, as if we're in the same room together. "It's not ripping the skin, abrading it or anything..." He keeps easing off the tape. "Soooo far, soooo good...There we go...! Got it, thank you, God!"

He holds up the strip for all to see.

"Good job, I can stop holding my breath," Marino says.

"I think you can handle it without me from this point on," I let Doug know, and Benton turns off the monitor.

CHAPTER 31

I unzip Rachael's black pouch, her body mummy-like in layers of white paper sheets. She's fully rigorous now, stiff as a board as they say, and refrigerated cold. She dully thuds against steel as I pull her onto the table. I cut through the paper with scissors, spreading the sheets open, sliding them out from under her.

"If you don't mind folding them, placing them inside a plastic bag," I say to Benton. "We'll send it up to trace evidence along with the bags from her hands and feet, her clothing and anything else that should be checked."

Palpating the injured side of her head, I can't feel anything significant. She didn't survive long enough to mount much of a tissue response, and clicking on the surgical lamp, I pick up a scalpel. I snap in a new blade, and shave away some of Rachael's lovely long hair, black as volcanic glass.

"You can barely see the contusion." I direct the light at a dusky red area of her scalp about the size of a silver dollar.

Benton looks on as I make tiny cuts, verifying that the discoloration is from blood seeping into tissue after her skull was fractured.

"She definitely has a bruise," I tell him. "And she didn't survive long, possibly a few minutes."

"Not too many things make you drop like a shot." He leans closer, staring at the patch of shaved scalp that I'm glad Rachael can't see.

"The microwave energy she was hit with must be very powerful," I reply. "I suspect she was affected so quickly that she didn't have time to think about finding a chair. Or even sitting down on the floor. No doubt she was in massive pain, ripping off her jewelry, confused and terrified as she lost consciousness."

"That's not the way I want to go." Benton begins selecting the appropriate forms and body diagrams from a wall of cubbyholes.

He's been inside many autopsy rooms during his career, not all of them mine or nearly as nice, which isn't saying much. But he's not squeamish. He more than gets the point, and is keenly aware of what my work involves. We've been a team since the beginning of our time together, having an easy rhythm that isn't deliberate or conscious. We understand each other, and don't care who's right as long as somebody is.

He clamps the necessary paperwork into one of our Masonite clipboards. Each has MORGUE gigantically written on it in permanent marker. Fabian makes sure of it lest anyone think of pinching something. String tied to the hole in the metal clamp is attached to a grease pencil that works fine on damp or gory paper.

Turning my attention to the paper bags and their rubber bands, I uncover Rachael's hands. Then her feet, and I focus on what's all over the bottom of her expensive sneakers.

"I wonder when she was outside," I say to Benton as he takes photographs. "And if it was at some point yesterday, because that's my suspicion."

"Based on the microwave signals Lucy and Tron picked up we're assuming Rachael was attacked between three-forty and four P.M.," he says. "Obviously, if she went out it was before that. And it wasn't a location she entered into the GPS, assuming she drove somewhere."

"She claimed she was working from home yesterday, or that's the story we've been given," I reply. "The way she was dressed, the absence of makeup and perfume are consistent with her being low-key and alone."

I point out that Rachael wasn't wearing an expensive timepiece or much jewelry, nothing that might make you think she was meeting someone. But that doesn't mean she never left the house.

"It doesn't mean she didn't leave Chilton Farms, and I'm thinking she did." I pick up a pair of fine-point forceps.

I scrape the dark purplish substance off the bottom of one of her sneakers and onto a piece of sterile blotting paper. Under the magnifier light, the bits of crushed vegetation are tacky with sap. Benton and I rinsed the treads of our shoes last night so we didn't track similar plant debris into his car. But that wasn't at Chilton Farms. It was at Belle Haven Market.

Jacaranda trees are native to Virginia. Benton and I have plenty of them on our property, and this year the season is late, the trees still in full blossom. They grow wild in meadows and along roadsides, and are popular in landscaping. But they shed a lot, and it's no wonder Wally kept his prize antique Chevy wagon protected by a carport. Otherwise, the paint would have been ruined eventually.

"There's not a single jacaranda tree at Chilton Farms," I tell Benton as we look through the magnifier together. "There hasn't been for decades. I know it for a fact."

"And you're sure what we're looking at isn't lilacs, maybe something else?" My husband may be a lot of things, but a gardener isn't one of them.

"What I'm seeing is more purplish-lavender," I explain as I seal plant debris in a paper envelope that I initial and label. "Annie's property has a lot of flowering trees but no jacarandas. That's what I believe this is from. We'll get it confirmed, but I have very little doubt."

When I first visited Chilton Farms during law school there was a jacaranda disease outbreak in Northern Virginia. I remember how upset Annie was when the family's glorious trees had to be dug up and burned.

"I've been to Chilton Farms enough to be certain," I add. "And I promise there's not a jacaranda tree to be found."

I think of the dense copses of them at Belle Haven Market. I ask Benton if the Secret Service has had any luck with Rachael's phone or other electronic devices.

"Maybe there are text messages that might tell us how she spent the day. If she went somewhere, and who she might have been in touch with before she was killed," I suggest.

"The short answer is no, we don't have her electronic devices," Benton says. "You might say we're being good partners and waiting our turn."

The CIA collected Rachael's computer, phone, pager, tablet, hotspot, any electronics in her possession. She was their employee. No doubt they showed up at the scene and spirited away such things, explaining why I didn't see them when Marino and I arrived. That's not what Benton says. But it's what he's telling me.

"Bottom line, I'm not going to have a clue what's on any of those devices for a while, if ever," I assume.

"That's right. Most details you're not going to know," Benton replies as I begin undressing the body. "But this much I can tell you from phone records so far. She tried to call Flagler several times yesterday, no big surprise. She wished him luck in court, said she loved him, and he didn't call her back. If she went somewhere, there's no reference."

As he's telling me all this it's as if Rachael is listening and fighting me like mad. She stubbornly forces me to break the rigor mortis in her arms or I can't manipulate them. She's unyielding as I work off her warm-up suit, her lingerie. Then she's naked on my table, and I fold her clothing, placing it and her shoes inside paper bags while Benton continues making notes and taking pictures.

■ ■ ■

Long-legged and big-bosomed, Rachael died in perfect shape, it seems, except for her curiously bloated belly. I don't notice tattoos or body piercings, no scars from past injuries or surgeries.

I see no signs of cosmetic procedures such as injectable fillers. She had the sort of sensuous beauty that would stop traffic, as the cliché goes, and she came by it naturally. Maybe she touched up her hair and availed herself of Botox, but that was about the extent of it, I have a feeling. Except for her laxatives and other compulsions, she seemed to have everything she wanted effortlessly.

The overhead surgical lamp shines harshly on her dead face, her eyes and lips barely parted, dry and darkened. I ironically think of the countless times I've heard her referred to as *drop-dead gorgeous*. Annie's been saying it ever since I can remember. I look at every inch of the body, making sure I see nothing out of the ordinary. I find no other injuries except for the burns.

I show Benton the ones around her neck, on her earlobes, and a finger, caused by her jewelry heating up. I check under her breasts, finding ones caused by the underwire in her sports bra. I measure the distance between the tiny red burns, and it's approximately five inches.

"Two-point-three-oh-five gigahertz, or a little more than five inches," I tell Benton as he takes pictures. "That's the approximate distance between the repeating wave peaks."

"What we're seeing wasn't caused by a pesticide," he replies.

"Definitely something conductive that heated up anything metal she had on."

I take off my gloves. On the cinder block wall inside my partitioned work area is an old-fashioned push-button phone. Fabian's emphatic sign next to it reads:

CLEAN HANDS ONLY!!

I dial the extension for the histology lab, and Jane Slipper doesn't sound eager when she answers. I tell her the CT scan shows that Rachael Stanwyck has a traumatic brain injury.

"That of course will be apparent on gross examination once I open her skull," I explain. "But of more interest are any changes in neural cells, signs of degeneration and necrosis that might be heat-related."

"Are you thinking she died from hyperthermia?" Jane puzzles over speakerphone in her blunted Midwest accent. "Maybe a heatstroke or something? And she passed out, hitting her head?"

"Not exactly, and I don't think so. We're looking for evidence of damage such as lesions from radiant exposure," I reply. "Possible thermal cauterization of superficial blood vessels."

"That sounds pretty awful. Like what we see in fire deaths."

"Truth is, Jane, I don't know what we might expect to see," I explain. "What we're dealing with is something we don't fully understand."

I don't mention microwaves, and she knows better than to ask invasive questions. She has no interest unless it's related to whatever it is I'm looking for in a given case, and which histological stains make the most sense. We decide the areas of the brain I should remove blocks of tissue from, and that I'll include a section of the spinal cord.

"I assume Fabian mentioned that I need you to stop by the autopsy suite to pick up the sections." I give my histologist the bad news she's been expecting. "I should be ready for you in about fifteen minutes."

"I'd rather not." Jane Slipper says it flatly.

"I can't bring anything to you for quite a while. It could be hours before I can get to your lab, and we need to get started," I reply over the "clean hands only" wall phone inside my partitioned workstation. "Cover up in PPE, and I don't want you anywhere near my table."

"I'd really rather not come inside, especially on a busy morning like this," she says, and any morning is too busy.

There's never an occasion when Jane would choose to step foot in the morgue. She stays away from the vehicle bay. She has no idea what our subterranean anatomical division looks like. If she did she'd never come back to her lab filled with paraffin shavings, and various stains with exotic names like Congo red, Prussian blue and Bodian silver.

"When we're ready, Benton Wesley will meet you outside the door with the samples." I suggest a compromise. "You two can exchange the appropriate paperwork."

I explain who he is, adding that he also happens to be my husband. Then I hang up, returning to the table. Benton has his gloves off, and I catch a glint of quiet anger behind his safety glasses. He's placed an antimicrobial protective plastic film over his phone, and is scrolling through messages.

"Now what?" I ask him.

"It's not a surprise, and was just a matter of time," he says. "But the fucking Bureau didn't need to do it now."

He explains that the FBI just issued a press release that they've officially reopened the investigation into the Colonial Parkway murders from twenty-two years ago. The medical examiner's role in particular is in question because of accusations raised during the Gilbert Hooke trial about Bailey Carter's competence.

"What a coincidence." I walk over to glass-doored wall cabinets.

"Patty Mullet's behind this, it's her doing and her M.O.," Benton says. "It's her way of letting me know who's got the power. In the process she's also giving bad people ideas, whether it's about lawsuits they might file or who they might punish. Publicity always cuts both ways, and I wouldn't have done what she just did."

I don't mention that Benton doesn't mind press statements as long as it's his people making them. All the same, the news is disappointing. It bodes poorly for the future when case after case falls under scrutiny, as most assuredly will happen. I worry there will be no end to it.

"Bailey screwed up April Tupelo's autopsy about as badly as anyone could, because there was something seriously wrong with him by then," I reply. "But it's ridiculous to think he did the same thing in the Parkway investigation, and I should know. I was the chief. I showed up and was hands on for all of it."

"I know that all too well, and can testify as much," Benton says, because he was there working the serial murders with me.

Opening a cabinet, I pull out a white box, a physical evidence recovery kit, or PERK, as we call it. Inside is a prepackaged collection of items used to examine patients for evidence of sexual assault. I have no reason to think Rachael was raped or that it was attempted. It's unlikely she had physical contact with her killer, but it would be negligent not to check.

Opening the PERK, I pull out two black plastic combs, the cheap kind we were given when school pictures were taken. I arrange test tubes, swabs, glass slides and other items on a clean sheet as Benton continues giving me the latest news updates. He says that Channel 5 is running the Annie Chilton special tonight, and ads for it are on the Internet. The sensational story promises to be the very publicity I avoid like the plague.

"Don't let it get to you, Kay," Benton says.

"I'm going to ignore it just like I always do," I reply, taking pubic hair combings. "I hope Annie will be all right."

I pluck out head hair samples. I swab every orifice. If Rachael hasn't suffered enough indignity, I scrape under her perfectly manicured fingernails. I cut them to the quick, collecting them in an envelope, not expecting to discover anything significant. I doubt she scratched anyone. There's no reason to think she struggled with her killer. Or touched him.

Picking up the scalpel, I cover Rachael's face with a towel, an old habit going back to my earliest years of training. When the patient is someone familiar, it's a sign of respect if nothing else. It's my way of apologizing as I commit all sorts of outrages in the name of justice and medical science.

CHAPTER 32

I begin the Y-incision, slicing down from each clavicle, detouring around the navel. Reflecting back the skin, I retrieve stainless steel shears from the surgical cart. Benton takes photographs as I snap through ribs, removing the breastplate of them.

Placing the bloc of organs on a cutting board, I isolate the distended stomach. That's the first nagging question I intend to answer, and I retrieve a pair of surgical scissors.

"I think we might know what Rachael did yesterday." I empty her gastric contents into a carton. "I'll confirm but I'm fairly confident she wasn't pregnant."

The food barely began to digest, and there's a lot of it, some eight hundred grams, or almost a quart. Rachael drove to Belle Haven Market yesterday and had the lunch special. She might have had more than one of the roast beef and chutney sandwiches and cups of gazpacho. I recall what Benton told me about the cash register receipt under the drawer partition.

"Maybe you took a picture of it?" I ask him, and he sets down the clipboard. "I'd like to see if we can tell when she might have come in and bought at least one special. Probably more. And who knows what else, and not long before she died, it would seem. The food is undigested for the most part."

I envision the bottoms of her sneakers, remembering the jacaranda blossoms behind the market near the picnic tables. I think of the crumbs inside her red Mercedes sports car. Benton drops his gloves in the biohazard trash can. He digs under his Tyvek, pulling out his phone again. Going through the camera roll, he finds what he's looking for. The fifty-dollar gift card was used at Belle Haven Market's gas pump at 2:37 P.M. yesterday, he says.

Putting down the surgical knife, I wipe my bloody gloved hands on a towel as Benton holds the phone close. He shows me photographs he took of the cash register receipt, and I find the very transaction I'm looking for. At 2:29 P.M., eight minutes before the killer charged gas to a stolen gift card, someone was inside the store. This person purchased two lunch specials, and a package of four lightbulbs.

The total amount was $29.45. It was paid in cash, and that had to be Rachael Stanwyck. She was at the market as the killer was filling his tank. She probably drove right past him as he was doing it, parking in back where she had privacy.

"I'm betting she wanted to sit in her car and eat undisturbed," I explain. "It was her secret pleasure, her compulsion."

"She was expecting the caretaker to come by Chilton Farms to change a lightbulb at five P.M.," Benton says. "She probably ran the errand as an excuse to buy food. The same thing people do when they go to the store for milk and while they're at it pick up booze or cigarettes."

"If the police haven't already done it they need to check the trash barrels outside the market," I reply. "Especially the ones in back. We didn't find anything in Annie's kitchen that might make you think someone had been to Belle Haven Market in recent memory. Possibly Rachael was careful about carrying her trash home with her. She threw away the evidence."

"Her secret pleasure, as you put it," Benton says as I make quick nicks through connective tissue. "Or a ritual that caused shame, and she didn't want Annie noticing what was in the trash at the house."

"I wonder if Annie knew about it anyway." I place her sister's heart in the hanging scale. "Two hundred and eighty grams," I tell Benton, and he writes it on the form clamped to his clipboard. "Why Rachael? Wrong place, wrong time?"

"That's probably closer to the truth than you know. The bad guy's coming from the failed attack near Ivy Hill Cemetery." Benton continues telling me what he thinks happened yesterday. "His adrenaline is going full tilt. He's in an uproar and enraged because the big coup was foiled. He was going to be the next Lee Harvey Oswald, the next Sirhan Sirhan. And it didn't happen."

I crosscut the coronary arteries, then slice the heart like a loaf of bread, not finding scarring or other anomalies. Unscrewing the lid from a glass jar of formalin, I drop in sections of cardiac muscle. I start on the lungs while Benton explains that the killer pulled up to the market with the intention of hitting the place. He was going to rob it at gunpoint after taking out the electrical power with his microwave weapon.

"He's not going to leave witnesses while making an example out of the old man he intends to savagely murder." Benton says this as if it's more than hypothetical. "But he decided to get gas first."

Once he took out the power that wouldn't be possible anymore, and he couldn't resist the temptation to fill up his tank. Maybe he was dangerously low on gas. We'll likely never know, but what he did was risky. He took a chance, and Rachael showed up unexpectedly. The killer hadn't anticipated this, and it was a problem.

"She likely saw him at the gas pump but didn't think anything of it. She may not have paid any attention, her compulsion propelling her," Benton says. "She parked in back, walked around to the front, entering the store to run her errand."

"Explaining the jacaranda blossoms all over the bottom of her shoes." I pull down the power cord from the overhead reel. "The parking lot behind the market in particular is covered in them."

"She purchases her two lunch specials," Benton says. "She buys the lightbulbs."

"Possibly paying with cash that she might have gotten from the ATM inside the market." I recall the crisp twenty-dollar bills sticking together in her wallet.

"She eats in the car, throws away her trash and drives home. Then the killer powers up his microwave weapon. He takes out the cameras, enters the store and confronts Wally Potter," Benton says as I drop what's left of Rachael's internal organs into a plastic bucket.

The assailant assumed that when he microwaved the store any trace of him having been there would be destroyed. And so far, that seems to be true. Nothing has been recovered from the cameras, and Benton doubts that will change. But the killer overlooked the paper receipt of the day's total that Wally tucked under the cash drawer the old-fashioned way.

"He was probably sitting at the checkout counter as the bad guy was getting gas," Benton says. "As soon as he paid with the gift card, Wally closed out the register. He saw whoever was out there at the pump, and so did Rachael. I'm betting it was someone they'd seen before or might be acquainted with."

"Maybe you're right." I remove the towel covering her face. "When all is said and done, he had to kill them. They knew too much even if they weren't aware of it."

"That's not the only reason or the biggest one," Benton says. "He did it because he felt like it. He needed to take back his power."

It was careless getting spotted at the gas pump. It was careless getting gas there to begin with, especially with a stolen gift card that could be traced.

"By now he's only more enraged," Benton says. "And the more out of control he gets, the more impetuous and violent."

■   ■   ■

Holding the scalpel like a pencil, I run it along the hairline, around the ears and the nape of the neck. I pull the face and scalp down like a rubbery Halloween mask, the exposed skull as white as an egg. Turning on the Stryker saw, I press the oscillating blade against bone, loudly grinding through it.

Moments later, Benton carries plastic containers to the autopsy suite door, handing them to Jane Slipper. He's meeting her in the corridor so she doesn't have to step inside. To speed up the process, she'll use undiluted formaldehyde as the fixative. She'll embed the sections in paraffin before making thin slices with a microtome.

But there's only so fast the process can go. I won't be looking at any microscopic slides today. Benton returns to the table as I'm placing what's left of sectioned organs inside a heavy-duty plastic bag. This goes into the empty chest cavity, everything returned to the body except for the sections and samples I need.

The "clean hands only" wall phone rings, and Benton takes off his gloves to answer.

"Morgue," he says, pushing the button for speakerphone.

"Who the hell is this?" trace evidence examiner Lee Fishburne asks in his Texas drawl.

Benton explains who he is and why he's answering the phone in the autopsy suite. He turns up the volume as high as it will go.

"Kay is right here," he says.

"I know what you're in the middle of and wouldn't bother you unless it's important," Lee replies. "Clark Givens and I are working on your dust bunny. We divided the evidence, and he's started Rapid DNA testing on skin cells and other biological debris."

The dust bunny was too big for the scanning electron microscope (SEM). The specimen holder that we commonly call a *stub* is only half an inch in diameter, and goes inside the SEM's small vacuum chamber. Lee had to divide the evidence into small portions before analyzing it with extreme magnification and energy-dispersive x-ray spectroscopy.

"I thought you'd want to know that what I'm seeing likely isn't indigenous to Belle Haven Market." He tells us why he's calling.

"What's made you decide that so quickly?" I'm threading a surgical needle with cotton twine.

"There's gold and silver." Lee's voice from the old wall phone's tinny speaker.

As in the precious metals, he says. Also, fragments of copper and aluminum that have some sort of gold tint, he says as Benton listens while sending text messages.

"These bright little bits you noticed in the dust bunny, Kay. That's what they are, tiny bits of different metals," Lee explains. "Weirdly, the fragments are laminated in thin layers that may have been sputter-coated with metals."

"What would be the purpose?" I suture with long sweeps of the needle and cotton twine, closing the Y-incision.

"I don't know, but it's not normal finding all this, whatever it is,"

Lee says. "Maybe some sort of research experiment? Or from some-thing being manufactured?"

He's counted thirty-three metallic particles so far. He says the next step will be to analyze them with gas chromatography/mass spectrometry for chemical compositions. He's conferred with toxicologist Rex Bonetta, who's getting started in his lab.

"That should give us a better idea what this shiny material is and might have been used for," Lee says. "There's a lot of other stuff in the dust bunny like silica, paper and cotton fibers, rust, gunpowder, saw-dust, glass, mineral and seashell fragments."

He promises to get back to us when he knows more, and Benton ends the call on the wall phone.

"I've got to go." He takes off his PPE, explaining he's been summoned to an emergency meeting at the Pentagon.

Lucy has been busy with her forensic software, analyzing yesterday's recordings from signal analyzers. She's triangulated the locations where the 2.305 GHz frequency was picked up.

"She's factoring in not just signals that she and Tron detected with the portable analyzers they carry in their backpacks." Benton drops his PPE into the trash. "But also from ones in fixed locations, and we have additional information."

He tells me that Lucy's software has sifted through the noise floor and found other rapid energy bursts that might lead to the terrorists' camp. Possibly, it's some thirty miles south of here in a rural area of Virginia near the Marine Corps base at Quantico. The Secret Service, the FBI may know where the terrorists have been living and training for the past few years.

After Benton leaves, I return to my lonely task, and it's not the job of the medical examiner to make a patient presentable. We don't offer hair and makeup like a funeral home, and I continue closing up Rachael Stanwyck's body. I line up the notch I made when removing the skull cap, fitting it back into place with a soft click. I suture the incision around her head.

Parallel-parking the gurney next to the autopsy table, I spread open the pouch all the way, lining it with a clean sheet. I slide the body inside, zipping it up. I place racks of test tubes and cartons of tissue and organ sections on the dumbwaiter. Pushing the button for the third floor, I send them up to the toxicology lab. Moments later I'm steering the gurney along the corridor and tucking it back inside the cooler.

I stop by the evidence room, placing Rachael's shoes and clothing inside a drying closet. Returning to the locker room, I remove my PPE, washing my face and hands, retrieving my belongings. Then I'm pushing through the fire exit door, taking the stairs to the second floor where my administrative corridor is quiet and empty.

It's almost noon, and everyone is in the morgue or out somewhere. I'm mindful of a vacant feeling in the air that wasn't here before. I pass the empty breakroom, the conference room, and ahead is Maggie Cutbush's shut door. I walk past it to my office, hearing the TV playing inside. I recognize the voices, my temper spiking.

I open the door, angry it wasn't locked, because that's not how I left it. I didn't leave the lights or television on either, and am confronted by Elvin Reddy talking to Dana Diletti on the Channel 5 midday news. She's interviewing him at his Richmond headquarters, and it's maddening to hear his self-serving bullshit.

"...Yes, Dana, it's been very sad indeed. Yet another dark stain on our fine medical examiner system." Elvin is seated at his big desk before a wall of glass, the skyline soaring around him. "When the FBI contacted me, I said we'd do whatever it takes to comply. I promised

I would personally see to it that Doctor Scarpetta cooperates to the fullest..."

He's in one of his hand-tailored suits, his bald head as shiny as polished stone. He looks appropriately disappointed and grim as he discusses why the Colonial Parkway murders have to be reopened. I turn off the TV in disgust, and I'm not sure what I'm noticing next to my desk. Then I can't believe it.

"No, no, no...!"

A volt of shocked disbelief runs through me.

"You didn't...!"

My heart hammers as I drop my briefcase to the floor. My fiddle leaf fig tree, my orchids aren't dead, but they will be if I don't come to their rescue immediately.

"NO! NO...!"

I knew my secretary was evil. But I didn't think even she would stoop this low. The plants were office-warming gifts from Benton and Lucy. I'm fastidious about their care, and Maggie has unpotted them. She's crammed them into the trash basket next to my desk. Her parting shot. I can't prove she did it. But who else?

I don't realize tears are running down my face until they splash on my bare hands as I scoop rich potting soil off the floor, returning it to the hand-painted ceramic pots left upside down next to my desk chair. I carry the plants, the tree into the bathroom, trickling water through their clumped roots.

I repot them, setting the orchids on my conference table, and the fiddle fig nearby. They're bedraggled like birds missing feathers, but should survive. Worried what other damage I might find, I open the door connecting Maggie's office to mine. I can feel her absence before I turn on the light.

CHAPTER 33

She's cleared her walls and desk of artwork and photographs. Missing are her various educational degrees, including from the University of Oxford, where she studied English language and literature, she never lets me forget.

Maggie had more self-important commendations and certificates displayed than I do, and there's nothing left but bare hooks. I slide open the desk drawers, and they're empty. She's quit. Either that or she's been fired by someone other than me. As I'm looking around her office, I realize that someone is inside mine.

"I'm in here!" I call out, and then Pete Marino is walking through the connecting doorway.

He scans Maggie's empty walls and bookcase, the overflowing wastepaper basket, the desk with nothing on it but her unplugged computer.

"Holy shit," he says.

"Did you have any idea?" I ask.

"Nope. But if it's true, good riddance. Fuck her."

"It's true. It is now if it wasn't before," I promise with cold fury as I envision what she did to my fig tree and orchids.

"Ding-dong, the witch is dead." Marino goes on to call her other names that don't bear repeating. "You watch how this joint gets whipped into shape without her around anymore."

"How's Wally Potter coming along?"

"He didn't aspirate blood," Marino says. "You were right about him being already dead. And the duct tape has a mother lode of shit sticking to it."

He follows me as I return to my office.

"There's a lot of microscopic stuff, including glitter that Lee Fishburne says could be bits of metal," Marino says. "Maybe the same stuff he's found in the dust bunny. The good news is the cash pouch was still in the cooler, in the hiding place where Wally kept it. The killer never got the five thousand dollars locked up in there..."

While he's telling me this he's noticing the potting soil on the floor near my desk. He sees the flower petals and leaves in my trash can. He's looking at the orchids and fiddle fig tree convalescing.

"Holy shit. What is this? *Fatal Attraction*?" He understands what my secretary did as her final petty act.

It's unfortunate that Maggie was given the chance to do damage, to get in the last ugly word. I know who was foolish enough to permit it. The only person I have to blame is myself. I should have gotten rid of her long ago, and won't make the same mistake again.

"Let's make sure Wyatt, Fabian, that everyone knows she doesn't work here anymore," I tell Marino. "She didn't leave on friendly terms, and isn't allowed on the premises. If she tries to return to our parking lot or building, security is to be notified immediately. If she pushes her luck, I'll have her arrested."

"I'm sending Wyatt a note right now," Marino says almost gleefully. "I'll let him be the one to spread the word since he's such a big fan of hers."

I unlock a drawer in my credenza, lifting out the thick files I placed there when the Hooke trial was getting under way in the spring. Accusations were made early on about Bailey Carter's credibility. His entire professional legacy was being brought into question, most of all the Colonial Parkway murders of four young couples twenty-two years ago. I wanted the materials here in my office, locked up and in easy reach.

I had Marino bring the original records here to Alexandria so I could refresh my memory, and I fear the worst as I start looking through the paperwork. I flip through the eight homicide cases, and the photocopies appear to have been made hastily, sloppily. The original documents and photographs are missing.

Also gone are Post-its and other slips of paper that were attached to reports, and this is most unfortunate. Not every scrap of information makes it into electronic format or is photocopied. The smallest note can be important, and without the original hard copies I can't know what's missing. Possibly for good.

"I don't know when this happened, as I've not looked at these records in weeks," I explain to Marino. "But I think it's obvious what Maggie's done."

"More of her damn sabotage," he says. "By disappearing the original files she's just left you another pile of shit. It looks really suspicious. Maybe people will think you're the one who took them because you have something to hide."

"While I dictate Rachael Stanwyck's autopsy report, maybe you could try to track down Piper Carter for me. Bailey Carter's widow," I reply.

"Yeah, I remember her like yesterday. She was always nice and friendly to me," Marino says.

"I'd like to talk to her, and we may have to pay her a visit."

"Pay a visit when?"

"It depends on what I find out. And please pull up the electronic record of her husband's suicide and send it to me so I can have it in front of me," I reply, and Marino disappears through the doorway connecting my office to Maggie's.

I didn't have Bailey's original case brought here because until now I wasn't concerned that something nefarious might happen to it. As worried as I've been about Maggie's access and agendas, obviously I wasn't worried nearly enough. Bailey's records should be at my Tidewater district headquarters in Norfolk where his autopsy was performed.

But I'm not trusting anything, and I call Dr. Rena Peace, the Tidewater deputy chief who went to the suicide scene and performed the autopsy. Bailey retired soon after April Tupelo's death in mid-October of 2020. Elvin Reddy hired Rena as Bailey Carter's replacement after he became impaired. She didn't know Bailey. They never met until he hanged himself inside his boathouse.

"Do you have questions about his death? I've been following the trial up there in Alexandria. Better you than us," Rena is saying. "Originally it was supposed to be here in Norfolk."

"You should be grateful it's not," I agree. "Life is anything but normal in Old Town. At the moment I wouldn't call it safe."

"I couldn't handle the angry mobs of protesters," she says.

While we talk I'm watching them on my wall-mounted security monitors as they march around my headquarters.

"But I know you didn't call me to chat," Rena adds. "What can I help you with, Kay?"

"I assume you have Bailey Carter's original case file there," I reply. "That's my question. I'm just confirming it's there where it should be..."

"Well, no. It's not at the moment..."

"What do you mean?"

"Elvin Reddy took it," she says. "He's not returned it yet."

Rena informs me that Elvin paid an unannounced visit to the Norfolk office last week, and left with Bailey's original records. He explained that the FBI had questions about his suicide and the Colonial Parkway murders. There likely would be many other cases reopened because of allegations about his incompetence that now span decades, as Rena puts it.

She got this directly from Elvin. He claimed the governor in particular demanded answers, and is worried about being politically embarrassed. It was at this point that Rena informed him about Marino collecting the original Parkway murder cases and bringing them to my Northern Virginia office.

"Elvin was most unhappy," Rena tells me over speakerphone. "He wanted to have his hands on those files. He wanted the originals. He was insistent about it, and got quite cross when I said I couldn't do anything about it. The original files are with you."

I don't offer that they're not anymore.

"And you didn't think his behavior was a little strange?" I reply, and I'm getting a good idea of the timing.

Elvin showed up at the Norfolk office last week to collect the original Parkway murder records he was interested in reviewing and no doubt intending to tamper with. He didn't realize that the files were in Alexandria, inside my credenza. He must have alerted Maggie to take care of the problem, and she did. There's no telling where the originals are now or if they even still exist.

"In the future no such thing is to be done without my permission," I tell Rena with far more diplomacy than I'm feeling. "Elvin shouldn't have walked off with original paperwork of any description. He shouldn't have been looking at Bailey's case to begin with. Certainly not without my knowing."

"But he's the health commissioner, Kay..."

"And I'm the chief medical examiner, Rena. I'm the legal custodian of all our records, and the buck stops with me, for better or worse. If Elvin really thought what he was doing was okay then why didn't he ask me directly? Why bypass me?"

"I didn't think about that. I assumed he'd discussed it with you." Rena feels bad about it, and she should.

■ ■ ■

I'm aware of Marino talking on the phone in Maggie's office, and it gives me a strange feeling. It's as if she's there. But he doesn't make the same sounds, his energy big and blunt as opposed to sneaky and sideways.

Logging onto my computer's autopsy protocol software, I begin working on Rachael Stanwyck's report. There's no point in dictating my findings when I no longer have a secretary to type them. I guess I'll have to manage on my own for a while like I used to do in the early days, and then Marino calls me on line one.

"I got Piper Carter," he says. "Don't get used to me acting like your freakin' secretary."

"Put her through, please."

I didn't know Bailey's wife well long ago when he and I worked together. I remember her as cheery and positive, warm and reassuring, while he was her polar opposite. Bailey never admitted that he struggled with anxiety and depression. But I sensed his heavy churning moods. I gave him space when he got sullen and offended by the latest inhumanity or cruel act of nature.

Murders. Negligent deaths. Suicidal leaps from buildings. Drownings. Shark attacks. Tornadoes. Insect stings and food allergies. I can see Bailey looking up at the heavens, angrily shaking his head, accusing the Almighty of sleeping on the job. He used to say that when he got to the *other side*, he planned to hold the creator of *all this mess to a meaningful conversation.*

"What original sin?" Bailey would say. "There's nothing original about what evil people do."

I'd hear stories about him isolating at work with his office door shut. He could be ungracious and critical, what Benton calls a curmudgeon. My Tidewater deputy chief was given to fits of pique and deep moroseness, and when we worked the Parkway murders he was like a wounded animal. His children were around the same ages as the victims. His insulation got pierced in a way it hadn't before.

He couldn't handle the serial murders, certainly not alone, and had I met him when he was in medical school I would have steered him away from his eventual profession. Forensic pathology takes you places you think you're fine to go but can't come back from. Bailey wasn't emotionally equipped to handle the exposure, his psyche forever kinked and broken by it.

"Hello, Piper." I put the call on speakerphone, writing the date and time in one of the notebooks I always carry. "I was very saddened to hear about Bailey, and I hope you got my letter."

"I did, and the beautiful flowers that you and Benton were so kind to send. Forgive me for not writing, but I wasn't myself for a while." She draws out her O's, her accent Eastern Shore, her tone more shadowed than before.

"How are you holding up?"

"As well as can be expected, life being what it is," she says. "I'm glad Bailey's not here to see what's happening in the world, to be honest. He has relatives on his mother's side who live in Ukraine. Or they did."

"I hope they're safe."

"Thanks to the kindness of strangers in Poland. I'm glad he's not here to see the news every night. It's such an irony that you're the chief again, Kay." Piper is struggling not to cry. "If things had turned out differently Bailey might be working for you all over again. I know how much that would have pleased him."

"It would have pleased me, too. I had a great deal of respect for your husband, still do," I reply. "I need to ask you a few questions about him, Piper. I want to talk to you about his death. I know it's not easy, and I regret having to probe. But it's important."

I explain that Bailey's cases are under a cloud of suspicion and distrust. As she likely has heard on the news, the Parkway investigation has been reopened by the FBI. I'm the first to say it's unmerited and a terrible waste for so many reasons.

"Mostly, it's about politics. It's about attorneys and others exploiting a vulnerability," I explain. "But we have to take the situation seriously. I have to prepare myself for what's to come, and you need to do the same."

"What they're saying about Bailey is bad enough already," Piper replies as I sit at my desk taking notes. "And I guess he'll be forever judged by the last things he did instead of all that went before. I heard your testimony on TV yesterday."

"I regret the necessity of it."

"I realize you had to say what you did about the mess he made of the April Tupelo case."

"And he did make a mess of it, a bad one, Piper." I'm not going to play games with her. "That's because he wasn't himself by then. But he didn't make mistakes in his earlier work. I know that firsthand because I was the chief in those days."

"He was only sixty-four, a very young sixty-four, when this terrible thing was done to him." Her voice shakes badly. "He had a mind like a steel trap until he didn't in the blink of an eye."

"What terrible thing are you talking about exactly?"

"He was fine when he went to the boathouse as the sun was going down. When he came home a few hours later he was completely altered," Piper says. "Nobody would listen to me. They thought I was hysterical. I've always believed somebody did something, maybe set up some sort of booby trap, probably something electrical, and Bailey walked into it."

What she's referring to happened almost two years ago on September 20, a Sunday, she says. It was getting close to six P.M. when Bailey headed out to the boathouse while she started dinner.

"What was he going there to do?" I assume he was taking his boat out for a sunset spin along the river behind their house.

Maybe he was checking on the crab pots, and I remember him telling me that fishing and crabbing were a way of relaxing. Sometimes he'd cruise alone in his boat as it was getting dark when there were few people out. But Piper replies that the boathouse was his home office, his private space. That Sunday night he'd gone there to be alone and work for a while as was his habit.

The waterfront residence she's talking about used to be their Norfolk getaway on Little Creek near the Bay Point Marina. She tells me that when the pandemic started, Bailey converted the boathouse into his office. He worked from there whenever possible, and they sold their home near his Tidewater district headquarters.

He'd drive to work only when his physical presence was necessary, typically to take care of autopsies. On the early evening Piper is telling me about, Bailey was inside the boathouse when he heard what sounded like a transformer blowing.

CHAPTER 34

Whatever it was, it knocked the power out," Piper is explaining. "He woke up on the floor in total darkness and terrible pain, not sure at first where he was. Or this is what he remembered. It's what he told me initially."

"Did you call the police? Was a booby trap or anything else checked for?" I inquire, double-underlining *power outage* in my notes. "Did you call for an ambulance?"

"We didn't call the police or anyone," she says. "I drove him to the hospital that night, and he had all sorts of tests. They figured it might have been a stroke, and then soon enough it was decided he had early dementia."

I scroll through the autopsy report that Marino's just e-mailed as Piper explains over the phone that her late husband was confused and difficult after that.

"Then he got angrier and more depressed," she says as I find the histological section of the electronic record. "He got stubborn and should have retired before he did. He should have done it instantly. But he refused to acknowledge that he wasn't himself. He wouldn't listen, and people around him were noticing and making comments."

The microscopic examination of Bailey's brain tissue shows diffuse white matter disease and cellular necrosis. It's probably similar to how Rachael Stanwyck's slides are going to look when they're prepared and I finally see them. Had she lived, she would have been severely impaired.

There's no question Bailey Carter was, that he had dementia. But now I may know how he got it. I have to wonder if his suicide the week of Thanksgiving in 2020 was due to an earlier attack in September that caused the brain damage I'm seeing. Also, who might have done such a thing? And why him?

"If someone knew your husband I'm assuming it would have been obvious that he was working from an office on your property," I say to Piper over the phone.

"Yes," she replies as I think of the implications. "Certainly, everyone he worked with knew what he was doing and where. Bailey wasn't hard to find. He was either at his downtown office here in Norfolk or the one at home. Other than his family and his boat, he didn't get out much, as they say."

Piper tells me that it was her late husband's therapy and ritual at the end of the day to spend a few hours alone inside his boathouse office. He'd look at the water while writing about his cases and whatever else was going on with him.

"It's how he'd sort himself out," she explains. "He had to exorcise the demons because of the unspeakable things he'd see. Just when he'd think nothing more awful could happen? Well, then he'd come home and go straight to the boathouse without talking to anyone. I used to hear in church that God won't give you more than you can endure. It's not true. But I don't blame God. I blame people."

She continues describing the night her husband supposedly had his stroke. It was around 7:30 when Bailey staggered back to the house. He was slurring his words, and talking about being abducted by extraterrestrials. That's what it felt like, he told Piper. The TV turned on, lights flickered, and sparks were flying. Then it was pitch dark and dead quiet.

"He didn't remember any other details except what I've described." His widow's voice follows me around my office as I go window to window closing the blinds. "He told me that he might have been unconscious briefly. Then he got somewhat better as days went by. But that's not saying a whole lot. He wasn't the Bailey I used to know, not the Bailey any of us knew. He never would be again."

"When the power went out in the boathouse, what about the main house? What was going on there?" I check on my abused orchids and fiddle fig tree, hoping they'll mend.

"It was fine. I was in the kitchen talking on the phone, and had no idea there was a problem. The lights in the house didn't even flicker. That's another reason I'd like to know what really happened to him. They found out there was no transformer that blew. It was only Bailey's boathouse that was affected. The main house was fine because it has a separate power box."

"What about the notes he was taking? I'm wondering what he might have at home, any files, his notebooks most importantly." I ask her what became of them.

"You're not the only one who's interested," she says. "When the FBI came poking around I knew exactly what they were after, and I made sure they didn't get it."

"When was this?" It's the first I've heard about the FBI paying her a visit.

"Just this past Wednesday," she says. "Day before yesterday. A woman agent appeared at my door unannounced, which I thought was rude and aggressive, I might add. I made her show me her badge, verifying she was really the FBI."

Otherwise, Piper wasn't going to let Patty Mullet inside the house. But she did, and they talked for several hours. She wanted to see where Bailey worked and died, and was shown the boathouse.

"She asked what I remember about him and the Parkway murders," Piper tells me. "She wanted to know if he'd ever said something about the DNA being a problem in those cases, and that it was covered up."

"The DNA was unusual, as you probably recall from the news at the time," I reply.

The suspected killer had undergone a bone marrow transplant that changed the DNA of his blood but not his other bodily fluids and tissues. Reopening the cases is further complicated by the suspect being shot to death before he could be questioned.

"The FBI agent implied that what really happened was my husband mixed up test tubes because of his carelessness and incompetence," Piper says. "She wanted me to admit it in an affidavit."

"You weren't the medical examiner, Piper." It's hard sitting on my anger. "You were married to one. There's nothing to admit because nothing's been covered up. You also don't have to tell Patty Mullet or anyone else anything at all about what you and Bailey discussed. Legally, it's privileged. It's protected because you were married."

"We still are." Her voice shakes.

"Legally, that's right."

"She demanded I turn over any original notes," Piper says angrily, her voice thick. "Not just in the Parkway murders but April Tupelo and every other case Bailey ever worked. And I acted like I didn't know what she was talking about."

The FBI is after Bailey's private notebooks, his therapeutic diaries. Patty Mullet claimed she knew for a fact that he kept them. It was mentioned in a newspaper story about him way back when he was first getting started. When she confronted Piper about this she played dumb.

Bailey's widow lied, in other words, and thank God or there may be no hope of proving what's true. His writings might be the only records that haven't been tampered with. They might be a touchstone for me in more cases than can be imagined right now, decades of them. I turn off my computer.

"What's happened to his diaries?" I ask her.

"They're still exactly where he left them."

"I'm extremely relieved to hear that." I take off my lab coat.

"There's probably about a hundred of them going back to his earliest days as a medical examiner."

Piper says she's never read them. She didn't while he was alive, and can't bring herself to do it now. I ask if I might have a look. I tell her certain original documents seem to have vanished.

"I'm not surprised," she replies. "You're now dealing with the same scoundrel that my husband did. The most useless chief in the history of the world is what Bailey thought of Elvin Reddy. And now he's the health commissioner. Isn't that something?"

．　．　．

Bailey would be happy for me to read what he had to say, Piper tells me. He'd want me to know his deepest thoughts, and it's fine with her as long as the diaries aren't removed from the boathouse. We agree to meet right away.

Inside my bathroom, I open the wooden locker where I keep a mid-sized tote bag packed with several changes of clothing, toiletries, PPE and other essentials. I hear footsteps and voices as DNA analyst Clark Givens and Marino walk into my office, both of them beaming.

"We've got a hit." Clark doesn't get excited often. "Actually, we've got two hits!"

Rapid DNA testing has produced five unknown profiles of individuals whose skin cells and other biological evidence were adhering to duct tape and the dust bunny in the Wally Potter case. The profiles have been run through the FBI's Combined DNA Index System (CODIS) database, and there are two matches verified so far.

"They're not telling us who," Marino explains. "But I think this new bunch of assholes that calls themselves The Republic is about to get locked up where the sun don't shine."

"I've got a lot of other tests to run but wanted you to be the first to know," Clark says, walking toward the elevator.

"Imagine if a terrorist organization is brought down by a fucking dust bunny." Marino couldn't be happier, and I pass on what I learned from Piper Carter.

"I don't know what Patty Mullet is up to," I explain, "but I'm not about to let the wrong people get hold of Bailey's original journals."

"Nobody's getting hold of them except us." Marino states it categorically.

It's now close to 1:30 P.M., and if we leave soon we can be in Norfolk by early evening, he says. We'll need to get hotel rooms, and it's not a bad thing if we avoid Old Town tonight. Benton won't be home. I doubt Lucy will be, either. I have no desire to stay at the house by myself with police parked out front.

Dorothy should be fine at their condo in its gated compound. The protesters aren't after her, and the more I convince myself she's safe, the guiltier I feel. Ever the dutiful older sister, I send her a text explaining that Marino and I have work to do on the Eastern Shore. I don't give her the slightest idea what or where.

We won't be back tonight, and I doubt Lucy will be home with everything that's happening. If Dorothy doesn't feel comfortable staying alone, maybe she should check into a Washington, D.C., hotel, and I'm sorry for any inconvenience. I regret we're not there to keep her company. She replies with emojis of a thumbs-up, a bottle of wine and a gun.

Marino and I head out to his truck, and marked cruisers have to escort us again with emergency lights flashing. The number of protesters has continued to grow, and the state police have been brought in. I don't look at the angry faces, and block out their hate speech as we drive away. We take I-95 South, for a while listening to coverage of the Hooke trial and other news.

Then Marino switches to his favorite oldies station. We listen to the Grass Roots, Three Dog Night and early Elton John. We're well into Fleetwood Mac when we reach Richmond, the skyline bringing back memories of a city that's nothing like it was when we were getting started. The redbrick Main Steet Station is now a shopping mall. Its clock tower displays the correct time, not a train in sight.

Nearby is the parking deck where my former headquarters used to be in a low-lying area that has a floodwall. My old building at 14th and East Franklin Streets was demolished not long after I moved away some twenty years ago. Now the medical examiner's central district office is in the middle of a biotech park, surrounded by private laboratories.

Dominating the skyline, the James Monroe Building rises twenty-nine stories, and in the early years the state office building was the tallest in Virginia. I envision Elvin Reddy inside his top-floor suite with its view of the James River. I think of the times he's summoned me there to ruin my day. My ring vibrates, and I don't put Benton on speakerphone. I'd like what little privacy I can have.

"I'm in the car and almost at my destination." His voice is in my earpiece, and he's not telling me where he is or going. "After that my phone's in a locker until God knows when."

He can't share details but indicates that arrests are imminent. The Secret Service and FBI have discovered where the terrorists are holed up, and they may have nipped something catastrophic in the bud that he'll explain later. As he's telling me this I'm alerted by a text from Lucy that a verdict has been reached in the Hooke trial.

"Got to go, and not sure when we'll talk next," Benton is saying. "Don't forget I love you."

I find live coverage on the radio, turning up the volume. Gilbert Hooke has been found not guilty on all counts. As the jury's decision is read by the foreman, I realize it's the same woman who interrupted my testimony to ask about diatoms.

"Not that I'm surprised, but the shit's going to hit the fan." Marino is digging in the ashtray for chewing gum again. "Imagine at the beginning of the holiday weekend? All those *Justice for April* people must be going berserk. I'm glad you and me got the hell out of Dodge."

As he's saying this I'm reminded of court reporter Shannon Park quitting the Hooke trial early to leave Old Town for this very reason. Opening my briefcase, I find the pink envelope she gave me yesterday. It's been out of sight and mind in the side pocket where I tucked it, and I decide to see what's so important.

I slide out a greeting card that has rainbows and dragons on it. Taped inside is a pink thumb drive. Shannon has written me a note in pink ink, and I read it out loud:

"Kay, you're surrounded by treachery, if you've not figured it out by now. It's high time you had an administrative assistant who can kick some arse. You and Marino could use a little help from a friend, and I'm ready for a new challenge. Included is my résumé."

"Fastest fingers in the East." Marino always says this about her. "She could probably type the damn autopsy report before you've even finished dictating it, speedy as she is. And she knows everybody who's anybody in law enforcement, the court system. Plus, she's loyal and knows when to shut her piehole."

"Don't think I won't talk to her," I reply as I see from the breaking news that two terrorist arrests have been made in Northern Virginia.

One of the suspects is the man who kicked me in the ankle, Clark Babbitt, a fifty-three-year-old roofer with a criminal history of domestic and other violence. He's now in federal custody, as is a former Army mechanic named Joel Ramekin, forty, and the picture of him storming the Capitol on January 6, 2021, is vaguely familiar. Other arrests are expected to follow swiftly.

Benton probably is locked up in a situation room filled with data walls. I imagine him surrounded by satellite images of the terrorists' camp, their compound, their vehicles, who knows what else. As I'm relaying the details to Marino, my chief toxicologist, Rex Bonetta, calls with an update, he says, and I sync him with the truck's speakers.

"Polyethylene terephthalate." He tells us the results of gas chromatography/mass spectrometry.

"Maybe speak English for once," Marino replies, driving with his mirrored sunglasses on, chewing Teaberry.

"Mylar," Rex says. "The metal-coated plastic film used to make balloons, space blankets, the insulation for satellites."

The shiny bits of metallic-looking glitter in the dust bunny and also on the duct tape are bits and pieces of Mylar, he says. It's been ironed together in layers, and heat-sealed, he explains. As suspected, in some instances the material has been sputter-coated with copper, even silver and gold, he adds.

"Do we have any idea what this might be used for?" I ask.

"No, but clearly somebody's experimenting, fabricating something, doing stuff involving Mylar, which is associated almost exclusively with the aerospace industry," Rex replies. "I find that more than a little concerning when arrests are being made of suspected terrorists, and everything else I'm hearing."

I need to pass this along to Benton, but he's not going to answer. No doubt his phone is tucked away inside a locker at the Pentagon, the White House, wherever he is. He checks his messages between meetings, and it might be hours before he does it again.

CHAPTER 35

I try Benton's number, and it goes straight to voice mail as I knew it would. I leave him a simple message.

"The glittery stuff recovered is Mylar." That's all I say, and I leave the same voice mail for Lucy and Tron.

They'll understand. I don't need to tell them that the reason for coating plastic with metals such as aluminum is to make the material highly reflective. Anything fashioned from it has the properties of a Faraday cage, I continue explaining to Marino what I've learned from my work on the Doomsday Commission.

"If you suited up in Mylar like we do in Tyvek, it would protect you from microwave radiation as long as all of you is covered. But you wouldn't want to run around in clothing made out of a shiny silver space blanket. Not if you're trying to move about unnoticed. I imagine it also would be hot as hell this time of year."

"It's like what they do to cars these days," Marino says. "Vinyl wraps instead of painting them, and you can pick anything you want. A bright color, camouflage, matte black, even a mirror finish. I saw a Ferrari not long ago that looked like it had been dipped in twenty-four-karat gold."

"That might explain the variety of colors in the bits of metal-like material," I reply as we begin crossing the Chesapeake Bay. "Brown, gray, green, black. Those in addition to finding curious traces of metals like silver, gold, copper."

The wide expanse of deep blue water becomes the Atlantic Ocean to the east, and we're surrounded by the military. Behind us in the distance is the Norfolk Naval Station, the largest in the world, its gray battleships silhouetted against the low sun. My Tidewater district headquarters overlooks Willoughby Bay several miles west of here, and every few months I drop by.

During site visits when meeting inside our conference room, I have a ringside seat watching battleships and aircraft in and out. There's been a lot more military activity since Russia began its monstrous invasion of Ukraine. I'm grateful there are good people fighting evil.

"Camouflage," I explain to Marino as I think about what Benton told me.

Last month a mom-and-pop pharmacy was robbed in Arlington. The perpetrator knocked out the power. Then this person entered the store dressed in camouflage, a loose-fitting hood that had built-in mirrored goggles.

"We don't know that these people aren't making Mylar protective clothing. But they're onto something new that blends better and is simple, convenient, practical," I suggest to Marino. "Jumpsuits, coveralls that are lightweight and easy to put on and take off, something you can fold up or stuff into your backpack like a space blanket."

But Mylar doesn't have to be bright or gaudy. Old tarnished metal birdhouses and dull aluminum window screens deflect radiation just as well as mirrored finishes. The material just has to be metalized, and eventually such protective wear will look like everyday clothing.

"Not so different from your fishing shirts that have UV protection and built-in bug protection," I explain, staring out my window.

The Atlantic Ocean is ruffled blue-green with whitecaps, and on the horizon a cruise ship looks as big as a hospital. The sun is low over the water, the sky the washed-out blue of old denim at the beginning of the July Fourth weekend. Traffic is heavy as we follow the Norfolk shoreline, the beaches and parks we pass busy with picnics and barbecues.

Smoke rises from grills flaming, and live music throbs. People are parasailing, and racing around on Jet Skis. They're flying kites and throwing Frisbees. Past the Surf Motel, we turn inland toward Little Creek, where spacious properties are wooded and private. I've never visited the Carters' waterfront hideaway. But I've heard about it plenty because it was where Bailey was happiest.

Most of the homes are small and rustic. They were built in the fifties and sixties, the lots generous, with piers reaching across the water like long fingers. There are boathouses or decks, and I notice neighbors tending to their crab pots. Others are out walking their dogs, waving as we drive past. It makes sense why Bailey wanted to spend his time here. I understand why Piper hasn't left despite the painful memories.

Their driveway is unpaved, pebbles pinging and dust billowing. We park in front of the wood-sided cottage. She appears on the porch, wiping her hands on a dishtowel, wringing it nervously. But she's smiling and excited. At a glance you might think we're old friends dropping by to pay a social visit, not a care in the world.

"You're a sight for sore eyes," she says to me, and it's probably been twenty years.

"I can't tell you how much I appreciate you doing this, and on such short notice, Piper." I give her a hug, and can feel her trembling.

Thinner and more wrinkled than when I saw her last, she's dressed in painters pants, a University of Virginia T-shirt and worn-out

Topsiders. Her hair used to be long and blond. Now it's short and snow white, and her bright blue eyes and quick grin can't disguise her deep sadness.

"Back in the day he headed the homicide squad in Richmond." I introduce her to Marino because she might not remember him. "He was out this way often when we were dealing with the Parkway killings."

"Of course, you're not easily forgotten," Piper says to him. "But I don't recall you looking like this. You must live inside the gym." Admiring him from stem to stern. "Bailey was a fan of yours. And that's saying a lot because he didn't suffer fools. He'd tell me, *That detective doesn't miss much*, his exact words," she says to Marino.

"He didn't know me all that well," he jokes, flattered as hell.

"My husband was a perfectionist, if you've not figured that out."

"Yeah, I know what it's like to work for one of those" is Marino's response.

"Well, I do hope the two of you are planning to have a little supper." She leads us inside the house, charming with braided rugs on the heart pine flooring. "I just put cheese biscuits in the oven, and made a fresh batch of honey butter."

"You don't have to twist my arm." Marino would have invited us had she not asked, and they're getting along famously.

■　■　■

The living room has a stunning view of Little Creek and the graying pier stretching over it, the dark green–painted boathouse at the end.

"I'd live in a place like this if I had my way about it," Marino says, looking around.

He steps close to the picture window, and a great blue heron flaps off from the shore, swooping across the water. Ducks paddle away in a wake of ripples. Seagulls screech as if startled by the looming presence gazing wistfully through glass.

"It's nice where Dorothy and me are on the Potomac with a boat slip, the whole nine yards," he says. "But too many freakin' condos, everything freakin' brand-new, including the people. This is real peaceful, and I bet the fishing's good."

"I wish you could spend the night, but as you can see there's not much space," Piper says. "When we got this place long ago it was mostly for when the weather was nice and Bailey was in the mood. We didn't plan on living here full time. Then COVID happened, and he said things couldn't get worse. Well, he was wrong."

"I've not had a good crab-picking in a while." Marino can't take his eyes off the view. "And it's slack tide."

When the water level is at its lowest or highest, the tidal motion is the stillest. It's the ideal time for catching blue crabs and peelers. Marino tells Piper he's happy to help check her pots.

"I was hoping you'd say that," she replies. "I have five. That's the limit, you know. I baited them a little while ago with chicken necks, and have a feeling we'll have an embarrassment of riches. And I've got beer."

"Now we're talking," Marino tells her.

Piper leaves us in the living room, and I look out at the pier, at a creek as wide as a lake or a harbor. Sailboats cut against the darkening sky, and shorebirds wheel and cry. When she returns with three sweating bottles of Molson Golden Ale, we drink a toast to Bailey. We clink the bottles together, and then she takes us out the back door.

She's going to show us the home office he fixed up. He did most of the work himself, fashioning special cabinets of cedarwood for the storage of his private journals and papers. Bailey's undergraduate degree was in engineering at the Massachusetts Institute of Technology, and I'm not surprised he was good at fixing and building.

Our footsteps thud hollowly on the old pier with its curling boards and rusty nailheads. I can smell the brackish water, and it ripples when fish touch the surface. The blue heron has returned, or maybe it's a different one alighting on the shore, standing on stilt-like legs. Cypress trees and shrubs crowd the bank where a gaggle of Canada geese have gathered.

Shadows dapple grass and wildflowers, and I can imagine Bailey looking forward to coming out here at day's end. No doubt he felt soothed as he followed the long pier. I estimate it's some sixty feet from beginning to where it terminates at the boathouse. We step up on a porch that has fishing rod holders on the railing. Piper has to find the right key on the ring of them jingling in her shaky hands.

She unlocks the weathered front door, and the air inside is stagnant and musty. I can tell the place has been closed up for a long time as we follow her inside. She turns on the ceiling fans, a few lamps. I help her open the curtains, the downstairs small with overstuffed furniture, and wormy chestnut paneling.

In the ceiling are exposed oak rafters, and I find the one where Bailey looped the rope he used to hang himself. The details and photographs I've reviewed indicate he took an overdose of a benzodiazepine, wrapped a towel around his neck, then the noose. He sat on the floor, leaning forward, compressing his carotid arteries. Cutting off the oxygen to his brain, he died from hypoxia.

When it was time to make his exit, Bailey knew how. He may have been demented by then but was logical and exact, deciding no more. He did it quickly and relatively humanely, without leaving a bloody mess for his wife to confront.

"I've not been in here in a while." Piper looks around the room with a startled expression on her face, avoiding the area where that tragic scene took place.

"I just don't come in. Never did, you know. It was always his special spot, like a treehouse. No girls or anyone else allowed."

Bailey's antique burlwood desk is centered by a computer, and on a table his microscope is shrouded in translucent plastic. Next to it is a stack of cardboard microscopic slide folders, and an old-style cassette tape recorder for his dictations. Books are double and triple shelved, and he has a number of antique anatomical models and artwork.

Across from the recliner is a TV on a stand, the remote control on top. There's an antique Rock-Ola jukebox, a glass case of antique medical instruments, a dusty plastic fish aquarium. The anatomical skeleton on a stand watches with empty eyes as Piper explains that after the power was knocked out the night of September 20, 2020, the boathouse was rewired.

"Bailey continued coming out here daily," Piper says. "But the person he used to be was gone. I'd see him through the window, just sitting and staring at the water."

"Where did he keep his journals, Piper?" I ask because I'm not seeing anywhere they might be.

"They're still here, right?" Marino worries.

"You might not have thought it, but Bailey did have a little mischief in him," Piper says. "He had his own sense of the absurd. That added to him not trusting most people worth a damn, and for good reason. Just think of Alice stepping through the looking glass, and it still makes me smile." As she does tearfully, angrily wiping her eyes.

Attached to the wall on the far side of the living room is a large ornately framed full-length mirror, and she runs her hand along the bottom of it. I hear a click as a lock releases, and she opens the mirror like a door. Behind it is a steep narrow staircase that Marino barely can maneuver through.

It's airless, hot and stuffy as we follow her up to Bailey's secret alcove. The four cedarwood cabinets are neatly labeled with the years they cover from 1991 to the day he killed himself two years ago on November 24, the Tuesday before Thanksgiving. Piper pulls open shallow drawers to show us the black Moleskine notebooks, the same kind I've been using since medical school.

"The only one I've ever looked at is the last one he was keeping. I tried to read the final few pages to see if he said why..." She pulls the notebook out of the cabinet, handing it to me. "Well, I wondered if he left an explanation...Or if he simply said goodbye..." Dabbing her nose with a tissue. "Sorry it's so hot and dusty up here."

"No note," Marino assumes, and she shakes her head, wiping her eyes.

"It's rare when people leave them. Much rarer than believed," I reply.

"Nothing. Not a word about what he was planning," she says. "And Bailey's ramblings were hard to understand by that point, as you'll see for yourself. After the incident, he couldn't write or talk coherently. He got things awfully confused and garbled while suffering unbearable headaches."

"Did you show his diaries to the police?" Marino asks.

"They were interested in a note. That's what they asked about as you'd expect, and I said I didn't find one," she replies. "I saw no need to let them start digging through Bailey's private journals or anything else as if he did something wrong."

"Good girl," Marino says.

"Do you mind if I carry a few of the notebooks downstairs at a time?" I ask, because there's nowhere to sit up here, and she's right about the dust and heat.

"As long as they don't leave the property." She opens another cabinet, this one containing notebooks from more than twenty years ago. "The ones he kept during the Parkway murders are in here, and I'm assuming that's what you want to look at."

"I will eventually," I tell her. "But what I'm interested in this moment are his more recent entries. Not just this notebook." I indicate the one she handed me. "But others he kept the last few years of his life."

I want to see what was going on with him toward the end, and I gather a dozen journals covering from 2017 until his death. I tuck them inside my briefcase to carry downstairs, and Marino and Piper leave the boathouse. They get started on their maritime chores and adventures as I make myself comfortable on the living room sofa, the ceiling fans spinning.

Surrounded by windows, I watch them out on the pier pulling up the crab pots. They empty them in a Styrofoam ice chest, and it looks like the slack-tide timing did the trick. There will be plenty for supper. When the crab pots have been emptied, Piper and Marino head back to the house. I hear them laughing and talking nonstop as I close the curtains because it's getting dark.

Returning to the couch, I plump pillows behind me, and sneeze a few times. I skim through Bailey's writings, and it's obvious they were his therapy, as implied by the newspaper article long ago that Patty Mullet brought up. The small black notebooks were his only safe sounding board in this scary world that constantly brought death to his door.

He would carry his cases home with him emotionally. It was the small details that sent him spinning. The bag of groceries inside the crashed car. The stuffed animals scattered around the plane wreckage. The lucky rabbit's foot in the pocket of someone hit by a train. Bailey had an eye for poignant images, and he hated his job.

He didn't like the people in his office, and felt his best days were gone. Forensic pathologists weren't the purists they used to be, a lot of them not discreet and respectful anymore.

... They're too busy wanting to be talking heads on TV, he says. *Everybody wants to be famous. Well, I don't...*

CHAPTER 36

He decided the world had been overtaken by selfish wrongheaded people lacking in empathy, and I'm curious about his repeated references to *BFD*. The first mention I've seen is for August 17, 2020. The pandemic was in full swing, and Bailey was working inside the boathouse as much as possible.

But that morning there were nine autopsies, and he was more short-staffed than usual. Elvin Reddy was the chief then and treated his Tidewater district office as badly as the rest of them. Bailey was having budget and personnel problems that added to his growing aggravation.

He drove to his headquarters, and at 6:45 P.M. was back inside the boathouse making that day's diary entry:

. . . Terrible, terrible! There's no honor or decency anymore! Where is everything headed? No place good! This morning the bay door was left wide open again as if inviting any scoundrel to come in. BFD. The stairwell door on the first level wasn't locked again. BFD. . .

As in Big Fucking Deal, I suppose, and Bailey didn't swear beyond an occasional damn or hell. But he did pepper his conversations with euphemisms and an occasional acronym. He'd complain about the *G-D* this or that, and call criminals *S-O-Bs* and *A-holes* who could *go fork* themselves.

. . . I don't like to confront but did, making matters only worse, he

writes. *I'm reluctant to come into the office at all! The more the cat's away, the more out of control. As if the pandemic isn't hard enough. Then this sort of nonsense. Nobody listens or cares...*

Taking a swallow of beer, I realize it's not cold anymore, and I've been at this for a while. I get up from the sofa, checking my phone. It's almost 8:30. The sky is a fiery orange as the sun smolders over the horizon, and I touch base with Marino.

"Just wondering how things are going," I ask, hearing music in the background.

"We're picking crabs." He's in good spirits. "Piper's going to make her famous crab cakes. What a place. I wouldn't mind staying here a week or two. Maybe the entire summer. You about ready to take a break?"

"Let me get through a little bit more," I reply, and my vision is bleary. "Bailey's handwriting is tough to read. So far, I'm not finding much that's helpful unless you have a guess who or what he might have been referring to when he mentions *BFD*."

"Pretty obvious what that means," Marino says, and he asks Piper if she knows.

Her answer is rather much the same, and I suggest he confirm our hotel reservations. If it's all right with Piper, I'm going to need to come back here in the morning. I want an idea of everything in the journals before returning to Alexandria. Most of all, I'd like the chance to glance at what he had to say during the Parkway murders.

"I recommend we find a way to safeguard his diaries and papers," I summarize to Marino. "I think it's extremely risky having all of this here. Maybe you can sweet-talk Piper into letting me take them with us."

"I'll work on it. Don't stay there too much longer," he replies.

I return to the couch and the diary I was looking at a few minutes earlier, the last one Bailey kept. I find the final entry before he suffered his alleged stroke the night of September 20, almost two years ago. Again, he references *BFD*.

...As if the work isn't so grim enough routinely, and then the badness follows you through your own door. BFD. Secretly, I've been keeping an eye on the inventory, and this is four times now in the past six months. It's not a coincidence, and so I finally said something this morning. "Why do we keep losing the Niroflex...?"

Bailey suspected the pilfering at the Tidewater district headquarters had been going on for a while, possibly the better part of two years. Cleaners, PPE and other supplies ran out faster than usual. Expensive surgical instruments vanished without explanation. Most significant was the repeated disappearance of Niroflex mesh metal gloves that help prevent cuts and needle sticks during autopsies.

The chainmail-like gloves also would provide Faraday cage protection, at least for the hands, and that's convenient when experimenting with microwave weapons. The missing gloves Bailey references in his diary aren't inexpensive. Large purchases of them from the Internet could draw the wrong attention to the Lucys and Trons of the world.

Such orders and shipments were traceable. Stealing the metal mesh gloves from the morgue wasn't necessarily. Unless the person doing it got caught, and he might have.

...I made it clear we wouldn't be ordering any more of them..., Bailey writes at 8:35 that September night not quite two years ago. *"You think you're so smart" is the rude response I got. The same way I've been insulted in the past, and I said "well I'm smarter than you, that's for G-D sure." This can't continue. I'll take it up again with Elvin but nothing will come of*

The entry ends literally midsentence. There's nothing again for several days, and then Bailey's handwriting is barely recognizable. It looks as if he was drunk or had developed an uncontrollable tremor, and not much that he says is easy to follow. But he was keenly aware that something was terribly wrong.

...*Can't do this. Can't do this,* he writes repeatedly. *What happened to Midas? What happened to my poor fish...? What happened to me? So scared...!*

My attention wanders to the plastic aquarium on the other side of the living room. It still has rocks and plastic foliage in it. I have little doubt what Bailey was referring to, and the scenario gets only sadder. But there's no grim carcass left to collect this time. All the same, I need a confirmation, and I call Marino again.

"Ask Piper about a fish called Midas," I say to him.

"Hold on." He puts us on speakerphone, and I repeat my question.

"Bailey's goldfish. It died when the power went haywire," Piper says what I expect. "He was very upset about it, just heartbroken. He used to talk to Midas the same way he talked to his journals."

The goldfish had no protection in its non-metallic tank just as Bailey didn't in the rustic wooden boathouse with its unscreened windows and doors. I tell Piper and Marino that I'm packing up, and will be there shortly. Promising to return the diaries to their proper place, I pack them inside my briefcase. I climb the stairs to the alcove, smelling the cedarwood, feeling terrible for Bailey, for his fish and everyone.

I slide open a file drawer, and when the lights flicker it doesn't alarm me. When it happens a second time as I'm returning to the living room, the power goes out with a BOOM, throwing me into complete darkness. I feel sizzling heat and searing pain while hearing loud bangs and pops. Electricity sparks and arcs all around me like fireworks as I fumble like mad with the briefcase Lucy insists I carry.

Unfolding it, I shield myself while crouching behind the mirrored door. I smell hot metal, the television and antique jukebox blaring crazily. Music turns on and off, dialogue blurting...

Bailey's monotone voice sounds from the tape recorder on his desk...

"...Within normal limits..."

"...Liver weighs fifty-six hundred grams..."

"...Case is pending until further investigation..."

■ ■ ■

The air crackles as if on fire as I crouch behind my deployed messenger bag and the mirrored door. There's nothing I can do but hide, waiting for what's next. My heart thuds against my chest, pounding in my neck, my mouth as dry as paper...

BANG! BANG! BANG!

Then complete silence. I barely breathe. As I strain to listen. Thinking about my gun in the drawer at home. Startled when the door leading outside suddenly flies open, knocking loudly against the wall. I hear heavy feet stepping inside on the wooden floor. And stopping.

"Doc?" Marino's voice, and he sounds the most frightened I've ever heard him. "Doc? Are you in here?"

"Where else would I be?" I sound like somebody else as I step out from behind the door in the pitch darkness.

"Are you okay?"

"I'm not sure. I think so. But I don't know." My balance isn't good, and my ears feel stopped up, as if I've been swimming.

I lower my unfolded briefcase, and a flashlight shines across the living room. I can see Marino's silhouette as he directs the light near me but not in my eyes. The hot metallic odor is stronger.

333

"What's happened?" I ask as he comes closer. "I heard gunfire. I think I did. It's hard to know, there was so much noise..."

"Come on, Doc. Let's get the fuck out of here."

He puts his big arm around me, helping me through the door, outside into the warm brackish-smelling air, the tide quietly lapping. I'm shivering as if it's winter as he lights our way. I look up dazed at the star-spangled sky, the moon glowing through clouds like a skull. In the distance the main house is lit up cheerily, apparently undamaged.

It wasn't in the line of fire, and I remember Piper telling me the house has its own separate electrical box. Marino leads me along the pier, and then to a grassy area on the shore where I noticed geese earlier. The assailant was crouched in the cover of shrubs and cypress trees. From here he couldn't be seen easily, and the boathouse would have been an unobstructed target.

He knew just the right spot because he'd done this before in September of 2020 when Bailey suffered his alleged stroke, the power surging, his goldfish dying. Now the monster was back to ruin and kill some more, and Marino shines the light on the bloody bearded face, the open eyes blinding staring, the white gleam of the slightly bared teeth. I vaguely recognize the Raven Landing security officer named Dogg.

He aggressively rode our bumper when we were headed to Chilton Farms, and I envision his sunglasses boldly fixed on us. It was Dogg who told the Alexandria police about noticing Flagler's car in Annie's driveway. No doubt the private security officer noticed all sorts of things as he stalked and planned his terrorist activities while people treated him like a good guy.

His thick beard is streaked with gray, and soaked with blood from the bullet wound to his left temple. I bend closer, and in the glare of the flashlight, the hole is tangential, angled slightly down. That shot alone was a showstopper, and if I had to guess it was the first one Marino fired. Two more bullets penetrated Dogg's upper body, likely ripping through vital blood vessels and organs. Any one of the injuries would have been fatal, I suspect.

I resist the impulse to compliment Marino on a job well done, to tell him how relieved and impressed I am. I thank him for saving my life, and it's not the first time I've done it. Chances are it won't be my last. He paints his light over Dogg's camouflage coveralls. Nearby on the ground is the hood he didn't bother wearing, and Marino picks it up. It has mirrored built-in goggles.

"I can't swear to it," he says. "But it feels like Mylar."

The same with the coveralls, and he turns over the body. The seams are heat-sealed except for a small-toothed plastic zipper in back that's protected by a Velcro flap Marino rips open. Dogg didn't bother wearing a hood, eye protection, gloves or shoe covers as he unleashed bursts of high energy at the boathouse while I was inside it.

I don't know how long the attack lasted. It felt like forever but Marino says it was no more than a minute. Maybe two, he tells me as he unzips the coveralls, patting down the body, making sure nothing's left here that shouldn't be.

"How did you turn it off?" I'm not understanding what Marino did as I continue to shiver.

"When I shot him the first time he stopped holding the trigger" is his simple answer. "Then I checked that he was dead. I killed the power switch on the engine before running to the boathouse, making sure you were okay."

The bushes Dogg fired through are denuded of leaves and foliage. The Yagi antenna he was pointing like a gun barrel is attached to an electrical cable that disappears inside a big backpack. The weapon is strange-looking, a combination of *Star Wars* and Stone Age. The antenna is maybe four feet long. It's enclosed in a crude metal cone that directs the lethal energy at its target.

The coveralls make startling crinkly sounds as Marino checks what Dogg is wearing underneath. Camouflage cargo pants. A non-descript tan T-shirt. In pockets are a roll of hundred-dollar bills, a remote-start fob for a Ford vehicle, and other keys. Inside a fanny pack is a .40 caliber pistol, a suppresser and extra ammunition. Marino drops out the gun's extended magazine, clearing the round from the chamber.

He's not concerned about preserving the scene or contaminating evidence. It's no secret who shot Dogg and why. Assuming he fired a microwave gun at the boathouse that September night in 2020, it would appear he and Bailey knew each other. Maybe Dogg was a security guard at the medical examiner's office at the time. That would be my guess.

Or he might have worked in some other business that resulted in Bailey having regular contact with him. I was still living in Massachusetts then, and no longer privy to the nuances of the Virginia medical examiner system. Only that it had been all but destroyed by Elvin Reddy, adding considerably to Bailey's growing despair and disillusionment.

"...I came around the side of the house." Marino continues telling me what he did, and it's hard to pay attention, my thoughts sparking everywhere. "He had his back to me, was busy shooting his fucking weapon of mass destruction. It sounded like a microwave oven running. I could hear the motor but couldn't see anything firing out of the antenna..."

"We need to call Benton and Lucy before doing anything else." I'm coming out of my skin.

Fireflies glow and dim, and frogs are barking as we hover by the body, looking around. We don't have a signal analyzer. We don't know that Dogg was acting alone. Some other homegrown terrorist could be aiming a high-energy weapon at us right now, and my aching head is splitting. My mouth is dry and tastes like dust. I'm having a hard time stopping my teeth from chattering.

"I'm trying Lucy now." Marino's phone lights up in the dark as he makes the call.

It goes to voice mail, and he leaves an urgent warning. If we contact the local police, he says, they'll be crawling all over everything before the Secret Service gets the chance. There's no question that Lucy, Tron, and Benton won't want the cops or anyone else getting their hands on the microwave weapon or even knowing about it.

"We can't stay here," I tell Marino when he's off the phone. "We're dealing with a terrorist cell, and can't assume there's no one else out there..."

He's dripping sweat, his attention everywhere as we return to the house. Inside the kitchen, Piper sits like a statue at the newspaper-covered table scattered with shells and picking tools, a bowl of crabmeat in front of her. Cheese biscuits cooling on a cookie sheet smell wonderful.

"Oh my Lord," she says, her eyes wide and unblinking.

"Don't call nine-one-one," Marino tells her. "You haven't, have you?"

She shakes her head, no she hasn't. He places Dogg's pistol, the ammunition on the newspaper-covered table. Piper stares at them numbly as I close the blinds over the sink, shutting out the night. She watches blankly as I begin refolding my deployed briefcase.

"It's the same thing that happened to Bailey, isn't it?" she says.

"Very possibly," I reply. "Only he wasn't behind his mirrored door, and wouldn't have known to think of such a thing. And he didn't have this." I indicate my unassuming-looking messenger bag.

"Oh." She has no idea what I'm talking about. "I heard gunshots."

"That's right." Marino is proud of himself, and he should be.

"Who?" she asks.

"The name Dogg with two g's mean anything to you?"

She again shakes her head, never heard of him. But Bailey didn't bring his work into the house, she keeps repeating herself.

"Some private security dirtbag who works at a ritzy yacht club in Alexandria," Marino says. "No ID in his pockets, but we'd seen him before. He got here somehow, must have a vehicle parked out of sight nearby. But that's not for us to be sticking our nose into. It wouldn't be safe, for one thing."

"And he came here tonight because he knew you'd be here?" Piper is baffled and getting angry. "Is he the same person who ruined Bailey? Now he wants to ruin Kay?"

"I'm guessing he intended to take out all of us before he was done," Marino says, and Piper begins to sob. "Maybe he followed us," Marino decides, his pistol in hand and pointed down. "I don't know, but we need to leave, and you're coming with us, Piper. We're taking the damn journals and other shit while we're at it unless you don't want to ever see them again. The Norfolk cops, the FBI will grab them, and that's the end of it."

"He's right." I visibly jump when my ring vibrates, my phone working fine.

I pull it out of a compartment in my briefcase where I tucked it earlier, halfway expecting another automated complaint about how poorly I take care of myself. But it's Benton calling.

"Are you hurt?" He's steady and quiet, the way he sounds when frantic.

"I don't think so."

"No time to talk. We've got agents two blocks away, and they'll take care of things," he says. "As soon as they arrive, you, Marino, Piper are to get in his truck. You'll be escorted back to Old Town. We're making sure all of you are safe. Everything's going to be fine, I promise, Kay. Don't forget I love you."

ONE WEEK LATER

The *BFD* that Bailey Carter refers to in his diaries are Benjamin Franklin Dogg's initials. The fifty-four-year-old private security officer's unfortunate nickname was Benji, and he wasn't a big fucking deal.

But he desperately wanted to be at any price. That was one of many things fundamentally wrong with him. And maybe with a lot of people these days if you ask Benton. Based on what he's discovered so far, Dogg sold out to the devil the same way most people do. A little bit at a time. Going back to day one.

He made bad choices. Finally, he died the way he lived. Only he didn't suffer nearly as much as his victims, and I realize that medical examiners aren't supposed to have personal opinions. We aren't supposed to care about the who or why. Only the what and how it's tangible, provable, will hold up in court. I'm expected to have no vested interest in why the person did it. Or didn't.

My job isn't to be a judge or a jury. But I'd tell anybody who asked that I wish Benji Dogg hadn't been born. I'm glad he's *dead and Dogg gone,* as Lucy puts it. Otherwise, more lives would have been ruined. By all indications, he was far from done. In recent years and months, he'd become increasingly impulsive as he plotted slaughter and coups for The Republic's radical causes.

His expertise and obsessive interest were the fabrication of microwave guns and all that goes with them. He worked with these types of weapons constantly at the training camp near Quantico, having been associated with the terrorist organization since its inception. Described as quiet and shy, Dogg could be helpful and polite until he turned rageful when countered or slighted.

He sounds very much the way Benton predicted he would, the sort to shovel the snow off your driveway or change your flat tire. Someone you'd hardly notice unless he decided to get in your face. Like most bullies, he'd retaliate when his victim didn't have a fighting chance. He had no presence on social media, using aliases to monitor future hits.

"...Shopping mall parking lots. Live performances. Outdoor college graduations and political rallies...," Marino says, and it's a good thing he has a big voice as he talks above the music and noise.

Mollie's Underground is mobbed without an inch to spare. A young man with tattoos and a buzz cut is singing karaoke, a not-so-bad version of John Denver's "Country Roads." Our table is in a remote corner where the owner always puts us, and Lucy is on one side of me. Next to her is Annie Chilton, and across from them Marino and Dorothy.

"...By all appearances, he had a list that was just getting longer," Marino carries on. "Because if you dissed him, you were next. Exactly like he did to poor Bailey Carter..."

I invited Piper to join us tonight. But she's with family in Norfolk this weekend. Her husband's journals and papers are safely locked up in a gun vault where no one's going to mess with them.

"...What I keep wondering about is a girlfriend, a pal, maybe one of the other terrorists," Dorothy is saying. "He must have had *someone* he was close to."

"Nope," Lucy says. "A total loner. Not even his comrades really knew him. Just ask Benton."

The chair to my left is empty as I wait for him, and I keep checking the door. Benton is tied up at the Pentagon with Mollie's husband, U.S. Space Force commander General Jake Gunner. They should be here any minute.

"...Anything sacred and meaningful? And Deputy Dogg and his merry band of assholes planned to destroy it until no one wants to leave their fucking house anymore," Marino boisterously, defiantly says.

"When you depersonalize these people, it's no different than them objectifying us," Annie speaks up, and she and Marino aren't necessarily like-minded.

It's fair to say they wouldn't vote for the same political candidates. Or watch the same TV shows and movies. They wouldn't get along if stranded together on a desert island.

"I truly believe we're making matters only worse if we do to others what they're doing to us. That's not justice." The more Annie drinks, the more it sounds like she's instructing the jury. "That's stereotyping and bigotry. Benji Dogg isn't just a *goon*, an *asshole...*"

"Not anymore he ain't! But he sure as fuck was!" Marino retorts.

■ ■ ■

"People speak with their feet," Dorothy agrees. "Actions speak louder."

"Be careful about categorizing." Annie is suddenly somber.

"Both sides need to get together," I agree.

"Well, that's all fine and dandy to say." Dorothy wags her finger around the table. "But there's the problem of bad wiring..."

Character disorders aren't obvious like an electrical short or thrown circuit breaker, and there's no easy explanation for what creates a violent psychopath. Dogg had a superior IQ. He attended Old Dominion University in Norfolk, interested in engineering and astrophysics. His father had left the family, and money was a constant struggle.

While attending college classes, Dogg lived at home with his mother, a makeup artist who worked for a local TV station. After her husband left the family, she had a lot of men in and out of the house. The police assumed it was one of them who murdered her in the spring of Dogg's sophomore year. She was taking a walk just blocks from home as she routinely did after supper.

When she was stabbed to death it was in front of a church while choir practice was in full swing, preparing for the upcoming Easter concert. The music was so loud outside on the street that it's doubtful anyone could have heard her scream. A slender young male dressed in dark clothing and a hood was sighted running and ducking behind trees and buildings, vanishing in the shadows.

"...Like I've said before," Dorothy goes on. "Bad to the bone."

"Damn right," Marino says. "The scum bucket took out his own mother..."

Most recently Dogg was living in Quantico near Fort Belvoir, staying in a rented two-bedroom house. His Raven Landing private security Durango SUV was in plain view in the driveway when federal agents arrived. He kept his personal pickup truck inside the garage. But the night he died it was parked out of sight close to the Carters' waterfront property in Norfolk.

Inside the truck was a rucksack containing a tactical knife with Wally Potter's DNA on it. There was a roll of duct tape, and the strips recovered from his body were fracture-matched back to it. Trace evidence clinging to the adhesive was consistent with what we found in the dust bunny.

Touch-DNA on Wally's shirt was matched to Benjamin Franklin Dogg, as was DNA left inside Belle Haven Market's safe and on the office chair. Dogg was out of control, arrogant, and maybe he'd deluded himself into believing he was invincible. He wasn't in the FBI's CODIS database because he'd never been arrested, and that added to his false sense of security.

I had my Norfolk deputy chief Rena Peace work the death scene and conduct the postmortem examination. It wasn't for me to do. I thought it fitting since she'd taken care of Bailey Carter.

■　■　■

I toy with my *Martian Margarita,* one of the house specials. Tequila, a splash of water and pomegranate juice on the rocks.

"Well, it's no fun to think about." Dorothy is holding forth about the Colonial Parkway murders again, has been doing it nonstop, and I wish she wouldn't. "But how do you know he wasn't involved somehow in the horrible deaths of those poor young couples?"

"I have to admit, the same thought keeps crossing my mind," Annie says. "Maybe back then he was getting started, learning how to hunt humans. He was practicing."

"That's right." Dorothy nods her head. "And he very well could have partnered with what's-his-name, the person blamed for the murders? The one with the weird DNA who got shot to death? Maybe both of them were involved. Who's to say? Partners in the worst crimes imaginable. It would be easier for two people to control a couple..."

"There's a lot we don't know." I try to change the subject. "Suffice it to say that if Dogg had something to do with the Parkway cases, I have a feeling we'll find out eventually."

"He may not have kept notes or even photos. But I bet he kept souvenirs," Lucy says as she helps herself to jalapeño poppers called *Flash-Bangs*.

She passes the basket to Annie, who is dressed in her usual khakis and oversized safari shirt. Living at the Watergate seems to agree with her. She has no plans to relocate, and continues to employ Holt Willard, whom Lucy refers to as the only family the judge has left, her *faithful retainer*. Mostly he runs a few errands, helping out with minor chores.

He and Annie have coffee, talking about the old days, when she's not on the bench or otherwise engaged. Dana Diletti's TV investigative piece hasn't done any harm. If anything, it seems to have upped Annie's stock, based on editorials and news stories I've been following. From what I understand, Raven Landing is buying Chilton Farms, and my old friend won't be as poor as a church mouse ever again.

"...Well, the more I think of it," Dorothy slurs, "of far more concern is the *real* couple-killer still being out there somewhere, God forbid. What if he never was caught to begin with...?"

Elizabeth the bombshell hostess appears with another round nobody ordered or will turn down. Her live-in boyfriend Jack the bartender has a heavy pour, and Annie's not much of a drinker. She's on her second *Jack the Ripper's Bloody Mary*, made with non-Russian vodka. It's a good thing Lucy is the designated driver for Her Honor, and also for her mother and Marino.

"...What if reopening the cases goads him into action and he starts hunting down couples or who knows what?" Dorothy is on a roll. "Doing something awful all over again."

"You're talking twenty-two years ago. Whoever it is? He's probably too old by now," Annie decides.

"Nonsense," Dorothy objects. "Whoever committed those murders might be only in his fifties by now. The same age as the psycho Marino had to take out..."

"Yeah, you can't make assumptions about age. There are guys in their seventies and more who you sure as hell wouldn't want to mess with." Marino toys with his shot glass of bourbon, his biceps bulging. "I hate that Bailey ever got tangled up with the fucking *Dogg shit* with two g's. I keep thinking if the doc and I had been in Virginia at the time, it wouldn't have happened."

"It wouldn't have. Amen to that." Dorothy deeply nods her head as if she's in church.

"If we'd been right here in Virginia, we could have prevented it. Don't you agree, Doc?" He looks at me. "No fucking way things would have gone this far."

"I would hope not," I reply. "For sure, had Bailey complained to me the way he did to Elvin, I would have done something about it."

Dogg began working security at the Norfolk medical examiner's office the fall of 2019. By then, he already was involved with the fledgling terrorist cell that now calls itself The Republic, of which Gilbert Hooke was a founding member. They knew each other, and it's likely that Dogg encountered April Tupelo at some point.

She was well aware of Hooke's anarchist involvements and aspirations. She more than shared his views, and they were frequent visitors to the Northern Virginia training camp. Now she's dead, and Hooke is back behind bars, this time on terrorist charges after interviews with his comrades, and other evidence. If April were alive, she'd be locked up, too. Both of them would be charged with multiple crimes.

"...Theft of government property, and armed robberies that were happening in the Hampton Roads area not long before she died." Dorothy continues reciting what's been in the news about April Tupelo.

"...And you know what I say about her going overboard?" Marino raises another shot of bourbon, looking around the table. "*That was just life fucking throwing her back!*"

"I told you she and Gilbert were cut from the same cloth." My sister says this dramatically and loudly while she looks at me. "And it wouldn't surprise me if she had some help tripping and ending up in the ocean."

"Hooke could have pushed her while they were fighting, right, Doc?" Marino says. "As shitfaced drunk as she was? It wouldn't have been hard."

"He didn't strangle her to death." I help myself to another *Flash-Bang*, a sip of my drink. "But he could have pushed her overboard and left her to drown. It wouldn't have taken long. He may not have been able to save her even if he'd tried."

We'll never know. But nothing about April Tupelo's last day alive has been truthful. When she and Hooke were out in his trawler retrieving the crashed weather balloon on October 14, 2020, it was about more than helping NASA-Wallops recover a failed experiment. The balloon was constructed of enough Mylar to cover a football field.

Normally the damaged material would have ended up sold as surplus, but this never happened. After April and Hooke helped recover the ruined balloon, it vanished. Typical of government facilities with multiple overcrowded warehouses, nobody noticed. When the terrorists' camp and training grounds were raided, it was discovered that The Republic had quite a cottage industry. It included Mylar, ovens and industrial shredders.

The terrorists had been making construction tiles embedded with Mylar glitter, some of it sputter-coated with microscopic amounts of precious metals. The tiles were used in their own buildings, creating habitats with Faraday cage shielding. Camouflage protective clothing was fabricated, and they'd modified their phones using spread spectrum technology.

This explains why no one pinged on the terrorists when they attempted their attack on the president. Their phone signals were lost in the noise floor and didn't pop up, their communications undetected. The bad guys were careful, but Dogg wasn't when he went on to create murder and mayhem at Belle Haven Market and Chilton Farms. It was even more reckless when he showed up in Norfolk, not bothering with gloves, a hood or other protection.

He didn't worry that he might be spotted before he could finish what he started. Maybe he was cocky or too angry to use logic and good judgment. Or more likely he wasn't thinking clearly anymore, possibly from chronic exposure to radiation. It must not have occurred to him that Marino might be looking out a window when the lights flickered right before the boathouse went pitch dark.

"...I knew right away what was going down." Marino's recounting gets more dramatic as happy hour goes on. "I went out the front door and crept around the side of the house. I could make out the shape of the fucker on the shore in a clump of bushes. He must have sensed me, turning his head just enough for me to pop him in the left temple. Then twice more center mass..."

Elizabeth the hostess interrupts his latest recycled rendition. She's appeared with *Guardian Guacamole* with *Frag Chips,* and baskets of *Heat Seeking Fries.* Compliments of the house. She bends over far enough in her low-cut blouse for Marino to enjoy the view. My attention wanders across the room to Bose Flagler, this moment alone in his booth, and for an instant our eyes meet.

He stopped by the table after we got here, acting the way he always does, friendly, charming and witty while my sister stared at him carnivorously and Marino got pissy. The commonwealth's attorney is having dinner with Patty Mullet, just now returning from the ladies' room or wherever she went. Sliding back into her seat, she resumes a conversation with him.

The FBI special agent is considerably older, and based on Flagler's demeanor, I doubt they're on a date. She avoids looking in this direction, and probably won't say hello to Benton when he arrives. Her attempted investigative takeover was weakened further when the insect, animal and plant evidence I collected from Chilton Farms was negative for carbofuran. Not a trace of it or any other poison.

"...I'm getting the urge," my sister announces as the last karaoke contestant leaves the stage to a rowdy round of applause and cheers. "Somebody better do it first...Or I'm gonna..." She threatens it seductively.

The prize money is up to three hundred dollars, my sister increasingly interested as she drinks *Cosmic Cosmos*. The aged Haitian rum has just enough Goldschläger *Moondust* to add a little sparkle. I'm unpleasantly reminded of Mylar glitter and sputter coating. She's draped over Marino in his muscle shirt.

"I'm not kidding." Dorothy stares at the empty stage.

The seconds creep by slowly as nobody volunteers. I reach for my drink, knowing what's coming.

"Well, this is boring. Someone has to." Dorothy pushes back her chair, spotlights flaring on her.

She's decked out in a shiny silver onesie that looks very NASA or very terrorist, depending on who you ask. Her big earrings look like comets, and she pauses to wrap glow sticks around her wrists, turning them on.

"Oh God," Lucy says.

"She won't really." Annie reaches for the guacamole. "Nothing could make me go up there."

"Oh, she'll do it." Marino proudly watches his wife saunter toward the stage as the crowd begins to cheer.

She gives them a rock star wave that's been perfected after repeated vocal performances she rarely remembers. People begin clapping and stomping their feet. She isn't walking the straightest of lines, and then Mollie herself appears at our table. Always in motion, she alights like a bright butterfly, and General Gunner is pulling out the chair next to her.

He's in civilian clothing and stealthy. But you can't miss his face that seems carved of granite like an older version of Bruce Willis in *Armageddon*. Benton is here, and instantly a squadron of waitstaff is deployed. They surround us, setting down steaming bowls of Mollie's *Meatier Chili*, and *Glutton-Free Humdinger Hummus*, extra spicy.

I dig into the *Honey-Do* fried chicken, and *Fire in the Hole* smashed potato fritters. I fix plates for Benton and me, and he hands me his phone. I look at the e-mail to him from Governor Roxane Dare:

…Please inform Kay that this won't be announced for a while and is to be kept quiet until further notice. But I wanted her to know that it's in the best interest of all involved for appropriate parties to be relocated. I will take care of this in short order, allowing them to make other arrangements for their professional futures…

Elvin Reddy and Maggie Cutbush will resign from their current positions, and I don't like the choice of the governor's words. As I read between the lines I detect that what she intends is for Elvin and Maggie to be reshuffled. That's the same thing as not going away. Ensuring they'll turn up somewhere I don't like. From the frying pan into the fire is usually how that ends.

But for now, it will have to do. I tell myself it's better than nothing as Dorothy grabs the microphone, tap-tapping it. All eyes are on her as she TAP-TAPs some more, the volume turning up. Loudly, getting feedback and the room's complete attention, she leans over, precariously swaying, her gaudy outfit shining and flashing like a space station or a mirror ball.

She says something to the karaoke DJ, telling him what track to pull. And he nods. As the crowd approves deafeningly. Even though we don't know what she's picked. Probably the same thing she always does.

"Are we ready, everyone?" Her voice is all around.

She scans the audience as if we're in a massive arena, and the crowd goes wild. She holds the microphone close to her bright-painted lips.

"Let's do this!"

Then my sister is belting out Cher's "If I Could Turn Back Time." People are yelling, screaming, stomping their feet and whistling. Some get up to dance as she sings off-key to her vast sea of fans.

ABOUT THE AUTHOR

In 1990, Patricia Cornwell sold her first novel, *Postmortem*, while working at the Office of the Chief Medical Examiner in Richmond, Virginia. An auspicious debut, it went on to win the Edgar, Creasey, Anthony, and Macavity Awards as well as the French Prix du Roman d'Aventures—the first book ever to claim all these distinctions in a single year. Growing into an international phenomenon, the Scarpetta series won Cornwell the Sherlock Award for best detective created by an American author, the Gold Dagger Award, the RBA Thriller Award, and the Medal of Chevalier of the Order of Arts and Letters for her contributions to literary and artistic development.

Today, Cornwell's novels and iconic characters are known around the world. Beyond the Scarpetta series, Cornwell has written the definitive nonfiction account of Jack the Ripper's identity, cookbooks, a children's book, a biography of Ruth Graham, and three other fictional series based on the characters Win Garano, Andy Brazil and Captain Callie Chase. In recent years, Cornwell has been researching space-age technologies at NASA facilities, the U.S. Space Force and Secret Service. She's visited Scotland Yard and Interpol, always keeping up with what's current.

Cornwell was born in Miami. She grew up in Montreat, North Carolina, and now lives and works in Boston.